William Henry Hurlbert

General McClellan and the Conduct of the War

SALZWASSER
VERLAG

William Henry Hurlbert

General McClellan and the Conduct of the War

Reprint of the original, first published in 1864.

1st Edition 2022 | ISBN: 978-3-75259-207-8

Verlag (Publisher): Salzwasser Verlag GmbH, Zeilweg 44, 60439 Frankfurt, Deutschland
Vertretungsberechtigt (Authorized to represent): E. Roepke, Zeilweg 44, 60439 Frankfurt, Deutschland
Druck (Print): Books on Demand GmbH, In de Tarpen 42, 22848 Norderstedt, Deutschland

GENERAL McCLELLAN

AND

THE CONDUCT OF THE WAR.

BY

WILLLIAM HENRY HURLBERT.

NEW YORK

1864.

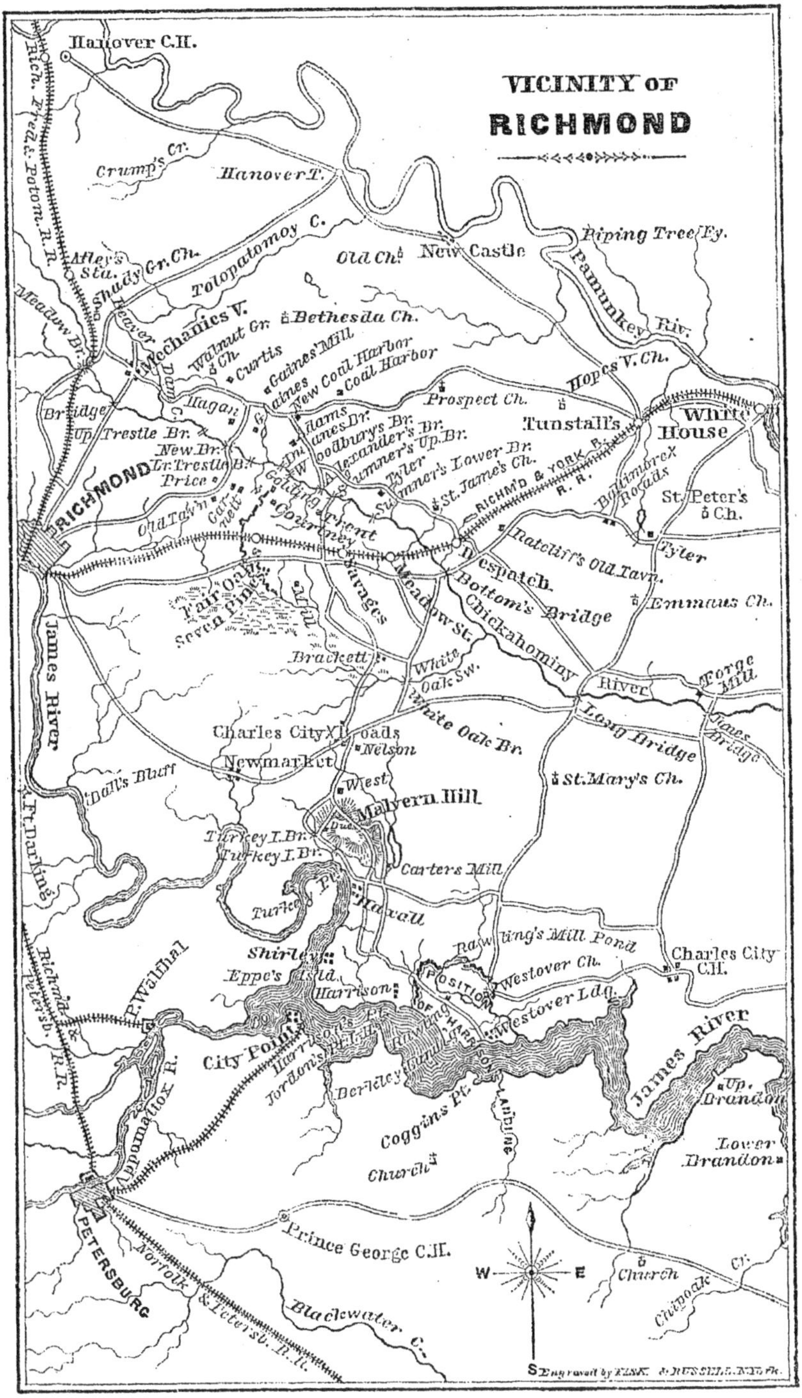
VICINITY OF RICHMOND
Hanover C.H.
Rich. Fred. & Potom. R.R.
Crump's Cr.
Hanover T.
Tolopatomoy C.
Old Ch.
New Castle
Piping Tree Fy.
Pamunkey Riv.
Atlee's Sta.
Shady Gr. Ch.
Meadow Br.
Mechanics V.
Beaver Dam C.
Walnut Gr. Ch.
Bethesda Ch.
Curtis
Gaines' Mill
New Coal Harbor
Coal Harbor
Prospect Ch.
Hopes V. Ch.
Tunstall's
White House
Hagan
Bridge
Up. Trestle Br.
New Br.
Lr. Trestle Br.
Price
RICHMOND
Woodbury's Br.
Alexander's Br.
Sumner's Up. Br.
Tyler
Sumner's Lower Br.
St. James's Ch.
RICHM'D & YORK R. R.R.
Baltimore X Roads
St. Peter's Ch.
Old Tavn.
Golding
Courtney
Trent
Despatch
Ratcliff's Old Tavn.
Tyler
Fair Oaks
Seven Pines
Savages
Meadow St.
Bottom's Bridge
Chickahominy
Emmaus Ch.
James River
Brackett
White Oak Sw.
River
Forge Mill
Charles City X Roads
Nelson
White Oak Br.
Long Bridge
Jones Bridge
Newmarket
Drill's Bluff
West
Malvern Hill
St. Mary's Ch.
Ft. Darling
Turkey I. Br.
Carters Mill
Turkey Pt.
Haxall
Shirley
Rawling's Mill Pond
Eppe's Isld.
Harrison
POSITION OF HARRISON LANDING
Westover Ch.
Charles City C.H.
Westover Ldg.
P. Walthal
Richmd. & Petersb. R.R.
City Point
Appomattox R.
Harrison's Pt.
Jordon's Pt.
Berkley
Coggins Pt.
James River
Up. Brandon
Lower Brandon
Church
PETERSBURG
Prince George C.H.
Norfolk & Petersb. R.R.
Blackwater C.
Church
Chipoak Cr.
W
E
S
Engraved by FISK & RUSSELL, N. York.

PREFACE.

I HAVE not attempted in this volume to write either a full biography of General McClellan or a complete history of his campaigns.

So far as the biography of a man yet living, and conspicuous in the political action of his time, can properly be written at all, this work has been admirably done, in respect to General McClellan, by Mr. George S. Hillard, of Boston. And the history of General McClellan's campaigns can only be completely written when the archives not of our own war department alone, but of the war department of the Confederate States also, shall have become accessible to the historian.

My object has been to depict, as fully and fairly as the documentary evidence before me would enable me to do, the parts played by General McClellan and by the administration of Mr. Lincoln, respectively, in the conduct of the war from its outbreak, in the spring of 1861, down to the final removal of General McClellan from the command of the Army of the Potomac, in November, 1862.

About two years ago my attention was specially directed to this subject by a remarkable article on the campaign of the Army of the Potomac, which appeared in the *Revue des Deux Mondes*, at Paris, in October, 1862, over the signature of A. TROGNON, and which was commonly attributed at the time to the pen of the Prince de Joinville. It is unnecessary to dwell here upon the reasons which make it desirable for a prince of the House of Orleans to refrain from signing with his own name papers published at Paris, under the imperial regime: but it is not, perhaps, improper for me to say that, in a letter on the subject of this article, the Prince de Joinville has thus expressed himself: "I assure you that I entirely partake the sentiments of respect and admiration entertained towards General McClellan by Mr. A. TROGNON."

I published a translation of this article at New York immediately after its appearance in Paris, and in a brief preface to that translation I took occasion to say that the paper must be considered to be substantially an indictment of the administration of Mr. Lincoln as the really responsible authors of the failure of the Peninsular expedition against Richmond.

All that has since been made known of the history of that expedition, as well by the reports of the Joint Congressional Committee on the Conduct of the War as by the reports of General McClellan himself, and of his subordinate commanders; by the journals of the time; and by various official and non-official publications on the subject, tends, it seems to me, to sustain and to reinforce this indictment.

Moved to the work by a protracted examination of these publications, I had made some progress, more than a year ago, in a "Historical Sketch of the Peninsular Campaign," when I was led by considerations of no moment to the reader to defer the completion of my design. Having been applied to by the Messrs. Sheldon & Co., the publishers of General McClellan's Report, to furnish them with a narrative of General McClellan's career as a commander of the national armies, I judged it best to elucidate as clearly as I could the peculiar relations sustained by General McClellan to the policy of the war as well as to its conduct in the field: and I have therefore embodied in the present volume much of the material prepared for use in a more full, careful, and elaborate work than this at all pretends to be.

NEW YORK, September 27, 1864.

CONTENTS.

CHAPTER I.

CHAPTER II.

CHAPTER III.

CHAPTER IV.

CHAPTER V.

CHAPTER VI.

CHAPTER VII.

CHAPTER VIII.

CHAPTER IX.

CHAPTER X.

CHAPTER XI.

CHAPTER XII.

CHAPTER XIII.

CHAPTER I.

BIRTH AND ANCESTRY OF GENERAL McCLELLAN. HIS TRAINING AT THE MILITARY ACADEMY AND IN THE WAR WITH MEXICO. HIS VISIT TO THE CRIMEA. HIS RESIGNATION FROM THE ARMY AND RETURN TO CIVIL LIFE.

MAJOR-GENERAL GEORGE BRINTON McCLELLAN was born in the city of Philadelphia, the seat of the Colonial Congress, the original capital of the American Union, the consecrated birthplace of our national greatness, on the 3d day of December, 1826.

His father, a physician of eminence, was a native of Connecticut, into which "land of steady habits" and of sterling men his ancestors had migrated from the mountains of Scotland, bringing with them the ancient Scottish love of liberty and of law, the just, tenacious nature of that hardy and heroic race which has bulwarked freedom and beaten back oppression on so many a hard-fought field from the days of Bruce and Wallace to our own.

The American people are not much given to inquiring into the ancestry of those who do the State service; but the faith which the republicans of old Rome held in the virtue of blood while still the Republic stood, was abundantly vindicated when the Roman people saw the shameless despotism of the worst of the Cæsars administered by men of base extraction and of corrupt birth. And wherever the permanence and the power of the commonwealth depend upon the virtue of its public servants, it should be no insignificant recommendation of a man to the confidence of his fellow-citizens that his fathers in their time were citizens of credit—"men, high-minded men," who knew alike their duties and their rights, and were as firm in maintaining the latter as they were faithful in fulfilling the former.

Such were those New England volunteers of the Revolution of whom the historian Bancroft tells us that, within a fortnight after the stand made at Lexington, there was scarcely a town in Connecticut that was not represented among the besiegers at Boston. The men who thus swarmed to the defence of their country were no reckless and revolutionary horde, delighting in war and careless of life. To use the words of the same historian, they were "men of substantial worth, of whom almost every one represented a household. The members of the several companies were well known to each other, as to brothers, kindred, and townsmen; known to the old men who remained at home, and to all the matrons and maidens. They were sure to be remembered weekly in the exercises of the congregations; and morning and evening in the usual family devotions they were commended with fervent piety to the protection of Heaven. Every young soldier lived and acted, as it were, under the keen observation of all those among whom he had grown up, and was sure that his conduct would occupy the tongues of his village companions while he was in the field, and perhaps be remembered his life long. The camp of liberty was a gathering in arms of schoolmates, neighbors, and friends; and Boston was beleaguered round from Roxbury to Chelsea by an unorganized, fluctuating mass of men, each with his own musket and his little store of cartridges, and such provisions as he brought with him, or as were sent after him, or were contributed by the people round about."

Of such a stock came George Brinton McClellan.

Removing from Connecticut to Pennsylvania, his father had achieved by his abilities and character a high position in the midst of that galaxy of accomplished medical men by whom the name of Philadelphia as the metropolis of physical science and the healing art in the New World was made illustrious throughout both hemispheres. It was the best reward of the life-long exertions of Dr. McClellan that he was thereby enabled to bestow upon his children all the advantages of education which the country could afford; and at the early age of thirteen George was entered as a student of the Freshman class in the University of Pennsylvania.

An inborn vocation, however, led him, as a like impulse a century before had led a certain young surveyor in Virginia, towards the life of an engineer and a soldier; and a cadet's warrant having been obtained for him, George Brinton McClellan in 1842 was sent to the Military Academy at West Point.

It is perhaps scarcely worth while to defend the Academy at West Point against the charges with which ignorance and passion have so often, in the course of the present war, assailed it. But the testimony of Gen. Barnard is so explicit in contradiction of the assertion that the influences exerted at the Academy upon the minds of the students have ever been unfavorable to the development of a large, loyal and intelligent patriotism, that it may well be quoted here. "That the greater part of the educated officers of the United States Army," says Gen. Barnard, in his treatise on the battle of Bull Run, "should have proved false to their flag, and gone over to the cause of secession, would imply that that cause had in it that which could justify a body of loyal and highly educated men, sworn defenders of the flag of their country, to espouse a cause which made flagrant war upon it. The facts are these: Of nine hundred and fifty-one officers of the Army, two hundred and sixty-two have proved disloyal. They (the disloyal) were, with a few exceptions, born in the seceding States; and it was not until their States had seceded, and placed themselves in hostile array, that such yielded (and most of them sorrowfully) to the supposed necessity of casting their lot with the section which gave them birth. Several of those who felt themselves called upon to relinquish their commissions in the army have declined to enter the Confederate service, and array themselves against their flag. Many more are known to have resigned with similar resolution, but returning to their native States, they have found themselves compelled to serve —compelled by influences which none but a martyr resists. The number of commissioned officers of the regular army borne on the Register for January, 1862, was two thousand and nine. Three hundred and three were born in the slave States, (District of Columbia included,) of whom one hundred and thirty were graduates of the Military Academy. Eighty-nine were born in seceded States, of whom forty-five were graduates of the Military Academy. More than half of these latter graduates were from Virginia, but all the seceded States, except Mississippi, were represented. The number of officers of the army born in the free States who went over to the rebel cause is small, and can be counted on the fingers."

At the Military Academy the young McClellan soon found himself thoroughly at home, distinguished himself in the exact studies to which he was called upon to apply his mind, and won the esteem of his superiors by his scholarlike and soldierly bearing. He was graduated with the second honors of his class in 1846; assigned to duty with a company of the Engineers, and ordered before the close of the year into active service on the line of the Rio Grande River.

The war with Mexico was then raging; and Lieutenant McClellan reached his post just after the battle of Monterey had been fought and won. It is a curious coincidence, and perhaps not altogether unworthy of notice, that although many years younger than Mr. Lincoln, General McClellan should have made his first appearance in the public service of the country simultaneously with the national debut of his actual competitor for the presidential chair.

Abraham Lincoln appeared for the first time on the stage

of national affairs in 1847, as a member of Congress from the State of Illinois; and although by no means prominent in the debates of the House of Representatives, he yet attracted attention by the pertinacity with which he denounced the national administration as having provoked the war with Mexico unnecessarily and wantonly, if not wickedly and with a sinister purpose. If we are to accept the cant of the present day, in deed the actual president of 1864 was in 1847 a most malignant and active Mexican "Copperhead."

In 1847 George Brinton McClellan also appeared for the first time on the stage of national affairs, as a soldier in the field upholding the honor of the national flag. After a brief period of service, at once obscure and arduous, on the banks of the Rio Grande, the young Lieutenant was ordered to Tampico in January, 1847, to take part in the concentration of troops then going on in preparation for the grand expedition which General Scott was about to lead in the footsteps of Cortez against the capital of Montezuma.

The future Commander of the Army of the Potomac was thus made an eye-witness at the outset of his career of the political difficulties and the personal spites which so often surround the path and thwart the plans of the truest patriots and the most accomplished military leaders. No one who is familiar with the history of his country needs to be reminded of the jealousies with which General Scott was forced to contend before he could set himself free to move against the public enemy; and the scenes which passed before the eyes of the young Lieutenant of Engineers during that fretful winter at Tampico must have often recurred to the mind of the Commander of the Army of the Potomac during that period of tremendous but unappreciated labor which intervened between the rout of General McDowell in July, 1861, and the marvellous proclamation made six months afterwards, *urbi et orbi*, to the city and to the world by Abraham Lincoln, of his deliberate intention to "crush" the great rebellion by a simultaneous advance of all the armies of the Union on the 22d of February, 1862.

In the beginning of the month of March, 1847, the army of General Scott at last disembarked from its transports to the west of the island of Sacrificios, and the memorable siege of Vera Cruz and San Juan d'Ulloa began.

It is not our purpose minutely to pursue the fortunes of Lieutenant McClellan through the wonderful campaign of which this siege was the initial chapter.

Who, indeed, can now find the heart to rewrite or even to reperuse the annals of that campaign, in which, if fanaticism and folly are to wreak their will upon us unchecked, American soldiers of the North and of the South, of the East and of the West, for the last time marched side by side to death and victory?

The executive documents of the Thirtieth Congress, in which the story of that glorious campaign lies embalmed, and awaits the historian's skillful hand, can be read now without overmastering emotion only by the fanatic or the fool, by him who is indifferent to his country's fate, or by him who rejoices in her ruin.

To these formal and official pages the course of subsequent events has given the painful interest of a tragedy. In them we read how, working with an equal zeal to serve one common cause, Lieutenants Beauregard and McClellan earned the commendation of their commander in the trenches before Vera Cruz; in them we read how the escort of Captain Robert E. Lee, engaging the skirmishers of Valencia in the Pedregal, opened that stern, unswerving march which led the stars and stripes, through storm and stress of strife and victory, up to their station of triumph on the heights of Chapultepec and the towers of the city of Montezuma. Heintzelman and Magruder, Kearney and Pillow, meet us, marching, manœuvering, fighting manfully together under the one old flag. One day Lieutenant T. J. Jackson, "the horses of his guns nearly all killed or disabled, his drivers and cannoniers cut up," gets one of his pieces from under the direct fire of Chapultepec, opens upon the enemy, and holds the battle till the castle is carried. Another day, Lieutenant Reno, "in the advance with his mountain howitzers," maintains against the superior artillery of the enemy so fierce a fire as saves the bold advance of "Lieutenant-Colonel Albert Sidney Johnston" with his voltigeurs. Now we have "Captain Hooker" riding gallantly down alone to reconnoitre the ground for Lieutenant-Colonel Hebert, of Louisiana; anon, "Lieutenant Grant, of the Fourth Infantry," pushed forward with a party to aid in securing advantages won by the troops of Tennessee and South Carolina.

Between these once fraternal names how wide a gulf has since been dug by passion, by madness, and by folly—a gulf which, in the providence of God, nothing surely but reason and justice can ever bridge again!

The peculiar importance of that arm of the service to which, in virtue of his distinction won at the Academy, Lieutenant McClellan was attached, naturally gave him a prominence in the operations of General Scott's advance to which his years and his rank would not otherwise have entitled him. He won his promotion to the rank of second lieutenant early in the campaign, and received his brevet as first lieutenant for gallant and meritorious conduct at the battle of Contreras on the 19th of August of the same year. The service of the engineers and the staff officers at Contreras was of the most arduous kind, testing in the highest degree the coolness, the personal bravery, and the powers of physical endurance, as well as the professional skill, of those engaged in it. General Valencia's position was infinitely more formidable from the broken, rough, and impracticable character of the country, than from the skill with which that pompous and wordy personage had selected and intrenched his camp, and the reconnoissance which determined the route taken by our troops to assault and overwhelm their enemy, had to be executed on a moonless night, over rocky and precipitous mule-paths, through a region of wild ravines and tangled forests.

Deserted in disgust by Santa Anna, whose advice he had scorned, and whom he hoped by a decisive victory over the American invaders to oust from power, Valencia was utterly bewildered by the attack to which this dangerous night reconnoissance opened the way; his troops, finding themselves inextricably involved, were stricken with a panic, and one of the most complete victories of the war rewarded the skill of our commanders and the valor of our troops.

When compared with the scale on which war has since been waged by American armies, the battles through which our soldiers fought their way to the city of Mexico may seem, indeed, but petty and insignificant combats. But the campaign of 1847 was, in truth, a most instructive school for the officers who passed through it. Not less by the mistakes and failures of the enemy than by our own successes were the capable and the thoughtful among those officers taught rightly to estimate the tremendous difficulties which attend a war of invasion, and the formidable advantages enjoyed by an army acting on the defensive in a country sparsely populated, broken, rugged, and densely wooded; nor is it easy to imagine the extent of the disasters which must have befallen the cause of the Union, in the outset of the existing war, had we possessed no officers qualified by such an experience to neutralize, in part at least, the follies and the presumption of the arrogant and ignorant civilians whose influence has been since so lamentably felt in the disturbance of well considered plans of campaign, and the waste of well organized resources.

The hard-fought action of Molino del Rey on the 8th of September, 1847, afforded Lieutenant McClellan an occasion to prove that his rapid promotion in his profession had not disturbed that conscientious love of justice which is one of the rooted qualities of his nature.

The conduct of the attack upon the Mexican positions at

Molino del Rey had been confided by General Scott to General Worth. The ostensible object of this attack was the destruction of a cannon foundry which the Mexicans were believed to have established at that point; but as General Worth found reason to anticipate such a resistance as might lead to a general action for the possession of the heights and fortress of Chapultepec, it was of the first importance for him to be thoroughly informed of the true nature of the defenses thrown up by Santa Anna at Molino del Rey, and of the true proportions of the force which the Mexican President would there array against him. Two serious reconnoissances were accordingly ordered by General Worth before the attack was made, and in these reconnoissances Lieutenant McClellan bore a distinguished part.

The conflict which followed assumed the character of a battle—the most fiercely contested battle, indeed, of the whole war—in which, after hours of desperate onslaught, an aggregate American force about three thousand five hundred strong assailed and drove from their formidable intrenchments a Mexican army numbering at least ten thousand men, with the loss to the enemy of four pieces of artillery and nearly a thousand prisoners. Lieutenant McClellan was offered the brevet rank of captain for his share in this victory, but declined to receive it on the ground that he was not fully entitled to it, having been concerned in the preliminary operations alone, and not in the actual assault and capture of the enemy's works. The maxim *palmam qui meruit ferat* is not often thus rigorously applied to his own case by a young and ambitious man actively engaged in the most exciting of professions. Within a week, however, the storming of Chapultepec, and the consequent occupation of the Mexican capital, gave the magnanimous young soldier a fresh opportunity of winning, by actual service and exposure in the stricken field, the rank which he disdained otherwise to wear. He was breveted a captain for these crowning operations of the campaign on the 14th September, 1847.

As Captain McClellan, he remained with the army in Mexico till the signing of the treaty of peace with that republic. The administration of a conquered city necessarily afforded to a soldier of his character and training many valuable opportunities of observation and reflection upon the true relations of the military with the civil authority. The impotence of mere force to maintain or restore a solid tranquillity in the social order is never so apparent to a clear and vigorous mind as when force is clothed with a temporary omnipotence; the beauty and the majesty of law are never so apparent as when the calm and constant operation of the law is for a time suspended in favor of the sword. As the Duke of Wellington learned during his long military mastery of the peninsula and his briefer practical dictatorship of Paris that profound dislike of all unnecessary military interference with civil affairs which, at a later day, when England was convulsed with civil commotion, made the veteran of a hundred victories the calmest, most forbearing, and most conciliatory of English statesmen, so we may be sure that his experience of conquest and of military rule in Mexico contributed mainly to fix in the mind of Captain McClellan those sound and moderate principles of policy which were afterward to develop themselves so wisely and so firmly in the proclamations and in the conduct of the victor of West Virginia and the leader of the Peninsula campaign.

In June, 1848, Captain McClellan returned to the United States, and was almost immediately ordered to the post at West Point, where, for three years, he remained in command of the company of sappers and miners. In June, 1851, he was removed to Fort Delaware to superintend the construction of the works, and early in the next year he fulfilled the common destiny of the officers of the regular army of the Union by joining an expedition for the exploration of the far western territory of the Red River, under the command of Colonel Marcy, whose daughter has since become his wife.

From the Red River he passed into Texas upon the staff of General Persifer F. Smith, and until March, 1853, was occupied in the survey of the Texan coast. From the sea-breezes of the Gulf and the lowlands of Texas he was suddenly transferred to the neighborhood of the Rocky Mountains, going to Washington Territory in the spring of 1853, and remaining there until May, 1854, in charge of the western division of the survey for the northern route to the Pacific Ocean. The vast extent, the magnificent possibilities, the grand unity in variety of our great national dominion, which are but sounding forms of words on the lips of so many a blatant orator, become simple realities to the intelligent American officer whose routine of duty thus leads him from one extremity to another of the imperial republic; and the sentiemnt of continental patriotism, which is so vague and passionate in the minds of most men, is thus made to him a substantial and controlling impulse of his nature.

But Captain McClellan's love and reverence of American nationality were to be intensified by a wider and still more impressive experience. In March, 1855, he was promoted to a full captaincy in the First Cavalry, and, with Major Delafield and Major Mordecai, was ordered to proceed to Europe, there to study the operations of the great war then raging between the western allies and the Russian empire. War on a scale which had become traditional in our time, war waged upon the principles of the Napoleonic era, but with all the appliances of modern progress, was now to pass under his inspection. When Captain McClellan and his companions reached the Crimea, in the early part of the summer of 1855, the most trying period of the great allied invasion had already been overpassed. The battle of the Alma had been fought and won; Sebastopol had been invested, so far as investment was practicable; victory had been snatched by the troops of

France and England from the very jaws of ruin, on the heights of Inkermann. But the spectacle which met the eyes of the American commissioners was far more instructive than any shock of battle could have been. In the course of his investigations into the organization and establishment of the allied forces before the Russian stronghold, Captain McClellan learned to estimate aright the tremendous hazards which, even in modern times, and with all the advantages given by a complete command alike of the sea and of all the "sinews of war," attend what may be properly called, as Mr. Kinglake has called it, a colossal "adventure of invasion."

As a means of training the future Commander of the Army of the Potomac, nothing more apt and admirable than this visit to the Crimea could well have been imagined.

England and France, the two greatest military and naval powers of modern times, after many years of uninterrupted intercourse with all parts of Europe, found themselves brought to the necessity of invading a remote and almost isolated province of the Russian Empire.

"Their fleets had dominion over all the Euxine Sea, home to the straits of the Kertch. They had the command of the Bosphorus, the Dardanelles, the Mediterranean, and of the whole ocean; and of all the lesser seas, bays, gulfs, and straits from the Gulf of Gibraltar to within sight of St. Petersburgh. The Czar's Black Sea fleet existed, but existed in close durance, shut up under the guns of Sebastopol." The expeditionary force of the Western allies numbered sixty-three thousand men, and a hundred and twenty-eight guns. The objective point of their campaign was a single city, held to be impregnable by sea, but by land wholly open to attack, and garrisoned, when the allies moved against it, by about forty-five thousand men. Yet such was the difficulty of obtaining accurate knowledge in regard to the condition and strength of this single city, though the embassadors of France and England and Constantinople, their generals and admirals, and the Foreign Offices of both countries, had been engaged for months with unlimited means in procuring it, that the French marshal, St. Arnaud, believed the enemy's force to be seventy thousand men, while the English Admiral Dundas supposed it to amount to one hundred and twenty thousand. Of the commander of the English army, Mr. Kinglake says: "It was natural, that a general who was within a few hours' sail of the country which he was to invade, and was yet unable to obtain from it any, even slight, glimmer of knowledge, should distrust information which had travelled round to him (through the aid of the Home government) along the circumference of a vast circle; and Lord Raglan certainly considered that, in regard to the strength of the enemy in the Crimea and the land defenses of Sebastopol, he was simply without knowledge."

From these inevitable incidents of a great errand of invasion, even in Europe, it had resulted that the commanders of the allied armies, after effecting an unopposed landing on the shore of the Crimea, and winning a brilliant victory within a day's march of Sebastopol, had found themselves compelled, by every consideration of military prudence, to such delays in their movement upon that place as afforded its Russian defenders time enough to avail themselves of the genius of a young engineer who, with pickax and spade, rapidly made their stronghold as formidable by land as it had before been by sea, and determined, by his achievements in a single siege, the whole modern system of fortifications.

All that it was the rare privilege of Captain McClellan to see and learn of the relations between politics and the military art, and of the practical operations of war conducted upon the grandest scale, during his visit to Sebastopol, might, however, let us here observe, have produced but an imperfect and inadequate effect upon his mind, had not his own previous and priceless, though comparatively limited, experience in Mexico prepared him intelligently to receive it, and fitted him to deduce from it the most solid instruction and the most durable convictions. The immediate fruit of his sojourn in Europe at this time was an elaborate and exhaustive report upon the constitution of the greater European armies, which was published under the authority of Congress in the early part of the year 1857, and which bears irrefragable witness to the pains and zeal with which the young officer had devoted himself to mastering the minutest details, as well as the broadest principles, of military organization. But of infinitely greater pith and moment to himself and to his country were the larger and deeper results of this military tour upon his mental constitution and his habits of thought.

The officers of the regular army of the United States, although most carefully trained in the principles of mathematical science and of the military art, during the four years of their academic course, have enjoyed for the most part in later life but few and limited opportunities of military experience. With the exception of the Mexican war, the lives of most of them now living had been passed, when the great rebellion broke upon us, in a routine of post and garrison duty between the peaceful sea-board of the Atlantic and the frontier forts of the Far West. A harassing but contemptible warfare with the roving Indian tribes of the trans-Mississippi educated them to practical skill in the handling of small detachments, but could do nothing, of course, toward familiarizing them with the spirit and the necessities of war on a grand scale. Many of them, inspired with a genuine zeal and love for their profession, were at great pains to master all that books could teach upon this subject. But as the most scientific and thoughtful of military authorities, Baron Jomini, has well observed, "war, practical war is not an affair of mathematical demonstrations; it is a *passionate drama*," and no study of military literature, however judicious and faithful, can teach in years so much available military truth as a soldier like McClellan must imbibe from a few weeks of actual living contact with the realities of war as he came upon and mingled with them in the Crimea. After the publication of this Report on the condition of the armies of Europe, in January, 1857, Captain McClellan resigned his commission in the army and went into civil life.

He was appointed chief-engineer of the Illinois Central Railroad, and upon the completion of that great enterprise was elected vice-president of the company, which post he continued to fill, residing at Chicago, until the month of August, 1860, when, having been chosen president of the Eastern Division of the Ohio and Mississippi Railroad, he removed to Cincinnati. Governor Dennison, of Ohio, in response to the first call of the President of the United States for volunteers to aid in the suppression of the rebellion and in maintaining the supremacy of the constitution, appointed George Brinton McClellan Major-General, to command the contingent of the State, being thirteen regiments of infantry. This commission was offered and accepted on the 23d of April, 1861.

On the 10th of May, 1861, the general government assigned General McClellan to the command of the Department of Ohio, embracing the States of Ohio, Indiana and Illinois, with his headquarters at Cincinnati. Four days afterward he was commissioned a Major-General in the regular army, which rank he now holds. From this appointment dates his entrance into active service in the present war.

CHAPTER II.

THE ORIGIN OF THE WAR OF 1861. CONDITION OF THE COMBATANTS AT THE OUTSET.

THE civil war which began with the surrender of Fort Sumter to the Confederate General Beauregard, in April, 1861, found the States of the South and of the North almost equally unprepared, in the condition of their treasuries and their armaments, for such a contest as the events of a very few months sufficed to develop into its true proportions.

Threats of disunion as a remedy for political evils not otherwise to be reached, had indeed been frequent in the history of the American Republic; but they had never led either the people of the States or the Federal Government seriously to consider and guard against the formidable consequences contingent upon a deliberate attempt to put those threats into effect. This is the more remarkable, that the history of the Union is the history, not of the gradual disintegration of that which had been at first a unit of feelings and of interests, but rather of the attempted consolidation of communities occupying an area of territory half as large as Europe; and divided, not only by distance and the difficulties of communication over so vast a region, but by their traditions, their habits, and the general economy of their life.

When the British Colonies combined, from the frontiers of Canada to the frontiers of Florida, in a common resistance to Parliamentary usurpation, the adherents of the Crown were not less confounded by the harmony in action of Virginia with New England, and of Pennsylvania with the Carolinas, than by the general spirit and energy with which the rebellious colonists confronted the metropolitan power of England, then advanced, by the triumphant administration of Chatham, to heights of imperial splendor unattained before in all her history.*

Under the stress of the Revolutionary War, the tendency to Union was naturally strengthened in the hearts of the peo-

* "Nothing has surprised people more than the Virginians and Marylanders joining with so much warmth with the New England Republicans, in their opposition to their ancient Constitution. . . . As there are certainly no nations under heaven more opposite than these Colonies, it would be very difficult to account for it on the principle of religion and sound policy, had not the Virginians discovered their indifference to both."—*Rivington's Gazette*—(Quoted by Fowler, Sect. Cont., p. 8.)

See, also, Irving's Life of Washington, vol. ii., p. 287. (*Ib.*) Franklin (Works, vol. iv., p. 27) uses the existence of independent communities united under the British flag, as an argument against the claims of Parliament. "In fact," he writes, "the British empire is not a single State, it comprehends many. . . . We have the same king, but not the same legislature."

As to the great differences of feeling that existed between the Colonies even in the high noon of the Revolutionary temper, a cloud of witnesses might be summoned up.

John Adams, in describing his journey to Congress, in 1774, records the fact that many of the New York patriots were "intimidated lest the leveling spirit of the New England Colonies should propagate itself in New York." "Phil Livingston," he says, "is a great rough mortal, who threw out hints about Goths and Vandals, hanging Quakers," and the like, for the benefit of the Eastern patriots. In Philadelphia, too, he found Massachusetts distrusted and scolded.

Patrick Henry's famous speech, in which he declared that he was "not a Virginian but an American," John Adams shows us, met with a tart and unsympathetic reply. "A little colony has its all at stake as well as a great one," exclaimed Major Sullivan.

Nor can there be any doubt that feelings of jealousy and distrust between the Colonies had much to do with the reluctance displayed by the Congress of the Colonies to take the decisive step of abolishing the royal supremacy. The only point distinctly settled by the inconsistent accounts which Adams and Jefferson have left of the genesis of the Declaration of Independence, is the fact that Massachusetts was compelled to surrender the leadership in the matter to Virginia, in order to conciliate the support of the Southern and Middle Colonies.

ple of the various Colonies, although abundant evidence exists to justify the emphatic assertion of the elder Adams, that "it required more serenity of temper, a deeper understanding, and more courage than fell to the lot of Marlborough, to ride in the whirlwind" of sectional passions and interests which convulsed not Congress and the country alone, but the army itself. With peace and independence these passions naturally became more clamorous, and these interests more antagonistic than ever. The inhabitants of thirteen British Colonies had acquired a fresh importance in their own eyes by becoming citizens of as many American States. It was the earnest hope of the wise and great men who presided over the foundation of the new Confederacy, that the general government might be so administered as gradually to wear away the centrifugal forces of local pride and prejudice and interest; and the earliest history of the Union is the history of their persistent and patriotic efforts to achieve this paramount object of statesmanship in America.*

The disruption in 1787 of that which in its articles of organization had been described as the "perpetual" Confederation, though in form a revolutionary act, was in substance an attempt to construct "a more perfect Union by dissolving that which could no longer bind, and leaving the separate parts to be united by the law of political gravitation to the centre."†

The Constitutional Convention of 1787, after discussing the

* In the Congress of the Confederation, it was announced as a matter of course by Mr. Graham, of Massachusetts, that the Eastern States, at the invitation of the Legislature of Massachusetts, were about to form a convention with New York, for "regulating matters of common concern." A debate arose hereupon, (April 1, 1788,) in which Hamilton and Madison earnestly insisted upon the peril to the Union of such conventions, which Mr. Bland, of Virginia, described as "young Congresses."

† John Quincy Adams. (Jubilee Oration, delivered in New York, on the fiftieth anniversary of the adoption of the Constitution.)

bases of this "more perfect Union," from May to November, finally adopted, as the sole alternative of a disorderly dissolution, a plan of Constitution which was very far from commanding the cordial and deliberate support of the delegates, and was with no little difficulty recommended to the favor of their constituents.* Four of the States, indeed, New York, Virginia, Rhode Island, and North Carolina, declined to join in this action; and though the first two of these States soon entered the new Confederacy, Rhode Island and North Carolina insisted upon trying the experiment of independence, and refused to accept the new terms of Union with their former confederates, the one for a little less and the other for a little more than three years. No men were more concerned as to the feasibility of maintaining and consolidating the Union thus framed and formed of such materials, than those who had taken an active and patriotic part in constructing it.

The fears that John Adams had expressed in 1775,† as to the consequences which might and probably would flow from the rooted "dissimilitude of character" between the people of the different Colonies, were felt as keenly in 1789 by men of the most widely different views on all other subjects. It was with a heavy heart that Washington left his home in Virginia to assume the presidential chair, and the scenes of popular joy and exultation through which he passed, on his way to the temporary capital of the newly founded nation, moved him to forebodings scarcely less melancholy than those with which the most gifted member of the cabinet of Wash-

* Secret Debates of the Constitutional Convention. By Luther Martin of Maryland, and Lansing of New York.

† "I dread the consequences of this dissimilitude of character, and without the utmost caution on both sides, and the most considerate forbearance with one another, and prudent condescensions on both sides, they will certainly be fatal."—*Adams' Works*, ix., 367.

John Adams hoped to see the danger conquered by an "alteration of the Southern Constitutions," but it was decreed that the cotton-gin, California, and Richard Cobden, should disappoint this hope.

ington has left it upon record, that he himself undertook "to prop the frail and worthless fabric."*

Under the administrtion of Washington, the conflict of sectional interests, as well as of sectional character, between the Northern and Southern States of the Union developed itself in discussions, which, although they were conducted for the most part, with candor and decorum, and in a temper of reciprocal respect, very clearly foreshadowed the dangers of the future. The institution of slavery at that time existed in most of the States of the Union, as well as throughout the British Colonial Empire. It was denounced by conspicuous statesmen at the South as well as at the North. The ordinance of '87, excluding slavery from the North-western Territory, was originated and passed by the South in the Congress of the Confederation; and the further introduction of slaves into Virginia had been prohibited by law in that commonwealth two years before the adoption in Massachusetts of that justly famous "Bill of Rights," by which slavery was afterwards judicially held to have been abolished in that State.† In the important agricultural States of the South, however, the number of slaves was greater, and their labor more productive than in the Middle and Northern States; and although the slavery question cannot properly be said to have been dangerously debated between the representatives of the South and of the North before the epoch of the "Missouri Compromise" in 1820, it undoubtedly contributed to the vivacity with which the differing commercial interests of the two sections were discussed in the Congress of the Union from the outset of its history.

But it was upon a great question of finance, the proposition

* "Perhaps no man in the United States has sacrificed or done more for the present Constitution than myself, and contrary to all my anticipations of its fate, as you well know, from the very beginning, I am still laboring to prop the frail and worthless fabric."—*Hamilton's Works*, vi., 530.

† Dunbar. Rise and Decline of Commercial Slavery in America. New York, 1863, pp. 212–16.

made by Mr. Hamilton, then secretary of the treasury, that the Federal government should assume the debts of the States, that the two great sections of the Union were, in 1790, for the first time arrayed against each other in an attitude sufficiently ominous of coming mischief to justify the earnestness with which Washington, in his farewell address, a few years afterwards, warned his countrymen against the organization of sectional parties. The Northern States supported, the Southern States opposed this measure with so much acrimony on either side, that when the proposition was finally rejected, Congress met and adjourned from day to day without doing anything; and the members from the Eastern States openly threatened the secession of those States from the Union, and the formation of an Eastern Confederacy.* A compromise was finally effected by the concession to the South of a site for the National Capital on the banks of the Potomac, in return for the reconsideration by the Southern members of the vote which had defeated the "Assumption Bill;" and American statesmanship received its first important lesson in the only policy which could be reasonably relied upon to confirm and consummate the union of the States. This lesson Mr. Jefferson, writing in 1792 to General Washington, declared had been lost upon the people of the Northern States, whose representatives in Congress had "availed themselves of no occasion of allaying the Southern opposition to the original coalescence"† of the States; and the objections of Washington to accepting a second presidential term were finally removed by the solemn consideration that the "continuance of the Union" depended upon the confidence which the people of both sections reposed in him, and in him alone.

The importance of this consideration became painfully obvious during the administration of the successor of Washing-

* Jefferson's Abridgment of Debates, vol. i., p. 250.

† Jefferson's Works, vol. i., p. 359.

ton. The resolutions passed in 1798 by the States of Virginia and Kentucky, in opposition to the high-handed policy of Mr. Adams, were couched in terms which clearly revealed the determination of those States to break asunder, in a certain contingency, the bond which united them with their Confederates.*

The policy of Mr. Adams, and the party by which that policy had been supported, were alike overwhelmed in the fresh political reaction of 1801, which carried Mr. Jefferson into power, and which that statesman styled the "peaceful revolution."† The conditions of American society, and the direction of American history, were profoundly affected by this revolution, and its most conspicuous immediate results were greatly to intensify the centrifugal forces of sectional feeling in the country, and greatly to widen the scope of the perils with which the Union was threatened by that force.

The territories west of the Alleghany were now becoming

* Upon the Resolutions of '98 Gouverneur Morris remarks: "During the administration of Mr. Adams, Virginia was almost in open revolt against the national authority, merely because a Yankee and not a Virginian was president."—*Life*, vol. iii., p. 196. The tone of this remark indicates a bitterness of sectional feeling in the writer, which is not less noteworthy than the remark itself. As to the extravagance of Mr. Adams' policy, Hamilton, a wiser witness than Morris, is strikingly explicit.—*Hamilton's Works*, vol. vi., p. 307.

† The opponents of Mr. Jefferson, in the New England States, regarded his election very much as the extreme men of the South regarded the election of Mr. Lincoln in 1860. When Jefferson was first a candidate in 1796, Oliver Wolcott, of Connecticut, declared that his election would justify the secession of New England. "I will say that if French agency places Mr. Jefferson in the seat of the chief magistrate (and if he is placed there, it will be by their intrigues,) the government of the United States ought at that moment to discontinue its operations, and let those who have placed him there take him to themselves: for although I am sensible, by our last revolution, of the evils which attend one, I sincerely declare that I wish the Northern States would separate from the Southern the moment that event shall take place, and never to unite with them, except it shall be necessary for military operations."—*Gibbs' Administration of Washington and Adams*, vol. i., p. 408.

occupied by an active and restless population. Pressed upon the north by England, and upon the south by Spain, the new communities of the West were courted by agents of both these powers. Great Britain sought to detach the West from the Union by promises of assistance in compelling Spain to open the lower Mississippi to Western enterprise and commerce; Spain, by offers to relax in favor of the West the severity of her colonial regulations, and to divide with it her monopoly of the splendid traffic of the Mexican Gulf. The Western people were by no means insensible to these advances.* And the enterprise of Burr, although it failed of success, pointed plainly to a new peril for the incipient Union—a peril which Mr. Jefferson by no means conceived himself finally to have conjured, but simply to have modified when the rupture of the peace of Amiens induced the First Consul of France to abandon his projects upon Louisiana, the cession of which he had obtained from Spain, and to transfer the magnificent territory of the Mississippi to the Union.†

The political opponents of Mr. Jefferson, in the Eastern States regarded the annexation of Louisiana as an ample justification of the secession of those States.

* Mr. Blount, a senator from Tennessee, was expelled from the Senate in 1797, for conspiring with British agents against the Spanish possessions.

† Mr. Jefferson considered himself to have done much for his country even in the event of a separate American republic growing up in the Louisiana territory. "If it should become the great interest of these nations to separate from this, if their happiness should depend upon it so strongly as to induce them to go through that convulsion, why should the Atlantic States dread it? . . . The future inhabitants of the Atlantic and Mississippi States will be our sons. We leave them in distinct but bordering establishments. We think we see their happiness in the Union, and we wish it. Events may prove it otherwise; but if they see their interest in separation, why should we take sides with our Atlantic rather than our Mississippi descendants? It is the elder and the younger son differing. God bless them both, and keep them in union, if it be for their good, but separate them if it be better." —*Jefferson's Works,* vol. iv., p. 499.

Propositions which had been entertained towards the end of the administration of John Adams, by distinguished New England statesmen, for the formation of an "Eastern Confederacy," to be bounded by the Hudson or the Delaware, and to be exempt from the operations of the "infamous Virginia policy," were revived and seriously discussed.* It was but natural that a party which had vainly endeavored to retain power in a confederacy confined to the States of the Atlantic, should shrink from the possibilities of a future so immense and indefinite as was thrown open to the politics of America by the acquisition of a new empire beyond the Alleghanies. The States of the South, on the other hand, dominant in the federal councils, and seeing in the geographical position of the new territory a guaranty of vast and direct advantages to accrue to themselves from its acquisition, hailed the treaty of cession as loudly as the people of the West.

The sectional hostility thus developed, was still further embittered by the measures which were adopted by the govern-

* Randall's Life of Jefferson, (vol. iii., p. 368;) Appendix, No. XXIV. In reply to a letter of inquiry from Harrison Gray Otis and others, President Adams wrote, Dec. 30, 1828: "This design had been formed in the winter of 1803–4, immediately after, and as a consequence of the acquisition of Louisiana. . . . The plan was so far matured, that the proposal had been made to an individual to permit himself, at the proper time, to be placed at the head of the military movements which it was foreseen would be necessary for carrying it into execution.' President Adams, in a subsequent letter to Gov. Plumer, states, that "three projects of boundary" for the New England Confederacy had been prepared. These were, "1. If possible, the Potomac. 2. The Susquehanna. 3. The Hudson." Plumer was an avowed disunionist. He wrote to New Hampshire from Washington, Jan. 19, 1804: "What do you wish your senators and representatives to do here? We have no part in Jefferson, and no inheritance in Virginia. Shall we return to our own homes, sit under our own vines and fig-trees, and be separate from the slaveholders?" He records, also, in his journal, a conversation with Timothy Pickering, in which the latter spoke of disunion as desirable; and when it was suggested that Washington had feared and deprecated such an event, added by way of assent and of criticism, "Yes, the fear was a ghost *that for a long time haunted the imagination of that old gentleman!*"

ment of Mr. Jefferson in defence of the American flag and of neutral rights, against the Commercial Decrees of the Emperor Napoleon, and the Orders in Council of the British government. New England regarded the Embargo Act of 1807, as a combined attack of the Southern and Western upon the Eastern States; "domestic convulsions" were threatened as its consequence by New England senators at Washington; and although that act was soon repealed, such was the vehemence of the sectional feeling which it had combined with other causes to excite, that Mr. Quincy, of Massachusetts, in opposing, four years afterwards, the admission of Louisiana as a State into the Union, was called to order for making the deliberate declaration, that by the admission of Louisiana the Union would be virtually dissolved.*

From the peace of Versailles to the annexation of the Louisiana territory, exactly twenty years had elapsed. During that time, the first experiment of union in America had utterly failed; and the real history of the second experiment was now about to begin under conditions and in circumstances seriously unlike those amid which its basis had been laid.

The overthrow of the Federal party coinciding in point of time with the acquisition of the vast territories of the Mississippi, had thrown open a new continent to the progress of new principles. The great development of American commerce and industry now began, and with it the growth of such a material prosperity as was calculated to educate coming generations in an increasing indifference to questions of pure politics. A tendency to centralization, involving in itself the seminal principle of absolutism, was rapidly to become paramount in the governments of the Union, and that efficient distribution of authorities among powers limiting, controlling, and

* "It will free the States from their moral obligations; and, as it will be the right of all, so it will be the duty of some to prepare for separation, amicably if they can, violently if they must."—*Journal, H. of R.*, January 14, 1811.

supporting one another, upon which the wisest framers of the American Constitution had relied for the stability of their work, was to be gradually undermined both in the practice of affairs, and in the affections of the people.

The results of Mr. Jefferson's foreign policy ripened, under his successor, into the second war with England. The States which had most strenuously opposed that policy and upon which its previous consequences had most heavily weighed, were roused by the crowning calamity of war into a fever of indignation and disgust. Influential orators, upon the platform and in the pulpit; able writers in the press; and men whose official station gave special weight to their words, united in calling upon the people of New England to refuse their support to the Federal government in the prosecution of "an unholy and unrighteous war." The menace of disunion was revived. The triumph of the party of Jefferson was attributed to that article of the Constitution which authorized a partial representation of the Southern negroes in Congress, and the institution of slavery was for the first time made the object of fierce sectional denunciations for a political purpose.

Early in the year 1814, a project which had been first publicly advanced in 1783, in the Congress of the Confederation, and which on several subsequent occasions had temporarily occupied the minds of leading men in New England, was carried into effect. A convention of delegates from all the New England States met at Hartford, in Connecticut, in response to a call from the legislature of Massachusetts, "for the purpose of devising proper measures to procure the united efforts of the commercial States to obtain such amendments and explanations of the Constitution as might secure them from further evils."* In this convention, among other things,

* "Men of the North! will you go on and for twelve long weary years see the commerce of the nation bound, her agriculture arrested, her coffers lavished, and her glory trampled in the dust by the *very men whom Southern slaves have lifted into office?*" —*Connecticut Journal,* 1802.

it was proposed to deprive the slave States of the partial representation of their slaves and to make a two-thirds vote of both houses of Congress necessary to the admission of any new State into the Union. The question of the dissolution of the Union was fully and ably discussed, and the general conclusion to which the convention came was, that if the political power of the agricultural and exporting States could be so reduced under the Constitution as to deliver the commercial States from the fear of a preponderance hostile to their interests it would be expedient that the Union should continue to exist. But "whenever it shall appear," said the convention in their report, "that the causes of our calamities are radical and permanent, a separation, by mutual arrangement, will be preferable to an alliance by constraint among nominal friends but real enemies."

The action of the Hartford Convention was considered at the time, both by those who approved and by those who disapproved it, as a distinct and deliberate movement towards the disruption of the Union and the formation of a new Confederacy. John Adams treated it as the retaliation upon the Southern States of the conduct of the latter during his own administration.* Harrison Gray Otis, of Massachusetts, who neither then, nor at any subsequent time, could be regarded as an enemy of slavery upon moral or social grounds, assumed the public responsibility of this ultimatum addressed to the South; and Gouverneur Morris, who had finally revised the phraseology of the Federal Constitution in the convention of 1787, openly encouraged New England to persevere in the course upon which she had entered, declared that New York must join with her, and maintained that the question of

Such extracts might be indefinitely multiplied, but one will suffice to show that the true animus of these early sectional assaults upon the institution of slavery was less detestation of slavery itself than jealousy of the political power which it was supposed to confer upon the slaveholder.

* Life and Works of John Adams, vol. x., p. 48.

boundary to be solved was "the Delaware, the Susquehanna, or the Potomac."*

On the other hand De Witt Clinton, of New York, denounced the convention as "treasonable," as threatening the "explosion of civil war," and simply giving vent and voice to the long-cherished designs of men who had attempted, at a previous time, to enlist Alexander Hamilton as the leader of the armies of a new Confederacy of the North.

The peace of Ghent arrested the progress of the events which must otherwise have followed from the action of the New England Convention. It was no longer necessary for the legislatures of the New England States, in the language of Governor Trumbull, of Connecticut,† "to interpose their protecting shield between the rights and liberties of the people, and the assumed power of the general government." The Hartford demonstration, which might have been, and threatened to be, the *Jeu de Paume* of the American Union, subsided into a factious and sectional manœuvre, which was considered to be more discreditable to those concerned in it than it was dangerous to the country. An "era of good feelings" set in, and men of patriotic minds congratulated themselves upon the prospect of a real and permanent consolidation of the Union in the sense of those illustrious men by whom that phrase had first been used.

But five years had not passed, when the question of preponderance in the Union was once more raised, in such a temper and upon such issues, as proved how vain had been all the efforts of statesmanship to make the principles of the American Constitution familiar, and of patriotism to make them dear to the popular mind. In the year 1819, the State of Missouri, a sovereignty erected out of the territory of Louisiana, demanded admission into the Union. The State had been largely peo-

* Spark's Life of Gouverneur Morris, vol. iii., p. 319. See, also, Letter to E. Benson, *Ib.*, p. 294.

† Messages of Governors of Connecticut.—*Fowler*.

pled by emigrants from the South, the institution of slavery existed within its borders, and the Southern States, no doubt, believed that its admission as a slave State would strengthen their own section in its relations with the Federal Government. This the Northern States also believed, and were determined accordingly to make the abolition of slavery a precedent condition of the admission of the new State. A sharp and positive division of Congress and of the country upon a strictly geographical line was the inevitable consequence of this antagonism. The questions of how a new State could be constituted, and of how far the interference of Congress in the domestic institutions of a new State could be lawfully pushed, were deeply considered and angrily debated at this time. But that the real issue made was an issue of sectional preponderance, is shown by the fact, that even after the question of the power of Congress had been practically settled by the passage of a resolution excluding slavery from all States to be formed out of territory lying north of 36° 30′, the Northern members in the House of Representatives, by a considerable majority, still refused to assent to the admission of Missouri, which lay to the south of that line.

The State was finally admitted, after more than two years of hot and perilous controversy, by a majority of no more than four votes in a House of Representatives of nearly two hundred members.

One man, at least, in America, fully comprehended the magnitude of the danger which lowered upon his country from the clouds of this fierce controversy. "The Missouri question," wrote Jefferson, on the 13th of April, 1820, to his old friend, disciple, and correspondent, William Short, "has aroused and filled me with alarm. . . . . . The coincidence of a marked principle, moral and political, with a geographical line, once conceived, I feared would never more be obliterated from the mind; that it would be recurring on every occasion, and renewing irritations, until it would kindle such mutual and mortal hatred as to render separation preferable to eternal discord. I have been among the most sanguine in believing that our Union would be of long duration. I now doubt it much."

So deeply impressed was Jefferson with the fears which he has here recorded, that, during the remainder of his life, he lost no opportunity of urging upon Virginia and the other Southern States the importance of preparing themselves for the exigency of a great revolutionary change.* The third President of the Union lived long enough to find in his own experience a striking illustration of the vanity of human plans and wishes. Out of his two great political achievements—the expansion of the territorial area of the Republic, and the enlargement of American democracy—had come up the fearful perils which so moved his mind and shook his heart. But for his successful diplomacy the question of the admission of Missouri had never perhaps been raised. But for his triumphant political theories that question, when raised, might have been debated in a calmer, more statesmanlike, and wiser tone. But the ranks of public life were even then filling up with recruits of a less noble type than that of the men whose counsels had originally made the Union possible. The discussion became a contest. It was marked on both sides by a more general disregard of mutual obligations and a more exasperating tone of sectional animosity than had ever before predominated in such a conflict. It came to an end, however, peacefully, and left the Union still unshattered.

But the little children of that time are the mature men of to-day. The earliest impressions of the generation which preceded them had been received from men who had fought together the battles of American Independence, and had labored

* He revived his favorite policy of non-intercourse, and especially warned his Southern fellow-citizens against sending their sons to the North "to imbibe opinions and principles in discord with those of their own country."—*Memoir, Correspondence, and Miscellanies of Jefferson*, vol. iv., p. 342.

together at the fabric of American Union. Their own earliest impressions were to be received from men inflamed to mutual dislike and distrust by an angry sectional contest. The generation which preceded them had learned in boyhood to merge the old provincial pride of the Carolinian and the New Englander, the New Yorker and the Virginian, in the new and grander pride of the American. They in their boyhood were to learn that the Carolinian had claims which the New Englander refused to recognize, that the Virginian had been denounced by the New Yorker as an enemy of human rights and a scandal to the American name.

The process of national crystallization had thus received a shock, the effects of which must necessarily long outlast the immediate oscillation of the system.

This was the more certain, that great and profound changes were going on in the character of the American people, and in the direction of the national destinies. This was more particularly the case at the South. The development of the cotton interest, which dates from the first years only of the nineteenth century, had been most powerfully stimulated by the opening of the western territory of the State of Georgia, and by the rapid settlement of the magnificent valley of the lower Mississippi. Arkansas was already pressing for admission to the Union, and this superb State, with Louisiana, Mississippi, and Alabama, seemed to offer to the people of the South, and to the institution of slavery, a new, imperial, and inexhaustible future. A party, small at first in numbers, but formidable by the fanatical and visionary character of the policy which it proposed to itself, began to be formed in the Southern States, which looked to disunion and to the constitution of a Southern Confederacy, precisely as the Gores and the Pickerings of an earlier day had looked to disunion and the constitution of an Eastern Confederacy.

The increasing power of the Northern States in Congress, and the development of manufactures in those States, which naturally kept pace with the development of agriculture at the South, led the politicians of the North to afford this party of disunion at the South the immense moral assistance of a new sectional issue.

This issue was seriously raised, for the first time, in 1824, upon the right of Congress to establish a tariff for the protection of domestic manufactures. It was again and more seriously made in 1828, when a new tariff was introduced into Congress.

The legislatures of the Southern States protested against the act, as the legislatures of Northern States had protested against the embargo of 1807. By the legislature of Georgia the act was denounced as having "already disturbed the Union and endangered the public tranquillity, weakened the confidence of the States in the Federal government, and diminished the affection of large masses of the people to the Union itself."

Mr. Berrien, afterwards eminent in the national councils, commented, in the legislature of the same State, upon the act as tending to precipitate the greatest trial to which the institutions of America could possibly be subjected. He implored all patriotic men to shrink from forcing upon the country "that experiment which shall test the competency of the government to preserve internal peace, whenever a question vitally affecting the bond which unites us as one people shall come to be solemnly agitated between the sovereign members of the confederacy." *

South Carolina, in which commonwealth the sentiment of dislike to the Union had, from reasons of local origin and application, made more progress than in any other State either at the South or at the North, assumed the leadership of the Southern opposition to the principle of the Federal tariff for protection.

Before the war of the Revolution, South Carolina had been

* Fowler's Sectional Controversy, p. 94.

relatively the wealthiest of the British American Colonies. The commerce of Charleston had been more important than that of Boston, Philadelphia, or New York. But notwithstanding the development of the cotton culture in which she found herself doubly interested, as a producer and as a factor, South Carolina had been gradually losing under the Union the prosperity which she had enjoyed under the crown. It might be easy to show that this fact ought to have been traced, in the main, to causes quite independent of the Union. But political economy is a science of modern origin, which has not yet made itself respected even in the most enlightened countries of the old world, and the people of South Carolina in 1828-9 were easily convinced that they had sacrificed to the Union much more than they had gained from it. This conviction operated upon their minds precisely as Henry Clay did not hesitate in his plea against nullification to assert that such a conviction would operate upon the minds of the New England and Middle States: "Let these States feel that they are the victims of a mistaken policy; let those vast portions of our country despair of any favorable change, and then, indeed, we might tremble for the continuance of the Union." *

The people of South Carolina believed themselves to be the victims of a mistaken policy, and they acted as the people of any other considerable section of the country, laboring under a similar belief, might have acted. They protested against the execution of the obnoxious laws, and having protested in vain they proceeded to make a show of force in maintenance of their protest.

President Jackson met these demonstrations with such a display of the Federal power as the means at his disposal per-

* Mr. Clayton, of Delaware, afterwards Secretary of State of the United States, was still more explicit. In 1833 that senator did not fear to say in his place in the Senate, "the government cannot be kept together if the principle of protection is to be discarded in our policy, and I would pause before I surrendered that principle EVEN TO SAVE THE UNION."—*Benton's Thirty Years' View*, vol. i., p. 321.

mitted, and applied to Congress for authority to reinforce those means. The authority which he asked was conferred upon him, but he was dispensed from the painful and perilous duty of employing it, by a timely congressional compromise, acceptable to South Carolina, and honorable to the government.

The party of disunion throughout the South was, at this time, too weak to afford any substantial support to the extreme views of South Carolina, but the most moderate Southern men, and those who looked with most disfavor upon the attitude of that State, admitted that had the sword been drawn by the President it would have been impossible to avert a general war between the combined Southern States and the Federal government.*

The election of Mr. Van Buren to the Presidency in 1836, avowedly as "a Northern man with Southern principles," afforded a striking illustration of the prominence which strictly sectional issues were rapidly assuming in American politics.

These issues were now about to be formidably influenced by the direct interference of an organized body of Northern men with the most distinctive social institution of the South.

A single man, William Lloyd Garrison, a man of humble origin and of fortunes as humble, animated by a fanatical hatred of slavery, and profoundly disgusted by the indifference with which that institution was regarded by the great masses of the Northern people, devoted himself to the task of setting on fire the moral instincts of the Northern people, and became the Hermit Peter of a Northern crusade against the "sum of human villianies." †

* Speech of B. Watkins Leigh, of Virginia, in U. S. Senate, 1833.

† The "Liberator" newspaper was founded by Garrison in Boston, in 1830. It was published in a mean form and at a small expense. When the government of Georgia placed a price on Garrison's head three years afterwards, Mr. Harrison Gray Otis, then mayor of Boston, truly informed the governor of Georgia that the publisher of the Liberator was an obscure person in a garret, of whom he had never so much as heard.

This man was a stranger to all political parties and combinations. He denounced the Constitution as a "covenant with death, and a compact with hell," because, as he had the capacity to perceive, and the candor to admit, it recognized the existence of slavery and guaranteed the rights of the slaveholder.

For this he was persecuted as a political blasphemer by the people of the North, reviled in the press, and assaulted by well-dressed mobs.

But this did not prevent the people of the South from regarding his course as an indication of Northern sentiment, or Southern fanatics from skillfully employing his most inflammatory harangues to encourage the growth of an intense sectional feeling of hostility to the North and to Northern men.

The then recent emancipation of the British West India slaves* gave a great impulse to this anti-slavery movement at the North. The flame of a succussful enthusiasm in old England communicated itself to the kindling enthusiasm of New England. Men who had "drunk delight of battle" on the platforms of Great Britain, the Varangians of the guard of Wilberforce, eagerly passed the Atlantic in quest of a new field of conflict.

The question of slavery soon began to fasten itself upon the politics of the Republic. Petitions seeking the abolition of slavery in the Federal District of Columbia, were introduced into Congress by members from the North.

The reception of these petitions was opposed by members from the South, on the ground that they violated at once the rights of the States by which the District had been ceded to the nation, and the principles of reciprocal comity and forbearance on which the Union itself was founded. The opposition was at first successful.† But the advocates of abolition returned again and again to the charge.

* August 1, 1830.

† Resolutions introduced into the House of Representatives by Mr. H.

On the 20th of December, 1837, just fifty years after the adoption of the Federal Constitution of the Union, motions were prepared by Mr. Rhett, of South Carolina, declaring it "to be expedient that the Union should be dissolved;" and calling for "a committee of two from each State to report upon the best means of peaceably dissolving it." These motions were intended to be presented as amendments to a motion made by Mr. Slade, of Vermont, to refer a certain petition to a committee with instructions "to report a bill abolishing slavery in the District of Columbia." They were not, however, presented, the original motion, after a hot and dangerous debate, being defeated by a two-thirds vote. But from this time onward the question was destined perpetually to recur in the halls of Congress. It had become complicated with the right of petition in the abstract, of which the venerable John Quincy Adams, a man hardly to be called an abolitionist, but vehement in point of character, and of a mind as narrow as it was vigorous, constituted himself the especial champion. The intemperance with which his position on this point was assailed by many of the Southern members, inflamed his passions, intensified his hereditary hatred of the South, and envenomed the sharpness of his rhetoric; and the debate upon this subject rapidly degenerated into gladiatorial conflicts, certain to exasperate the public sentiment in both sections of the Union.

While the moral relations of the people of the North and the South were in this angry and perilous state, influences most unfavorable to harmony and union were at work upon their political relations also. A great financial crisis in 1837 was followed by a contest, which rapidly assumed a strongly sectional aspect, upon questions of financial policy. The altered

C. Pinckney, of South Carolina, were passed May 25, 1836, declaring that Congress "ought not to interfere in any way with slavery in the District of Columbia," and ordering all papers in any way relating "to the abolition of slavery to be laid upon the table." These resolutions were adopted by a vote of 117 to 68.—*Fowler's Sectional Controversy*, p. 118.

circumstances of the country and of the world were about to invest this contest with a character entirely new. The prosperity of the Southern slaveholding States was about to receive a fresh and powerful impulse, the force and the results of which have only been fully revealed by the events of the existing war.

In 1845, the project of reannexing to the United States the magnificent Republic of Texas, formed out of territory originally included in the cession of Louisiana by France, but receded by the United States, in 1819, to Mexico, awakened a political tempest violent beyond all previous example. The cry of "Texas or Disunion" was raised in many parts of the South, while the legislatures and governors of some of the Northern States emphatically declared that the annexation of Texas would be a practical dissolution of the Union. All the passions before enlisted on the subject of slavery burst forth again upon Congress and the country with fresh fury. Propositions, looking to the abolition of the slave representation of the South, and even to the abolition of slavery itself within the Southern States, by congressional action, were introduced into Congress. These propositions were indorsed by State authority on the one side, and denounced by State authority on the other. Texas, however, was finally annexed to the American Union amid a tempest of moral indignation at the North, which became still more vehement upon the consequent declaration of war with Mexico. In many parts of the North, and particularly in New England, it was found to be practically impossible to raise volunteers for this war. The South and the West regarded the war with favor, and feelings of sectional jealousy and distrust developed themselves in the armies of the Republic actually in the field.

Under the administration of President Polk, the Southern views of financial policy won a substantial triumph in the passage of the tariff of 1846. In this tariff, the principle of revenue was substituted for that of protection, to the manifest advantage of the great agricultural States of the South; while almost at the same moment, the Northern States succeeded in demonstrating their determination to exclude the institution of slavery from those territories of the Union which were still in the process of development into States. So many new States had been created since the annexation of Louisiana, that the traditional dignity which had invested the original State sovereignties was already perceptibly wearing away. Nothing is more easy of development than the sentiment of provincial pride, which, in its origin, is simply pride of family; but time and the light of history are necessary to invest this pride with respectability and authority in the eyes of mankind. As State after State was added to the Union, the general pride of Americans in America must inevitably have overgrown and absorbed these sentiments of local patriotism, had not circumstances, as we have seen, unfortunately tended to group the States into two great sections, by alienations of temper and conflicts of interest.

When it became necessary, in 1846, to make arrangements for aggregating with the dominions of the Union the splendid territories about to be ceded by Mexico, a question at once arose whether the industrial institutions of the South should be suffered to establish themselves upon those territories. Mr. Wilmot, of Pennsylvania, introduced into Congress an amendment to a bill proposed by Mr. McKay, of North Carolina, for making peace with Mexico, which amendment provided for the exclusion of slavery from all territories to be acquired by the Union as a consequence of the peace.

The amendment of Mr. Wilmot was finally rejected in March, 1847, by a majority of five votes only, in a House of one hundred and ninety-nine members. There can be no doubt that the resolute support which the amendment of Mr. Wilmot received from the people, the press, and the legislatures of Northern States, was largely the result of a growing and genuine detestation of slavery. That institution had long since disappeared from Northern life. Men who recurred to the earlier annals of the Republic, found therein abundant proofs that the founders of the Union cordially disliked the institution of slavery, and looked upon it as an anomaly which, in the natural course of things, must soon disappear from the social order of America. That, in the sixtieth year of the history of the Union, this odious system should not only persist in the original States of the South, but should be extending itself over new territories, and claiming the protection of the general government, not for its maintenance alone, but for its progress, revolted the honest sensibilities and the thoughtful convictions of thousands of honest and thoughtful men. Unhappily for the peace and permanence of the Union, the intense moral indignation which was thus aroused, could only find expression through such an illegitimate sectional antagonism in politics, as necessarily excited the people of the South into the belief that their rights, their interests, and their honor were alike in jeopardy.

The imperial resources of Texas had immensely reinforced the slaveholding States. A vast and fortuuate future seemed opening before them. Before the flush of the visions which rose thence upon the mind of the South, the beauty and value of the Union began to pale.

The tone of American politics had for many years been neither elevated nor inspiring. At the North, men of passionate natures and vivid imaginations, recoiling from the corruptions or wearied with the tameness of partisan life and partisan ideas, had begun to examine into the necessity of upholding a Constitution which tolerated the existence of human slavery within the scope of its sanctions, and to agitate in the hearts of the people the revolutionary hope of a reformed Republic, rising like the commonwealth of England in the vision of John Milton, to a youth and a glory clean of this accursed thing. At the South, men of the same type, infuriated by what they regarded as the moral impertinence of Northern philanthropy, disgusted with the hypocrisy of men who made that philanthropy the mask of sectional selfishness and personal ambition, or inflamed with dreams of a grander policy and a loftier fate in the future of a new and more military confederacy, began to question the value of a Constitution which had certainly failed to command universal respect for its provisions, and to plan the disruption of a Union from which they had ceased to hope either for individual distinction or for general repose.

Events were rapidly flowing as these men in either section would have them. One after another, the great ecclesiastical bodies began to divide upon the issue of the toleration of slavery; it being manifestly impossible that men should continue to act together in the name of a common religious faith after it had become clear to any great proportion of their number that God required it of them to treat their fellow-believers as criminals of the deepest dye. Commercial conventions of the Southern States, such as had been stigmatized during the earlier days of the Republic as "young Congresses," began to be held. The proposition to admit California into the Union brought the two sections again into collision.

All the questions which had divided the opinions, all the interests which had fired the passions of the American people for twenty years, were engaged in the fierce debate which now arose. The marvellous golden wealth of the new dominion over which the angry sections contended, acted upon the imaginations of men as the discoveries of Columbus and the conquests of Cortez had acted upon the mind of Europe four centuries before. It was in vain that the chief statesmen of the Republic invoked the influences and appealed to the sanctions of an elder day. They were enabled, indeed, by supreme exertions, to accomplish a new compromise, to achieve the admission of California into the Union, with a Constitution prohibiting slavery, and to impose upon the Northern States a new and more stringent law enforcing the return of fugitives from slavery. But the people of the South chafed against the former measure as fixing a national brand upon their social order, and excluding them from the unreserved enjoyment of all their rights of property, in a region won by contributions of their own blood and their own treasure; while the people of the North revolted from the latter measure as an outrage upon their moral instincts, and an insult to the spirit of the age.

These antagonistic emotions rapidly became the life and impulse of two profound and hostile political movements. At the South the purpose of Southern independence, at the North the restriction of slavery, now began to enlist the strength and mould the future of either section. Such was the general prosperity of the people, however, and so gradual is the apparent advance of the most formidable revolutions, that neither at the North nor at the South was the tremendous power of these divergent forces at all appreciated.

No steps of importance were taken in either section to prepare for the fearful possibilities which were so swiftly ripening into certainty.

A tardy attempt to arrest the progress of disruption was made in 1854, by Mr. Douglas, of Illinois, a man of extraordinary abilities, trained in demagogic arts, and in no wise averse from their use, but filled with an earnest apprehension of the perils of the country, and animated by a patriotic desire to conjure away the coming storm. Mr. Douglas introduced into the Senate a bill repealing the Missouri Compromise of 1820, by which slavery had been excluded from the territories lying north of thirty-six degrees thirty minutes of north latitude, and referring the question of the establishment or the prohibition of slavery in all the territories of the Union to the people of those territories themselves. The purpose of this bill undoubtedly was to allay the passions alike of the North and of the South, by adopting a principle in regard to the occupation of the national domain which should relieve the States in Congress from the dangerous necessity of meeting in consultation upon the issues by which the nation had already been shaken to its centre. But these issues had now passed out of the reach of political measures into the passionate life of either section.

Removed from the halls of Congress and the conflicts of opinion, they were sure to be raised again at once under conditions more formidable still to the public peace, and to precipitate collisions of force.

The anti-slavery sentiment of the North had now penetrated the great religious masses of the Northern people. It had thoroughly colored the dominant literature of New England, and from New England as a centre it had radiated throughout the free States. The ecclesiastical and educational systems of New England had been reproduced from the Hudson to the Mississippi. The social and intellectual life of the Middle and Western States was mainly fed from the colleges, the seminaries, the printing-presses of New England. The sanctions of the ancient theology of New England, the illuminations of the modern philosophy of New England, contending at a hundred points beside, combined their forces against all further toleration of the existence of slavery within the borders of the model Republic.

Another influence of the first importance wrought to the same end. The recoil of the revolutionary wave of 1848 from the shores of Europe had flung upon the soil of the New World an immense emigration from the Continental States, and especially from the German Confederation. Such was the force of this influx that within ten years from the triumph of the reaction in Europe the city of New York alone contained a German population larger than that of any capital in Germany, excepting Vienna and Berlin. The population of German birth in all the Union, which in 1820 had fallen short of eight thousand in the whole, in 1860 had swollen to more than a million and a half of souls, and of this enormous number nearly a million were transferred to America during the six years which intervened between the revolutions of 1848 in

Europe, and the repeal of the Missouri Compromise. Nowhere in Europe had the revolutionary spirit of 1848 taken upon itself so hot and radical a temper as in Germany. Contempt of all things established and venerable had become to it a kind of religion. Thirty years of a stupid and selfish bureaucracy had made the very names of law and order odious to it. The pressure of social inequalities, exasperated by unenlightened legislation, had generated in the wildest and most passionate theories of social organization. Inflamed and embittered by defeat, the leaders of the German Democracy, self-exiled or banished to America, could scarcely be expected to treat the established Constitution of the United States more respectfully than the promised Constitution of Prussia. The great names of American history, the great principles of American polity, were as utterly destitute of authority and of influence over them and over the multitudes who swarmed with them into the promised land beyond the Atlantic, as the heroes of the Nibelungen Lied and the positions of the Pragmatic Sanction. It was enough for them to know that slavery was the converse of freedom, and that the social system of the South conferred upon a certain order of men special privileges and something very like an aristocratic position.

They became at once the deadly, vehement, and determined enemies of slavery itself, and of all guaranties, compromises, and concessions, transmitted from the past or imagined in the present for the protection of slavery.

Nor was the intensity of their enmity diminished by the consideration that the fairest and most fertile lands of the new continent trended southward and westward, beyond the Mississippi, beyond the Missouri, towards the temperate plains of the Indian Territory, the borders of Arkansas, and the distant opulence of Texas. The stream of Western emigration soon found that its most profitable course led it away from the further shores of the great lakes, and below the parallel which the compromise of 1820 had fixed upon as the terminal line of slave occupation.

Meanwhile the prosperity of the South had been advancing with gigantic strides. Slavery no longer languished along the Atlantic seaboard, but, swollen into a lusty and adventurous life, was dreaming of new domains, and asserting itself a legitimate inheritor of the earth.

The gold discoveries of California and Australia coinciding substantially in point of time with the adoption of the principle of Free Trade in the commercial legislation of England, and with liberal modifications in the commercial legislation of the United States, communicated a tremendous impulse to the commerce and the industry of mankind. It has been estimated that the commerce of the world more than doubled itself in the decade between 1850 and 1860. It is certain that the aggregate wealth of the United States alone, during that time, increased in a still greater ratio. In no region of the world did this sudden and immense development of human activity make itself more immediately, in few regions of the world did it make itself more profitably felt than in the slaveholding States of America. From the year 1847 to the year 1860, the civilized world may be said to have been in a conspiracy to stimulate the employment of slave labor in the cotton-growing States of the Union. While immigration and individual enterprise were sowing States broadcast over the prairies of the Northwest, commerce was inflaming the mind of the Southern planter with visions of indefinite empire, and of a "potentiality of wealth beyond the dreams of avarice."

The South, which in the main had been almost stationary during the earlier portion of the century, pressed forward in the race of prosperity during these eventful years with an impulse and an energy which are far from having been generally recognized, but which cannot be overlooked by him who would form a just and practical conception of the causes which led to the great national catastrophe of 1861, or a reasonable estimate of the resources which were brought by the South to the prosecution of the war.

The repeal of the Missouri Compromise throwing open the Territories of Kansas and Nebraska to the enterprise of North and South alike, a direct meeting of the antagonistic forces, and a direct trial of strength between them upon that ground, became inevitable. The collision was eagerly invited by the passions of either party. The South, possessed with a wide-spread and profound contempt of Northern prowess, was first in the field, and while the pulpit and the press of the North rang with appeals to the armed rescue of freedom, imperiled by slaveholding violence on the plains of Kansas, that Territory was invaded by reckless and desperate men from Missouri, and its soil stained with the blood of Americans, slain by Americans, in a contest for dominion over the destinies of an unborn American State.

In that supreme moment, if ever, it might have been expected that the shadow of the coming doom falling upon the minds of the legislators of what was still a Union of States, would have impressed upon them the solemnity and the patience, the mutual justice and the common patriotism, in which alone could any rational hope for the Republic still be found.

But from the halls of Congress came no oracular voice of wisdom and of warning. The clash of arms from the distant West went echoing back to the maddened combatants, mingled with clamors of legislative rage, and the sound of blows stricken in the very Senate of the nation.

In 1856, for the first time in the history of the Union, a great political party essayed to establish itself in power for the express purpose of compelling the slaveholding States to accept the condemnation passed upon the institution of slavery by the moral sense of modern Christendom. The avowal of this purpose made it wholly impossible for Southern men to afford the slightest sympathy or support to the party which avowed it. There were many men of worth and character throughout the

South who believed slavery to be a thing evil in its nature, and in its influences deadly; who were far from sharing the brilliant dreams of so many of their fellow-countrymen, as to the future of a great slaveholding Republic; and who ardently loved the American Union. The desire of such men as these was to see the question of slavery wholly eliminated from all political conflicts; and patriotic statesmanship at the North might have so wrought in harmony with them, as long to defer, if not finally to defeat, all projects of Southern independence; projects which, however flattering to the populations of the South Atlantic seaboard and the Gulf, were neither agreeable to the predominant opinions nor consonant with the interests of the northernmost slaveholding States.

To gain time in such extremities is a victory of the highest importance; and had the candidate who triumphed in the election of 1856 been equal to the great opportunity which Providence afforded him the evil day might perhaps have been long deferred. But Mr. Buchanan was a politician grown old in the small intrigues of party. Neither by nature nor by experience was he fitted to hold the even balance of a wise authority between the angry sections. His administration completed the ruin of the Republic. The question of the Territories, indeed, practically settled itself, but the organization of the Republican party was immensely strengthened by the official corruption and the administrative incapacity which reigned at Washington. That the most conspicuous leaders of the Republican party, during the revolutionary contest which began with the very inauguration of Mr. Buchanan, either designed, or, had they anticipated it, would have risked the overthrow of the Union, is grossly improbable. Faith in the stability of the Union had become an unreasoning instinct of the Northern people. The menaces and the warnings of the South were regarded with contemptuous incredulity and indifference; and politicians who looked upon the anti-slavery passion of the North with the kind of cynical scorn which men of affairs are apt to feel for all political emotions, did not hesitate to inflame that passion to the utmost, as an invaluable auxiliary in their contest for power.

The anti-slavery word was propagated far and wide throughout the land; and the force with which it had possessed the popular heart of the North was revealed in proportions which, to use an image of Jefferson, could not fail to rouse the people of the South "like a fire-bell in the night," when in the autumn of 1859, John Brown, a fanatical enthusiast, who had "done the Lord's work not negligently" in Kansas, attempted to set up the standard of revolt against slavery within the borders of the State of Virginia.

At the North this wild and visionary act was regarded by no inconsiderable part of the population as an inspiration of divine rage against a devilish wrong. The bearing of Brown, during the scenes which preceded his execution, was such as to command for him the almost idolatrous admiration of those who had gradually come to believe the abolition of slavery, at whatever cost, the immediate and paramount duty of all Americans worthy of the name. By the great majority of the Northern people, indeed, his conduct was condemned, but it was condemned in a vague, languid way, as by men who were too much occupied in their own affairs, and too wholly confident of the future to waste their thoughts or their feelings upon a mere "sensational" incident of the passing day. At the South, of course, the case was widely different. Quiet and conservative men were there startled into an indignation and alarm of which the extreme revolutionary party of the South availed themselves as earnestly and as adroitly as the politicians of the Republican party at the North turned to their own uses the exciting event itself.

For many years, the organization of the militia throughout the United States had been falling into decay. Military schools of a respectable character existed, indeed, in several of the Southern States, and in many of the Southern cities independent companies of volunteers were to be found, adequately equipped, and not inadequately trained to such service as volunteers might commonly expect to be called upon to render. But the habits of the Southern people and the distribution of population in the South were alike unfavorable to any general military organization. At the North, matters were in a somewhat better state. In Massachusetts especially, thanks to the somewhat ostentatious administration of Governor Banks, and in New York, at the time of the "John Brown raid," many regiments of militia were to be found not wholly unaccustomed to regimental action; while there is reason to believe that not more than one or two such regiments then existed in the whole extent of the South. Steps were immediately taken to improve the military organization of the Southern people in their several districts. Col. Jefferson Davis, then a senator of the United States from Mississippi, who had won distinction in the field during the Mexican war, and had acquired experience in military administration as secretary of war in the cabinet of President Pierce; Henry A. Wise, then governor of Virginia, a man almost insanely impetuous in temperament, but ingenious and indefatigable in the pursuit of his objects; and John B. Floyd, secretary of war in the cabinet of President Buchanan, an ardent and unscrupulous partisan of "Southern independence," devoted themselves with a particular zeal to this work. It was impossible that the measures necessary to success in such an effort should not heighten the animosity of the Southern people against the people of the North. The identification of the ideas of abolitionism and of the North had for several years been complete in the minds of the common people of the slaveholding States. A further step was now taken, and the "minute men" of the Southern States rapidly came to consider themselves the sentinels and body-guard of Southern society against the threatened invasions of a fanatical North. Upon this irritated and dangerous condition of the body politic the presidential election of 1860 supervened.

Four candidates were eventually presented to the people for their suffrages, by means of that new system of national conventions for nomination which had gradually established itself as a part of the political machinery of the American government. One of these candidates, Mr. Lincoln, was a politician of Illinois of no large national experience, who had adroitly advanced himself, and had still more adroitly suffered himself to be advanced into the front rank of the heterogeneous sectional party of which he was suddenly made the champion and representative. With a facility of habits and tastes, and an apparent simplicity of character, which commended him to the sympathy of the lower orders of his countrymen, he united a mystical fanaticism of temperament which commanded for him the confidence of those who aimed at a moral and political revolution in America, and a practised cunning which enabled him to extract from his double character of politician and of reformer the utmost possible advantage without committing himself absolutely to either.

The most formidable opponent of Mr. Lincoln was Mr. Douglas, also of Illinois, of whom mention has before been made. Mr. Douglas occupied a singular and trying position. He had incurred the personal animosity of President Buchanan, who exerted the whole force of his official influence to prevent the nomination of Mr. Douglas by the Democratic party. The ground taken by Mr. Douglas on the question of slavery was almost equally odious to the extreme representatives of Southern and of Northern passion. To himself the institution of slavery was morally indifferent, and this fact impaired his influence at the North with men who, while they condemned political abolitionism as being at once impolitic and unjust, were keenly alive to the shame and anomaly of the vigorous existence of slavery in the American Republic. At the South, while Mr. Douglas was detested by those who aspired after Southern independence, and disliked by the much larger body of those who desired to see the slave property of the South positively protected by the Federal authority beyond the limits of the States, he was popular with the numbers who cared more for the Union than for slavery, who regarded abolitionism as a sort of malignant invention which might and ought to be put down, and who shrank from the disruption of the confederacy either in a blind horror of all great political changes, or from a wise prescience of the calamities which must follow in its train. In the hope of propitiating the South, and harmonizing its own distracted elements, the Democratic party had appointed its Convention to be held at Charleston, in South Carolina. The Convention accordingly met in that city, April 23d, 1860. After a session of three weeks, the Convention adjourned in disorder, to meet in Baltimore, June 18th; the delegates of all the "Cotton States" having withdrawn from the body, nominally upon the refusal of the Convention to adopt the "platform" proposed by them, but really upon a question of candidates, the friends of Mr. Douglas insisting, in the face of his own remonstrances,* that he should be nominated, with some moderate Southern man, like Mr. Orr, of South Carolina, Mr. Fitzpatrick, of Alabama, or Mr. Johnson, of Georgia, as the vice-presidential candidate upon the same ticket.

When the Convention met again in Baltimore the temper of the members was found to be more uncompromising, and their differences were found to be more irreconcilable than before. The Border slave States, which had refused to leave the Convention at Charleston, abandoned it at Baltimore, Missouri alone declining so to do, and coalescing with the States of the

* There can be no doubt that the consent of Mr. Douglas to appear as a candidate was wrung from him by his friends. Had he been certain of election, his ambition must have made him prefer the immense power he would have wielded for four years, as the Democratic leader of the Senate, under a Democratic President, with the assurance of the "succession," at the end of that time; to four years of executive authority, accepted under circumstances peculiarly embarrassing, and leaving him, when they were fulfilled, a man still in the prime of life, but practically "shelved."

Gulf, conferred a presidential nomination upon Mr. Breckinridge, then vice-president of the Union; a man amiable and well-disposed, but infirm of will, and in politics vacillating, whose nomination, in the circumstances, was a simple offer to the North of the grand alternative of "Southern Rights" or secession.

The original Convention nominated Mr. Douglas, with Mr. Fitzpatrick of Alabama. The latter gentleman, after promising acceptance, gave way to private representations and declined the proffered honor, which was finally assumed by Mr. Johnson of Georgia.

Mr. Bell of Tennessee, a respectable politician of the school of Clay, was also made a presidential candidate, with Mr. Everett of Massachusetts as vice-president, by a "Constitutional Union party." These latter nominations were simply a cry of conservative despair.

In November, 1860, Abraham Lincoln of Illinois, was chosen president of the United States by an overwhelming majority of the electoral vote of the States. He received, however, a marked minority of the total popular vote of the Union, and his leading competitor, Mr. Douglas, fell but a little way behind him in the popular vote of the North itself.

This event was almost immediately followed by the formal secession from the Union of the State of South Carolina. Whether this secession, which took place Dec. 24th, 1860, was intended by all who assisted in bringing it about to be final; or whether a large number of influential men, even in South Carolina, hoped by this decisive act to compel a reconsideration of the past in American politics, and the eventual reconstruction of the Union upon principles more favorable to the peace of the slaveholding States, is a question certainly open to discussion, but not here to be discussed.

The majority of the people of South Carolina itself undoubtedly believed that a complete separation, political and fiscal, from the other States of the Union, as well Southern as Northern, would serve their local interests as much as it gratified their local passions. That the power of the Federal government would ever be employed to coerce them into accepting the authority of the newly chosen national executive, or that if so employed it could achieve such a result, few of them believed. In anticipation of the possibility of such an event, however, the State of South Carolina at once began military preparations, mainly for the defense of the harbor of Charleston, but these preparations were neither extensive nor formidable.

Immediately upon the passage of the ordinance of secession, the news of which was received at the North, at first with incredulity, and afterwards with derision, commissioners were appointed to visit the city of Washington and open negotiations with the Federal government for a peaceable separation. These commissioners, three in number, after being indirectly encouraged by President Buchanan to believe that informal communication would be held with them, addressed a letter to that functionary, January 3d, 1861, which was returned to them within three hours after it had been received, with an indorsement declaring that the president could not read or consider such a document. Upon this the commissioners, one at least of whom, Mr. Orr, there is reason to believe was honestly anxious for such an amicable arrangement of the terms of secession as might not wholly close the door against any subsequent revision of the whole matter, instantly returned to South Carolina. On their way home they passed through Richmond, where their account of the condition of affairs at once exhilarated the then small party of secession in Virginia, and alarmed the much larger party in that State of those who hoped that Virginia in virtue of her traditional influence and her actual importance might be enabled to control the rising tide of events, and avert the now impending peril of civil war.

It would be beside our present purpose to recite at length

and in detail the incidents which from this moment forward hurried on the action of the fatal drama.

One after another the States of Georgia, Alabama, Florida, Mississippi, Louisiana, and Texas, were swept into the pathway opened by South Carolina.

The sectional passion, of which we have sketched the origin and development, was unquestionably the impelling force of this formidable movement. But the resistance which it must otherwise have encountered was paralyzed by the conviction of numbers of honest and patriotic men in those States, that nothing less than a unanimous array of Southern strength, not so much in support of the attitude of South Carolina, as in assertion of her right to be unmolested in assuming that attitude, could prevent the Federal government from drawing the sword and committing the whole issue irrevocably to that dread arbitrament. That the people of South Carolina in the heat of their new-born independence were determined to accept this arbitrament, if forced upon them, was shown in the month of January, when the flag of the United States, flying from a steamer commissioned to relieve the Federal garrison in Charleston harbor, was fired upon by the shore batteries of the State, and the vessel herself compelled to return without fulfilling her errand. Upon this Mr. Thompson of Mississippi resigned his seat in the cabinet of Mr. Buchanan, declaring that the attempt to provision Fort Sumter was a breach of faith with South Carolina, and a violation of the president's understanding with his own advisers.

The people of the North, astounded by the turn which events were taking, accepted the apathy of the administration as a policy, in the absence of any authority able and willing to initiate a more decisive turn in affairs. A deep feeling of indignation against the seceded States began, however, to move the Northern heart. It is as true of nations as of men, that those who find themselves overtaken by a catastrophe which they ought themselves to have foreseen and averted are always particularly impatient and unjust towards the immediate authors of the mischief. The explosion which had now shaken asunder the arch of the Union began to be charged to the account of a few conspirators bent on self-aggrandizement at the expense of their country. A terrible misfortune, more directly attributable to the want of statesmanship and character in the national councils than to any other single cause, gradually assumed the aspect of an atrocious crime, to be remorselessly chastised. Those among the leaders of the incoming administration whose experience and whose capacity might have enabled them to impose upon their associates and upon the country a larger, and calmer, and wiser view of the position, were, unhappily, swayed by the delusion that as the whole matter had been in a great measure brought about by the manœuvres of politicians, it might be safely treated as a gigantic but ephemeral demonstration, to be met by counter-demonstrations as gigantic and as ephemeral.

By the force of this delusion all the good which perhaps might also have followed from the convocation at Washington, early in February, of the "National Peace Congress," was defeated. The deliberations of this "Congress" were presided over by an ex-president of the Union, John Tyler, of Virginia, and many men of mark took part in its deliberations. But the actual leaders of the hour at the North looked upon this Congress with mingled disgust and contempt. They regarded it as a device to secure, in the words of Secretary Chase, "the absolute submission and humiliation of the non-slaveholders of the country," and all hope of any practical result from its conferences was dashed by the ingenuity of a member from New York, entirely devoted to the passions and the purposes of those who believed, with a senator from Michigan, that "a little blood-letting" would do the country no harm.

The impression that the whole movement of secession might be safely dealt with as an ebullition of local petulance, inflamed by partisan passion, was greatly strengthened at the

North by the failure of the "unconditional secessionists" to secure a majority in the Virginia Convention, elected on the 4th of February, and by the refusal of the people of Tennessee and North Carolina to go into convention at all, and these facts, which ought to have fortified the party of conciliation at the North, were perverted to the service of this fatal impression.

There was, however, it must be said, not a little in the course and conduct of many of the seceding leaders themselves to foster this delusion. The seceding States sent delegates in February to a provisional Congress at Montgomery, in Alabama. Here a Constitution substantially modelled upon that of 1787, was provisionally adopted, and a provisional government chosen for the federal administration of the seceding States, under the style and title of the "Confederate States of America." Jefferson Davis, of Mississippi, was named provisional president, and Alexander H. Stephens, of Georgia, provisional vice-president of this new confederacy. The cabinet of Mr. Davis was at once made up of men by no means identified with the party of secession at the South. The most conspicuous advocates of "Southern Independence," indeed, were treated by their new president with a coldness and a refusal of confidence, which provoked an immediate and vehement outburst of disgust and indignation from their organs in the Southern press. Further to the North, the efforts of the secessionists of the border States to impel those powerful communities into following the course of their "Southern sisters," were sternly resisted by a majority of the population, and secretly impeded by the representatives of the "government" at Montgomery. While that government proceeded at once to take measures for raising a "provisional army" of one hundred thousand men, it did not desire, nor did it really expect to be forced into the field against the government of the Union. Extravagantly confident in the power of the cotton interest to compel an immediate recognition of the Confederacy by the greater European States, the Confederate authorities hoped to see the border States cling to the Union, at least long enough to impose a policy of forbearance and compromise upon the incoming administration of Mr. Lincoln. To this end, informal negotiations were carried on during the critical month of February, and the first part of the month of March, between certain leaders of the incoming Federal administration on the one side, and the conservative leaders of Virginia, which State believed herself to be the arbiter of the situation, on the other.

The most delicate and perilous feature of the situation at this time, was the occupation by the United States' troops, under Major Anderson, of Fort Sumter, in Charleston harbor. Down to the day of the secession of South Carolina, Fort Sumter had been practically unoccupied; the Federal garrison holding Fort Moultrie, a more interior defence of the harbor. It had been understood between the government of the Union and that of South Carolina, that no change should occur in the military situation at Charleston. This, at least, was claimed by Mr. Floyd, secretary of war under President Buchanan. During the night of the 20th of December, however, Major Anderson silently transferred his garrison from Fort Moultrie to Fort Sumter, having previously taken such hasty measures as the time and the circumstances permitted for dismantling the former stronghold. This act was regarded by the South Carolinians as an act of war, and they immediately proceeded to occupy the deserted fortress, at the same time declaring that they were willing to treat for the evacuation of Fort Sumter; that, pending the result of negotiations upon this subject, they would suffer the post to be supplied from Charleston,—but that any attempt on the part of the Federal government to throw into it either men or provisions, would be resisted by them at all risks. It was in pursuance of this declaration that the steamer "Star of the West," as we have already stated, was fired upon by the South Carolinian batteries, on the 9th of January. President Buchanan having failed to take, and the people of the Union having failed to demand that he should take, any steps in response to the challenge thus thrown down to the government, the question of Fort Sumter met the administration of President Lincoln at the threshold.

As making an issue between the seceding States and the Federal government upon the right of the former to the possession of the Federal fortresses and property within the limits of their territory, this was by no means an isolated question. Nor did it offer that issue in the most offensive form, or in the circumstances most galling to the self-respect of the Federal authorities. Between the 20th of December, 1860, and the 20th of February, 1861, many forts and arsenals of the United States had been seized in the States of South Carolina, Georgia, Florida, Alabama, Mississippi, Louisiana, and Texas. In several cases, the garrisons of these forts and arsenals had been compelled to surrender, and to lower the flag of the Union before a superior force. In the State of Texas, a general of the Federal army, Twiggs, had taken advantage of his position to put the troops and the property confided to his charge at the mercy of the State authorities.

It is not at all probable that, in transferring his small garrison from Fort Moultrie to Fort Sumter, Major Anderson had any intelligent apprehension of the consequences which were to flow from his action. He seems to have been moved by a sort of blind instinct, such as in many other supreme crises of history, has determined steps in themselves apparently insignificant, but destined, in the great chain of causes and effects, to decide the direction of changes infinitely momentous.

As February wore away, it became apparent to all thoughtful observers that the immediate issues of peace and war lay involved in the settlement of this question of Fort Sumter. The people of the Union were entirely uncommitted upon the matter, and awaited in a kind of incredulous amazement the signal of some decisive action by the government. The president elect preserved an obstinate and absolute silence upon the point, veiling his views and his intentions under a studied display of levity and unconcern, which contrasted strangely enough with the hot and positive breathings of Southern passion. Some of those who believed themselves, or affected to believe themselves, the future masters of the presidential policy, threw out, however, intimations as positive as intimations can ever be said to be, that no issue of force would be made upon the occupation or evacuation of the South Carolinian fortress. Down to the day of the inauguration of Mr. Lincoln, March 4th, 1861, these intimations were authoritatively, though unofficially, conveyed to the "Union" men of Virginia, by whom they were effectively used in thwarting the projects and disarming the appeals of those who were bent upon driving that great commonwealth into an act of secession.

The extreme men of the South, many of whom still remained at Washington, labored incessantly, both there and at Montgomery, to discredit these intimations; to commit not only Virginia, but Kentucky, Tennessee, North Carolina, and Maryland to the new Confederacy, before the administration of Mr. Lincoln should be established in power; and to precipitate an attack on Fort Sumter. These men, of whom Senator Wigfall, of Texas, was a leader and a type, had, with difficulty, been restrained during the early winter from organizing and executing plots for the seizure of Washington and Baltimore; for the occupation of Norfolk and Fortress Monroe, both of which important points might easily have been mastered by small bodies of desperate and determined men; and for the abduction of General Scott, who, with the able and efficient co-operation of Colonel, since Brigadier-General Charles P. Stone, of Massachusetts, an accomplished officer, called by him from the civil life to which he had retired, had taken such measures, during the month of February, for the protection of the Federal capital against their enterprises, as must have insured their utter failure, had they ever been seriously attempted.

The more temperate leaders, into whose control the direction of the Southern movement had fallen, shrank from forcing the crisis of the great events which had lifted them into a position at once of so much power and of so much peril. They clung to the hope of peace, believing that, if the disruption of the Union could be accomplished without a resort to arms, an immense revulsion would set in of the popular feeling in the North and West, which would compel the resignation of Mr. Lincoln, and bring about a convention of all the States for the purpose of reconsidering the past, and reorganizing the national government upon a new and more permanent basis, adapted to the profound changes which had taken place in the condition of all sections of the country.

On the 4th of March, 1861, Mr. Lincoln took the oath of office as President of the United States. For the first time in the history of the Republic, its chief magistrate passed along the streets of Washington to the Capitol under an escort of armed men. Cannon commanded the approaches to the city; a cloud of cavalry encircled the presidential equipage, and the elect of the nation entered the Senate House between files of the sappers and miners, the *corps d'élite* of the small Federal army. The Inaugural Address of the president had been communicated to those who were to appear in history as his confidential advisers only a few hours before it was actually delivered; and, while the burden of the discourse seemed to be eminently in harmony with the professions of forbearance and conciliation which had been so abundantly put forth by the most conspicuous of those advisers, the single assertion which it contained on the point of the president's future policy plainly revealed, to those who had ears to hear, his deep and settled determination to drive the South from the position which it had sought to assume. The president declared it to be his intention to "hold, occupy, and possess the forts and places belonging to the government." By this declaration, the government of the Union was brought face to face with the governments of the seceded States and of the newly formed Confederacy, which were already in possession of many "forts and places belonging" to the former government, and which maintained their right, as representing the people of the seceded South, to the possession of all such "forts and places" within the limits over which their authority was claimed to extend.

The Confederate government, at Montgomery, at once dispatched commissioners to Washington for the purpose of opening negotiations upon this point, and upon all other points arising, or to arise, between the people of the "Union" and the people of the "Confederacy." Mr. Seward, secretary of state, put himself into communication with these commissioners through Judge Campbell, of the Supreme Court of the United States, by whom it is asserted that he was made the instrument of equivocations and false dealing with them, for the purpose of gaining so much time as might be necessary for completing the preparations which the government of Mr. Lincoln was meanwhile making to execute the declared intention of the president. It is quite as probable, however, that the president had taken exclusively upon himself the responsibility of opening his own policy without making that fact known to the secretary of state; that he abstained entirely from committing himself to any part in the action taken by this minister, and that he began his official career by ordering the reinforcement of Fort Sumter within a few hours of his formal installation in the presidential chair. Whatever confidence may have been felt by Mr. Davis and his cabinet in the representations which were made to them from Washington of the intended evacuation of Fort Sumter, and of the pacific dispositions of the Federal administration, no efforts were spared by them to prepare for the worst. The organization of the Confederate army was pushed forward as rapidly as the mutual jealousies and the extravagant pretensions of the different seceded States would permit. Neither arms nor munitions of war were lacking in the Southern States, and the resignation, by a considerable number of officers of Southern birth, of their commissions in the Federal army, enabled the Confederate government, and the governments of the seceded States, to provide the volunteers, who pressed forward into their service, with a reasonably efficient staff of leaders.

One of the most prominent of these officers, Major Pierre Toutant Beauregard, of Louisiana, a man still in the flower of his years, who had distinguished himself as an engineer and in action during the Mexican war, had been sent, immediately after the inauguration of Mr. Lincoln, with the rank of general, to superintend the fortifications, offensive and defensive, of Charleston harbor. General Beauregard found the enthusiastic volunteers of South Carolina ardently engaged in preparing for themselves the certainty of a speedy doom so soon as the Federal fire should open from Fort Sumter upon their inaccurate and inadequate works. Under his practised and skillful supervision the aspect of affairs rapidly underwent a radical change; and when, in the beginning of April, the preparations of the Federal government for the reinforcement of Fort Sumter were completed, and the fleet which bore with it the fate of the Republic steamed out from the port of New York, the issue of any serious attempt to relieve the beleaguered fortress was no longer doubtful.

It is charged by the South Carolinian authorities that an unfair and dishonorable use was made of the permission to visit Fort Sumter which was accorded by them to an agent of the Federal government on the 6th of April, and that this agent communicated to Major Anderson the plan which had been devised at Washington for reinforcing him. Be this as it may, the squadron detailed for the relief of Fort Sumter appeared off Charleston harbor on the 8th of April; and on the same day the government at Montgomery was startled into comprehending the intentions of President Lincoln by a telegraphic message from General Beauregard, announcing that he had received notice of the determination of the Federal authorities to send provisions to Fort Sumter, "peaceably, if they could; forcibly, if they must."

Upon this the secretary of war of the Confederates, Mr. Walker of Alabama, a hasty and hot-headed man, powerful by his family connections, but himself of little weight or influence, telegraphed to General Beauregard an order instructing him to demand the evacuation of Fort Sumter, and should the summons be disregarded to open fire upon it at once. The demand was made accordingly, and Major Anderson in a quiet and spirited reply refused to comply with it.

The issue had at last been made and met. Those who made it were far from believing that it would be thus promptly and peremptorily met. Those who met it had but a dim and vague conception of the gigantic consequences involved in the action they were now about to take. In the Northern cities the vast majority of the population laughed to scorn the notion that a fleet of the Union, advancing to the relief of a fortress of the Union, would really be attacked by the batteries of the South Carolinians, the "Gascons" of America, as from their persistent and petulant boastings they had long since come to be considered. In Charleston, on the contrary, the electric anticipation of battle thrilled the popular heart with a kind of Berserk madness. The accumulated passion and contempt of years blazed out in an ecstasy of fierce rapture at the prospect of an actual collision with the despised and detested "Yankees" of the North.

On the 12th of April, in the gray of the early morning, the boom of the cannon broke upon the lightly slumbering city. Half the night through the men and the women of Charleston had listened for that sound—the few in sadness, soberness, and solemnity of heart; the many with an almost delirious impatience.

As gun after gun rang out upon the still spring air the

people hurried from all quarters of the city to the points of view which best commanded the strange and exciting spectacle. All day long the conflict was kept up between the fortress and the batteries, the squadron of relief, meanwhile, steaming idly to and fro off the bar.

The batteries of General Beauregard had been skillfully constructed, and their guns were served with precision, but the fortress still held out when night fell upon the scene. The attack was renewed the next morning; by noon the fortress was in a blaze, and in the afternoon of Saturday, April 13th, the news of the surrender of Fort Sumter to the Confederate forces was telegraphed throughout the Union.

At the North this news was received at first with blank incredulity; and when it had become no longer possible to doubt, men stared one upon the other "with a wild surmise," as ignorant and unresolved what next to expect, or to suggest, or even to wish.

At the South the tidings everywhere set on fire the inflammable temper of the already excited population. In all the leading towns and cities of the South, the bells were rung in peals of joy; bonfires reddened the sky, and the standards of the new Confederacy and of the States were raised by exulting crowds.

The astonishing fact that throughout the two days of conflict between the fortress and the batteries no human life had been lost was hailed as a merciful interposition of Providence, lending thus to the new-born Republic the consecration of a bloodless parting from its old associates.

The amazement of the North, and the jubilation of the South, were of brief duration. On Sunday, April 14th, President Lincoln issued a proclamatiou, declaring that the execution of the laws of the United States were obstructed in the States of South Carolina, Georgia, Alabama, Florida, Mississippi, Louisiana, and Texas, by "combinations too powerful to be suppressed by the ordinary course of judicial proceeding, or by the powers vested in the marshals by law," and calling upon the States of the Union to furnish their militia to the aggregate number of seventy-five thousand men, for the purpose of suppressing these combinations. This proclamation was modelled upon a proclamation issued by Washington in 1792, and there can be no doubt, either that the execution of the laws of the United States was really obstructed in the States mentioned, or that the president was legally clothed with power to call out the militia of the States for the purpose of enforcing such execution. An interesting controversy might well be maintained, however, as to whether it was intended by the framers of the Constitution that, in circumstances such as had now arisen, or in any circumstances, the president should possess the right to march the militia of one State into another for this purpose, without an express demand made upon him to that effect by the government of the invaded State.

In times of revolutionary excitement, however, acts are arguments. The people of the North rallied at the call of the National Executive, the more enthusiastically that neither the Executive nor the people at all comprehended the true proportions of the events which had provoked it. Never before, in the history of the new world, had so vast a force been so suddenly summoned under arms. The battles of America had been fought, from the wars of King Philip to the conquest of Mexico, by armies the greatest of which scarcely outnumbered a strong European division. To the popular imagination a host of seventy-five thousand men presented an image of irresistible strength.

Thousands of Northern citizens who would have shrunk back in horror and dread from the anticipation of a civil war, and who firmly believed the movement of secession to be a tumult evoked by ambitious demagogues, and odious even to the masses of those who were for the moment swept onward in its rush, hailed the proclamation of the president as opening the prospect of a speedy and pacific settlement of the difficulty. The army which he had called into the field was regarded as a magnificent demonstration of the national police, by the sheer moral weight of which the illegal combinations dominant in the seceded States must be immediately broken up and dispersed. It was fully believed, too, at the North, that the States of the South which had, down to this time, resisted the impulse of secession, would contribute their quotas to this demonstration; and while the comparatively small party of those who at the North had gradually learned to hate the Southern people in hating Southern institutions, rejoiced in the hope of taming the Carolinian pride, and curbing the recklessness of the great Southwestern States, the nursing-mothers of "fillibustering" and lawless foreign adventure, the conservative majorities of the North, animated by a passionate and unreasoning devotion to the idea of American unity, burned with a less unfraternal zeal to chastise the unscrupulous enemies and to reinforce the overawed disciples of that idea in the South.

But the foresight which thirty years before had so earnestly deprecated the perils of any attempt to impose the national will by force of arms upon States acting in their sovereign capacity, was abundantly justified by the effects of the proclamation of April 14th throughout the entire body of the Southern commonwealths.

The governors of Virginia, North Carolina, Kentucky, Missouri, Arkansas, and Tennessee, responded to the appeal of the President by refusing, in language ranging from the courtesy of remonstrance to the contempt of flat denunciation and defiance, to furnish the government with troops for the purpose of aiding in what Governor Ellis, of North Carolina, styled a "wicked violation of the laws of the country," and Governor Jackson, of Missouri, an "inhuman and diabolical" project.

Maryland alone proffered, by her governor, the quota asked of her by the President; but in a published proclamation the governor of that State also invited the people to elect for themselves between the United and the Confederate States.

On the 17th day of April, 1861, the proudest and most illustrious of the American States, the great commonwealth of Virginia, withdrew from the Union which Virginians had been foremost in founding, and over whose history a long line of conspicuous Virginians—statesmen, soldiers, and jurists—had shed the light of their patriotism and their genius. It might have been expected that an act so solemn and so sad would be accomplished by the actors with solemnity and sadness, and that it would have imposed, at least, a brief moment of awe upon all sections of the great people whose destinies it was, for good or ill, so tremendously to affect.

But the tragic proprieties of history exist mainly in the imagination of historians. The secession of South Carolina had been prepared with a deliberate eye to dramatic effect, and had been put upon the stage with all the pomp and circumstance within the resources of the State. The ordinance of secession of Virginia was hurried through an excited and agitated convention, amid the shouts of a noisy and uproarious populace. During the few days which immediately preceded the passage of this ordinance, Richmond had been subjected to a reign of terror. The governor of the Commonwealth, and a majority of the members of the Convention, were known to be hostile to the measure, but not a few of the more conspicuous among these friends of the Union were men whose want of personal character and moral courage infected the whole party to which they belonged with vacillation and timidity. The more respectable among them, too, had laid such stress upon the representations made to themselves, by friends of the administration at Washington, concerning the policy of forbearance about to be pursued by Mr. Lincoln, that the sudden contradiction given by events to all their assurances paralyzed at once their spirit and their influence. Those who had accepted office from Mr. Lincoln, in Richmond, were hastily driven into resigning their posts. Men of Northern birth were insulted by vagrant deputations from irresponsible vigilance committees; and throughout the State a strange spasm of lawlessness and violence accompanied the resumption by the "Old Dominion" of that complete "independence" which Virginia, of all the American commonwealths, should have been the most careful to assert, if assert it she must, with decency, with dignity, and with composure. In truth, a certain dim consciousness of the peril which they were incurring now began to mingle with the passion of the Virginian secessionists. No adequate preparations had been made in Virginia for the contingency which had now overtaken her. Neither Harper's Ferry, the great arsenal of the nation, nor Norfolk, one of its chief naval stations, nor Fortress Monroe, commanding the waters of the Chesapeake and the James River, all of which were within her territory, had she taken any measures to secure. While the more extreme States of the South had been denouncing Virginia as indifferent, if not false, to the Southern cause, the secessionists of Virginia had been too much occupied in bringing the popular feeling up to the work which they had planned, to find much time for providing the materials necessary to the success of that work when once begun. Before they could throw the force of the State into an active disposable form, Harper's Ferry had been evacuated and partially destroyed by the Federal commander of the post; Norfolk had been evacuated, and a vast quantity of the stores there accumulated, with several men-of-war, had been consigned to the flames; and Federal reinforcements had been thrown into Fortress Monroe.

Without committing herself at once to the Confederacy of the South, Virginia rapidly threw herself upon the defensive. Colonel Robert E. Lee, a soldier of marked ability and experience, although avowedly and sorrowfully averse from the policy of South Carolina and the extreme secessionists, felt himself constrained by the withdrawal of Virginia from the

Union to resign his commission in the Federal army, and to take service with his native State. He declined to receive a commission from the government at Montgomery, and was appointed by the governor of Virginia to the chief command of the "Virginia forces."

Meanwhile the republican journals of the North rang with ridicule of the anile and impotent commonwealth which had assumed to clothe secession with the faded terrors of her countenance. It was satisfactorily shown by the returns of the census that the "Mother of States and of Presidents" was decidedly in her dotage, that her financial condition was hopelessly involved, and her military strength contemptible. The vision of a victorious invasion, sweeping over the graves of Washington, of Jefferson, of Henry, and of Madison, to plant again the banner of the Union above the humbled standard of Virginia, was contemplated, not as men contemplate a stern and painful necessity, but with a certain riotous and exuberant levity, the sole and poor excuse of which is to be sought in the unhappy inability of the people fully to comprehend the realities upon which they were rushing.

By the secession of Virginia, the slaveholding States of the West and the State of North Carolina may be said to have been taken in the flank and rear. If that secession was to be maintained in arms against an assault in arms, it was clearly impossible that North Carolina, Tennessee, Kentucky, Arkansas and Missouri could hope to escape from the necessity of acting with one or the other of the contending parties. The position of Maryland excepted that State from this double pressure, at once political and military, while it exposed her to analogous pressure from the power of the North and West. Although the institution of slavery had long been decaying in Maryland, the habits and feelings of the people were still deeply tinged with its influences, and by a thousand ties of association, tradition, and political opinion, the most influential classes of Maryland were inclined to sympathize with the

States beyond the Potomac. A powerful party existed in Maryland bent upon effecting the secession of the State. This party was particularly strong in the city of Baltimore; and there is reason to believe that upon the strength of promises of assistance in the way of men and of arms, made to them by the eager and headlong secessionists of Virginia, the leaders of this party had made no inconsiderable progress towards preparing a revolutionary movement in Baltimore, when all their plans were disconcerted, and all their hopes dashed to the ground, by the discovery that Virginia, once in secession, had neither men nor arms to spare. Simultaneously with this discovery, events occurred in Baltimore which at once precipitated the full power of the Federal government upon that city, and fixed it as in a vice.

On the 19th of April, a regiment of volunteers from Massachusetts, passing through Baltimore, on their way to the defence of the national capital, were compelled to leave the train in which they were travelling, by a barricade of stones and rubbish hastily thrown up on the track, and to march through the streets of the city. Their appearance was the signal for a popular demonstration. An angry crowd, chiefly made up of the dregs of the Baltimore populace, thronged about them with taunts and cries, waving the flag of the Confederates, and assailing their columns with missiles of all descriptions. The march soon became a *mêlée*, and when the troops finally reached the station at which they were to reëmbark for Washington, a desperate attempt was made to block up the track and convert the *mêlée* into a massacre. The troops, however, finally moved off, firing from the windows of the cars, and killing, by one of their last volleys, a gentleman who had taken no part in the riot save as a spectator. Other citizens, the number was never definitely ascertained, and two of the soldiers, had been slain in this affray. Upon whom the original responsibility for this most unhappy collision ought to rest, it is not easy nor is it at this time important to decide. That the real leaders of the secession movement in Maryland should have deliberately planned it, is altogether improbable. Those leaders were perfectly well aware that they were destitute of the means of arming even a small proportion of their own party, and it would have been sheer madness in them thus to invite the establishment of the Federal power by force in Baltimore, and thus to impress upon their projected enterprise, at its outset, a character of lawlessness and mob violence. To them and to their plans, indeed, the riot of April 19th was a fatal blow. Once again the telegraph, which had already played so tragical a part in the grand catastrophe of the nation, by concentrating and condensing the passions of the most widely separated communities, drew the natural excitement and just indignation of the whole North into a single thunder-burst. Years before, Mr. Jefferson, writing to Destutt de Tracy,* had congratulated his country on the hope of permanence for its institutions afforded by "its great extent, and the small portion, comparatively, which could ever be convulsed at one time by local passion."

"When frenzy and delusion," he had said, "like an epidemic, gain certain parts, the residue remain sound and untouched, and hold on till their brethren can recover from the temporary delusion." But the steam-engine and the telegraph, the boasted ministers of peace and good-will, harmony and mutual understanding, among mankind, now lent themselves to the service of the passions most fatal to peace and good-will, to harmony and to mutual understanding. They had annihilated the wholesome action of time and deliberation in this supreme crisis of national affairs.

The smoke had hardly lifted from the streets of Baltimore, when a cry for vengeance—blind, immediate, and overwhelming—went up from all the North. The press, which had long since ceased to lead the public mind and contented itself with giving voice to the extremest passions of the hour, rang with

* Jefferson's Works, vol. v., p 570.

appeals to arms. "Through Baltimore or over it," was the unreflecting response of the North to the madness of a mob as unreflecting.

For the moment, the government of Maryland, and the municipal authorities of Baltimore, were entirely paralyzed. All travel southward through Baltimore was for some time suspended, and the volunteers, who from all parts of the North hurried forward at the summons of the "Capital in danger," were forced to make their way to Washington by a circuitous route through Annapolis.

Measures, however, of a summary and despotic character were soon adopted by the Federal authorities for reducing Baltimore. The success which attended those measures, and the indifference with which the contest for the possession of Maryland was abandoned by the Confederates, must be attributed, in part, to the rapid development of the Northern determination to uphold the policy of the president, and assert the supremacy of the laws of the Union; in part to the chaotic and uncertain condition of affairs at the South; and in part, also, to an aversion then general throughout the South, from the prospect of seeing Maryland introduced into the Southern Confederacy.

This aversion had its origin in a variety of considerations.

Those among the Southern leaders who, like President Davis and a majority of his cabinet, regarded secession as a grand political expedient to result "in a suitable political and civil union, adequate to the security of both sections at home and abroad,"* hoped that Maryland, remaining in the Union, might exert upon the policy of the Federal government an influence favorable to peace, forbearance, and compromise. The chiefs of the party which aimed at a permanent separation, and the foundation of a great Southern Confederacy, felt

* Judge Campbell, of Alabama, in "A Statement and Vindication of Certain Political Opinions." (By the Hon. Wm. B. Reed, of Philadelphia.) Philadelphia, 1863.

that Maryland was rather in name than in fact a slave State; nor had they any desire to see so prosperous a commercial city as Baltimore embraced within the borders of their new Republic, there to compete with the less powerfully developed mercantile interest of the further South, for the control of that magnificent commerce which they believed must rapidly flow in from every quarter of the globe upon the seaboard towns of the Confederacy.

Visions, plans, theories, and schemes of all sorts, however, were destined now to disappear on both sides, under the swiftly advancing realities of war. On the 9th of May the Confederate president issued a proclamation declaring that war existed between the United and Confederate States, and notifying mankind of his intention to issue letters of marque and reprisal in response to the blockade of the Southern ports.

Before the end of the month Tennessee, Arkansas, and North Carolina, with Virginia, had joined the Confederacy of the South, and accepted in its provisional character the provisional government established at Montgomery, which had already raised, without difficulty, a loan of five millions of dollars, and was distributing military commissions, and pushing forward military organizations throughout the Southern States.

Partly as a military measure, and partly, no doubt, for the purpose of controlling the conflicting political elements which threatened to paralyze the movement of secession in its inception, the government of Jefferson Davis was suddenly transferred, on the 21st of May, to Richmond, in Virginia, a point at which the main lines of communication running through the South and Southwest converged, and affording an excellent base of operations, whether offensive or defensive, in the face of the Federal forces now rapidly assembling at Washington and in the State of Maryland.

The reception which the Confederate president met with in Richmond was very far from being satisfactory. He found the Virginian authorities neither friendly to himself personally, nor disposed to abdicate the control of affairs in favor of his administration on the plea of military necessity. For many days those about his person trembled for his safety whenever he appeared in public; and the Confederate secretary of war, who had made himself ridiculous at Montgomery by a speech delivered on the day of the surrender of Fort Sumter, in which he prophesied the invasion and subjugation of the North, found the "Virginia forces" no more disposed to accept orders from his department, or from officers commissioned by the Southern president, than were the New England troops of 1775 to acquiesce in the appointment of Washington to the supreme command of the colonial armies. The greatest efforts were accordingly made to bring forward into Virginia, in the shortest possible time, the largest possible force of troops from other States of the Confederacy.

The carrying capacity of the Southern railways was taxed to the utmost, and from the end of May to the end of June, soldiers, from all parts of the South, arrived in Richmond at the rate of from fifteen hundred to two thousand men daily.

These were the flower of the Southern populations; stalwart mountaineers from Tennessee, the descendants of those bold borderers who had fought for the independence of the State of Franklin; staunch Presbyterians from the highlands of North Carolina, the heirs of those whose Mecklenburg protest against Parliamentary usurpation antedates the Declaration of Independence itself; gigantic up-countrymen from Georgia and South Carolina; high-spirited planters from the seaboard and the lower Mississippi; fire-breathing citizens from Charleston and Savannah, Mobile and New Orleans.

Of arms and equipments these new levies had no lack, and of the war spirit more than a sufficiency. But their discipline was in most cases deplorable, and although many of their officers were men of respectable military training and experience, the army as a whole was in truth little better than a brave and clamorous mob. Their confidence in their own invincibility was only equalled by their contempt for the soldiery of the North. The conviction which possessed the minds of the leading men of the Confederate government that the war could not outlast a few months at furthest was universal among them, and contributed, with the novel excitements of the crisis, and with the military pomp, parade, and circumstance of the hour, to maintain them in a kind of rapture of reckless expectation.

Meanwhile the war fever was raging with an equal heat at the North. The troops called out by President Lincoln had been summoned into the field for three months, and it was generally believed that sixty days would see them returning in an almost bloodless triumph from the overthrow of the pretended government at Richmond. The great West and the New England States vied with each other in the vehemence of their zeal for this "short, sharp, and decisive" war, which was summarily to chastise the treason in which Southern insolence had finally culminated. In this tempest of passion all hope, and even all desire, of a tolerant and reasonable settlement of the national difficulties soon disappeared. Each section felt itself to be absolutely in the right, and neither consequently cared or would for a moment essay to comprehend the objects or do justice to the position of the other.

The great majority of thinking men at the South believed, with Madison in his reply to Patrick Henry, that the national government was intended "to be binding on the people of a State only by their own separate consent," and they necessarily, therefore, looked upon the coercive invasion of a State by the Federal forces as a wicked assault upon the very life of the Constitution. The masses of the Southern people sharing this belief, and imbued also with an intense conviction of the abolitionist tendencies of the North, rose as one man to repel what they regarded as a deliberate attempt to extirpate the institutions and annihilate the prosperity of the South.

On the other hand that great majority of the people of the North which cherished no animosity against the South on the question of slavery, was inflamed by a passionate love of the Union, and filled with a very genuine amazement and horror by the idea that its disruption should be seriously attempted.

No time or opportunity was to be afforded for bringing about a truce of intelligence between these great populations, thus fiercely and suddenly thrown the one against the other by the wave of events.

Everything was done, on the contrary, which could be done, to excite the passions of either section, and to widen the breach between them. A reign of terror began both at the North and at the South.

At the South, "Vigilance Committees" and "Committees of Public Safety" set themselves to the task of driving out of the country all whose fidelity to Southern principles, and whose loyalty to Southern institutions, could be possibly called in question. In some of the States, the State governments attempted to curb this irresponsible violence; but without much success. In Virginia, an act was passed by the convention, which substantially conferred upon the governor of that commonwealth the power of abrogating all the guaranties of personal liberty in the case of Northern citizens whom he might think proper to suspect of designs against the State. The Confederate government was powerless either to inflict injustice or to prevent its infliction; and for many months life and liberty, in many parts of the South, were held at the caprice of private malignity and of popular passion.

In the more densely populated and more highly civilized North, the excitement of the people vented itself more rarely in the form of popular outrages upon individuals. It poured itself through the body corporate of the government, and rapidly infused into the administration of the Republic all the unscrupulous and untrammelled vigor of a military despotism. Since the day when the dispatches of the American commissioners in Paris stung the nation to its feet with the news that the Directory of France had dared pretend to levy tribute in

America, no such abdication of all other considerations in behalf of strengthening the government had been witnessed in the United States. As in 1798, so again in 1861, the people and their rulers underwent a common effervescence of mingled fear and rage, in which, however, the element of rage now enormously predominated over the element of fear. "Every thing was thought possible, and every thing justifiable." To speak of compromise was disloyalty, to deprecate the policy of war was to embrace the hopes of treason. Men were arrested without a warrant, imprisoned without a hearing, discharged without a trial. The mails were violated; domiciliary visits were made in the dead of night; a vast machinery of espionage and of denunciation shook the confidence of private life, and silenced in public the wholesome voices of political debate.

As the tide of passion rose on either side, all the influences most hostile to the public interest and to general peace rose with it to the surface of affairs. The armies which either government had been authorized to raise were large beyond all precedent in America; and as few persons in either section had yet at all divined the proportions of the evil that was coming upon them, all that was adventurous and ardent, all that was scheming and ambitious, in either section, pressed forward for a place in the front of war.

The prowess of the South was ridiculed at the North, the prowess of the North was ridiculed at the South. The great wars which mark our time, the war of the Crimea and the war of Italy, have aroused the military spirit again throughout the world, and nowhere has its recrudescence been more signal than in America. Thousands of young men in both sections responded to the blare of the trumpet and the roll of the drum in a sort of martial infatuation, while thousands more rushed to the field, impatient to vindicate, in a single conclusive ordeal by battle, the impugned valor of the section to which they belonged.

The president of the Confederates was himself a soldier, and, so far as circumstances would permit, he secured to his own armies the important advantage of a body of officers, selected with some regard to their military knowledge and experience.

The North was less fortunate in this particular. Many partisans of the new Federal administration, who had necessarily been disappointed of political preferment in the distribution of a patronage of which the offices disposable were in proportion to those seeking them as one to thirty, eagerly pressed upon President Lincoln their claims to military appointments; and the president thankfully seized upon so happy an opportunity of liquidating past obligations and securing future support. That it was impossible to make a man a judge or a collector of customs, was accepted as an excellent reason for appointing him a brigadier-general.

On either side the most respectable, the most odious, and the most ridiculous traits of human nature, were thus impartially enlisted to precipitate the dread collision of war between the now widely sundered sections of the American nationality.

CHAPTER III.

COMMENCEMENT OF THE WAR. CONDITION OF PUBLIC SENTIMENT, AND OF THE MILITARY FORCE IN THE TWO CONTENDING SECTIONS. THE CAMPAIGN OF WESTERN VIRGINIA. GENERAL McCLELLAN CALLED TO WASHINGTON.

The two great sections into which the American States had by the force of circumstances been gradually divided, having at last, under the stress of political passions and social exasperation, become engaged in arms, the one against the other, it rested mainly with the more powerful of the two, and with the one which claimed to represent the true idea of the national unity, to decide how and for what objects the impending war should be waged.

The majority of the Northern people, as we have seen, had no very definite views, nor, indeed, any very positive feelings on this point. They were content to accept the policy of the government whatever that might be. A well-considered apprehension of the probable results, immediate and remote, of the secession of the Southern States upon Northern greatness and Northern progress, might and no doubt would have dictated a policy to the people themselves. But no such well-considered apprehension existed or could exist among a people to whom the whole of the great drama upon which they were entering was an amazement and a dream.

With the exception of the small and insignificant minority of those who sympathized with the secessionists of the South, the whole North and West were united in the determination to meet force by force, and uphold at all hazards the authority of the Union. But as to the true condition of the South, and the best steps to be taken in carrying out this determination, great diversities of opinion existed. Into the details of these diversities it is unnecessary for us here to enter. Let it suffice to say, that two grand theories of action were evolved from them, each of which had its partisans and supporters in or about the immediate body of the administration.

The first of these theories recognized the facts of secession as they actually existed; the second accepted them as they appeared in the mist of popular astonishment and sectional passion at the North. According to the first theory, the organization of eleven States, containing a population three times as large as that of the Colonies which revolted against the British crown in 1776, and embracing an area of territory half as large as Europe, under a regular system of Federal government, able to command all the resources of those States in money and in men, was a reality too formidable to be lightly dealt with. Those who adopted this view of the position, insisted that the military preparations of the government to assail and overthrow the antagonist authority, thus erected and established, should be at least as carefully considered and as effectively carried out as they would be were it the intention of the government to invade the American possessions of Great Britain or the Republic of Mexico. And they insisted upon this the more strenuously that political considerations of the highest importance were involved in the case actually before them, which would by no means enter into the case of an invasion of the British territories or of Mexico. The object of the war against the South being simply the restriction of the South within the limits of its constitutional obligations, it was evident that if the war were not so conducted as to secure this object, with the least possible loss of life and property, and the least possible inflammation of popular feeling at the South, the war must inevitably aggravate the mischief it was expected to abate.

To this end, they maintained, it was essential that no blow should be struck unless with a moral certainty of success; and that it would be better to spend many months in the preparation of an army which should be reasonably adequate to the enormous work it was to attempt, than to risk the indefinite prolongation and extension of the conflict by such an ill-advised opening of the war as must, in all military probability, result in the failure of the Federal invasion.

Those who thus reasoned, were fortified in their conclusions by the further reflection, that the secession of the Southern States was not a well-organized act of revolution, but an explosion of popular passion. They saw nothing in the Constitution of the Confederacy to which the secession had given birth, to encourage the belief that it could long commend itself to the support of the majority of the States which composed it. They recognized the existence of such an essential antagonism of interests and tendencies between the Southern States of the lower Atlantic and the Gulf on the one hand, and the Southern States of the border on the other, as must infallibly make itself felt at once in the councils of the new federation; and they believed it to be the course of true wisdom to allow these internal forces to work for the disruption of the ties so hastily and so passionately formed. At the same time they perceived that the Northern people also needed to be disciplined and schooled by calmer reflection than is possible to any people amid the heats and clamors of actual war, into a proper comprehension of their own mistakes and their own responsibilities in this matter.

In a word, with men of this way of thinking, the maxim laid down by Lieutenant-General Scott, in a remarkable letter on the prospects of the country, addressed by him to President Buchanan, on the 30th of October, 1860, still held good. They believed, with the only American who had ever successfully conducted a war of invasion, a veteran whose life's experience embraced the most critical periods of the nation's history, that it was "a great object to gain time" for the cooling of the popular passions and the precipitation of the popular reason.

But these men were confronted in the government by an overwhelming majority of the adherents of a totally different theory, in which the movement of secession and the establishment of the Southern Confederacy appeared as the impotent and contemptible uprising of a handful of demoralized politicians against the colossal power of a great people and of its government. Those who looked upon matters in this light, were fully convinced that, to the immediate annihilation of all resistance to the Federal authority, nothing more would be necessary than the dispersion of the bands of insurgents assembled at Richmond for the protection of the arch-conspirators engaged in this audacious treason. They regarded the rebellion of the South as a riot, and the army of the South as a mob.*

The almost universal ignorance of the real nature and necessities of war which existed in America, contributed at once to strengthen these convictions, and to increase the influence of these men. The educated military men of the United States were few in number, and quite destitute of influence as a class. Their own experience of war, indeed, was for the most part of the most limited character. Few of those highest in rank among them had ever seen an army arrayed for actual service; fewer still had ever borne a part in the operations of a grand campaign conducted against a powerful enemy. The military traditions of the nation, too, bore very much the same relation to the realities of its military history, as the legends of the Paladins of Charlemagne bear to the realities of the Pyrenean fights between the Saracens and the Franks.

* Two years after the outbreak of the war we find Governor Andrew of Massachusetts announcing, with the air of a discoverer, to his people at Worcester, that we are "engaged in a war and *not* in putting down a riot"!

Remote from the contact of powerful neighbors, and marvellously favored by the accidents of climate, soil, and geographical position, the people of the United States had been educated into an overweening self-confidence, a contempt of probabilities, and an indifference to the laws of success, which were now about to bear their bitter but wholesome fruit of disaster and disappointment. The popular voice was at the command of those who were ready to brand prudence as cowardice, forbearance as disloyalty, and patience as poverty of spirit.

For a time, however, the execution of the policy of war determined upon by the government was necessarily confided to the man of the largest military experience in America. Lieutenant-General Scott, in virtue of his position at the head of the national army, was charged, in name at least, with the organization of the troops called by the president into the field, and with the planning of the campaign in which those troops were to be employed.

Mainly in consequence of the representations of Lieutenant-General Scott, the president was induced to issue, on the 4th of May, a second proclamation, supplementary to his proclamation of April 14th, and to call upon the States to furnish more than forty thousand additional troops, to be enlisted for three years or for the war. An increase of the regular army was also ordered by the president in advance of the action of Congress, summoned to meet at Washington, in an "extra session," on the 4th of July, 1861.

Assuming that the war about to be waged was to be, indeed, a war, it was evident that success was only to be looked for by the armies of the Union from a strict obedience to the principles of the art of war.

To assail the armies of the Confederates from the Atlantic coast, and drive them back upon the mountain fastnesses of the interior, commanding so great and fertile an extent of territory, the very heart of their strength and hope, was manifestly absurd. The United States possessed but one positive military advantage over the States in rebellion, and this was the control of the sea. Treating the coast line of the Confederacy as a strong position held by the Union forces, it was evidently the dictate of sound strategic principles so to combine the land assaults of the Federal armies as to drive their adversary, when defeated, outward upon this coast line.

It was in accordance with this simple and comprehensive view of the position that Lieutenant-General Scott endeavored to organize his first plans of campaign. But he soon found that whatever deference might be paid to him, there were certain objects which he would be positively compelled to aim at without any regard to their harmony or their discord with his general intentions.

Foremost among these objects was the reduction of Richmond.

The government of the Confederates had scarcely established itself at Richmond before it became evident that the main force and virulence of the approaching contest would be concentrated upon the attack and defence of that capital.

Though the border States from the mountain line of Western Virginia to the frontiers of Kansas were in a state of fermentation and confusion, and it was already becoming apparent that the fury of the war must soon blaze out along the course of the Mississippi and in the central West, the Confederate government pressed forward the great majority of the forces raised throughout the South into Tide-water and Piedmont Virginia. It is probable that Lieutenant-General Scott, had he been left to his own judgment, would have acted upon the Napoleonic maxim of refusing to meet his enemy where that enemy invites the attack, and "for the simple reason that he there invites the attack." But he was not permitted to do this; and in the end of May he proceeded to organize an invasion of Eastern Virginia.

The forces assembled at Washington under the orders of

Lieutenant-General Scott, and now to be thus employed, were respectable in point of numbers; but such was their condition in all other particulars, that they scarcely deserved to be styled an army.

Many of the regiments had reached the capital without arms, and much delay had occurred in arming them. Their field and line officers were, for the most part, entirely destitute of military habits and experience; and nothing at all resembling an orderly hierarchy of command existed among them. The hopeful nucleus of this heterogeneous body was a small force of regular troops; but the organization of this force, small as it was, had been seriously deranged by the secession from the Federal army of many officers who had occupied positions upon its general staff.

The "Grand Army of the United States" encamped about Washington, at the beginning of June, 1861, was an army without a quartermaster's department, without a commissary's department, without a medical department, without a general staff. It had no adequate force of cavalry; and no adequate force of efficient artillery. Its communication with the North were protected by the military occupation of Baltimore, but its positions at Washington were not properly intrenched; and if it was to be moved upon a campaign of invasion it must move without a fortified base of operations, and, substantially, without a reserve.

The preparations, meanwhile, of the Confederates for the defense of Virginia against this army were not much more formidable.

The Southern president, Mr. Davis, a man of military experience and military intelligence, was hampered in the work of perfecting these preparations by a number of influences. The jealous disinclination of Virginia to commit her sword into his keeping gravely interfered with the unity of plans and of command in the Confederate camp.

A like disinclination existed in other States, and particularly in Georgia, the governor of which commonwealth refused to arm or equip any troops going forward to Virginia unless they moved under his own commission.

Cherishing still the hope that actual war might after all be averted, and indisposed to confide in men whose political views differed from his own, Mr. Davis hesitated in his distribution of important commands. Notwithstanding the evident concentration of the Federal power upon Virginia, the end of May found the Confederate forces in that State scattered without any combination of positions, and the Confederate leaders still without any general plan of defense.

Batteries had been thrown up on the banks of the Potomac and the lower James, although so late as in the end of April the city of Richmond had been thrown into a panic by the reported approach of a single Federal war-steamer. The hostile visitor proved to be a passenger steamer, from Norfolk, which narrowly escaped annihilation from a six-pounder cannon hastily dragged to a height near the city. But so entirely without defense was the river throughout its course, that had a single Federal war-steamer been indeed dispatched upon the errand, there can be no doubt that it might have compelled the surrender of Richmond almost without firing a shot.

Norfolk was occupied by a small Confederate force. Colonel J. B. Magruder, formerly of the Federal army, held a position near Hampton and Fortress Monroe, with about two thousand troops, mainly from North Carolina and Eastern Virginia.

The defense of Western Virginia had been assumed by General Lee, commander-in-chief of the Virginia forces, who had dispatched to that part of the State Colonel Porterfield, with instructions to raise a volunteer force, and to hold the line of the Baltimore and Ohio Railroad. Between the extreme east and the extreme west of Virginia lay the main body of the Confederates. General Joseph E. Johnston, a cool, wary, and experienced officer, distinguished in the Federal army by his thorough knowledge of his profession and his great personal gallantry, had been sent with a force, chiefly from Tennessee and Mississippi, of less than nine thousand men and thirty guns, by Jefferson Davis, to the important advanced position of Harper's Ferry. Alexandria was held by a small body of Virginia cavalry. The bulk of the Confederate forces were concentrating at Manassas Junction, a plateau of moderate elevation, twenty-five miles west of Alexandria, which commands the intersection of the great line of railway leading from Washington to Richmond with a branch road, called the Manassas Gap Railway, which runs westward through the Blue Ridge to the valley of the Shenandoah river. This plateau, flanked by two small but deeply bedded streams, the river Occoquan and the now world-famous Bull Run, was admirably fitted for the purposes of the Confederates. The broken and wooded country which surrounds it is traversed, like all northern Virginia, both east and west of the Shenandoah Valley, by few, and for the most part, miserable roads. The Warrenton turnpike, a good Macadamized road, which leads from Alexandria west to Centreville, twenty-two miles distant, turns at that place to the South, and crosses Bull Run at a point now become historical, and known as Stone Bridge.

The Confederate troops here assembled were left under the orders of General Bonham, of South Carolina, until the nature and proportions of the Federal campaign became irresistibly clear, when General Beauregard, who had been previously appointed to the defense of the lower Mississippi, was suddenly recalled to Virginia, and sent to this important command.

Lieutenant-General Scott, being required to invest and invade Virginia, made the best disposition possible of the forces under his command. To Fortress Monroe he sent Major-General Butler, a lawyer of Massachusetts, who had been a conspicuous supporter of the policy of Mr. Jefferson Davis in the Democratic party, but who had thrown himself eagerly into the war, and happening to be sent into Maryland immediately after the Baltimore riots of April 19th, had astonished the government and the country by a kind of unscrupulous Bow-street energy, which raised him at once to the rank of a popular hero.

Major-General Patterson, of Pennsylvania, an officer of some experience, was moved through Maryland towards Harper's Ferry, at the head of a column of twenty thousand men.

Lieutenant-General Scott himself, with the main body of the Union forces, threatened, from Washington, Manassas and the road to Richmond.

The invasion of Western Virginia was committed to Major-General McClellan, who was left substantially to take care of himself, make his own plans, and pursue his own policy.

On the 23d of May, 1861, the Virginia pickets, on duty upon the Virginia shore of the Potomac, near Washington, were driven from their posts by the midnight advance of the "advance guard of the grand army of the United States."

For some days a Federal war-steamer had been lying off Alexandria. Her officers had been exchanging pleasantries and courtesies freely enough with the Virginians; and the latter were evidently quite at their ease as to the perils which frowned upon them from Washington. The advance of the Federal army drove this careless and confident garrison without a blow from the city. They fell back upon the positions at Manassas, leaving this important gateway of Virginia to be occupied in force by the Federal troops.

Ten days after the occupation of Alexandria, on the 3d of June, Colonel Porterfield, then lying with eight hundred men at Philippa, a village of Western Virginia, was surprised in the night by a body of Ohio troops, from the army of General McClellan.

Notwithstanding repeated requests made to him by General Johnston, commanding the Confederates at Harper's Ferry, to communicate with that post on the subject of the advance of the Federal forces, Colonel Porterfield had refused to co-operate in any way with that officer. His own command was in a miserable condition, and after its dispersion by the Federals, it disappeared in the forests of Western Virginia, and was heard of no more, till Colonel Porterfield appeared in Richmond, to report in person to General Lee the results of his campaign.

This disaster, while it depressed to a certain degree the high-wrought popular feeling at the South, materially helped the Confederate cause by making the Virginians more willing to consolidate their forces with those of the other "allied republics;" and it was not long afterwards balanced in their minds by the ignominious defeat at Bethel Church, in Eastern Virginia, of a force pushed forward by General Butler, from Fortress Monroe and Newport News, to attack the North Carolinians of Colonel Magruder in their intrenchments. The action was in itself insignificant, but it produced a profound impression throughout both sections. The Confederates had lost but one man killed and seven wounded; the Federals nearly one hundred wounded and thirty killed. The confidence of the South was inflamed by the victory; and the dread fact that Northern men had fallen in battle by Southern bullets, struck home for the first time something like a sense of the realities of war upon the heart of the North.

A few days after the fight at Bethel Church, on the 15th of June, Harper's Ferry was evacuated by General Johnstone; the combined advance of General McClellan from the west, and of General Patterson from the northeast, making it necessary for that commander to throw himself upon the road of Patterson at Winchester, in order to keep open his communications with General Beauregard at Manassas Junction.

The first really important action of the war was now about to be fought, and in Western Virginia.

This was the battle of Rich Mountain. On the 16th of May, George B. McClellan, previously commissioned as a major-general by the governor of Ohio, had been raised to the same rank in the army of the United States. He had already, as a major-general of volunteers, been put in command of the "Department of the Ohio," comprising the States of Ohio, Illinois, Indiana, with portions of Pennsylvania and Virginia. Finding the government of the United States unable to afford him any practical help in the organization of a force for active operations, General McClellan twice called the governors of the States embraced in his Department into consultation with himself, and eventually succeeded in moving a respectable force of troops, mainly from Ohio and Indiana, into Northwestern Virginia. On the 25th of April, he occupied the considerable town of Parkersburg, and on the next day issued a proclamation, in which he assured the citizens of Virginia that they and their property of all descriptions should be protected by the army under his command, since he came simply to execute the laws, and neither to break nor to make them. The effect of this proclamation was excellent; and when the army of General McClellan, more efficiently equipped and prepared for service, took the field a month later in Western Virginia, it found the Union sentiment of that region a substantial reality.

The Confederates, however, were not disposed to abandon so important a bulwark of their cause without an effort. General Garnett was appointed in June to the command of the Confederate troops in Western Virginia, and finding General McClellan pressing in upon him in force, he proceeded to intrench himself in the strong positions of Rich Mountain and Laurel Hill, where he could dispute with the Federal commander the passage by Huttonsville, through the Alleghanies, into Eastern Virginia.

On the 29th of June General McClellan in person reached Clarksburg, twenty-two miles from Grafton, and on the 1st of July he moved with eight thousand men, thirty miles, to Buckhannon, a point from which he could turn the positions of General Garnett at Laurel Hill, Rich Mountain, and Carrick's Ford. Of these positions Rich Mountain was the key, and was held by Colonel Pegram, of Virginia, with about two thousand men, and seven pieces of artillery.

The march of Gen. McClellan from Clarksburg to Buckhannon led him through a wild and wooded country filled with points from which a serious opposition might with ease have been made to his advance. No attempt was made by the Confederates to avail themselves of these opportunities.

From Buckhannon Gen. McClellan rapidly combined his plans for the capture of Rich Mountain and Laurel Hill.

At daybreak on the 11th of July, Brigadier-General Rosecrans, with four regiments of infantry, and a troop of cavalry from Ohio, moved from the position of General McClellan, in front of Rich Mountain, to the attack of Colonel Pegram's force, which was strongly intrenched at the foot of the mountain. Led by a guide of the country, and by Colonel, afterwards General Lander, of Massachusetts, a bold and adventurous pioneer, familiar for years with Rocky Mountain life, the column of General Rosecrans took its way for five miles through a pathless forest. The trees and the dense underbrush were thoroughly wet with the heavy rain of the night before, and when the column emerged at noon in a road upon the edge of a clearing at the summit, the rain was pouring down with renewed violence.

News of their march had, however, preceded them. A dragoon sent after the column with dispatches had fallen, about seven o'clock, into the hands of the Confederates.

Colonel Pegram had instantly notified General Garnett of General McClellan's intentions, and urging it upon him to occupy a designated point on the road between Rich Mountain and Beverly for the purpose of checking the advance of General McClellan, had dispatched a force of about five hundred men with three guns to occupy the summit of Rich Mountain.

This force opened fire from its hastily constructed intrenchments upon the troops of General Rosecrans as soon as they made their appearance on the edge of the forest. The Union troops, availing themselves of the cover of the woods, returned the fire with spirit, and after an irregular but animated action the Confederates, their line of breastworks being turned by an Indiana regiment, gave way in disorder and fled; one man alone standing his ground and loading and firing a field-piece, until he was shot with a revolver at his post.

General Rosecrans, the field being won, re-formed his troops in line of battle and waited events. Colonel Pegram, finding himself not attacked by Rosecrans, and learning that the advance of General McClellan had not been delayed, attempted to make his escape, taking with him reinforcements which had been sent forward to him from Beverly. A part of his force, dispersed in the trackless forests of the mountains, made its way to a place of safety; but Colonel Pegram himself, with about six hundred men, caught upon the banks of the Cheat River, with no means of escape, sent in a flag of truce and made his surrender to General McClellan on Saturday, July 13th.

The inaction of General Rosecrans after the engagement at Hart's farm, on Rich Mountain, enabled General Garnett to evacuate Laurel Hill during the night. He attempted to make his way by the Huttonsville pass to the Staunton road, but in consequence of some strange misrepresentation, misdirection, or misconception of orders, Colonel Scott, who had been ordered by General Garnett, in conformity with the suggestion of Colonel Pegram, to hold the key of the Beverly road, had failed so to do. General Garnett was accordingly compelled to retreat through the mountains to the southwest. His forces were twice overtaken and attacked by the troops of General McClellan; and in the second of these affairs, General Garnett exposing himself with reckless gallantry, to encourage his men, was killed. His little army was, however, brought off in safety after a most difficult and painful march through a mountain wilderness.

The prostration of the Confederate power in Western Virginia was complete. General McClellan telegraphed to Washington the inspiring news of the capture of a thousand prisoners, with all the stores, baggage, and artillery of the enemy. "Secession," he added, "is killed in this country." This proved to be no empty boast.

The judicious measures which General McClellan had six weeks before taken to appease the alarms and make easy the submission to law of the West Virginia population now bore their fruit abundantly. The armed force which had represented the rebel government being entirely dispersed, and the army of General McClellan conducting itself as in a friendly country, the yeomanry of the mountains, never very warmly disposed towards the great slaveholding interest of the further South and of Eastern Virginia, rapidly made up their minds to stand by the Federal authority.

After accepting the surrender of "John Pegram, Esquire, styling himself Colonel in the Provisional Army of the Confederate States," General McClellan treated his prisoners with marked kindness and consideration, and eventually paroled them all. The effect of this course was greatly to indispose the majority of these prisoners to the further prosecution of hostilities, and for many subsequent months the most passionate organs of public opinion in the Confederate States took frequent occasion to point out the evil influence upon the Confederate army of conduct so entirely in contrast with the popular convictions on the subject of Northern feeling towards the South.

The moral advantages of the victory of Rich Mountain to the cause of the Union, great as they were, were not greater than its material consequences might have proved to be, had not the successes of the Federals in Western Virginia been practically nullified by the terrible disaster which was about to overtake them in the East.

Immediately after the battle of the 11th of July, General McClellan advanced his headquarters to Huttonsville, where he held the only pass available in that region, for many miles, by which an army could be successfully moved into Eastern Virginia. From Huttonsville a decent road leads to Staunton, sixty miles distant, a point of great strategic importance, lying in the rear both of Winchester, and of Richmond, and commanding the lines of the James River canal, and of the Virginia and Tennessee Railway.

Had any unity of design existed at Washington as to the prosecution of the war, it is easy to see how favorable an opportunity was here presented for new and formidable movements against the enemy in Eastern Virginia. As things actually were, however, no such results were to be looked for; and General McClellan, learning that the position of affairs in the Kanawha Valley was far from satisfactory, prepared himself at once for an effort in that direction, and was on the point of moving in person to the assistance of General Cox, there commanding, when he was suddenly summoned to Washington.

CHAPTER IV.

GENERAL McCLELLAN TAKES COMMAND IN WASHINGTON. THE BATTLE OF BULL RUN, AND THE CONDITION OF THE ARMY. CHANGE IN THE PROSPECTS OF THE WAR. REORGANIZATION OF THE FORCES. GENERAL McCLELLAN APPOINTED TO THE CHIEF COMMAND UPON THE RESIGNATION OF GENERAL SCOTT.

GENERAL McCLELLAN, on arriving in Washington, found himself called upon not merely to assume the command of an army shattered and demoralized by defeat, but to construct a military system for a continent at war.

The persistent opposition of Lieutenant-General Scott to any advance of the army at Washington upon the positions of Beauregard at Manassas had been overcome by the "pressure" which politicians and the press had brought to bear upon the president and his cabinet. General Scott knew the true condition of that army; he was opposed, to use his own words, "to a little war by piecemeal," and he desired time enough to organize a force in some degree proportionate to the work which was to be done before attempting to do that work. Of the whole force called into the field under the president's proclamations of April 17th and May 3d, and which amounted in the aggregate to about one hundred and fifty thousand men, including eighteen thousand sailors, much more than one half, or seventy-five thousand men, had been summoned under arms for three months only; the president's most conspicuous advisers, if not the president himself, having expected that before the expiration of this term the rebel government at Montgomery would have ceased to exist, and the seceding States have been restored to their places in the Federal system.

Of these troops it was perfectly idle to expect anything like effective service in a campaign of invasion. The testimony taken by the Committee on the Conduct of the War in respect to the battle of Bull Run conclusively proves that it was hardly worth while to seek for strategic explanations of the results of that battle elsewhere than in the simple fact of its having been fought at all. General McDowell, who commanded the expedition, and with whose plan of operations it is not easy to find any substantial fault, testifies: "I had had no opportunity to test my machinery, to move it around and see whether it would work smoothly or not. In fact, such was the feeling, that when I had one body of eight regiments reviewed together, the general censured me for it, as if I was trying to make some show." "I wanted very much a little time; all of us wanted it. We did not have a bit of it. The answer was, 'You are green, it is true, but they are green also; you are all green alike.' We went on in that way."

Of such a way there was but one end.

The country could not understand, ignorant as it was of war and war's requirements, how it could possibly be true that after three months of preparation and of parade an army of thirty thousand men should be still utterly unfit to move thirty miles against a series of earthworks held by no more than an equal number of other men. Those whose duty it was to enlighten the country were as much in the dark on the subject themselves as their fellow-citizens, and the few military men who pleaded for patience and practical measures got neither justice nor comprehension at their hands. Not all military men, it is true, did so plead. Professional rivalry, jealousy, envy; the desire of promotion and of conspicuous command; in some cases a mere craving for the popularity to be so easily won by falling in with the public clamor of the hour, led some men who should have known better, and probably did know better, into reinforcing the "pressure" which was driving so many brave but undisciplined men to useless slaughter.

The battle was fought. A "foolish affair," to use the language of Gen. Barnard, which preceded it on the 18th of July, contributed greatly to heighten the confidence of the enemy and to disturb the *morale* of the advancing army. But so far as the troops actually engaged on the 21st of July were led and manœuvred into fighting, they fought for the most part gallantly and well, with the bravery which is common to their race. There were exceptions, of course, as in the case of that regiment of which Major Barry testifies: "When I rode in among them and implored them to stand, telling them that the guns would never be captured if they would only stand, they seemed to be paralyzed, standing with their eyes and mouths wide open, and did not seem to hear me."

But in the great majority of instances the men broke because nobody "rode in among them and implored them to stand." New troops, unaccustomed to being killed, and confused by the noise and the sudden movements incident to a battle, cannot very safely be left to the light of nature. Captain Griffin testifies: "A great many of our regiments turned right off the field as they delivered their fire, turning even as they delivered their volleys. They did not go off in any system at all, but went right off as a crowd would walking the street, every man for himself, with no organization at all."

Colonel Davis, himself a volunteer officer, testifies: "I can tell you what I think is the cause of the whole defeat of that day. The troops were raw; the men had been accustomed to look to their colonels as the only men to give them commands. They did not understand the command devolving in succession upon the lieutenant-colonel, major, and the captains in their order of rank. The officers themselves did not know what to do; they were themselves raw and green. Every man went in to do his duty, and knew nothing about anybody else. When the colonels were killed or wounded the subordinate officers did not know what to do, and the men did not know whether to obey them or not. When they lost their commanding officers, or those to whom alone they had been instructed to look for commands, they supposed they had a right to leave the field. That, I think, was the cause of many regiments retiring from the field; not from any cowardice or fear of fighting, but because, having lost their colonels, they supposed they were out of the battle."

The battle once over and definitely lost, the army, of course, morally speaking, became a mob. Much fault has been found, not, perhaps unnaturally, with the very vivid colors in which Mr. Russell of the London Times has painted the retreat from Manassas; and it is certainly but fair that justice should be done to the firm front displayed by the Union reserves at Centreville. But the victorious enemy, exhausted by the conflict, did not make any serious pursuit on the day of the victory; and they were prevented by political considerations, against which General Beauregard indignantly but vainly contended, from following up their advantage by an attempt upon Washington.* Had they made such an attempt the real extent of the demoralization suffered by the Union army in consequence of the disastrous day of Manassas would have been fully and terribly revealed.

General Keyes, who of course did not understand at that time the reasons which withheld the enemy from moving upon

* "In conclusion, it is proper, and doubtless expected, that through this report my countrymen should be made acquainted with some of the sufficient causes that prevented the advance of our forces and a more vigorous pursuit of the enemy to and beyond the Potomac. The war department has been fully advised long since of all those causes, *some of which only are proper to be here communicated."—Gen. Beauregard's Official Report of the Battle of Manassas. Southern History of the War. Richardson, New York*, p. 31. This report of General Beauregard was not made public at the South until the winter of 1862, and it was well understood that the Louisiana general, in the first draft of his report, had been much more explicit in his allusions to the policy of President Davis.

the capital, testified before the committee on the conduct of the war in January, 1862: "There was a striking want of generalship on the other side for not following us. If they had followed us they might have come pell-mell into the capital.' The same witness declared that "the troops then were not in a state of sufficient discipline to enable any man living to have had an absolute command of them."

The defeat at Manassas, in short, was not an ordinary defeat of an army. It was the breaking down of a system.

From the outbreak of the war Lieutenant-General Scott, in virtue of his position at the head of the regular army of the Union, had been at the head also of all the forces called into the field. But he had by no means been permitted to handle these forces as an army, to count upon them in the organization of any complete plan of campaign, or even to organize any such plan. It being considered certain that the war would soon be over, the leading organs and leading politicians of the administration had not shrunk from the responsibility of controlling its conduct. General McDowell testifies before the Committee on the Conduct of the War: "I had begged of the Secretary of War, *and the Secretary of the Treasury, who at that time was connected with the Secretary of War in many of the plans and organizations going forward*, that I should not be obliged to organize and discipline and march and fight all at the same time. I said that it was too much for any person to do. But they could not help it, or did not help it, and the thing went on until this project of the march on Manassas was broached."

The same witness testifies that General Scott's plans were discussed in the Cabinet, and adds in respect to one of those plans: "I do not think well of that plan, and was obliged to speak against it in the Cabinet;" thus revealing to us the fact that great military operations, which could only be successfully conducted on the condition of an absolute unity of command and a consequent absolute secresy in respect to their object and their details, were made the theme of Cabinet meetings where the commander-in-chief was forced into elaborate debate with Aulic councillors, military and civil.

The disaster of Manassas suddenly changed the aspect of affairs. The most careless and ignorant and noisy of the politicians who surrounded the President; the Senators, like Mr. Chandler, of Michigan, whose sufficient theory of the war was summed up in the conviction that "it was a bragging, lying force that the enemy were exhibiting along our lines;" and the representatives who had voted for an adjournment of Congress to enable them to go to the front and see the spectacle of the overthrow of the rebels at Manassas, were silenced for the moment by the new and ominous look of things.

It became evident that the march to Richmond was to be something more serious than a promenade; that the post of a brigadier-general was likely to be more dangerous if not more honorable than a private station; that plans of warfare organized by secretaries of the treasury, cabinet councils, and vehement journalists, might entail mischief upon their authors as well as upon the country.

It was felt that we were about to have war in earnest; that we must meet it with a real army; and that this army must have a real head.

The spirit of the people rose magnificently to meet the emergency. The indignation which had been excitedly the capture of Fort Sumter, had been unattended by any feeling of humiliation. The flag of the Union had been lowered there indeed to the cannon of an enemy. But it had been lowered only after a gallant resistance to an overwhelming force.

The defeat at Manassas on the contrary was a sectional if not national humiliation. President Davis and his advisers, in restraining General Beauregard from an advance upon Washington, have been commonly held to have done the cause of the Union an unintentional service. It may perhaps be doubted whether they might not have done the cause a far greater service had they suffered the fiery Creole to work his will. Sternly and swiftly as the Northern people rose in arms to re-assert their character for conduct and courage in battle, so shamefully impugned at Manassas, their uprising would probably have been still sterner and more swift had the crowning disgrace of the loss of the capital been inflicted; while that revolution in the military policy and management of the administration, which was only partially effected by the sharp lesson of the 21st of July, 1861, might in that case have been made complete and final.

The appointment of General McClellan to the command vacated by the defeat and the consequent though unjust disgrace of General McDowell, was made at the suggestion of Lieutenant-General Scott. But the general voice of the country reinforced the advice of the veteran commander, and smoothed the President's transition to a saner and more practical system of military administration.

For a time everything was committed to the hands of the young general; for the secretaries of the treasury, Aulic councillors, and vehement journalists who had managed and mismanaged the whole military machinery of the country from the appointment of hospital nurses up to the nomination of major-generals, before the awful day of Manassas, could by no means see their way clearly through the chaos which had since supervened; and were in no wise indisposed to shift the burden of organizing the war upon competent and responsible shoulders.

The work was indeed a labor of Hercules. General McClellan has given but the merest outline of its colossal proportions in the following simple statement of the condition of things at the time when he entered upon the duties of his new position:

"When I assumed command in Washington on the 27th of July, 1861, the number of troops in and around the city was about 50,000 infantry, less than 1,000 cavalry, and 650 artillerymen, with nine imperfect field-batteries of thirty pieces.

"On the Virginia bank of the Potomac the brigade organization of General McDowell still existed, and the troops were stationed at and in rear of Fort Corcoran, Arlington, and Fort Albany, at Fort Runyon, Roach's Mills, Cole's Mill, and in the vicinity of Fort Ellsworth, with a detachment at the Theological Seminary.

"There were no troops south of Hunting Creek, and many of the regiments were encamped on the low grounds bordering the Potomac,—seldom in the best positions for defence, and entirely inadequate in numbers and condition to defend the long line from Fort Corcoran to Alexandria.

"On the Maryland side of the river, upon the heights overlooking the Chain Bridge, two regiments were stationed, whose commanders were independent of each other.

"There were no troops on the important Tenallytown road, or on the roads entering the city from the south.

"The camps were located without regard to purposes of defence or instruction; the roads were not picketed, and there was no attempt at an organization into brigades.

"In no quarter were the dispositions for defence such as to offer a vigorous resistance to a respectable body of the enemy either in the positions and numbers of the troops, or the number and character of the defensive works. Earthworks in the nature of 'têtes-de-pont' looked upon the approaches to the Georgetown aqueduct and ferry, the Long Bridge, and Alexandria by the Little River Turnpike and some simple defensive arrangements were made at the Chain Bridge. With the latter exception, not a single defensive work had been commenced on the Maryland side.

"There was nothing to prevent the enemy shelling the city from heights, within easy range, which could be occupied by a hostile column almost without resistance. Many soldiers had deserted, and the streets of Washington were crowded with straggling officers and men, absent from their stations without authority, whose behavior indicated the general want of discipline and organization."

To this let us add, that it was necessary to organize completely and, as the Prince de Joinville very justly says, "without any assistance from the past," the administrative services for provisions, munitions and transports, the artillery reserves, the engineer corps, the pontoon corps, the topographical brigade, the telegraphs and the hospital system for an army of three hundred thousand men, and we may begin to form some fair conception of the task which General McClellan undertook when he accepted the distinction conferred upon him at the end of July, 1861.

Such a conception it is necessary for every man to form, who honestly wishes to understand the part which General McClellan has played in this great war, and to do justice to the ability and the success with which that part has been filled.

The subsequent career of General McClellan as a commander in the field is far more likely to fix the public attention than the story of the months which he passed at Washington, in the later summer and the autumn of 1861, in bringing order out of confusion, system out of chaos, plans and a purpose out of incoherent passion and vainglorious optimism.

But the whole future of the war, so far as concerned its material machinery, was in those months of colossal and almost unrecognized toil. It was in those months that our Western as well as our Eastern armies were planned and moulded into form. Fort Donelson and Vicksburg, Stone River and Chattanooga, as well as Williamsburg and Fair Oaks, Malvern Hill and Antietam, were then preparing, then were made possible.

It may be said by those who have made up their minds not to believe anything good of a general who has become a Democratic candidate for the presidency, that some other commander in the place of General McClellan at this time might have done as well as he the great work which then was done; and this is one of those assertions of which in the nature of things it is idle to attempt to prove a negative. All that we positively know is, that if the foundations of our military successes had not been laid deeply and well during those critical months which followed the disaster of Manassas, we never should have had any military successes at all.

If Manassas had not been fought and lost; if the system, or want of system, which gave us that action as the result of three months of planning and preparation, had been pushed into the autumn of 1861, the spring of 1862 would have found us without an army worthy of the name, either in the East or in the West. What the consequences of such a condition of affairs, as well to the domestic as to the foreign aspects of the war for the Union, might have been, it is not very easy to say. What they probably would have been it is certainly far from pleasant to imagine.

We all know now how full of brilliant promise for the arms of the Union the whole field of operations began to seem a few months after the general organization of the war had been confided to the young general from Western Virginia. But the identification of General McClellan's name and fortunes with those of the army which he himself led into the field has become so complete that much less than justice is commonly done, even when no injustice is meant to be done to him, in respect to those vast preliminary labors and their results on the destiny of campaigns in which he took no active and apparent part.

The records of the War Department, however, will one day bear out the assertion made by the New York *Times* of April 13, 1862, at least so far as concerns the honorable revelations concerning General McClellan which sleep in their huge files:

"There are important facts connected with the history of the Army of the Potomac that will cover General McClellan with glory, and smite certain civil and military officials with the blackest infamy. This chapter cannot now be written. It is sufficient at present to say that Halleck and Buell will not be wanting when the time comes to do that justice to McClellan for the part he took in procuring the victories of Fort Donelson and Fort Henry, Bowling Green and Island No. 10, which has so honorably distinguished General Burnside in his recent report to the War Department."

The report of General Burnside here referred to is his report of the operations in North Carolina. These operations had been planned and suggested by General McClellan early in September, 1861, he being then in command simply of the Army of the Potomac, but being constantly called upon by the government for advice in regard to the whole scope of our military operations. When in November, 1861, General McClellan was formally appointed to the chief command of the armies of the Union, his plan for these operations underwent of course some very important modifications; and his own account of the whole matter may well be inserted here.

THE NORTH CAROLINA EXPEDITION.

The records of the War Department show my anxiety and efforts to assume active offensive operations in the fall and early winter. It is only just to say, however, that the unprecedented condition of the roads and Virginia soil would have delayed an advance till February had the discipline, organization and equipment of the army been as complete at the close of the fall as was necessary, and as I desired and labored, against every impediment, to make them. While still in command only of the Army of the Potomac, namely, in early September, I proposed the formation of a corps of New Englanders for coast service in the bays and inlets of the Chesapeake and Potomac, to co-operate with my own command, from which most of its material was drawn.

On the 1st of November, however, I was called to relieve Lieutenant-General Scott in the chief and general command of the armies of the Union. The direction and nature of this coast expedition, therefore, were somewhat changed, as will soon appear in the original plan submitted to the secretary of war, and the letter of instructions later issued to General Burnside, its commander. The whole country indeed had now become the theatre of military operations from the Potomac to and beyond the Mississippi, and to assist the navy in perfecting and sustaining the blockade, it became necesssry to extend those operations to points on the sea-coast, Roanoke Island, Savannah and New Orleans. It remained also to equip and organize the armies of the West, whose condition was little better than that of the Army of the Potomac had been.

The direction of the campaigns in the West, and of the operations upon the seaboard, enabled me to enter upon larger combinations, and to accomplish results the necessity and advantage of which had not been unforeseen, but which had been beyond the ability of the single army formerly under my command to effect.

The following letters and a subsequent paper to the Secretary of War sufficiently indicate the nature of those combinations to minds accustomed to reason upon military operations.

HEADQUARTERS ARMY OF THE POTOMAC,
WASHINGTON, Sept. 6, 1861.

HON. SIMON CAMERON, *Secretary of War:*

SIR: I have the honor to suggest the following proposition, with the request that the necessary authority be at once given me to carry it out: To organize a force of two brigades of five regiments each of New England men, for the general service—but particularly adapted to coast service. The officers and men to be sufficiently conversant with boat service to manage steamers, sailing vessels, launches, barges, surf boats, floating batteries, &c. To charter or buy for the command a sufficient number of propellers or tug-boats for transportation of men and supplies, the machinery of which should be amply protected by timber: the vessels to have permanent experienced officers from the merchant service, but to be manned by details from the command. A naval officer to be attached to the staff of the commanding officer. The flank companies of each regiment to be armed with Dahlgren boat guns, and carbines with water-proof cartridges; the other companies to have such arms as I may hereafter designate, to be uniformed and equipped as the Rhode Island regiments are. Launches and floating batteries, with timber parapets of sufficient capacity to land or bring into action the entire force.

The entire management and organization of the force to be under my control, and to form an integral part of the Army of the Potomac.

The immediate object of this force is for operations in the inlets of Chesapeake Bay and the Potomac: by enabling me thus to land troops at points where they are needed, this force can also be used in conjunction with a naval force operating against points on the sea-coast. This coast division to be commanded by a general officer of my selection. The regiments to be organized as other land forces. The disbursements for vessels, &c., to be made by the proper department of the army, upon the requisitions of the general commanding the division, with my approval.

I think the entire force can be organized in thirty days, and by no means the least of the advantages of this proposition is the fact, that it will call into the service a class of men who would not otherwise enter the army.

You will immediately perceive that the object of this force is to follow along the coast, and up the inlets and rivers, the movements of the main army when it advances.

I am, very respectfully, your obedient servant,

G. B. McClellan, Maj.-Gen. Comdg.

Owing chiefly to the difficulty in procuring the requsite vessels, and adapting them to the special purposes contemplated, this expedition was not ready for service until January, 1862.

When in the chief command I deemed it best to send it to North Carolina with the design indicated in the following letter:

HEADQUARTERS OF THE ARMY,
WASHINGTON, January 7, 1862.

Brig.-Gen. A. E. BURNSIDE, *Commanding Expedition:*

GENERAL: In accordance with verbal instructions heretofore given you—you will, after uniting with flag-officer Goldsborough, at Fort Monroe, proceed under his convey to Hatteras Inlet, where you will in connection with him, take the most prompt measures for crossing the fleet over the bulkhead into the waters of the sound. Under the accompanying general order constituting the Department of North Carolina, you will assume command of the garrison at Hatteras Inlet, and make such dispositions in regard to that place, as your ulterior operations may render necessary—always being careful to provide for the safety of that very important station in any contingency.

Your first point of attack will be Roanoke Island and its dependencies.

It is presumed that the navy can reduce the batteries on the marshes, and cover the landing of your troops on the main island, by which, in connection with a rapid movement of the gunboats to the northern extremity—as soon as the marsh battery is reduced—it may be hoped to capture the entire garrison of the place. Having occupied the island and its dependencies, you will at once proceed to the erection of the batteries and defences necessary to hold the position with a small force. Should the flag-officer require any assistance in seizing or holding the debouches of the canal from Norfolk—you will please afford it to him.

The commodore and yourself having completed your arrangements in regard to Roanoke Island, and the waters north of it, you will please at once make a descent on Newbern; having gained possession of which, and the railroad passing through it, you will at once throw a sufficient force upon Beaufort, and take the steps necessary to reduce Fort Macon, and open that port. When you seize Newbern, you will endeavor to seize the railroad as far west as Goldsborough—should circumstances favor such a movement. The temper of the people, the rebel force at hand, &c., will go far towards determining the question as to how far west the railroad can be occupied and held. Should circumstances render it advisable to seize and hold Raleigh—the main north and south line of railroad passing through Goldsborough, should be so effectually destroyed for considerable distances north and south of that point, as to render it impossible for the rebels to use it to your disadvantage. A great point would be gained in any event, by the effectual destruction of the Wilmington and Weldon Railroad.

I would advise great caution in moving so far into the interior as upon Raleigh. Having accomplished the objects mentioned—the next point of interest would probably be Wilmington, the reduction of which may require that additional means shall be afforded you. I would urge great caution in regard to proclamations. In no case would I go beyond a moderate joint proclamation with the naval commander, which should say as little as possible about politics or the negro, merely state that the true issue for which we are fighting is the preservation of the Union, and upholding the laws of the general government, and stating that all who conduct themselves properly, will, as far as possible, be protected in their persons and property.

You will please report your operations as often as an opportunity offers itself.

With my best wishes for your success,

I am, &c., &c., G. B. McClellan,

Major-General Commanding in Chief.

It will be observed that in his instructions as commander-in-chief issued to General Burnside for the conduct of this expedition, General McClellan dwells upon the occupation and destruction of the Weldon Railroad, at which General Grant has now for months been assiduously laboring, as a chief object to be aimed at.

When the expedition was actually in the field, General McClellan had ceased to be commander-in-chief; and Mr. Lincoln, who had then assumed the duties of that office, thought proper to divert the North Carolina expedition to the somewhat different object of organizing a provisional State government somewhere on the coast of that commonwealth.

The consistency of the principles upon which General McClellan instructed General Burnside to base his political course in an invaded country with those upon which General McClellan himself had so successfully acted in Western Virginia, will be remarked. This consistency was plainly a matter of military sagacity and common sense, quite as much as of political conviction; and it is not very flattering to the intelligence of the American people that a large and active political party should seize upon such instructions as these as "a means of convincing them that General McClellan secretly sympathized" with "slavery and with the South" from the first.

Immediately upon his arrival in Washington, General McClellan had been requested by the President to prepare a general view of the prospects of the war, together with such suggestions as he might think proper to make in respect to the way in which it ought to be prosecuted. The following memorandum was handed in by the General, in obedience to this request, on the 4th of August, 1861.

"The object of the present war differs from those in which nations are usually engaged, mainly in this: That the purpose of ordinary war is to conquer a peace, and make a treaty on advantageous terms. In this contest it has become necessary to crush a population sufficiently numerous, intelligent, and warlike to constitute a nation. We have not only to defeat their armed and organized forces in the field, but to display such an overwhelming strength as will convince all our antagonists, especially those of the governing, aristocratic class, of the utter impossibility of resistance. Our late reverses make this course imperative. Had we been successful in the recent battle, (Manassas,) it is possible that we might have been spared the labor and expense of a great effort; now we have no alternative. Their success will enable the political leaders of the rebels to convince the mass of their people that we are inferior to them in force and courage, and to command all their resources. The contest began with a class; now it is with a people, our military success can alone restore the former issue.

"By thoroughly defeating their armies, taking their strong places, and pursuing a rigidly protective policy as to private property, and unarmed persons, and a lenient course as to private soldiers, we may well hope for a permanent restoration of a peaceful Union. But, in the first instance, the authority of the government must be supported by overwhelming physical force.

"Our foreign relations and financial credit also imperatively demand that the military action of the government should be prompt and irresistible.

"The rebels have chosen Virginia as their battle-field, and it seems proper for us to make the first great struggle there. But while thus directing our main efforts, it is necessary to diminish the resistance there offered us, by movements on other points, both by land and water.

"Without entering at present into details, I would advise that a strong movenent be made on the Mississippi, and that the rebels be driven out of Missouri.

"As soon as it becomes perfectly clear that Kentucky is cordially united with us, I would advise a movement through that State into Eastern Tennessee, for the purpose of assisting the Union men of that region, and of seizing the railroads leading from Memphis to the east.

"The possession of those roads by us, in connection with the movement on the Mississippi, would go far towards determining the evacuation of Virginia by the rebels. In the meantime all the passes into Western Virginia, from the east, should be securely guarded; but I would advise no movement from that quarter toward Richmond, unless the political condition of Kentucky renders it impossible, or inexpedient for us to make the movement upon Eastern Tennessee, through that State. Every effort, should, however, be made to organize, equip, and arm as many troops as possible in Western Virginia, in order to render the Ohio and Indiana regiments available for other operations. At as early a day as practicable, it would be well to protect and re-open the Baltimore and Ohio Railroad.

"Baltimore and Fort Monroe should be occupied by garrisons sufficient to retain them in our possession. The importance of Harper's Ferry and the line of the Potomac, in the direction of Leesburg, will be very materially diminished so soon as our force in this vicinity becomes organized, strong and efficient, because no capable general will cross the river, north of this city, when we have a strong army here, ready to cut off his retreat.

"To revert to the West; it is probable that no very large additions to the troops now in Missouri, will be necessary to secure that State.

"I presume that the force required for the movement down the Mississippi will be determined by its commander and the President. If Kentucky assumes the right position, not more than 20,000 troops will be needed, together with those that can be raised in that State and Eastern Tennessee, to secure the latter region and its railroads, as well as ultimately to occupy Nashville.

"The Western Virginia troops, with not more than 5,000 to

10,000 from Ohio and Indiana, should, under proper management, suffice for its protection. When we have reorganized our main army here, 10,000 men ought to be enough to protect the Baltimore and Ohio Railroad and the Potomac. Five thousand will garrison Baltimore, 3,000 Fort Monroe, and not more than 20,000 will be necessary, at the utmost, for the defense of Washington.

"For the main army of operations, I urge the following composition:

250	Regiments of infantry, say	225,000	men
100	Field Batteries, 600 guns	15,000	"
28	Regiments Cavalry	25,500	"
5	" Engineer troops	7,500	"
	Total	273,000	

"The force must be supplied with the necessary engineer and pontoon trains, and with transportation for everything save tents. Its general line of operations should be so directed that water transportation can be availed of from point to point by means of the ocean and the rivers emptying into it. An essential feature of the plan of operations will be the employment of a strong naval force, to protect the movements of a fleet of transports intended to convey a considerable body of troops from point to point of the enemy's sea-coast: thus either creating diversions, and rendering it necessary to detach largely from their main body, in order to protect such of their cities as may be threatened, or else landing and forming establishments on their coast at any favorable places that opportunity might offer. This naval force should also co-operate with the main army, in its efforts to seize the important seaboard towns of the rebels.

"It cannot be ignored that the construction of railroads has introduced a new and very important element into war, by the great facilities thus given for concentrating at particular positions, large masses of troops from remote sections, and by creating new strategic points and lines of operations. It is intended to overcome this difficulty by the partial operations suggested, and such others as the particular case may require. We must endeavor to seize places on the railways, in the rear of the enemy's points of concentration, and we must threaten their seaboard cities, in order that each State may be forced, by the necessity of its own defence, to diminish its contingent to the Confederate army.

"The proposed movement down the Mississippi will produce important results in this connection. That advance, and the progress of the main army at the East, will materially assist each other by diminishing the resistance to be encountered by each. The tendency of the Mississippi movement upon all questions connected with cotton is too well understood by the president and cabinet to need any illustration from me. There is another independent movement which has often been suggested, and which has always recommended itself to my judgment. I refer to a movement from Kansas and Nebraska, through the Indian Territory upon Red River and Western Texas, for the purpose of protecting and developing the latent Union and free State sentiment, well known to predominate in Western Texas, and which, like a similar sentiment in Western Virginia, will, if protected, ultimately organize that section into a free State. How far it will be possible to support this movement by an advance through New Mexico from California, is a matter which I have not sufficiently examined to be able to express a decided opinion. If at all practicable, it is eminently desirable, as bringing into play the resources and warlike qualities of the Pacific States, as well as identifying them with our cause, and cementing the bond of Union between them and the general government.

"If it is not departing too far from my province, I will venture to suggest the policy of an intimate alliance and cordial understanding with Mexico; their sympathies and interests are with us; their antipathies exclusively against our enemies and their institutions. I think it would not be difficult to obtain from the Mexican government the right to use, at least during the present contest, the road from Guaymas to New Mexico. This concession would very materially reduce the obstacles of the column moving from the Pacific. A similar permission to use their territory for the passage of troops between the Panuco and the Rio Grande, would enable us to throw a column of troops, by a good road from Tampico, or some of the small harbors north of it, upon and across the Rio Grande, without risk, and scarcely firing a shot. To what extent, if any, it would be desirable to take into service and employ Mexican soldiers, is a question entirely political, on which I do not venture to offer an opinion.

"The force I have recommended is large, the expense is great. It is possible that a smaller force might accomplish the object in view; but I understand it to be the purpose of this great nation to re-establish the power of its government, and to restore peace to its citizens, in the shortest possible time. The question to be decided is simply this: shall we crush the rebel lion at one blow, terminate the war in one campaign, or shall we leave it for a legacy to our descendants?

"When the extent of the possible line of operations is considered, the force asked for the main army under my command cannot be regarded as unduly large. Every mile we advance carries us further from our base of operations, and renders detachments necessary to cover our communications, while the enemy wlll be constantly concentrating as he falls back. I propose with the force which I have requested, not only to drive the enemy out of Virginia and occupy Richmond, but to occupy Charleston, Savannah, Montgomery, Pensacola, Mobile and New Orleans; in other words, to move into the heart of the enemy's country, and crush out the rebellion in its very heart.

"By seizing and repairing the railroads as we advance, the difficulties of transportation will be materially diminished. It is perhaps unnecessary to state, that in addition to the forces named in this memorandum, strong reserves should be formed, ready to supply any losses that may occur.

In conclusion, I would submit that the exigencies of the treasury may be lessened by making only partial payments to our troops, when in the enemy's country, and by giving the obligation of the United States for such supplies as may there be obtained.

GEO. B. McCLELLAN, Major-General.

Upon this memorandum General McClellan remarks in his report:

"I do not think the events of the war have proved these views, upon the methods and plans of its conduct, altogether incorrect. They certainly have not proved my estimate of the number of troops and scope of operations too large. It is probable that I did under-estimate the time necessary for the completion of arms and equipments. It was not strange, however, that by many civilians intrusted with authority there should have been an exactly opposite opinion held in both these particulars."

The President was so much impressed with the propriety and practical force of the views set forth in this memorandum, that he urged General McClellan to address a letter embodying its substance to Lieutenant-General Scott, whose own plans for the next campaign, as we have seen, had been frequently submitted by him to discussion at cabinet meetings, in the presence of General McClellan's predecessor in the command of the Department of the Potomac.

Lieutenant-General Scott took umbrage at the submission to him by letter of views which he expressed himself as perfectly ready to "entertain and discuss," if "presented by General McClellan in person;" and he accordingly addressed a note on the subject to the secretary of war, in which he declared, that feeling himself "to be an incumbrance to the army as well as to himself," he must ask to be placed on the retired list.

Shocked at the idea that he could be supposed capable of wantonly or carelessly wounding the sensibilities of the venerable head of the army, General McClellan on learning what had happened, at once addressed the following letter to the President:

WASHINGTON, Aug. 10, 1861.

The letter addressed by me under date of the 8th inst. to Lieutenant-General Scott, commanding the United States army, was designed to be a plain and respectful expression of my views of the measures demanded for the safety of the government in the imminent peril that besets it at the present hour. Every moment's reflection and every fact transpiring, convinced me of the urgent necessity of the measures there indicated, and I felt it my duty to him and to the country to communicate them frankly. It is therefore with great pain that I have learned from you this morning, that my views do not meet with the approbation of the Lieutenant-General, and that my letter is unfavorably regarded by him. The command with which I am intrusted was not sought by me, and has only been accepted from an earnest and humble desire to serve my country in the moment of the most extreme peril. With these views I am willing to do and suffer whatever may be required for that service. Nothing could be farther from my wishes than to seek any command or urge any measures not required for the exigency of the occasion, and above all, I would abstain from any conduct that could give offence to General Scott, or embarrass the President or any department of the government.

Influenced by these considerations, I yield to your request and withdraw the letter referred to. The government and my superior officer being apprised of what I consider to be necessary and proper for the defence of the national capital, I shall strive faithfully and zealously to employ the means that may be placed in my power for that purpose, dismissing every personal feeling or consideration, and praying only the blessing of Divine Providence on my efforts. I will only add that as you requested my authority to withdraw the letter, that authority is hereby given, with the most profound assurance of my respect for General Scott and yourself.

Very respectfully, your obedient servant,

GEORGE B. McCLELLAN.

The President at once called upon General Scott to ask him to withdraw in his turn his letter to the secretary of war; but this General Scott declined to do, on the ground as stated by himself that—

"The original offence given me by General McClellan seems to have been the result of deliberation between him and some of the members of the cabinet, by whom all the greater war questions are to be settled without resort to or consultation with me, the nominal general-in-chief of the army."

The "freedom of access to and consultation with portions of the cabinet," enjoyed by the junior general, added General Scott, "have very naturally deluded him into a feeling of indifference towards me." The veteran accordingly ended this unfortunate correspondence with a reiterated expression of his wish to retire from the service rather than risk undignified collisions with a general so "supported," and, as he added, the justice of the soldier constraining him to the tribute, "who besides possessed very high qualifications for command."

General McClellan could not permit matters, however, so to rest; and such was the force of his intrinsic honesty of feeling and purpose that this difficulty which, had it occurred with a man more vain, arrogant, or inconsiderate than himself, must have occasioned permanent pain and annoyance to a chieftain entitled to the reverence of all Americans, and might possibly have inflicted some serious damage on the cause of the Union, passed off quietly and honorably to both parties.

It was not until the 1st of November that General Scott reiterated his application for leave to withdraw from active service upon the single ground of his advanced years and his many infirmities.

"With the retirement of General Scott," says Mr. Lincoln, in his first annual message to Congress, "came the executive duty of appointing in his stead a general-in-chief of the army. It is a fortunate circumstance that neither in council nor country, was there, so far as I know, any difference of opinion as to the proper person to be selected. The retiring chief repeatedly expressed his judgment in favor of General McClellan for the position, and in this the nation seemed to give a unanimous concurrence. The designation of General McClellan is, therefore, in a considerable degree, the selection of the country as well as of the executive; and hence there is better reason to hope there will be given him *the confidence and cordial support thus, by fair implication promised, and without which he cannot, with as full efficiency, serve the country.*"

Pregnant words! upon which the conduct of the President himself was within a few short weeks to furnish a most painful and instructive commentary!

On taking the Command-in-Chief of the Armies of the Union, General McClellan issued a general order, in which, after paying a simple and noble tribute to the merits and the services of the "great soldier of our nation," he made this touching appeal to the army:

"While we regret his loss, there is one thing we cannot regret, the bright example he has left for our emulation. Let us all hope and pray that his declining years may be passed in peace and happiness, and that they may be cheered by the success of the country and the cause he has fought for and has loved so well. Beyond all things, let us do nothing that can cause him to blush for us. Let no defeat of the army he has commanded embitter his last years, but let our victories illuminate the close of a life so grand."

Swords were now voted to the young commander; speeches

were made to him; he was compared in the newspapers to Napoleon the Great. A few words, spoken by him in reply to one of these many assaults upon his modesty and his manhood, completely paint at once the man himself and the true duty of a people towards one whom they have elevated to such a position:

"I ask in the future only forbearance, patience, and confidence. With these we can accomplish all."

CHAPTER V.

GENERAL McCLELLAN AS COMMANDER-IN-CHIEF. CONSEQUENCES OF THE VICTORY OF MANASSAS AT THE SOUTH. PREPARATIONS FOR THE GENERAL ADVANCE OF THE ARMIES OF THE UNION IN THE SPRING. POPULAR IMPATIENCE. MR. LINCOLN SUPERSEDES GENERAL McCLELLAN AT THE END OF TWO MONTHS.

It is essential not merely to a just comprehension of the true responsibility of General McClellan for the successes and failures which attended the effort to re-establish the Federal authority by force of arms while he remained in the active service of the Union; but to a fair understanding of the course of events, that we should now briefly consider the way in which military affairs had been administered at Washington during the interval between the nomination of General McClellan to the command of the Army of the Potomac, and the retirement of General Scott.

During these three months the new army of the Union had been organizing; the defenses of Washington had been constructing; and the general character of the military work done had been such as to offer little temptation to mere amateurs. It is only when a fine army stands ready at hand to execute itself and their will that the inspired and uninstructed masters of the art of war take a real pleasure in the exercise of their genius. For the most part, therefore, the military affairs of the United States were directed during the months of August, September and October, 1861, by military men, Lieutenant-General Scott being nominally at the head of the army.

By the 15th of October the total force of troops in and about Washington, including the garrisons of Alexandria and

Baltimore, had been raised to 152,051 men. As these troops had gradually been gathered in from all parts of the country, they had been organized into brigades of four regiments each, and after this organization had been well established into divisions of three brigades each. The organization of the artillery and cavalry necessarily went on more slowly and needed to be still more carefully prosecuted than the organization of the infantry.

As week after week passed by with no decisive demonstrations either on the part of the enemy or on that of the army of the Union, the civilians at headquarters who were impatient of results, and from whose minds the severe lesson of Bull Run was gradually fading out, had begun first to wonder and then to murmur at what they regarded as the "inaction" of the forces. They saw the steady increase in the number of the defenders of the nation, and gliding easily into the error of confounding fullness of the ranks with fitness for service, they gradually fell into their old way of planning brilliant campaigns and demanding decisive measures.

What the educated and competent officers of the army itself thought of this temper growing up around them, and what their judgment was as to the efficiency of the army at this time, was well expressed by General McCall, of Pennsylvania, an officer who afterwards highly distinguished himself in the campaign of the Peninsula.

General McCall was examined by the Congressional committee on the conduct of the war on the 28th of December, 1861, in reference to the affair of Ball's Bluff, which took place October 21st, and of which we shall presently have occasion again to speak.

In the course of his examination Senator Chandler, of Michigan, a legislator of unusually warlike tastes and fancy, who seems to have made up his mind that General McClellan had missed a noble opportunity for annihilating General Johnston by massing his own troops, and compelling the enemy to do as much at Leesburg, a point which neither general had considered important enough to occupy in force, put the following questions to General McCall, and received from him the following answers:

The Senator. Suppose you had been ordered up, Smith's division had been ordered up, and other divisions next to them had been ordered up along there, Stone's division had been ordered over, and Banks' division ordered over also, so as to be able to meet any force they could have brought from Manassas or Centreville into the open field, would not that have been a good time to have done it?

The General. No, sir.

The Senator. If they had failed to come out then, you would have cut their left wing up entirely?

The General. That would have brought on the general battle of the campaign, and McClellan was not ready to fight that battle at that time.

The Senator. Why not?

The General. He had not the force. His men were not disciplined, as they were new. It would have been, I consider, a very imprudent thing. And I have not the smallest doubt that McClellan saw that at once, and he knew that if an affair of one or two brigades took place there, the probability was that it would have brought on the general battle of the campaign, and terminated, perhaps, the campaign. He was not prepared for it, and did not want to fight there. I am almost certain of that, judging from my knowledge of the man, and from what I think I should have done myself under the circumstances.*

* I cannot refrain from inserting here an exquisitely characteristic passage from the close of this examination of General McCall by Mr. Chandler, a passage which would be as amusing as it is characteristic had not the interference of such persons as Mr. Chandler with the civil and military policy of the nation entailed so much misery upon us. Utterly dissatisfied with the General's replies to his military inquiries, the mortified senator suddenly turns upon him thus:

This disastrous affair of Ball's Bluff had occurred, as we have seen, but a few days before President Lincoln conferred the supreme command of the forces upon General McClellan. Of course the President cannot possibly have considered General McClellan to have been in any way responsible for the mishap; and the circumstances which attended it ought to have impressed his excellency's mind anew with the truth of his own maxim, that "one bad general is better than two good ones."

In the beginning of the month of October General McClellan had found reason to believe that the enemy were preparing to evacuate their positions at and about Manassas Plains. Watching the whole field of operations with an instructed and intelligent eye, he had not failed to perceive that the victory of July 21st, while it had given prestige and spirit to the army of the Confederates actually in their service, had indisposed the Southern people in general to making any particular efforts to increase their army or to strengthen the hands of their government. They had been lapped by the successes of that day into a condition of careless self-confidence, which must have proved eminently advantageous to the cause of the Union if the renewal of active hostilities could have been postponed by the army of the Union until it had become strong enough to take the offensive at one and the same time against all the great points of Southern resistance. Little had been done towards adequately fortifying the Southern seaports, or adequately constituting the Southern armies for the defence of the vast extent of territory which the Confederates had undertaken to hold. Neither the war minister nor the naval minister of

The Senator. What disposition are you now making of the contrabands that come into your lines?

The General. I have been ordered to receive all that come in and send them to Washington.

The Senator. You do not send them back to their owners?

The General. No, sir!

Jefferson Davis commanded the confidence of the Southern people, and neither had done or seemed disposed to do anything to deserve confidence. The Confederacy was soon to be recognized by a world famishing for the lack of cotton; and close upon that auspicious moment must come peace with all her blessings.

In his report on the surrender of New Orleans the Confederate General Mansfield Lovell states that upon assuming command of his department he had applied in vain for guns of heavy calibre to be mounted for the defence of the city, but could obtain none, "the general impression being that New Orleans would not be attacked by the river;" nor was he able during the whole of the fall and winter months of 1861–62 to procure effective small-arms for arming more than twelve hundred men when the crisis came in the fate of the commercial metropolis of the South. The same languor hung upon the naval preparations for holding the lower Mississippi.

The coast defences of South Carolina and Georgia were confided by the Confederate government to a certain General Gonzalez, an adventurer of Cuban and Nicaraguan notoriety, who came to Richmond and reported Hilton Head "impregnable," about a fortnight before that place surrendered to the Union fleet.

When General Albert Sidney Johnston was ordered to the command of the Confederates in the West he found but about fifteen thousand men at Bowling Green, the "western Manassas," as it was called, nor could he obtain any attention to his repeated representations of the precarious condition of the rebel cause in the great central region of the Tennessee and the Cumberland till the thunder of the Union guns began to speak more loudly than his letters and dispatches.

This being the general state of military affairs at the South while General McClellan was organizing the national armies and preparing them for decisive action, General Joseph Johnston's force at Manassas was kept well in hand to fall back upon and cover Richmond at the first intimation of a new Federal movement for its capture. It was doubted at Richmond whether any such movement would be made at all, but it was not at all doubted that if made, and made under a competent commander, it would be made either by the way of the Shenandoah valley, the lower Rappahannock, or the James and York Rivers.

The value of the Confederate positions at Manassas as a base of offensive operations against Washington had passed away with the foregone opportunity of July, and the Southern army at that point had suffered too much from disease and from defective organization during the months of August and September to assume the offensive and attempt to create a new opportunity of the same kind.

In the improbable contingency that General McClellan should suffer himself to be hurried by non-military influences into making the lamentable blunder of an advance against Manassas, General Johnston had accordingly prepared himself to retreat at once towards his true base at Richmond.

Nothing of this was commonly understood at the North, where the continued presence of Johnston at Manassas was perpetually denounced as an insult, a menace, and a peril to Washington and to the Union; and President Lincoln began again to be besieged with entreaties, more or less imperious, to command a direct movement upon the enemy.

On the 19th of October General McClellan, clearly conceiving the true state of the case, ordered General McCall to cover a grand reconnoissance in force to be made the next day from Drainesville. This reconnoissance was successfully made; and on the next day, October 20th, General Stone, occupying Poolesville in Maryland, was ordered to make a feint of crossing the Potomac in order to feel the enemy at Leesburg, in Virginia, which place the enemy had held in no great force, and which General McClellan believed them to be, as they in fact were, on the point of abandoning. This feint was made;

but in making it General Stone employed an officer whose direct personal relations with the President, and whose official rank as a senator of the United States, seems to have misled him into adventuring further than it was expected or intended he should go; and the events of next day, October 21st, converted the simple reconnoissance of Edwards' Ferry into the disastrous battle of Ball's Bluff, a battle fought certainly without the knowledge or the orders of the commanding general, fought where there was no direct military purpose to be gained even by a victory, and fought with so little skill and judgment that it resulted in the complete and humiliating defeat of our troops by a body of the enemy largely inferior in point of numbers and of artillery.

All that could possibly have been won by a successful issue of this unhappy movement would have been a stimulation of the public appetite for "brilliant and exciting intelligence" and a powerful reinforcement of the rapidly increasing Aulic Council of military civilians by whom the government was now again surrounded and the commanding general beset.

Its failure confirmed the exulting confidence of the Southern troops in their own invincibility, and cast another shade of gloom over the banners which the defeat of Bull Run had already clouded.

Good might, however, have come out of this evil had the President but read in it a fresh lesson of the absolute necessity of trusting the control of the armies implicitly to their nominal commander and of abstaining himself, and causing others to abstain, from ignorant and impatient interference with operations which imperatively demanded time for their ripening and unity of authority for their successful execution.

Immediately upon taking command of the armies of the Union, General McClellan addressed letters of instruction to Generals Halleck, Buell, Sherman and Butler, commanding respectively the departments of Missouri and Ohio, and the expeditions of the South Atlantic and the Gulf. In these letters the whole field before the army as we shall see was surveyed with masterly judgment, and the special part to be taken in those operations by each commander sketched out for him, with clearness and with precision, and, as subsequent events have proved, with an almost marvellous sagacity. The restoration of public confidence in Missouri by a thorough reform in the military administration of that State, and by the chastisement of official corruption: the conciliation of the well-disposed population of Kentucky by a "religious respect for the rights of all:" the prompt and decisive occupation of Knoxville and East Tennessee—cutting off all communication between Virginia and the Mississippi; the reduction of Fort Pulaski on the Savannah River, and the organization of a formidable attack upon Charleston. These were the principal measures which General McClellan proposed to himself as the constituent points of his grand campaign for the reduction of the seceded States to their allegiance to the Union.

Had these measures been carried into effect simultaneously in the spring of 1862, under the untrammelled supervision of a single military mind, and with forces adequate, as well in point of preparation as in point of numbers, to the work, it is difficult to resist the conviction that they must have resulted in the complete prostration of the organized force of the Confederate States.

As we have already seen, such was the condition of the Confederate armies at the time when General McClellan was maturing his plans, that the premature, hastily prepared, and somewhat hurriedly executed movements which, in February and March, were made in the West under the direct authority of President Lincoln, sufficed to make an impression upon the front of Confederate resistance in that quarter, which, had it been accompanied by an equal impact upon the eastern and southern bulwarks of the then loosely jointed Confederate system, could hardly have failed to determine a speedy issue of the war. Won as they were, these isolated and premature triumphs in the West simply aroused the Confederates to a full sense of their danger. The great scheme of the war was broken up by them, and the nation expiated in more than a year of desperate and costly efforts to master the Mississippi, and open a way into Eastern Tennessee, the impatience which refused to recognize the infinite advantages of the delay which perfects concentration, over the desultory and incoherent energy which spends itself in ill-combined blows and in spasmodic effort.

The period during which General McClellan really held command of the armies of the Union, and was really in a position to enable him to plan and prepare a campaign proportionate to the area of the war, extended over but a little more than two months. He was called, as we have seen, to fill the post vacated by Lieutenant-General Scott in November, 1861. Incessantly occupied with the details of the organization of the main army, which was to be directly commanded by himself, General McClellan was at the same time burdened with the duty of supervising all the military preparations of the Union, and of elaborating the vast plan of campaign already sketched.

It is not surprising that while sparing neither body nor brain in this colossal task, the young commander-in-chief should have overtaxed even his vigorous constitution. Towards the middle of December he contracted a serious illness, which for a short time confined him to his headquarters at Washington.

During this time the political pressure upon the President for an advance of the armies became daily more and more vehement. The secretary of war, Mr. Cameron, left the cabinet, and was succeeded by Mr. Stanton, who, while he professed the warmest regard for the young general in command of the armies, gave his most strenuous efforts in support of the external clamor which was driving the President toward a practical nullification of his influence and his authority.

Before General McClellan had fully recovered his health, and without any consultation whatever had with him, the President finally, on the 27th of January, 1862, succumbed to these demoralizing forces, and assumed himself the command of the national forces.

On that day he issued from the Executive Mansion the following War Order:

"*Ordered*, That the twenty-second day of February, 1862, be the day for a general movement of the land and naval forces of the United States against the insurgent forces. That especially the army at and about Fortress Monroe, the army of the Potomac, the army of Western Virginia, the army near Mumfordsville, Kentucky, the army and flotilla at Cairo, and a naval force in the Gulf of Mexico, be ready to move on that day.

"That all other forces, both land and naval, with their respective commanders, obey existing orders for the time, and be ready to obey additional orders when duly given.

"That the heads of departments, and especially the secretaries of war and of the navy, with all their subordinates, and the general-in-chief, with all other commanders and subordinates of land and naval forces, will severally be held to their strict and full responsibilities for prompt execution of this order. ABRAHAM LINCOLN."

From the moment of the promulgation of this most extraordinary order, the general, whom it so peremptorily and so insultingly superseded, ceased of course to be responsible for the conduct of any military operations not carried on directly under his own eyes, and specially committed to his own direct control.

It is necessary to remember here that the armies thus directed to be set in motion upon a given day, which was thus publicly announced to foes and friends alike, were made up of many thousands of men entirely unfamiliar with war, and commanded for the most part by officers as inexperienced as themselves. The few "veterans" of this host were men whose nominal service under arms had a date of but from four to five months. As to the condition of those great branches of the military service, on which the practicability of moving such a force must have been absolutely dependent, had the troops been troops of the line, inured to war, no one could possibly form an intelligent notion excepting the commanding general under whom they had been organized, but who was not so much as consulted upon the subject.

Viewed in the light of these considerations this singular order would seem as unaccountable in itself as it is certainly unique in the history of human warfare, were not an adequate, if not a satisfactory, explanation of its origin and its intent furnished to us by one of the ablest and most intrepid defenders of Mr. Lincoln and of his administration.

In his Life of President Lincoln, Mr. Raymond, of New York, thus simply and clearly states the case:

"As winter approached without any indications of an intended movement of our armies, the public impatience rose to the highest point of discontent. The administration was everywhere held responsible for these unaccountable delays, and was freely charged by its opponents with a design to protract the war for selfish political purposes of its own, *and at the fall elections the public dissatisfaction made itself manifest by adverse votes in every considerable State where elections were held.*"

From the moment when considerations of political and partisan expediency thus invaded the great question of the conduct of the war in the mind of the President all harmonious concert of action between that functionary and General McClellan necessarily came to an end. With such considerations General McClellan, as an honest and single-minded soldier, laboring for the defeat of the armed enemies of the Union, had and could have nothing whatever to do. It is by no means foreign to the course of our narrative to observe that the "public dissatisfaction" which "made itself manifest by adverse votes" in the fall elections of 1861 had its origin in many other causes besides the delays in the movement of our armies. The civil administration of the government had been conducted with an extraordinary recklessness alike of the laws of the land and of the liberties of the citizens, while the bare fact of the persistent existence of the civil war itself necessarily shook the public confidence in the statesmanship of a party whose leading representatives had openly laughed the possibility of such a war to scorn; and the "premier" of whose elected President had repeatedly predicted the complete restoration of order throughout the nation within "sixty days" from the passage of the ordinance of secession by the State of South Carolina. To concentrate this "public dissatisfaction" if possible upon the delays in the movement of our armies; to brand these delays as "unaccountable;" and to fix the responsibility of them upon the commander of the forces, was perhaps a clever move in partisan tactics. Clever or foolish, it seems to have tempted the administration into entire forgetfulness of the fatal consequences which it must entail upon the public service and the welfare of the State.

It would appear, too, that a singular confidence in his own capacity as a military leader was at the same time growing up in the mind of the President. For, not content with assuming the general command, by proclamation, of the armies of the Union, Mr. Lincoln at once proceeded to assume the direct control of the campaign of the Army of the Potomac in particular.

On the 31st of January, 1862, appeared the President's Special War Order, No. 1, couched in the following terms:

"EXECUTIVE MANSION, January 31, 1862.

"*Ordered*, That all the disposable force of the Army of the Potomac, after providing safely for the defence of Washington, be formed into an expedition for the immediate object of seizing and occupying a point upon the railroad southwestward of what is known as Manassas Junction, all details to be in the discretion of the commander-in-chief, and the expedition to move on or before the twenty-second day of February next.

"ABRAHAM LINCOLN."

Had the civil war been suddenly brought to an end by the submission of the South before a single movement had been made in the campaign of 1862 this "Special War Order, No. 1" might doubtless live in history simply as the most grotesque document which ever emanated from a man elevated by his fellow-men to a position of great trust and grave responsibility.

The accredited biographer of Mr. Lincoln informs us that he distinguished himself in his early life by his bravery and skill in conducting the defence of a flatboat on the Mississippi River against an attack made upon it by seven negroes. The remembrance of the exploit does not seem to have impelled the president to relieve our naval commanders of the responsibilities of their profession; and it is highly improbable that it would ever have occurred to the President, had he found himself on board of the Monitor during her remarkable conflict with the Merrimac, to assume the command of that gallant little craft and prescribe manœuvres of battle to Lieutenant Worden. Yet the brief land campaign against the Indians in which we are assured that Mr. Lincoln once took a creditable part as a captain of militia appears to have inspired him with the belief that he might reasonably and respectably undertake to handle one of the largest armies of modern times engaged in one of the most formidable and difficult invasions upon record.

General McClellan has many times in the course of his career exhibited a power of self-command, and a forgetfulness of all merely personal considerations in behalf of his obligations to his country and to the troops under his command, which entitles him to a high place among those heroes who, like England's Iron Duke, have dared to feel that

> "The path of duty is the way to glory."

But never surely were these qualities more keenly tested than they must have been by this "war order," which at once shocked his common sense as a soldier and outraged his self-respect as an officer high in command.

Before this "order" was issued, General McClellan had explained to the President the plan of campaign which he intended to pursue in Virginia. Like the immortal Dutch commissioners who harassed the soul of Marlborough with their incessant interferences in his campaign, the President certainly had a right in virtue of his position to know what operations the general in command of his armies was about to undertake; but like those high and mighty marplots also, his excellency committed the blunder of interpreting this right into a warrant for assuming the control of those operations, objecting to them, and modifying all the conditions essential to their success. Had Mr. Lincoln consulted General Halleck on the subject of these pretensions of his, that officer, who has done his country the service of translating Baron Jomini's great work on the art of war, might have enlightened him as to the limits of executive duty, with the following passage, upon which the campaign of 1862 on the Peninsula was destined to furnish a commentary more striking than any which the older history of warfare has bequeathed to us.

"In my judgment," observes Baron Jomini, discussing the part taken by the Executive Aulic Council of Vienna in directing the operations of the Austrian armies, "the only duty which such a council can safely undertake is that of advising as to the adoption of a general plan of operations. Of course I do not mean by this a plan which is to embrace the whole course of a campaign, tie down the generals to that course, and so inevitably lead to their being beaten. I mean a plan which shall determine the objects of the campaign, decide whether offensive or defensive operations shall be undertaken, and fix the amount of material means which may be relied upon in the first instance for the opening of the enterprise, and then for the possible reserves in case of invasion. It cannot be denied that all these things may be, and even should be, discussed in a council of government made up of generals and of ministers; but here the action of such a council should stop; for if it pretends to say to a commander-in-chief not only that he shall march on Vienna or on Paris, but also in what way he is to manœuvre to reach those points, the unfortunate commander-in-chief will certainly be beaten, and the WHOLE RESPONSIBILITY OF HIS REVERSES WILL REST UPON THOSE WHO, TWO HUNDRED MILES OFF FROM THE ENEMY, PRETEND TO DIRECT AN ARMY WHICH IT IS DIFFICULT ENOUGH TO HANDLE WHEN ACTUALLY IN THE FIELD."

CHAPTER VI.

GENERAL McCLELLAN AS COMMANDER-IN-CHIEF. HOLDS THAT POSITION FOR ABOUT TWO MONTHS. GENERAL PLAN OF CAMPAIGN AND POLITICS OF THE WAR.

WHEN General McClellan accepted the formal command of the armies of the Union on the 1st of November, 1861, of course he accepted that most responsible position with the understanding that he was to enjoy in the discharge of its duties "the confidence and cordial support, thus by fair implication promised, and without which he could not" (it is President Lincoln, be it remembered, who speaks) "with so full efficiency serve the country."

The meaning of the words "confidence" and "cordial support," as we shall now see, must undergo a serious modification before either of these terms can be fitted to the treatment which General McClellan did actually receive from the executive of the Union.

From the moment when General McClellan was thus made responsible for the general progress of the war, the campaign of the Potomac necessarily ceased to be the exclusive subject of his care. The more extended power now conferred upon him authorized, and indeed required him, to devote himself to perfecting and developing, in a systematic plan of operations, those suggestions of movements to be made on many other points of the circle of hostilities, which he had before thrown out at the request of the President, and in a merely advisory way.

Still regarding the capture of Richmond, and the defeat of

the main rebel army in Virginia, as the leading object to be aimed at, and determining to conduct in person that part of the operations he was about to direct, the new commander-in-chief undertook a complete review of the political and military elements of the problem before him. The results of this labor are fully presented in the letters of instructions which he addressed to the different generals by whom the different parts of the general scheme of operations upon which he had resolved were intended to be carried out.

We give these letters in full, for a fair understanding of the whole history of the war subsequently to the first of November, 1861, can only be obtained by a careful perusal of them.

It will be observed that three of these letters bear date from the 7th to the 11th November, 1861, while the two others, and these not the least important, are dated on the 14th and 23d of February, 1862, respectively. The instructions comprised in them all belong to one system of action; but it is of vital consequence for the reader to bear in mind that the position of the writer had become materially modified by circumstances, which will be fully considered in the progress of this sketch, during the interval between the 12th of November, 1861, and the 14th of February, 1862.

The operations of the armies in the departments of the Ohio and of Missouri, which are treated of in the letters written in November, 1861, and the operations of the armies on the South Atlantic and on the Gulf, which are treated of in the letters written in February, 1862, were intended to be actively begun at one and the same time, when the general plan of operations was drawn up by General McClellan in November, 1861. The position of affairs in the departments of the Ohio and of Missouri, however, was such, in the month of November, 1861, the whole region embraced in those departments being then substantially under the control of our arms, that a judicious political administration of our military force was the imperative need of the moment there.

In the departments of the South Atlantic and the Gulf, on the contrary, we had our whole way still to make; and it was altogether undesirable therefore, from a military point of view, that any important directions should be issued, or any important movements undertaken in that part of the scene of action, until the opening of the season for general and combined operations.

Before the opening of that season came, General McClellan, as we have seen, had been virtually deprived of the authority necessary to the execution of his plans. On the 23d of February, 1862, he still retained indeed the nominal command of the armies of the Union, but he had been publicly notified, and the armies and the people of the Union with him, that he no longer enjoyed the "confidence," and could no longer expect the "cordial support," without which it was impossible for him to discharge the duties of command.

The President, who had seen fit thus to violate his pledged faith to the commander-in-chief within less than three months from the day when it was given, proceeded to deal with the plan of operations adopted in November, 1861, according to his pleasure.

In so far as concerns the politics of war, the principles of the plan laid down by General McClellan in his letters of instruction were entirely abandoned by the President. General McClellan, in his memorandum presented to the President on the 4th of August, 1861, had recognized the new and dangerous character likely to be impressed upon the war of secession by the results of the Confederate victory at Manassas. "The contest," he had then said, "began with a class, now it is with a people; our military success alone can restore the former issue." In his letters of instruction to the commanders of departments he dwelt earnestly upon the importance of taking all possible pains to prevent the complete and permanent impression of this new and dangerous character upon the war.

"National wars," observes Baron Jomini, "are of all wars

the most formidable. This name can only be given to those which are carried on against a whole population animated with the fire of independence. In such wars every step is contested with a combat. The army which enters such a country holds only the ground on which it encamps: it can only supply itself at the point of the sword: its trains are everywhere threatened or destroyed."

"To succeed in such a war," continues the same authority, "is always difficult. To display, in the first place, a mass of force proportionate to the resistance and the obstacles to be encountered; *to calm popular passions by all possible means; to let them wear out with time; to display a great combination of policy, of gentleness, and of severity; but above all things the greatest justice:* these are the first elements and conditions of success."

Of the truth of these sage counsels, the condensed results of the experience of civilization, General McClellan was profoundly convinced. To be convinced of them, indeed, it was only necessary to understand the principles on which the Union of these States had been formed, and to see with unclouded vision the successive departures from those principles on the part of extreme and passionate, of ignorant and reckless men in both sections, by dint of which secession and the war had been made possible.

In his instructions to the commanders of departments the general-in-chief had accordingly endeavored to infuse into those commanders the spirit of these counsels, as their supreme rule of conduct in dealing with the population around around them.

But no such rule of conduct could be observed if the violent destruction of the social institution of slavery was to be considered either a legitimate means or a legitimate end of the warfare to be waged in the name of the Constitution and the Union. And President Lincoln therefore completely abandoned the military politics of General McClellan's plan.

Of the strictly military programme embraced in that plan the President, on the contrary, unhesitatingly availed himself. Entirely ignorant, however, of the art of war, and consequently unable to appreciate intelligently the mutual relations of the different operations foreshadowed in the scheme, the President introduced into it such modifications, and imposed such delays upon the execution of its different parts, as, in the general result, have combined now with the effects of the presidential system of military politics to protract the conflict through now nearly four years.

We have already seen how, after permitting General Burnside to commence an attack upon the coast-line of North Carolina in accordance with a subsidiary part of General McClellan's programme, the President, upon taking general command of the army, so far suspended the execution of General McClellan's ulterior orders to that officer that the occupation of the Weldon and Wilmington Railroad, which General McClellan had intended should be accomplished in the early winter of 1862, has absorbed the attention and wasted the forces of the grand army of General Grant during the summer and autumn of 1864.

We shall now see that General Buell was intrusted by General McClellan, in November, 1861, to prepare for the immediate occupation of Eastern Tennessee, and for the cutting of the communications between Virginia and the Mississippi, neither of which objects has President Lincoln, since he assumed the command of the armies, in January, 1862, been able to achieve, although much costly time, much treasure, and many valuable lives have been lavished upon disconnected and inconsequential efforts to effect them.

We shall see, also, that it was the intention of Genera McClellan, had he retained the supreme command of which he was deprived substantially in January, 1862, and formally in March, of the same year, to have pressed forward the forces under General Butler immediately after the capture of New

Orleans, (in respect to which capture he anticipated, with rare sagacity, as "more than probable" precisely what did occur, "that the navy unassisted could accomplish the result") against "Jackson in Mississippi," for the purpose of "opening a communication with the Northern column" by the river.

This part of General McClellan's plan President Lincoln entirely neglected, permitting General Butler to waste many months in the "civil administration" of the city of New Orleans, which had surrendered to the fleet and was so entirely at the mercy of its guns, that, as General Butler himself testifies, having only two hundred and fifty men within the city limits, "we never had any trouble after the first day." General Butler made no movement to communicate with Grant until June, when sickness had set in, and then with but four thousand or five thousand men.*

How easily General McClellan's programme might have been carried out to the letter we now know. The Report of Major-General Mansfield Lovell of the "Confederate States Army," dated at Vicksburg, May 22, 1862, informs us that this officer upon the fall of New Orleans retreated upon Jackson and Vicksburg, at the head of no more than "four thousand five hundred troops, newly raised and equipped." These troops were "nothing but infantry and two batteries of field artillery," and were not fully armed and equipped at the time of the capture of the city. The result of a vigorous movement of General Butler's force of eighteen thousand men, cavalry, infantry, and artillery, in pursuit of General Lovell upon the points indicated by General McClellan, would have been to prevent the establishment of those batteries at Vicksburg, before which the fleet and army of the West afterwards consumed themselves for more than a year, and which were finally turned and taken by General Grant, in July, 1863, by a bold and hazardous movement upon the very line which, as General

* The capture of New Orleans. Report on Conduct of the War. Part III., p. 353.

McClellan had anticipated, was opened to the Army of the Gulf by the surrender of New Orleans, in April, 1862.

With these preliminary remarks I now submit to the reader the following Letters of Instruction, grouped under two appropriate headings.

I.—OPERATIONS IN THE WEST.

HEADQUARTERS OF THE ARMY,
WASHINGTON, D. C., November 11, 1861.

Maj.-Gen. H. W. HALLECK, U. S. A.,
Comd'g Depart. of Missouri:

GENERAL:—In assigning you to the command of the Department of Missouri, it is probably unnecessary for me to state that I have intrusted to you a duty which requires the utmost tact and decision.

You have not merely the ordinary duties of a military commander to perform; but the far more difficult task of reducing chaos to order, of changing probably the majority of the personnel of the staff of the department, and of reducing to a point of economy consistent with the interests and necessities of the state, a system of reckless expenditure and fraud perhaps unheard, of before in the history of the world.

You will find in your department many general and staff officers holding illegal commissions and appoiniments not recognized or approved by the President or secretary of war, you will please at once inform these gentlemen of the nullity of their appointment, and see that no pay or allowances are issued to them until such time as commissions may be authorized by the President or secretary of war.

If any of them give the slightest trouble, you will at once arrest them and send them under guard, out of the limits of your department, informing them that if they return they will be placed in close confinement. You will please examine into the legality of the organization of the troops serving in the department. When you find any illegal, unusual, or improper organizations you will give to the officers and men an opportunity to enter the legal military establishment under general laws and orders from the War Department; reporting in full to these headquarters any officer or organization that may decline.

You will please cause competent and reliable staff officers to examine all existing contracts immediately, and suspend all payments upon them until you receive the report in each case. Where there is the slightest doubt as to the propriety of the contract, you will be good enough to refer the matter, with full explanations, to these headquarters, stating in each case what would be a fair compensation for the services or materials rendered under the contract. Discontinue at once the reception of material or services, under any doubtful contract. Arrest and bring to prompt trial all officers who have in any way violated their duty to the government. In regard to the political conduct of affairs, you will please labor to impress upon the inhabitants of Missouri and the adjacent States, that we are fighting solely for the integrity of the Union, to uphold the power of our national government and to restore to the nation the blessings of peace and good order.

With respect to military operations, it is probable, from the best information in my possession, that the interests of the government will be best served by fortifying and holding in considerable strength, Rolla, Sedalia, and other interior points, keeping strong patrols constantly moving from the terminal stations, and concentrating the mass of the troops on or near the Mississippi, prepared for such ulterior operations as the public interests may demand.

I would be glad to have you make, as soon as possible, a personal inspection of all the important points in your department, and report the result to me. I cannot too strongly impress upon you the absolute necessity of keeping me constantly advised of the strength, condition, and location of your troops, together with all facts that will enable me to maintain that general direction of the armies of the United States which it is my purpose to exercise. I trust to you to maintain thorough organization, discipline, and economy throughout your department. Please inform me, as soon as possible, of everything relating to the gunboats now in process of construction, as well as those completed.

The militia force authorized to be raised by the State of Missouri for its defence, will be under your orders.

I am, General, &c., &c.,
GEORGE B. McCLELLAN,
Maj.-Gen. Com. U. S. A.

HEADQUARTERS OF THE ARMY,
WASHINGTON, November 7, 1861.

Brig.-Gen. D. C. BUELL,
Comd'g Depart. of the Ohio:

GENERAL:—In giving you instructions for your guidance, in command of the Department of the Ohio, I do not design to fetter you. I merely wish to express plainly the general ideas which occur to me in relation to the conduct of operations there. That portion of Kentucky west of the Cumberland River is, by its position, so closely related to the States of Illinois and Missouri that it has seemed best to attach it to the Department of Missouri. Your operations, then, in Kentucky will be confined to that portion of the State east of the Cumberland River. I trust I need not repeat to you that I regard the importance of the territory committed to your care as second only to that occupied by the army under my immediate command. It is absolutely necessary that we shall hold all the State of Kentucky; not only that, but that the majority of its inhabitants shall be warmly in favor of our cause, it being that which best subserves their interests. It is possible that the conduct of our political affairs in Kentucky is more important than that of our military operations. I certainly cannot overestimate the importance of the former. You will please constantly bear in mind the precise issue for which we are fighting—that issue is the preservation of the Union, and the restoration of the full authority of the general government over all portions of our territory. We shall most readily suppress this rebellion and restore the authority of the government by religiously respecting the constitutional rights of all. I know that I express the feelings and opinions of the President when I say that we are fighting only to preserve the integrity of the Union, and the constitutional authority of the general government.

The inhabitants of Kentucky may rely upon it, that their domestic institutions will in no manner be interfered with, and that they will receive at our hands every constitutional protection. I have only to repeat that you will, in all respects, carefully regard the local institutions of the region in which you command, allowing nothing but the dictates of military necessity to cause you to depart from the spirit of these instructions.

So much in regard to political considerations. The military problem would be a simple one, could it be entirely separated from political influences; such is not the case. Were the population among which you are to operate wholly or generally hostile, it is probable that Nashville should be your first and principal objective point. It so happens that a large majority of the inhabitants of Eastern Tennessee are in favor of the Union; it therefore seems proper that you should remain on the defensive on the line from Louisville to Nashville, while you throw the mass of your forces, by rapid marches by Cumberland Gap or Walker's Gap, on Knoxville, in order to occupy the railroad at that point, and thus enable the loyal citizens of Eastern Tennessee to use, while you at the same time cut off, the railway communication between Eastern Virginia and the Mississippi.

It will be prudent to fortify the pass, before leaving it in your rear. I am, &c.,

GEO. B. McCLELLAN,
Maj.-Gen. Com. U. S. A.

HEADQUARTERS OF THE ARMY,
WASHINGTON, Nov. 12, 1861.

Brig.-Gen. D. C. BUELL,
Comdg. Dept. of the Ohio:

GENERAL: Upon assuming command of the department, I will be glad to have you make, as soon as possible, a careful report of the condition of your command. The main point to which I desire to call your attention, is the necessity of entering Eastern Tennessee as soon as it can be done with reasonable chances of success, and I hope that you will, with the least possible delay, organize a column for that purpose, sufficiently guarding at the same time the main avenues by which the rebels might invade Kentucky. Our conversations on the subject of military operations have been so full, and my confidence in your judgment is so great, that I will not dwell further on the subject, except to urge upon you the necessity of keeping me fully informed as to the state of affairs, both military and political, and your movements.

In regard to political matters, bear in mind that we are fighting only to preserve the integrity of the Union, and to uphold the general government; as far as military necessity will permit, religiously respect the constitutional rights of all. Preserve the strictest discipline among the troops, and while employing the utmost energy in military movements, be careful so to treat the unarmed inhabitants as to contract, not widen, the breach existing between us and the rebels. I mean by this, that it is the desire of the government to avoid unnecessary irritation by causeless arrests and persecution of individuals. Where there is good reason to believe that persons are actually giving aid, comfort or information to the enemy, it is of course necessary to arrest them; but I have always found it is the tendency of subordinates to make vexatious arrests on mere suspicion. You will find it well to direct that no arrest shall be made except by your order, or that of your generals, unless in extraordinary cases, always holding the party making the arrest responsible for the propriety of his course. It should be our constant aim to make it apparent to all that their property, their comfort, and their personal safety, will be best preserved by adhering to the cause of the Union.

If the military suggestions I have made in this letter prove to have been founded on erroneous data, you are, of course, perfectly free to change the plan of operations.

I am, &c., &c.,

G. B. McClellan,

Maj.-Gen. Com. U. S. A.

II.—OPERATIONS IN THE SOUTH.

Headquarters of the Army,
Washington, Feb. 14, 1862.

Brig.-Gen. T. W. Sherman,
Comd'g. at Port Royal, &c.:

General: Your dispatches in regard to the occupation of Dawfuskie Island, &c., were received to-day. I saw also to-day, for the first time, your requisition for a siege train for Savannah.

After giving the subject all the consideration in my power, I am forced to the conclusion that, under present circumstances, the siege and capture of Savannah do not promise results commensurate with the sacrifices necessary. When I learned that it was possible for the gunboats to reach the Savannah River above Fort Pulaski, two operations suggested themselves to my mind, as its immediate results.

First. The capture of Savannah by a "*coup de main,*" the result of an instantaneous advance and attack by the army and navy.

The time for this has passed, and your letter indicates that you are not accountable for the failure to seize the propitious moment, but that, on the contrary, you perceived its advantages.

Second. To isolate Fort Pulaski, cut off its supplies, and at least facilitate its reduction by a bombardment.

Although we have a long delay to deplore, the second course still remains open to us; and I strongly advise the close blockade of Pulaski, and its bombardment as soon as the 13-inch mortars and heavy guns reach you. I am confident you can thus reduce it. With Pulaski, you gain all that is really essential; you obtain complete control of the harbor, you relieve the blockading fleet, and render the main body of your force disposable for other operations.

I do not consider the possession of Savannah worth a siege, after Pulaski is in our hands. But the possession of Pulaski is of the first importance. The expedition to Fernandina is well, and I shall be glad to learn that it is ours.

But, after all, the greatest moral effect would be produced by the reduction of Charleston and its defences. There the rebellion had its birth; there the unnatural hatred of our government is most intense; there is the centre of the boasted power and courage of the rebels. To gain Fort Sumter, and hold Charleston, is a task well worthy of our greatest efforts, and considerable sacrifices. That is the problem I would be glad to have you study. Some time must elapse before we can be in all respects ready to accomplish that purpose. Fleets are *en route*, and armies in motion, which have certain preliminary objects to accomplish, before we are ready to take Charleston in hand. But the time will before long arrive, when I shall be prepared to make that movement. In the meantime, it is my advice and wish that no attempt be made upon Savannah, unless it can be carried with certainty by a "*coup de main.*"

Please concentrate your attention and forces upon Pulaski, and Fernandina. St. Augustine might as well be taken by way of an interlude, while awaiting the preparations for Charleston. Success attends us everywhere at present.

Very truly yours,

GEO. B. McCLELLAN,

Maj.-Gen. Com. U. S. A.

HEADQUARTERS OF THE ARMY,
WASHINGTON, Feb. 23, 1862.

Maj.-Gen. B. F. BUTLER,
U. S. Volunteers:

GENERAL: You are assigned to the command of the land forces destined to co-operate with the navy, in the attack upon New Orleans. You will use every means to keep your destination a profound secret, even from your staff officers, with the exception of your chief of staff, and Lieutenant Weitzel, of the engineers. The force at your disposal will consist of the first 13 regiments named in your memorandum handed to me in person, the 21st Indiana, 4th Wisconsin, and 6th Michigan, (old and good regiments from Baltimore.)

The 21st Indiana, 4th Wisconsin, and 6th Michigan, will await your orders at Fort Monroe.

Two companies of the 21st Indiana are well drilled as heavy artillery. The cavalry force already *en route* for Ship Island, will be sufficient for your purposes.

After full consultation with officers well acquainted with the country in which it is proposed to operate, I have arrived at the conclusion that (2) two light batteries fully equipped, and (1) one without horses, will be all that are necessary.

This will make your force about 14,400 infantry, 275 cavalry, 680 artillery; total, 15,255 men.

The commanding general of the Department of Key West is authorized to loan you, temporarily, 2 regiments; Fort Pickens can probably give you another, which will bring your force to nearly 18,000.

The object of your expedition is one of vital importance the capture of New Orleans. The route selected is up th Mississippi River, and the first obstacle to be encountered (perhaps the only one,) is in the resistance offered by Forts St. Philip and Jackson. It is expected that the navy can reduce these works; in that case, you will, after their capture, leave a sufficient garrison in them to render them perfectly secure;

and it is recommended, that on the upward passage, a few heavy guns, and some troops, be left at the Pilot Station, (at the forks of the river,) to cover a retreat in the event of a disaster. These troops and guns will, of course, be removed as soon as the forts are captured.

Should the navy fail to reduce the works, you will land your forces and siege train, and endeavor to breach the works, silence their fire, and carry them by assault.

The next resistance will be near the English Bend, where there are some earthen batteries; here it may be necessary for you to land your troops and co-operate with the naval attack, although it is more than probable that the navy, unassisted, can accomplish the result. If these works are taken, the city of New Orleans necessarily falls. In that event, it will proba bly be best to occupy Algiers with the mass of your troops, also, the eastern bank of the river above the city; it may be necessary to place some troops *in* the city to preserve order, but if there appears sufficient Union sentiment to control the city, it may be best for purposes of discipline, to keep your men out of the city.

After obtaining possession of New Orleans, it will be necessary to reduce all the works guarding its approaches from the east, and particularly to gain the Manchac Pass. Baton Rouge, Berwick Bay, and Fort Livingston, will next claim your attention.

A feint on Galveston may facilitate the objects we have in view. I need not call your attention to the necessity of gaining possession of all the rolling stock you can on the different railways, and of obtaining control of the roads themselves The occupation of Baton Rouge by a combined naval and land force, should be accomplished as soon as possible after you have gained New Orleans. Then endeavor to open your communication with the northern column by the Mississippi, always bearing in mind the necessity of occupying Jackson, Mississippi, as soon as you can safely do so, either after, or before you have effected the junction. Allow nothing to divert you from obtaining full possession of all the approaches to New Orleans. When that object is accomplished to its fullest extent, it will be necessary to make a combined attack on Mobile, in order to gain possession of the harbor and works, as well as to control the railway terminus at the city.

In regard to this, I will send more detailed instructions as the operations of the northern column develop themselves.

I may briefly state that the general objects of the expedition are: *First*, the reduction of New Orleans and all its approaches: then Mobile and its defenses: then Pensacola, Galveston, &c. It is probable that by the time New Orleans is reduced it will be in the power of the government to reinforce the land forces sufficiently to accomplish all these objects: in the meantime you will please give all the assistance in your power to the army and navy commanders in your vicinity, never losing sight of the fact, that the great object to be achieved is the capture and firm retention of New Orleans.

I am, &c.,

GEO. B. McCELLAN,

Maj.-Gen. Com. U. S. A.

"The plan indicated in the above letters," quietly observes General McClellan in his Report, "comprehended in its scope the operations of all the armies in the Union, the Army of the Potomac as well. It was my intention, for reasons easy to be seen, that its various parts should be carried out simultaneously or nearly so, and in co-operation along our whole line. If this plan was wise, and events have failed to prove that it was not, then it is unnecessary to defend any delay which would have enabled the army of the Potomac to perform its share in the execution of the whole work."

That in truth which needs defence in that period in the history of the war upon which we are now entering is not any delay in the preparations making to enable the army of the

Potomac to perform its share in the execution of General McClellan's plan of operations.

It is the breaking of the faith pledged, not to General McClellan alone, but to the whole people of the Union when he was appointed to conceive and prepare a plan of operations, that in doing this duty he should receive the "confidence" and the "cordial support" necessary to his success.

"I have no accusation against him"—said President Lincoln in a speech on the subject of General McClellan's change of base to the James River, delivered by him in Washington on the 6th of August, 1862, "I have no accusation against him. I believe he is a brave and able man, and I stand here, as justice requires me to do, to take upon myself what has been charged on the secretary of war, as withholding from him."

General McClellan, in his turn, brings no accusation against President Lincoln. The official proprieties of his position as a Major-General in the army of the United States, forbid him so to do.

But it is perfectly certain that either against President Lincoln or against General McClellan the armies and the people of the United States have a very serious "accusation" to bring. Against whom that accusation shall be brought must be decided by a single consideration, "by whom were the conditions under which the campaign of the army of the Potomac, in the spring of 1862, was commenced and prosecuted, finally and supremely controlled?"

CHAPTER VII.

CONGRESS AND THE WAR. THE JOINT COMMITTEE AND THE NEW WAR SECRETARY, MR. STANTON. THE PRESIDENT ASSUMES COMMAND OF THE ARMIES, AND SUPERSEDES GENERAL McCLELLAN. PRELIMINARY HISTORY OF THE CAMPAIGN OF THE PENINSULA.

About the end of the year 1861, General McClellan, worn down with incessant and exhausting labor was prostrated with a severe illness. On his recovery towards the middle of January he found that his relations with the civil executive were likely to be seriously modified by two important events which had occurred in the interval.

Shortly after the meeting of Congress in December, a joint committee on the conduct of the war had been appointed by that body. The proper sphere of duty of such a committee would of course have been a candid and systematic inquiry into things actually accomplished. The members of the committee, however, did not so limit their notions of their functions. They considered themselves to be a sort of Aulic Council clothed with authority to supervise the plans of commanders in the field, to make military suggestions, and to dictate military appointments. This is evident from their own report of their proceedings; and it is necessary therefore to notice here the constitution of the committee, and its competency to the work to which at this most critical moment of the war, its members addressed themselves.

The committee consisted of six members, two from the Senate and four from the House of Representatives. With the

MAP OF THE PENINSULA
WILLIAMSBURG
College
Queens Cr.
Jamestown Id.
College Cr.
Ft. Magruder
Whittiker
Allan's
Wharf
Kings Cr.
Church
Kings Cr.
Grove Wharf
Halfway Ho.
Skiff's Cr.
Gloucester Pt.
YORKTOWN
Brick Ch.
Course of Warwick River
Wynn's Mill
Mulberry Point
Mulberry Island
Saw Mill
Moore
Lee's Mill
Garrow
Riv.
False
Warwick
Church
Dr. Powers
Brick Ch.
Back Cr.
Mulberry Wharf
Warwick C.H.
Cheesman Cr.
Adams
Cockletown
Howard's Br.
Pequosin R.
Deep Cr.
Church
Halfway Ho.
Big Bethel
North West Br.
Watt's Cr.
Little Bethel
Newmarket Br.
New Br.
Back River
South West Br.
HAMPTON
Newport News
FORTRESS MONROE
Light Ho.
HAMPTON ROADS
Rip Raps
Ft. Calhoun, now Ft. Wool
Willoughby Pt.
Sewall's Point
0 1 2 3 4 Miles
JAMES RIVER
YORK RIVER
CHESAPEAKE BAY
W
E
S

exception of a single representative from New York, these gentlemen belonged to the Republican party, and the most conspicuous of them, Mr. Wade, of Ohio, and Mr. Chandler, of Michigan, to the extreme section of that party.

None of them were possessed of any military experience. They had, however, extremely well-defined and positive notions in respect to the "politics of war," and that these notions were diametrically antagonistic to those held upon the same subject by the commander-in-chief of the forces, will sufficiently appear from the following extract from a majority report in relation to the conduct of the war under General Fremont in Missouri.

"That feature of General Fremont's administration which attracted the most attention at the time, and which will ever be most prominent among the many parts of interest connected with the history of that department, is his proclamation of emancipation. Whatever opinion may be entertained in reference to the time when the proclamation of emancipation should have been inaugurated, or by whose authority it should have been promulgated, there can be no doubt that General Fremont at that early day rightly judged in regard to the most effective means of subduing this rebellion. In proof of that it is only necessary to refer to the fact that his successor, when transferred to another department, issued a proclamation embodying the same principle.* And the President, as commander-in-chief of the army and navy, has applied the same principle to all the rebellious States, and few will deny

* This successor was General DAVID HUNTER, who, having been transferred to the command in South Carolina, issued there a proclamation "embodying the principle" of emancipation. Whether the effectiveness of this "means of subduing the rebellion" was "proved" by the publication of General Hunter's proclamation may perhaps be questioned when we consider that the rebellion has not yet been subdued in South Carolina nor even in Missouri, and that General Hunter, after issuing his "proclamation" was removed from the former department, as he had been from the latter, leaving no trace of his presence in a single military or political advantage gained for the cause of the Union.

that it must be adhered to till the last vestige of treason and rebellion is destroyed."

That a committee on the conduct of the war holding such views of the politics of war should bestow either "confidence" or "cordial support" upon a commander-in-chief whose whole military policy was based on the principle that everything ought to be done to quiet and nothing to inflame those passions of the people of the seceded States in which resided the real strength of their armies in the field, it was of course absurd to expect. It became, therefore, a matter of vital importance to the future of General McClellan's operations, that this committee should in no manner be suffered to interfere with the active management of military affairs.

During the interval which had witnessed the first reaching-forth of this committee after the control of the war, another change, not less momentous, had occurred in the administrative machinery at Washington.

Mr. Cameron had retired from the war office, and had been succeeded by Mr. Stanton.

Mr. Stanton brought with him to the duties of this most arduous and responsible post no administrative experience, but an established reputation for activity, energy, and all those indefinable, but easily recognizable, qualities which are commonly spoken of as "talents for business;" qualities which, in such a field of duty as that to which Mr. Stanton was now called, may make a man either the most useful or the most mischievous of ministers, accordingly as they are, or are not, under the control of a well-balanced character, of a liberal mind, and of a disposition naturally just.

Mr. Stanton was appointed secretary of war on the 14th of January, 1862. Seven days afterwards, on the 21st of January, the new secretary permitted the chairman of the committee on the conduct of the war to address to him the following letter:

Sir:—I am instructed by the joint committee on the conduct of the present war, to inquire of you whether there is such an office as commander-in-chief of the armies of the United States, or any grade above that of major-general? If so, by what authority is it credited? Does it exist by virtue of any law of Congress, or any usage of the government? Please give us the information asked for at your convenience.

I remain, &c., B. F. Wade, Chairman.

Edwin M. Stanton, Secretary of War.

Had General McClellan been aware of the fact that such a letter as this had been addressed to the new secretary he could scarcely have failed to understand that a deliberate attack was about to be made by the joint committee of Congress, in conjunction with that minister, upon his own position at the head of the armies, and upon the "confidence" and "cordial support" which had been pledged to him by the President.

The letter, too, was a direct insult to the President, who had appointed General McClellan in November to fill the office of which this committee question the existence, so direct an insult, that one is at a loss to understand how the newly appointed secretary should have ventured to risk his official position by making himself a party to it, unless, indeed, the whole matter had been concerted and brought about with the full knowledge and consent of the President himself.

Of the intellectual fitness of the new secretary for his new position, he himself gave the public a safe measure in a letter which he addressed to the New-York *Tribune*, about a month after his appointment; and by the reflected light of which we may now fairly estimate the temper which he must have brought, in January, to the grave questions of command then about to be decided. This letter was written on the occasion of some slight advantage won over a handful of the enemy by an enterprising officer at the head of a small body of men:

SIR:—I cannot suffer undue merit to be ascribed to my official action. The merit of our recent victories belongs to the gallant officers and men that fought the battles. No share of it belongs to me.

Much has been recently said of military combination and organizing victory. I hear such phrases with apprehension. They commenced in infidel France with the Italian campaign, and resulted in Waterloo. Who can organize victory? Who can combine the elements of success on the battle-field? We owe our recent victories to the spirit of the Lord that moved our soldiers to dash into battle, and filled the hearts of our enemies with terror and dismay. The inspiration that conquered in battle was in the hearts of the soldiers and from on high. Patriotic spirit, with resolute courage, in men and officers, is a military combination that never failed.

We may well rejoice at the recent victories, for they teach us that battles are to be won now, and by us, in the same and only manner that they were ever won by any people, or in any age since the days of Joshua—by boldly pursuing and striking the foe. What, under the blessings of Providence, I conceive to be the true organization of victory and military combination to end this war, was declared in a few words by General Grant, made to General Buckner, "I propose to move immediately on your works."

The official who could venture to print such a farrago of furious cant as this in February, it may well be believed, was in no condition to comprehend, in January, the patient, practical and thorough combinations of the commander-in-chief, to the effectiveness of whose "organization of victory," interrupted though it was now about to be, the country was destined to be indebted for the opportunity afforded to General Grant of moving immediately upon the enemy's works.

In his first interviews with the new secretary, General McClellan, of course, heard nothing of the machinations then going on for the overthrow of his plans. The secretary urged upon him, in these interviews, the propriety of attempting two operations, the practicability of which had been often before considered by General McClellan in concert with the government, and which it had been repeatedly shown that it would be in the last degree unwise to undertake until the armies was in readiness for grander and more decisive movements.

These operations were the re-opening of the Baltimore and Ohio Railroad, and the raising of the blockade of the Potomac by the rebel batteries on its banks.

However annoying the presence of the enemy on these great lines of communication might be, it was no more annoying in January, 1861, than it had been for five months previously; and as the general-in-chief had been permitted to reserve his force up to this time for the great operations, one admitted consequence of which was to be the complete accomplishment of these secondary objects, it is difficult to understand what possible practical motive there can have been to urge the tardy suspension of preparations, fast ripening to perfection, and the diversion of the army upon such expeditions. The true state of the case, in respect both to the blockade of the railroad and the blockade of the river is clearly given by General McClellan in his report, and so much of his remarks on these subjects as is necessary to a clear understanding of them may well be transferred to these pages.

THE ENEMY'S BATTERIES ON THE POTOMAC.

The attention of the navy department, as early as August 12, 1861, had been called to the necessity of maintaining a strong force of efficient war vessels on the Potomac.

HEADQUARTERS DIVISION POTOMAC,
WASHINGTON, August 12, 1861.

Hon. GIDEON WELLES, *Secretary U. S. Navy:*

SIR,—I have to-day received additional information which

convinces me that it is more than probable that the enemy will, within a very short time, attempt to throw a respectable force from the mouth of Acquia Creek into Maryland. This attempt will probably be preceded by the erection of batteries at Mathias and White House Points. Such a movement on the part of the enemy, in connection with others probably designed, would place Washington in great jeopardy. I most earnestly urge that the strongest possible naval force be at once concentrated near the mouth of Acquia Creek, and that the most vigilant watch be maintained day and night, so as to render such passage of the river absolutely impossible.

I recommend that the Minnesota, and any other vessels available from Hampton Roads, be at once ordered up there, and that a great quantity of coal be sent to that vicinity, sufficient for several weeks' supply. At least one strong war vessel should be kept at Alexandria; and I again urge the concentration of a strong naval force in the Potomac without delay.

If the naval department will render it absolutely impossible for the enemy to cross the river below Washington, the security of the capital will be greatly increased.

I cannot too earnestly urge an immediate compliance with these requests.

I am, sir, very respectfully, your obedient servant,

G. B. McClellan, Major-General Commanding.

It was on the 27th September, 1861, that General Barnard, chief engineer, in company with Captain Wyman, of the Potomac flotilla, had been instructed to make a reconnoissance of the enemy's batteries as far as Mathias Point. In his report of his observations he says: "Batteries at High Point and Cockpit Point, and thence down to Chopawampsic, *cannot* be prevented. We may, indeed, prevent their construction on *certain* points, but along here, somewhere, the enemy can establish, in spite of us, as many batteries as he chooses. What is the remedy? Favorable circumstances, not to be anticipated nor made the basis of any calculations, might justify and render successful the attack of a particular battery. To suppose that we can capture *all*, and by mere attacks of this kind prevent the navigation being molested, is very much the same as to suppose that the hostile army in our own front can prevent us building and maintaining field-works to protect Arlington and Alexandria by capturing them one and all as fast as they are built."

In another communication upon the subject of crossing troops for the purpose of destroying the batteries on the Virginia side of the Potomac, General Barnard says:

"The operation involves the forcing of a very strong line of defence of the enemy, and all that we would have to do, if we were really opening a campaign against them there. It is true we hope to force this line by turning it, by landing on Freestone Point.

'With reason to believe that this may be successful, it cannot be denied that it involves a risk of failure.

"Should we then, considering all the consequences which may be involved, enter into the operation merely to capture the Potomac batteries? *I think not.*

"Will not the Ericsson, assisted by one other gunboat, capable of keeping alongside these batteries, so far control their fire as to keep the navigation sufficiently free as long as we require it? Captain Wyman says yes."

It was the opinion of competent naval officers, and I concur with them, that had an adequate force of strong and well-armed vessels been acting upon the Potomac from the beginning of August, it would have been next to impossible for the rebels to have constructed or maintained batteries upon the banks of the river.* The enemy never occupied Mathias Point,

* See remarks of Lieutenant Wise, U. S. N., in Russell's "Diary North and South." "The navy are writhing under the disgrace of the Potomac blockade." *Ibid., Dec.* 12, 1861.

nor any other point on the river, which was out of supporting distance from their main army.

When the enemy commenced the construction of these batteries, the Army of the Potomac was not in condition to prevent it; their destruction by our army would have afforded but a temporary relief, unless we had been strong enough to hold the entire line of the Potomac. This could be done either by driving the enemy from Manassas and Acquia Creek by main force, or by manœuvring to compel them to evacuate their positions. The latter course was finally pursued, and with success.

THE BALTIMORE AND OHIO RAILROAD.

I had often observed to the President, and to members of the cabinet, that the reconstruction of this railway could not be undertaken until we were in a condition to fight a battle to secure it. I regarded the possession of Winchester and Strasburg as necessary to cover the railway in rear, and it was not until the month of February that I felt prepared to accomplish this very desirable, but not vital purpose.

The whole of Banks' division, and two brigades of Sedgwick's division, were thrown across the river at Harper's Ferry, leaving one brigade of Sedgwick's division to observe and guard the Potomac from Great Falls to the mouth of the Monocacy. A sufficient number of troops, of all arms, were held in readiness in the vicinity of Washington, either to march via Leesburg or to move by rail to Harper's Ferry, should this become necessary in carrying out the objects in view. The subjoined notes from a communication subsequently addressed to the war department will sufficiently explain the conduct of these operations:

"When I started for Harper's Ferry I plainly stated to the President and secretary of war that the chief object of the operation would be to open the Baltimore and Ohio Railroad, by crossing the river in force at Harper's Ferry; that I had collected the material for making a permanent bridge by means of canal-boats; that from the nature of the river it was doubtful whether such a bridge could be constructed; that if it could not I would at least occupy the ground in front of Harper's Ferry, in order to cover the rebuilding of the railroad bridge, and finally, when the communication was perfectly secure, move on Winchester.

"When I arrived at the place I found the bateau bridge nearly completed; the holding ground proved better than had been anticipated, the weather was favorable, there being no wind. I at once crossed over the two brigades which had arrived, and took steps to hurry up the other two, belonging respectively to Banks' and Sedgwick's divisions. The difficulty of crossing supplies had not then become apparent. That night I telegraphed for a regiment of regular cavalry and four batteries of heavy artillery to come up the next day, (Thursday,) besides directing Keyes' division of infantry to be moved up on Friday.

"Next morning the attempt was made to pass the canal-boats through the lift lock, in order to commence at once the construction of a permanent bridge; it was then found for the first time that the lock was too small to permit the passage of the boats, it having been built for a class of boats running on the Shenandoah canal, and too narrow by some four or six inches for the canal-boats. The lift locks above and below are all large enough for the ordinary boats. I had seen them at Edwards' Ferry thus used; it had always been represented to the engineers by the military railroad employees and others that the lock was large enough, and the difference being too small to be detected by the eye, no one had thought of measuring it, or suspected any difficulty. I thus suddenly found myself unable to build the permanent bridge. A violent gale had arisen, which threatened the safety of our only means of communication; the narrow approach to the bridge was so crowded and clogged with wagons that it was very clear that under existing circumstances nothing more could be done than to cross over the baggage and supplies of the two brigades; of these, instead of being able to cross both during the morning, the last arrived only in time to go over just before dark. It was evident that the troops under orders would only be in the way should they arrive, and that it would not be possible to subsist them for a rapid march to Winchester; it was therefore deemed necessary to countermand the order, content ourselves with covering the reopening of the railroad for the present, and in the mean time use every exertion to establish, as promptly as possible, depots of forage and subsistence on the Virginia side, to supply the troops and enable them to move on Winchester independently of the bridge. The next day (Friday) I sent a strong reconnoissance to Charleston, and under its protection went there myself. I then determined to hold that place, and to move the troops composing Lander's and Williams' commands at once on Martinsburg and Bunker Hill, thus effectually covering the reconstruction of the railroad.

"Having done this, and taken all the steps in my power to ensure the rapid transmission of supplies over the river, I returned to this city, well satisfied with what had been accomplished. While up the river I learned that the President was dissatisfied with the state of affairs—but on my return here, understood from the secretary of war that, upon learning the whole state of the case, the President was fully satisfied. I contented myself, therefore, with giving to the secretary a brief statement about as I have written it here."

The design aimed at was entirely compassed, and before the 1st of April, the date of my departure for the Peninsula, the railroad was in running order. As a demonstration upon the left flank of the enemy, this movement no doubt assisted in determining the evacuation of his lines on the 8th and 9th of March."

After discussing these questions with General McClellan, Mr. Stanton inquired into his general plan of campaign, and particularly into that part of the plan which was to be executed by the Army of the Potomac, and effect the reduction of Richmond. General McClellan having explained his designs on this subject verbally to the secretary, that official requested him to develop them more fully to the President.

Already unavowedly at odds with the general-in-chief in respect to his notions of the politics of the war, the President now revealed his disposition to put a serious practical construction on his own official rank as commander of the army and navy of the Union. He listened to the plan of General McClellan, raised objections to it, and sketched one of his own, which he suggested to the admiration and the adoption of his interlocutor.

It would seem that from a very early period in the history of the war the President had been visited with military illuminations. It has already been shown from the testimony of General Irwin McDowell, given before the joint committee on the conduct of the war, that during the operations preliminary to the first battle of Bull Run the President was in the habit of discussing and passing sentence upon the military projects of Lieutenant-General Scott; and a singular passage from the diary of the London *Times* correspondent, Mr. W. H. Russell, informs us that in the very outset of hostilities the President gave direct orders for a naval movement which, had it been attempted, must have almost certainly inflicted a serious misfortune upon our naval force, and that, too, at a moment when we could ill have afforded the loss of a single gun afloat.*

* This passage is so extremely curious, and seems to have excited so little attention, that I transcribe it. Under the date of August 31st, 1862, Mr. Russell writes: "I dined with Lieutenant Wise, and met Captain Dahlgren, Captain Foote, and Colonel Fletcher Webster. * * Incidentally I learned from the conversation—and it is a curious illustration of the power of the President—that it was he who ordered the attack on Charleston Harbor, or, to speak with more accuracy, the movement of

The events of July 21st, 1861, appear to have quieted for a time the military aspirations of Mr. Lincoln. But they were now reviving, whether by the sheer force of nature, or under the manipulations of a secretary of war, who believed in battles by a divine inspiration, and of a joint committee confident in the military efficacy of exasperating proclamations it is not now material to inquire; and General McClellan, after holding the position of commander-in-chief of the armies for nearly three months, and preparing a complete and thorough plan of operations against the enemy, with the distinct understanding that all the time and materials and authority necessary to its successful execution would be secured to him by the "confidence" and "cordial support" of the President, found himself called upon to submit one of the most material features of that plan to the uninstructed revision of that great functionary.

While this cloud still lowered upon the spirits of the young general, and upon the military hopes of the country, the President, as has been heretofore shown, suddenly took the whole matter into his own hands, and assumed the command of the armies in the following war order, which I have already given, but which I give again, as essential to this part of the narrative:

EXECUTIVE MANSION,
WASHINGTON, January 27, 1862.

PRESIDENT'S GENERAL WAR ORDER, No. 1.

Ordered: That the 22d day of February, 1862, be the day for a general movement of the land and naval forces of the United States against the insurgent forces.

the armed squadron to relieve Sumter by force if necessary; and that he *came to the conclusion it was feasible, principally from reading the account of the attack on Kinburn by the allied fleets.* There was certainly an immense disproportion between the relative means of attack and defence in the two cases; but, at all events, the action of the Confederates prevented the attempt."

That, especially,
The army at and about Fortress Monroe,
The army of the Potomac,
The army of Western Virginia,
The army near Mumfordsville, Kentucky,
The army and flotilla at Cairo,
And a naval force in the Gulf of Mexico, be ready to move on that day.

That all other forces, both land and naval, with their respective commanders, obey existing orders for the time, and be ready to obey additional orders when duly given.

That the heads of departments, and especially the secretaries of war and of the navy, with all their subordinates, and the general-in-chief, with all their commanders and subordinates of land and naval forces, will severally be held to their strict and full responsibilities for prompt execution of this order. ABRAHAM LINCOLN.

Of course neither Mr. Lincoln himself, nor Mr. Stanton, nor even the joint committee on the conduct of the war, can have regarded this "order" as a serious war measure. Couched in a style which recalls the heraldic recitation of a great English nobleman's titles of honor and dignity over his grave ere the steward breaks his wand of office, and the dust is left in peace with its kindred dust: appointing with dramatic affectation a popular anniversary for the achievement of military impossibilities, this order No. 1 would go down into history simply as a model of the grotesque in executive assumption, had not many subsequent events given to it a melancholy significance as the first autographic evidence of Mr. Lincoln's personal and fatal interference in the military conduct of the war.

It was followed up four days afterwards by the Special War Order No. 1, in which the President, having already resumed the active command of the armies in general, next resumed the active command of the Army of the Potomac in particular. This order, it will be recollected, ran thus:

EXECUTIVE MANSION,
WASHINGTON, January 31, 1862.

PRESIDENT'S SPECIAL WAR ORDER, No. 1.

Ordered: That all the disposable force of the Army of the Potomac, after providing safely for the defence of Washington, be formed into an expedition for the immediate object of seizing and occupying a point upon the railroad southwestward of what is known as Manassas Junction, all details to be in the discretion of the commander-in-chief, and the expedition to move on or before the 22d day of February next.

ABRAHAM LINCOLN.

Whether the new commander-in-chief of the United States army and of the Army of the Potomac, when he thus gave General Johnston a three weeks' warning of his intention to march upon Manassas Junction, supposed that the Confederate general and his army, paralyzed by fear of their impending fate, would helplessly await his onset in a state of exanimation, or whether he imagined that the rebels, excited by the fear of losing the earthworks which, as the New York *Tribune* and other radical journals declared at the time they had mounted only with "Quaker guns," would hurry forward all their forces to the place by him appointed, and there, upon the day by him appointed, open a grand tournament to decide the issues of the war, cannot now be clearly settled.

Puerile as the order was in itself, and supremely ridiculous as it must have seemed to the enemy, it was portentous of mischief to the Federal cause. General McClellan lost no time in seeing the President, and requesting to know definitely whether it was expected that he should abandon all consideration of the plan of campaign upon which he had himself decided, and adopt the project set forth in this new and special order. The President graciously gave him permission to set forth in writing his reasons for desiring to adhere to his own well-matured designs.

Before the paper, which General McClellan in accordance with this permission at once began to draw up, was prepared, he received from the President the following characteristic note:

EXECUTIVE MANSION,
WASHINGTON, February 3, 1862.

MAJ.-GEN. McCLELLAN,—

MY DEAR SIR,—You and I have distinct and different plans for a movement of the Army of the Potomac. Yours to be done by the Chesapeake, up the Rappahannock to Urbanna, and across and to the terminus of the railroad on the York River: mine to move directly to a point on the railroad south-west of Manassas.

If you will give me satisfactory answers to the following questions, I shall gladly yield my plan to yours:

1st. Does not your plan involve a greatly larger expenditure of *time* and *money* than mine?

2d. Wherein is a victory *more certain* by your plan than mine?

3d. Wherein is a victory *more valuable* by your plan than mine?

4th. In fact, would it not be *less* valuable in this; that it would break no great line of the enemy's communications, while mine would?

5th. In case of disaster, would not a retreat be more difficult by your plan than mine?

Yours truly,
ABRAHAM LINCOLN.

Rarely, if ever, in the history of the world, have the honesty and the patriotism of a military commander been subjected to so trying a test as this letter applied to General McClellan.

The President had now openly taken upon himself the direction of the national armies. Had General McClellan been a commonly selfish man, had he not wholly sunk all consideration of the slight and injustice put himself in his fear and concern for the safety of his brave army, and of the cause to which, and not to the President, he had given his sword, he might now have waived the unequal contest with arrogance and incapacity in the seat of power: he might have accepted, in the really subordinate position to which the President had so cavalierly reduced him, the presidential plan of campaign: he might have contented himself with attempting, as the lieutenant of this new and most eccentric general, to put it into execution.

But this General McClellan could not do.

He went on manfully with the ungrateful task of stating his reasons for doing what by every consideration of decency, justice, good faith, and common sense, he was entitled to do unchallenged and unquestioned. Those reasons he embodied in the following letter, handed to the secretary of war on the same day on which Mr. Lincoln's "note of inquiry" reached him:

HEADQUARTERS OF THE ARMY,
WASHINGTON, Feb. 3, 1862.

HON. E. M. STANTON,
Sec'y of War,—

SIR,—I ask your indulgence for the following paper, rendered necessary by circumstances:

I assumed command of the troops in the vicinity of Washington on Saturday, July 27, 1861, six days after the battle of Bull Run. I found no army to command; a mere collection of regiments, cowering on the banks of the Potomac, some perfectly raw, others dispirited by the recent defeat. Nothing of any consequence had been done to secure the southern approaches to the capital by means of defensive works—nothing whatever had been undertaken to defend the avenues to the city on the northern side of the Potomac. The troops were not only undisciplined, undrilled, and dispirited;

they were not even placed in military positions; the city was almost in a condition to have been taken by a dash of a regiment of cavalry.

Without one day's delay, I undertook the difficult task assigned to me; that task the honorable secretary knows was given to me without my solicitation or foreknowledge. How far I have accomplished it will best be shown by the past and the present. The capital is secure against attack; the extensive fortifications erected by the labor of our troops enable a small garrison to hold it against a numerous army; the enemy have been held in check; the State of Maryland is securely in our possession; the detached counties of Virginia are again within the pale of our laws, and all apprehension of trouble in Delaware is at an end: the enemy are confined to the positions they occupied before the disaster of the 21st July: more than all this, I have now under my command a well-drilled and reliable army, to which the destinies of the country may be confidently committed: this army is young and untried in battle, but it is animated by the highest spirit, and is capable of great deeds. That so much has been accomplished, and such an army created, in so short a time, from nothing, will hereafter be regarded as one of the highest glories of the administration and the nation. Many weeks—I may say many months ago, this Army of the Potomac was fully in condition to repel any attack; but there is a vast difference between that and the efficiency required to enable troops to attack successfully an army elated by victory and intrenched in a position long since selected, studied and fortified. In the earliest papers I submitted to the President, I asked for an effective and movable force far exceeding the aggregate of that now on the banks of the Potomac. I have not the force I asked for. Even when in a subordinate position, I always looked beyond the operations of the Army of the Potomac. I was never satisfied in my own mind with a barren victory, but looked to combined and decisive operations.

When I was placed in command of the armies of the United States, I immediately turned my attention to the whole field of operations, regarding the Army of the Potomac as only *one*, while the most important, of the masses under my command. I confess that I did not then appreciate the total absence of a general plan, which had before existed—nor did I know that utter disorganization and want of preparation pervaded the Western armies. I took it for granted that they were nearly, if not quite, in condition to move toward the fulfilment of my plans; I acknowledge that I made a great mistake. I sent at once, with the approval of the executive, officers I considered competent to command in Kentucky and Missouri—their instructions looked to prompt movements—I soon found that the labor of creation and organization had to be performed there; transportation, arms, clothing, artillery, discipline, all were wanting; these things required time to procure them. The generals in command have done their work most creditably—but we are still delayed. I had hoped that a general advance could be made during the good weather of December; I was mistaken. My wish was to gain possession of the Eastern Tennessee Railroad as a preliminary movement—then to follow it up immediately by an attack on Nashville and Richmond, as nearly at the same time as possible. I have ever regarded our true policy as being that of fully preparing ourselves, and then seeking for the most decisive results. I do not wish to waste life in useless battles—but I prefer to strike at the heart. Two bases of operations seem to present themselves for the advance of the army of the Potomac. 1*st*. That of Washington, its present position, involving a direct attack upon the intrenched positions of the enemy at Centreville, Manassas, &c., or else a movement to turn one or both flanks of those positions; or a combination of the two plans. The relative force of the two armies will not justify an attack on both flanks; an attack on his left flank alone involves a long line of wagon communication, and cannot prevent him from collecting for the decisive battle all the detachments now on his extreme right and left. Should we attack his right flank by the line of the Occoquan, and a crossing of the Potomac below that river, and near his batteries, we could, perhaps, prevent the junction of the enemy's right with his centre, (we might destroy the former,) we would remove the obstructions to the navigation of the Potomac, reduce the length of wagon transportation by establishing new depots at the nearest points of the Potomac, and strike more directly his main railway communication.

The fords of Occoquan, below the mouth of Bull Run, are watched by the rebels; batteries are said to be placed on the heights in rear, (concealed by the woods,) and the arrangement of his troops is such that he can oppose some considerable resistance to a passage of that stream. Information has just been received, to the effect that the enemy are intrenching a line of heights, extending from the vicinity of Sangsters, (Union Mills,) towards Evansport. Early in January, Sprigg's Ford was occupied by General Rhodes, with 3,600 men and eight guns. There are strong reasons for believing that Davis' Ford is occupied. These circumstances indicate, or prove, that the enemy anticipates the move in question, and is prepared to resist it. Assuming, for the present, that this operation is determined upon, it may be well to examine briefly its probable progress. In the present state of affairs, our columns (for the movement of so large a force must be made in several columns, at least five or six) can reach Accotinck without danger; during the march thence to the Occoquan, our right flank becomes exposed to an attack from Fairfax Station, Sangsters and Union Mills. This danger must be met by occupying, in some force, either the two first-named places, or, better, the point of junction of the roads leading to the village of Occoquan. This occupation must be sustained so long as we continue to draw supplies by the roads from the city, or until a battle is won.

The crossing of the Occoquan should be made at all the

fords from Wolf's Run to the mouth, the points of crossing not being necessarily confined to the fords themselves. Should the enemy occupy this line in force we must, with what assistance the flotilla can afford, endeavor to force the passage near the mouth, thus forcing the enemy to abandon the whole line, or be taken in flank himself.

Having gained the line of the Occoquan, it would be necessary to throw a column, by the shortest route, to Dumfries, partly to force the enemy to abandon his batteries on the Potomac, partly to cover our left flank against an attack from the direction of Acquia; and, lastly, to establish our communication with the river by the best roads, and thus give us new depots. The enemy would, by this time, have occupied the line of the Occoquan above Bull Run, holding Brentsville in force, and, perhaps, extending his lines somewhat further to the southwest.

Our next step would be to prevent the enemy from crossing the Occoquan between Bull Run and the Broad Run, to fall upon our right flank while moving on Brentsville. This might be effected by occupying Bacon Race Church and the cross-roads near the mouth of Bull Run, or still more effectually, by moving to the fords themselves, and preventing him from debouching on our side.

These operations would probably be resisted, and it would require some time to effect them. As nearly, at the same time, as possible, we should gain the fords necessary to our purposes above Broad Run. Having secured our right flank, it would become necessary to carry Brentsville at any cost, for we could not leave it between our right flank and the main body. The final movement on the railroad must be determined by circumstances existing at the time.

This brief sketch brings out in bold relief the great advantage possessed by the enemy in the strong central position he occupies, with roads diverging in every direction, and a strong line of defence, enabling him to remain on the defensive with a small force on one flank, while he concentrates everything on the other for a decisive action.

Should we place a portion of our force in front of Centreville, while the rest crosses the Occoquan, we commit the error of dividing our army by a very difficult obstacle, and by a distance too great to enable the two parts to support each other, should either be attacked by the masses of the enemy, while the other is held in check.

I should, perhaps, have dwelt more decidedly on the fact that the force left near Sangsters must be allowed to remain somewhere on that side of the Occoquan until the decisive battle is over, so as to cover our retreat, in the event of disaster; unless it should be decided to select and intrench a new base somewhere near Dumfries, a proceeding involving much time.

After the passage of the Occoquan by the main army, this covering force could be drawn into a more central and less exposed position, say Brimstone Hill, or nearer the Occoquan.

In this latitude the weather will, for a considerable period, be very uncertain, and a movement commenced in force, on roads in tolerably firm condition, will be liable, almost certain, to be much delayed by rains and snows. It will, therefore, be next to impossible to surprise the enemy, or take him at a disadvantage by rapid manœuvres. Our slow progress will enable him to divine our purposes, and take his measures accordingly. The probability is, from the best information we possess, that the enemy has improved the roads leading to his lines of defence, while we will have to work as we advance.

Bearing in mind what has been said, and the present unprecedented and impassable condition of the roads, it will be evident that no precise period can be fixed upon for the movement on this line. Nor can its duration be closely calculated; it seems certain that many weeks may elapse before it is possible to commence the march. Assuming the success of this operation, and the defeat of the enemy as certain, the question at once arises as to the importance of the results gained. I think these results would be confined to the possession of the field of battle, the evacuation of the line of the upper Potomac by the enemy, and the moral effect of the victory; important results, it is true, but not decisive of the war, nor securing the destruction of the enemy's main army, for he could fall back upon other positions and fight us again and again, should the condition of his troops permit. If he is no condition to fight us again out of range of the intrenchments at Richmond, we would find it a very difficult and tedious matter to follow him up there, for he would destroy his railroad bridges, and otherwise impede our progress through a region where the roads are as bad as they well can be, and we would probably find ourselves forced at last to change the whole theatre of war, or to seek a shorter land route to Richmond, with a smaller available force, and at an expenditure of much more time than were we to adopt the short line at once. We would also have forced the enemy to concentrate his forces, and perfect his defensive measures at the very point where it is desirable to strike him when least prepared.

"II. The second base of operations available for the army of the Potomac, is that of the lower Chesapeake Bay, which affords the shortest possible land route to Richmond, and strikes directly at the heart of the enemy's power in the east.

"The roads in that region are passable at all seasons of the year.

"The country now alluded to is much more favorable for offensive operations than that in front of Washington, (which is *very* unfavorable,) much more level, more cleared land, the woods less dense, the soil more sandy, the spring some two or three weeks earlier. A movement in force on that line obliges the enemy to abandon his intrenched position at Manasses, in order to hasten to cover Richmond and Norfolk. He must do this; for should he permit us to occupy Richmond, his destruction can be averted only by entirely defeating us in a battle, in which he must be the assailant. This movement, if successful, gives us the capital, the communications, the supplies of the rebels; Norfolk would fall; all the waters of the Chesapeake would be ours, all Virginia would be in our power; and the enemy forced to abandon Tennessee and North Carolina. The alternative presented to the enemy would be to beat us in a position selected by ourselves; disperse or pass beneath the Caudine Forks.

"Should we be beaten in a battle, we have a perfectly secure retreat down the Peninsula upon Fort Monroe, with our flanks perfectly covered by the fleet. During the whole movement our flank is covered by the water, our right is secure, for the reason that the enemy is too distant to reach us in time; he can only oppose us in front; we bring our fleet in full play.

"After a successful battle, our position would be, Burnside forming our left, Norfolk held securely, our centre connecting Burnside with Buell, both by Raleigh and Lynchburg, Buell in Eastern Tennessee and Northern Alabama, Halleck at Nashville and Memphis.

"The next movement would be to connect with Sherman on the left, by reducing Wilmington and Charleston; to advance our centre into South Carolina and Georgia, to push Buell either towards Montgomery, or to unite with the main army in Georgia, to throw Halleck southward to meet the naval expedition from New Orleans.

"We should then be in a condition to reduce at our leisure, all the southern seaports; to occupy all the avenues of communication, to use the great outlet of the Mississippi; to reestablish our government and arms in Arkansas, Louisiana and Texas; to force the slaves to labor for our subsistence, instead of that of the rebels; to bid defiance to all foreign interference. Such is the object I ever had in view; this is the general plan which I hope to accomplish.

"For many long months, I have labored to prepare the Army

of the Potomac to play its part in the programme; from the day when I was placed in command of all our armies, I have exerted myself to place all the other armies in such a condition, that they too could perform their allotted duties.

"Should it be determined to operate from the lower Chesapeake, the point of landing which promises the most brilliant results, is Urbanna, on the lower Rappahannock. This point is easily reached by vessels of heavy draught, it is neither occupied nor observed by the enemy, it is but one march from West Point, the key of that region, and thence but two marches to Richmond. A rapid movement from Urbanna, would probably cut off Magruder in the Peninsula, and enable us to occupy Richmond before it could be strongly reinforced. Should we fail in that, we could, with the co-operation of the navy, cross the James and show ourselves in rear of Richmond, thus forcing the enemy to come out and attack us, for his position would be untenable, with us on the southern bank of the river.

"Should circumstances render it not advisable to land at Urbanna, we can use Mob Jack Bay—or the worst coming to the worst, we can take Fort Monroe as a base, and operate with complete security, although with less celerity and brilliancy of results, up the Peninsula.

"To reach whatever point may be selected as a base, a large amount of cheap water transportation must be collected, consisting mainly of canal-boats, barges, wood-boats, schooners, &c., towed by small steamers, all of a very different character from those required for all previous expeditions. This can certainly be accomplished within thirty days from the time the order is given. I propose as the best possible plan that can, in my judgment, be adopted, to select Urbanna as a landing-place for the first detachments. To transport by water four-divisions of infantry with their batteries, the regular infantry, a few wagons, one bridge train, and a few squadrons of cavalry, making the vicinity of Hooker's position the place of embarkation for as many as possible. To move the regular cavalry and reserve artillery, the remaining bridge trains and wagons to a point somewhere near Cape Lookout, then ferry them over the river by means of North River ferry-boats, march them over to the Rappahannock (covering the movement by an infantry force near Heathsville) and to cross the Rappahannock in a similar way. The expense and difficulty of the movement will thus be very much diminished (a saving of transportation of about 10,000 horses) and the result none the less certain.

"The concentration of the cavalry, &c., in the lower counties of Maryland, can be effected without exciting suspicion, and the movement made without delay from that cause.

"This movement, if adopted, will not at all expose the city of Washington to danger.

"The total force to be thrown upon the new line would be, according to circumstances, from 110 to 140,000. I hope to use the latter number by bringing fresh troops into Washington, and still leaving it quite safe. I fully realize that in all projects offered, time will probably be the most valuable consideration. It is my decided opinion, that in that point of view, the second plan should be adopted. It is possible, nay, highly probable, that the weather and state of the roads, may be such as to delay the direct movement from Washington, with its unsatisfactory results and great risks—far beyond the time required to complete the second plan. In the first case we can fix no definite time for an advance. The roads have gone from bad to worse—nothing like their present condition has ever been known here before; they are impassable at present, we are entirely at the mercy of the weather. It is by no means certain that we can beat them at Manassas. On the other line, I regard success as certain by all the chances of war. We demoralize the enemy by forcing him to abandon his prepared position for one which we have chosen, in which all is in our favor, and where success must produce immense results.

"My judgment as a general, is clearly in favor of this project. Nothing is certain in war, but all the chances are in favor of this movement. So much am I in favor of the southern line of operations, that I would prefer the move from Fort Monroe as a base—as a certain though less brilliant movement, than that from Urbanna—to an attack upon Manassas.

"I know that his excellency the President, you and I, all agree in our wishes, and that these wishes are to bring the war to a close, as promptly as the means in our possession will permit. I believe that the mass of the people have entire confidence in us. I am sure of it. Let us then look only to the great result to be accomplished, and disregard everything else.

I am, very respectfully, your obedient servant,

G. B. McClellan,
Major-General Commanding.

General McClellan, in his Report, simply says of this letter: "It must have produced some effect upon the mind of the President, since the execution of his order was not required, although it was not revoked as formally as it was issued."

In his history of President Lincoln's administration, Mr. Raymond, better informed as to the secrets of the presidential mind, remarks: "The President was by no means convinced by General McClellan's reasoning: but in consequence of his steady resistance, and unwillingness to enter upon the execution of any other plan, he assented to the submission of the matter to a council of twelve officers, late in February, at head-quarters."

Dates are here witnesses of great importance: and these witnesses unfortunately fail to bear out Mr. Lincoln's authorized version of his own conduct in this great emergency.

General McClellan's letter was read by the President on the 3d of February. As he had now declared himself commander-in-chief, it was the President's imperative duty to come to an immediate decision on the subject. To hesitate was a crime. The winter was slipping away. Already, by the President's orders, the execution of a part of General McClellan's plan of operations had been precipitated at the West. Why was the army of the Potomac to be kept waiting by Mr. Lincoln upon his decision? Mr. Raymond's language conveys the impression that the President steadily postponed action until late in February, when he summoned a council of twelve officers to aid him in taking it. If this impression were strictly in consonance with the facts, it would still convict the President of a weak and dangerous hesitation to impose his authority upon a subordinate of whose plans he disapproved.

But the facts in the case are these:

The President substantially acquiesced in General McClellan's conclusions, and thereby substantially authorized him to begin the campaign of the peninsula, early in February. To the purposes of this campaign it was essential that an extraordinary amount of water transportation should be provided on the Potomac, and no time ought to have been lost in procuring the vessels for this work. Already, early in January, before the President had superseded him, General McClellan, on leaving his sick-room, had summoned to Washington a gentleman well and widely known for his familiarity with the transportation service of the country, and had consulted him as to the feasibility of obtaining a complete water transportation at one time for an army of 50,000 men, with horses, guns, and all the usual equipment of such a force. This gentleman, Mr. John Tucker, of Philadelphia—for a time assistant secretary of war—had reported a few days afterwards that the thing which the general had asked could certainly be done.

In repeated interviews with the President, as well as with General McClellan, Mr. Tucker was consulted by both as to the shortest time in which this transportation service could be got ready, and he had repeatedly assured them that thirty days at least would be required to complete the outfit.

Upon the 27th of February, finally, *no council of generals whatever having been held upon the matter, the secretary of war, by authority of the President, instructed Mr. Tucker that the movement of the army by water to the Peninsula was finally decided upon, and required him at once to procure the necessary steamers and sailing craft.*

It is plain, therefore, that the President, after yielding his assent to the proposed plan of campaign early in February, hesitated over the necessary preparations for it until the end of that month, and thereby interposed a delay of at least three weeks in the movement.

Let it here be stated that in the space of thirty-seven days from the 27th of February, Mr. Tucker, acting in concert with General McClellan, had chartered and assembled no fewer than 113 steamers, 188 schooners, and 88 barges; and upon them had transported from the Potomac to Fortress Monroe an army of 121,500 men, with 44 batteries, 74 ambulances, 1,150 wagons, and 14,592 animals, besides pontoon bridges, telegraph materials, and the enormous quantity of equipage required for such a force. All this was done with the loss only of eight mules, and of nine barges, the cargoes of which were saved; and Mr. Tucker is certainly warranted in his assertion, "that for economy and celerity of expedition this movement is without a parallel on record."

A few days before the directions for procuring transportation service were given to Mr. Tucker, General McClellan left Washington for Harper's Ferry, to take order in regard to affairs at that point. He returned on the 28th of February, and, upon the reiterated urgency of the President and the secretary of war, set about organizing an expedition against the Potomac batteries of the enemy; although he did this with reluctance, for the reasons stated in the brief memorandum on the subject which has been given above.

On the 8th of March, on which day a meeting of the Divisional Generals had been called by General McClellan at his headquarters, for the purpose of giving them their instructions in respect to this expedition against the batteries, the President sent for him at a very early hour. His Excellency, to the great surprise of the General, renewed all his old objections to the plan of the movement against Richmond by water,—the plan which he had countermanded in January—to which he had assented again and again, throughout the month of February, and all the costly preparations for which were now, by his own order, in the full course of execution. Again General McClellan went over the whole question, and again the President expressed himself as satisfied with the expedition. Learning, however, that the divisional generals were to meet at General McClellan's headquarters that day, he urged it upon the general to submit the plan to them in council.

All military precedents ruled against such a proceeding in a case so grave as that of the grand plan of a campaign of invasion. Without impugning the honor or the wisdom of any one of their number, a general-in-chief might well be excused for thinking the secret of such a plan safer in the hands of one general than of thirteen generals.

The President, however, insisted.

The meeting was held; the plans of General McClellan were laid before the generals, and they were fully approved by seven out of the twelve generals present; an eighth also giving them his conditional approbation.

It is a curious circumstance that every one of the generals who upon this occasion voted by implication against the superiority of the President's plan of campaign, has, since that time, upon one or another pretext, been eliminated from the army of the Potomac, if not from the service. They were Generals W. F. Smith, Fitz-John Porter, Naglee, Franklin, McCall, Andrew Porter, and Blenker—men who certainly proved themselves, in the subsequent serious work of the war, not the least upon the rolls of Federal valor and conduct.

Not less curious perhaps is it that the four generals who by implication countenanced the President's plan, were on the same day advanced by the President to the high distinction of commanders of army corps. These were Generals McDowell, Sumner, Heintzelman, and Keyes.

For, having, at last, to use the language of Mr. Raymond, "consented to the submission" of General McClellan's plan to a council of twelve generals nearly a fortnight after he had himself given the final positive orders for carrying it into execution, the President at once proceeded to take that plan entirely into his own hands; and without consulting the commander who had conceived it, who was to carry it out on the field, and upon whom he intended to fix the entire responsibility of its results, he issued on this very day of its adoption by the council, two more war orders of the greatest importance in regard to it.

The first of these orders directed the organization of the Army of the Potomac into four army corps, and appointed four generals to the new commands: the second revealed to the enemy and the world General McClellan's intention of moving the Army of the Potomac to a new base, and tied up the whole movement with restrictions fatal to the commanding general's freedom of action.

Both of these orders demand particular attention. We begin with the second:

EXECUTIVE MANSION,
WASHINGTON, March 8, 1862.

PRESIDENT'S GENERAL WAR ORDER, No. 3.

Ordered: That no change of the base of operations of the Army of the Potomac shall be made without leaving in and about Washington such a force as, in the opinion of the general-in-chief, and the commanders of army corps, shall leave said city entirely secure.

That no more than two army corps (about fifty thousand troops) of said army of the Potomac shall be moved *en route* for a new base of operations, until the navigation of the Potomac, from Washington to the Chesapeake Bay, shall be freed from the enemy's batteries and other obstructions, or until the President shall hereafter give express permission.

That any movement, as aforesaid, *en route* for a new base of operations, which may be ordered by the general-in-chief, and which may be intended to move upon the Chesapeake Bay, shall begin to move upon the bay as early as the 18th of March, instant, and the general-in-chief shall be responsible that it so moves as early as that day.

Ordered: That the army and navy co-operate in an immediate effort to capture the enemy's batteries upon the Potomac, between Washington and the Chesapeake Bay.

AB. LINCOLN.

L. THOMAS, Adjt.-Gen.

Upon this order it is to be remarked, that the clause holding General McClellan responsible that the movement on the bay should begin as early as the 18th of March was issued directly in the face of the facts which were perfectly well known to the President, though not to the public, that the assistant secretary of war, charged with procuring transportation for this movement, had stated it to be impossible to procure such transportation in less than thirty days' time, and that the said assistant secretary of war had never received permission from the President to begin the work of procuring such transportation until the 27th of February.

The clause of this order, therefore, can only be regarded as a deliberate attempt to make the general commanding the expedition responsible before the country for a delay of which the President, who issued the order, knew himself, when he issued it, to have been the cause.

But the whole order exposes its author to a still more formidable imputation than is here implied.

The Prince de Joinville, in commenting upon the submis sion by the President's orders of General McClellan's plans to a council of twelve, observes that on the "next day these plans were known to the enemy. Informed, no doubt, by one of those thousand female spies who keep up his communications into the domestic circles of the Federal enemy, Johnston evacuated Manassas at once." It was dangerous, of course, to make the plans of the commanding general known to so many of his subordinate officers; but the President's order, intimating the imminence of a movement of the Army of the Potomac by water to a new base, was such a sufficient notification of impending events, as abundantly to dispense General Johnston from an absolute reliance upon "female spies."

The first presidential order issued on this fatal 8th day of March was in its way quite as significant to the enemy, and breathed a spirit quite as mischievous to the success of the Federal cause, as the one which we have considered.

By this "General War Order, No. 2," the four most important commands in the Army of the Potomac were given to generals not of General McClellan's selection; and the enemy were informed that General Banks was to be intrusted with a separate fifth command of his own.

General McClellan had never objected to the organization of the army into army corps, nor is there anything to show that if left to his own judgment, he might not have selected for such commands the officers named to them by the President.

But General McClellan had always insisted that the organization of the army corps ought to be deferred "until some little experience in campaign, and on the field of battle, should show what general officers were most competent to exercise these high commands, for it must be remembered that we then had no officers whose experience in war on a large scale was sufficient to prove that they possessed the necessary qualifications.* An incompetent commander of an army corps

* See testimony of General McDowell, Report on the Conduct of the War, Part II., p. 38.

might cause irreparable damage, while it was not probable that an incompetent division commander could cause any very serious mischief."

In spite of these obviously sensible considerations, the President by his own motion, and without so much as hinting his intentions to the commander of the expedition, by this order suddenly broke up the Army of the Potomac into four great corps, putting at the head of these corps four generals, all of whom had expressed themselves unfavorably to the plan of campaign which they were thus clothed with the power vitally to forward or fatally to thwart! The way in which these generals subsequently conducted themselves cannot be alleged here in extenuation of this worse than blunder on the part of the President and his counsellors. Their action put General McClellan and his enterprise practically at the mercy of four generals who could not command his full confidence, since they had pronounced unwise the plans which he himself believed to be the wisest he could adopt: it gave these generals the dangerous consciousness of executive support against their military head; and it therefore exposed them to all the temptations of jealousy, envy, and personal ambition.

"It happens much more frequently than is supposed," says Baron Jomini,* "that a general-in-chief is deceived by his lieutenants, who, listening only to their egotism, forget that they betray not him alone, but their country and the army, through the influence of the lowest jealousy and the guiltiest ambition. The incapacity of a lieutenant, unable to conceive of the merits of a manœuvre which has been ordered, and committing consequently grave mistakes in the execution of it, would have the same results as his envy or his jealousy in overthrowing the finest combinations."

If General McClellan's plan of campaign was destined to escape such dangers as these, it was none the less exposed to them by the President's General War Order No. 2, which

* *Précis de l'Art de la Guerre.* Bruxelles, 1841. Tome 2d, p. 228.

must therefore be set down as one of the most significant steps in the steady progress of the government towards the utter prostration of all the hopes which the country and General McClellan had built up on the basis of that plan.

And why, now, were these orders issued, in this untoward way, and at this most unpropitious moment?

In commenting upon the President's War Order, No. 1, issued January 27th, 1862, Mr. Lincoln's biographer, Mr. Raymond, makes this naive statement as to its origin:

"As winter approached without any indications of an intended movement of our armies, the public impatience rose to the highest point of discontent. The administration was everywhere held responsible for these unaccountable delays, and was freely charged by its opponents with a design to protract the war for selfish political purposes of its own; and at the fall elections the public dissatisfaction made itself manifest by adverse votes in every considerable State where elections were held.

"Unable longer to endure this state of things, President Lincoln put an end to it on the 27th of January, 1862, by issuing" his War Order, No. 1.

It is not possible to add one word to the complete revelation which is here made of the President's willingness to sacrifice his armies and their generals to a fancied political exigency. For what purpose was Mr. Lincoln clothed with the great powers of the presidency if not that he might interpose those powers between an ignorant popular impatience and those faithful servants of the State to whom he himself but a few weeks before had solemnly pledged the "confidence, and his cordial support" necessary to their success in the execution of their vast plans for the public good?

What mattered the charges of the "opponents of the administration;" what the "adverse votes of every considerable State in the fall elections," in comparison with the tremendous issues of national life and national death dependent on the freedom of the commander of the national armies to perfect his plans and put them safely into execution?

How much of the "public dissatisfaction" which Mr. Lincoln thus found himself "unable to endure" arose from the delays of the army, and how much from the illegal, arbitrary, and violent conduct of the administration in civil matters, as well as from that general loss of confidence in the Republican party which was but the natural consequence of their failure to arrest the civil war, it is not perhaps worth while for us here to attempt to decide. The events of 1861 had certainly given the country abundant reasons for doubting the prescience of Mr. Seward, and with it the sagacity of the great party which looked up to him as its teacher, its founder, and its intellectual chief.

As the President had issued his General War Order, No. 1, to check the flow of "adverse votes," so, under the incipient pressure of the joint committee on the conduct of the war, and of the new secretary of war, he issued his General War Orders, Nos. 2 and 3.

In his History of President Lincoln's Administration, Mr. Raymond gives us the following letter, "never before," as he says, "made public." The letter was addressed to General McClellan; and it is a striking illustration of the patience and forbearance with which General McClellan has adhered to the strictest standard of official propriety in all his publications on the subject of the war that this letter should first have seen the light through an oversight on the part of the friends of the writer, and not through any act of General McClellan or his friends.

FORTRESS MONROE, May 9, 1862.

MY DEAR SIR,—I have just assisted the secretary of war in forming the part of a dispatch to you relating to army corps, which dispatch, of course, will have reached you long before this will. I wish to say a few words privately to you on this subject. *I ordered the army corps organization not only on the unanimous opinion of the twelve generals of division, but also on the unanimous opinion of every military man I could get an opinion from, and every modern military book, yourself only excepted.* Of course, I did not on my own judgment pretend to understand the subject. *I now think it indispensable for you to know how your struggle against it is received in quarters which we cannot entirely disregard. It is looked upon as merely an effort to pamper one or two pets, and to persecute and degrade their supposed rivals. I have had no word from Sumner, Heintzelman, or Keyes.* The commanders of these corps are of course the three highest officers with you, but I am constantly told that you have no consultation or communication with them, that you consult and communicate with nobody but Fitz-John Porter, and perhaps General Franklin. I do not say these complaints are true or just; but, at all events, it is proper you should know of their existence. Do the commanders of corps disobey your orders in anything?

When you relieved General Hamilton of his command the other day you thereby lost the confidence of at least one of your best friends in the senate. And here let me say, not as applicable to you personally, that senators and representatives speak of me in their places as they please without question; and that officers of the army must cease addressing insulting letters to them for taking no greater liberty with them. But to return, *are you strong enough, even with my help, to set your foot upon the neck of Sumner, Heintzelman, and Keyes, all at once? This is a practical and very serious question for you.*

Yours truly, A. LINCOLN.

The entire absence throughout this letter of any consciousness that a general holding in his hands the lives of a hundred thousand brave men and the hope of a nation might perhaps regard with disgust and contempt such appeals, from his sense of what was best for his army and for his campaign to his concern about his personal popularity in "quarters which he could not entirely disregard," and to his fears of losing the confidence of his "friends in the senate," is highly noteworthy, and lets in a lamentable light upon the inner chambers of the history of this great war.

But on the special question of the War Orders, Nos. 2 and 3, the evidence of this letter is final and conclusive when taken in connection with the following passage from the Journal of the Joint Committee on the Conduct of the War:

"February 26, 1862.

"Pursuant to previous arrangement, the committee waited upon the President at eight o'clock on Tuesday evening, February 25. They made known to the President that, having examined many of the highest military officers of the army, their statements of the necessity of dividing the great army of the Potomac into *corps d'armée* had impressed the committee with the belief that it was essential that such a division of the army should be made—that it would be dangerous to move upon a formidable enemy with the present organization of the army. The application was enforced by many arguments drawn from the usages in France and every other military nation in Europe, and the fact that, so far as the committee could learn, all our military officers agreed that our army would not be efficient unless such an organization was had.

"The President observed that he had never considered the organization of the army into army corps so essential as the committee seemed to represent it to be; still he had long been in favor of such an organization. General McClellan, however, did not seem to think it so essential, though he had at times expressed himself as favorable to it.

"The committee informed the President that the secretary of war had authorized them to say to him that he deemed such an organization necessary."

From all which it appears that the armies of the United States in general, and the Army of the Potomac in particular, were commanded on the 8th day of March, 1862, by the following persons:

ABRAHAM LINCOLN, *President;*
EDWIN M. STANTON, *Secretary of War;*
BENJAMIN F. WADE, ⎫
ZACHARY CHANDLER, ⎭ *Senators;*

and four members of the House of Representatives, making up, with these senators, a joint committee of Congress.

It was under the auspices and the control of these six commanders-in-chief, assisted by an Aulic council of senators, representatives, and military men, quite indefinite as to numbers, that the active commander in the field of the Army of the Potomac, Major-General McClellan, set out upon his expedition for the capture of Richmond.

"If such a council presumes not only to say to a general-in-chief that he is to march on Vienna or on Paris, but also how he is to manœuvre and handle his army, the unfortunate general will be infallibly beaten, and the whole responsibility of his reverses will rest on those who at two hundred leagues' distance from the enemy pretend to direct an army which it is quite difficult enough to direct when one is actually in the field." *

* Jomini. *Précis de l'Art de la Guerre,* tome ii. p. 47.

CHAPTER VIII.

THE ARMY OF THE POTOMAC IN MOTION. RETREAT OF JOHNSTON FROM MANASSAS. THE DEFENCE OF WASHINGTON, AND OF THE SHENANDOAH VALLEY. THE MOVEMENT TO THE PENINSULA.

THE 8th of March, 1862, was a notable day in the history of the war.

On that day, as we have seen, the whole system of warfare, which General McClellan had been laboring so earnestly to perfect and put in operation, was shattered by two war orders of the President.

On that day, also, the Federal ship of war *Merrimac*, raised from the bottom of Norfolk harbor, where she had been sunk on the abandonment of that port to the enemy, and refitted by the Confederates for a new and terrible experiment in naval warfare, suddenly made her appearance in the waters of the lower James.

She assailed the Federal fleet there lying, shattered and scattered the ships, and for the moment rode supreme over the mouths of the Chesapeake, threatening Fortress Monroe itself.

The engagement which followed next day, between the *Merrimac* and the *Monitor*, though it restored the prestige of the Federal navy, and secured the safety of Fortress Monroe, failed to recover for the North the control of the James River. General McClellan's plan of campaign thus received a serious blow. He could no longer count upon the James River, but must modify all his calculations upon the theory that the York

River alone was to make his line of water communications with his base at Fortress Monroe.

On the 9th of March Johnston began to evacuate Manassas and Centreville. During the night of that day General McClellan ordered a general movement of the army towards the abandoned positions, less of course with the hope of being able to inflict any serious loss upon the enemy than in order to prepare the troops for their entry upon the great campaign before them. The observations which this movement enabled the general to make of the strength of the enemy's positions confirmed him in the belief that an advance upon those positions during the winter would have been extremely dangerous to the untried army of the Union. He became satisfied also that these positions, strong as they were, had been held so long only in order that Johnston might ascertain distinctly from what quarter Richmond was likely to be menaced. General McClellan's own language on this subject has acquired a weight from the subsequent course of events which demands its reproduction here:

"New levies, that have never been in battle, cannot be expected to advance without cover under the murderous fire from such defences, and carry them by assault. This is work in which veteran troops frequently falter, and are repulsed with loss. That an assault of the enemy's positions, in front of Washington, with the new troops composing the Army of the Potomac, during the winter of 1861–2, would have resulted in defeat and demoralization, was too probable. The same army, though inured to war in many battles hardly fought, and bravely won, has thrice, under other generals, suffered such disasters as it was no excess of prudence then to avoid.

"My letter to the secretary of war, dated February 3d, 1862, and given above, expressed the opinion that the movement to the Peninsula, would compel the enemy to retire from his position at Manassas, and free Washington from danger.

"When the enemy first learned of that plan, they did thus evacuate Manassas. During the Peninsular campaign, as at no former period, northern Virginia was completely in our possession, and the vicinity of Washington free from the presence of the enemy. The ground so gained was not lost, nor Washington again put in danger, until the enemy learned of the orders for the evacuation of the Peninsula, sent to me at Harrison's Bar, and were again left free to advance northward, and menace the national capital. Perhaps no one now doubts that the best defence of Washington is a Peninsular attack on Richmond."

While this movement on Centreville and Manassas was going on, another complete and formal change in the organization of the army was made by the President; the order making it, like all his preceding orders, being published without consultation with General McClellan, and coming this time to his knowledge through one of his aids-de-camp, who, having seen it in the *National Intelligencer* of March 12th, 1862, telegraphed a copy of it to the general at Fairfax Court House. The order ran as follows:

EXECUTIVE MANSION,
WASHINGTON, March 11, 1862.

PRESIDENT'S WAR ORDER, No. 3.

Major-General McClellan, having personally taken the field at the head of the Army of the Potomac, until otherwise ordered; he is relieved from the command of the other military departments, he retaining command of the Department of the Potomac.

Ordered further, That the departments now under the respective commands of Generals Halleck and Hunter, together with so much of that under General Buell as lies west of a north and south line indefinitely drawn through Knoxville, Tennessee, be consolidated and designated the Department of the Mississippi, and that, until otherwise ordered, Major-General Halleck have command of said department.

Ordered also, That the country west of the Department of the Potomac, and east of the Department of the Mississippi, be a military department, to be called the Mountain Department, and that the same be commanded by Major-General Fremont.

That all the commanders of departments, after the receipt of this order by them, respectively report, severally and directly, to the secretary of war, and that prompt, full, and frequent reports will be expected of all and each of them.

ABRAHAM LINCOLN.

When it is remembered that the President had permitted General McClellan to "take the field" two days before this order was issued, without the slightest intimation that any such change in the organization of the army was contemplated, it would certainly seem to be unnecessary to look elsewhere than to the habitual state of mind of the chief executive of the nation for an adequate explanation of the "unaccountable delays," disappointments, and deceptions which have so unhappily marked the course of the war under Mr. Lincoln's administration of affairs.

General McClellan, under this new and peculiarly insulting blow, bore himself with the same quiet dignity which he had displayed during the trying weeks which preceded it, and to which the Prince de Joinville pays this eloquent tribute :—

"As the day of action drew near, those who suspected the general's project, and were angry at not being informed of it, those whom his position had excited to envy, his political enemies, (and who in America is without them?) in short all those who beneath him or beside him who wished him ill, broke out into a chorus of accusations of slowness, inaction, incapacity. McClellan, with a patriotic courage which I have always admired, disdained these accusations and made no reply. He satisfied himself with pursuing his preparations in laborious silence."

He now addressed a brief note to the President, in which he used these words:—

"I believe I said to you some weeks since, in connection with some Western matters, that no feeling of self-interest or ambition should ever prevent me from devoting myself to the service. I am glad to have the opportunity to prove it, and you will find that under present circumstances I shall work just as cheerfully as before, and that no consideration of self will in any manner interfere with the discharge of my public duties."

The premature disclosure of General McClellan's plans, precipitating the retreat of General Johnston, had made all notion of any effective pursuit at that season of the year, through the always impracticable country about Washington and Manassas Junction, absurd. The Prince de Joinville gives a graphic picture of the fearful condition of the roads over which, on the 14th of March, General Stoneman, with a reconnoitering force, attempted to follow up the retiring enemy.* Stoneman found "the railroad bridges all burned down to Warrenton Junction, saw two regiments of cavalry and three bodies of infantry on the other side of Cedar Run; had we crossed we should not have been able to get back for high water."

All the energies of General McClellan were now concentrated on the expedition to the Peninsula. Some of the elements most important to the success of that expedition, as we have seen, had already been eliminated from the calculation by the

* General Bell, (Major-General Bell, R. A., who commanded the Royals in the Crimea,) went round the works with General McClellan, and expressed his opinion that it would be impossible to fight a great battle in the country which lay between the two armies—in fact, as he said, "a general could no more handle his troops among those woods than he could regulate the movements of rabbits in a cover."—*W. H. Russell. My Diary North and South.* Vol. II., p. 349, English edition.

action of the President and his counsellors, and it was ominously doubtful whether the navy department, which had never been able to clear the Potomac of the enemy's batteries, would be able to fulfil its promise of neutralizing the *Merrimac* and opening the James River to the expedition. Mr. Assistant Secretary Tucker, however, was vigorously pushing forward the transportation service, and much might still be done if but an ordinary dependence could be placed upon the good faith and the intelligence of the government.

A council of generals was held at Fairfax Court House March 13th, at which it was agreed that if the *Merrimac* could be neutralized and the transportation service speedily put in readiness, the operations against Richmond from the base of Fortress Monroe should at once be commenced.

The proceedings of this council were submitted to the new commander-in-chief, the President, by whom they were approved, upon condition that "Washington should be made entirely safe, and Manassas Junction occupied in sufficient force to prevent the return of the rebels;" the said rebels, as General Stoneman had discovered, having burned the railroad bridges, by the help of which they might have returned to Manassas Junction had they been so minded.

Manassas was occupied for the time by a part of General Sumner's corps, and before this force was relieved at the end of March the reconnoissances of its commander had revealed the fact that the Rappahannock bridge had been blown up by the rebels, and the line of the Rappahannock and Manassas Gap Railway thus left secure from any important menace by the enemy.

On the 16th of March General McClellan issued his instructions to General Banks for holding Manassas Junction and covering the line of the Potomac River and Washington.

A force of the enemy under General Stonewall Jackson, which had occupied Winchester at the time of the evacuation of Manassas, fell back before the advance of General Banks's troops, and pursued by General Shields, had retreated, by the 19th of March, to a point twenty miles south of Strasburg. In accordance with General McClellan's instructions of the 16th, General Banks concentrated on Manassas; Jackson returned upon his steps, and on the 23rd suffered a severe defeat at Winchester, after which he made the best of his way southward again. Had the instructions given to General Banks and Colonel Alexander, of the engineers, by General McClellan been followed out after this, not only would Manassas have been placed in such a condition for defence as to have prevented General Pope's disaster of August, 1862, but the Union forces would probably have been enabled to hold the Shenandoah country completely clear of the enemy. How it came to pass that they were not so followed out we shall presently see. The defences of Washington were committed to Brigadier-General Wadsworth.

The true defence of Washington, as General McClellan maintained, and as the subsequent course of events has abundantly proved lay in the energetic and successful prosecution of the expedition against Richmond. Washington had been surrounded, during the summer and autumn of 1861, with numerous and strong fortifications. It had become, indeed, a fortified capital, such a capital as Napoleon declared could always be defended with a force of 50,000 men against an attack by an army of 300,000 men, or by a force, that is, standing to the assailants in the proportion of one to six.

For the immediate garrison of Washington General McClellan provided a force of 18,000 men with 32 guns.* As the strongest force of the enemy which ever made its appearance in Northern Virginia during the Peninsula campaign, was General Jackson's movable column of, at the most, 20,000 men; and as the forces left by General McClellan in the Shenandoah and at Maryland amounted to between 50 and 60,000

* Report of General Barry, Chief of Artillery, contradicting statement of Hon. Z. Chandler, in the United States Senate.

men, with more than 70 guns, it would seem that the President's anxiety in regard to the safety of Washington might well have been laid to rest.

So in fact it seemed to be until after General McClellan had taken his departure for the Peninsula, when it blazed up anew and with fatal consequences to the cause and army of the Union.

On the 1st of April, 1862, General McClellan embarked, with his headquarters, at Alexandria, and reached Fortress Monroe the next day.

A few days before his embarkation, General McClellan had met the President by appointment, and had been informed by him that a strong "pressure" had been brought to bear at Washington to procure the detachment of General Blenker's division of 10,000 men from the Army of the Potomac, in order that it might be attached to the department of General Fremont. "His excellency was good enough," says General McClellan, "to suggest several reasons for not taking Blenker's division from me." I assented to the force of his suggestions, and was extremely gratified by his decision to allow the division to remain with the Army of the Potomac." The command in the Shenandoah Valley, however, was however now given to General Fremont, who thus became responsible for the fortunes of the startling campaign shortly afterwards carried on against the Union troops in that region by General Stonewall Jackson.

On the very day before he left Alexandria the following note was handed to General McClellan:

EXECUTIVE MANSION,
WASHINGTON, March 31, 1862.

MAJOR-GENERAL McCLELLAN.

MY DEAR SIR:—This morning I felt constrained to order Blenker's division to Fremont; and I write this to assure you that I did so with great pain, understanding that you would wish it otherwise. *If you could know the full pressure of the case, I am confident you would justify it, even beyond a mere acknowledgment, that the commander-in-chief may order what he pleases.*

Yours, very truly, A. LINCOLN.

To this imperial statement of the "master of all the legions" of the Union what reply could be made?

"I answered in substance," observes General McClellan, "that I regretted the order, and could ill-afford to lose 10,000 troops, which had been counted upon in forming my plan of campaign, but as there was no remedy I would yield, and do the best I could without them. In a conversation with the President a few hours afterwards, I repeated verbally the same thing, and, expressed my regret that Blenker's division had been given to Fremont, from any 'pressure' other than the requirements of the national exigency. I was partially relieved, however, by the President's positive and emphatic assurance that I might leave, confident that no more troops beyond these 10,000 should, in any event, be taken from me, or in any way detached from my command."

This was on the 31st of March.

On the night of the 3d of April a telegram from the adjutant-general reached General McClellan, at Fortress Monroe, to inform him that, "by order of the President," he was deprived of all control over General Wool and his division of 10,000 men at Fortress Monroe, and its dependencies. Besides the reduction of force entailed by this order, it took away from General McClellan the command of his own base of operations.

"Of the causes which led to this order," says General McClellan in his report, "I am to this day ignorant," and as not even Mr. Lincoln's biographer has thought it best to throw any light upon them, the student of this extraordinay history is left to conjectures which can hardly lead him very far wrong.

One immediate and most disastrous result of this act of the "commander-in-chief who could order what he pleased," was to deprive the Army of the Potomac of all accurate and authoritative means of information as to the enemy in its front, their force and their positions. General McClellan could obtain no maps; he learned that General Magruder held Yorktown, but with how many troops General Wool could not pretend to say.

In the New-York *Times* of April 5th, 1862, General Wool is made to telegraph to the war department, "The Army of the Potomac will not find many rebels to fight in its front."

In the same journal of April 6th, 1862, General Wool is made to telegraph, that General Magruder "has 30,000 men."

Nothing was known at Fortress Monroe of the formidable lines of the enemy across the Warwick River.

Reconnoissances were pushed forward at once, and the advance began on the 4th of April. The roads were in a terrible state. On reaching Lee's Mills, which he had been instructed to carry, General Keyes discovered the strength of the positions on the Warwick, found they could not be carried, and was brought to a stand.

Almost at this moment the following telegram reached General McClellan:

ADJUTANT-GENERAL'S OFFICE,
April 4th, 1862.

GEN. McCLELLAN:—

By direction of the President, General McDowell's army corps has been detached from the force under your immediate command; and the general is ordered to report to the secretary of war; letter by mail.

L. THOMAS,
Adj't-Gen.

A new department, that of the Rappahannock, had been created for General McDowell!

The following are General McClellan's comments upon an order which paralyzed all his operations at their very outset, and, as the Prince de Joinville very justly says, converted a brilliant and rapid movement into a long, wary and wearying advance:

"The President, having promised in our interview following his order of March 31st, withdrawing Blenker's division of 10,000 men from my command, that nothing of the sort should be repeated, that I might rest assured that the campaign should proceed with no further deductions from the force upon which its operations had been planned, I may confess to having been shocked at this order, which, with that of the 31st ult., removed nearly 60,000 men from my command, and reduced my force by more than one-third after its task had been assigned, its operations planned, its fighting begun. To me the blow was most discouraging. It frustrated all my plans for impending operations. It fell when I was too deeply committed to withdraw. It left me incapable of continuing operations which had been begun. It compelled the adoption of another, a different, and a less effective plan of campaign. It made rapid and brilliant operations impossible. It was a fatal error."

The duty to which the magnificent corps of McDowell had been assigned was to turn Yorktown by West Point on the York River. This operation had now to be abandoned, and, through a tangled wilderness, traversed by countless streams, while the rains incessantly fell, and storms of wind detained the transports in Hampton Roads, the army had to feel its way blindly forward against the front of the enemy's positions.

In what light those who were near the headquarters of his excellency the commander-in-chief, who had the best opportunities for knowing the truth, and who had no motives for misrepresenting the spirit of the "pressure" under which he thus inflicted upon General McClellan this persistent and fatal interference with his plans, viewed the matter, we may learn from the journals of the time.

General McClellan in his Report tells us that—

"The council, composed of four corps commanders, organized by the President of the United States, at its meeting on the 13th March, adopted Fort Monroe as the base of operations for the movement of the Army of the Potomac upon Richmond.

"For the prompt and successful execution of the projected operation, it was regarded by all as necessary that the whole of the four corps should be employed, with at least the addition of ten thousand men drawn from the forces in the vicinity of Fortress Monroe: that position and its dependencies being regarded as amply protected by the naval force in its neighborhood, and the advance of the main army up the Peninsula, so that it could be safely left with a small garrison."

The President having thus been clearly informed, not merely by General McClellan, but by the four corps commanders whom he had himself selected from among the divisional generals for promotion, that "for the prompt and successful execution of the projected operation," it was *necessary* that the whole of the four corps commanded by these officers, with at least ten thousand additional men from Fortress Monroe, should be employed, how did it come to pass not only that one of these corps, and that the strongest of them, was withdrawn bodily from General McClellan's expedition, but that the general commanding it was nominated to the command of a new and independent department created expressly for him? To withdraw nearly one-third of the force "necessary" for the prompt and successful execution of a great military movement, was for the President to take upon himself the terrible responsibility of the failure of that movement. Ignorant as the President was of all military matters, and surrounded by counsellors no more enlightened than himself, some dim sense of this formidable truth, one would suppose, might have dawned upon his mind. By what influence was the healing ray obscured?

"The order creating a new department for General Irwin McDowell," says the well-informed New York *Times* of April 7th, 1862, "is but the culmination of a long cherished plan of the progressive Republicans."

In other words, the President of the United States deliberately assumed the dread responsibility of ruining the most important campaign of the most important army of the nation, for the sake of propitiating the "progressive" and impatient and annoying members of his own political party. This was so distinctly understood at the time in Washington, that it was the subject of public as well as private conversation; and the following extract from the New York *Times* of April 6th, 1862, will show the pleasant and humorous light in which the trifling of a commander-in-chief who could "direct whatever he pleased," and of "progressive Republicans" who could control the commander-in-chief, with the lives of soldiers, the honor of their generals and the hopes of the nation, was regarded by those who were at home behind the political scenes:

"It looks now very much as though the two Macs had been pitted against each other, and it would be a good joke, after all, if Banks's dashing movement down the valley should frighten the rebels out of Gordonsville and drive them precipitately out of Virginia, thus cheating both Macs out of a fight." *

* The language here used is much more significant than any more labored and serious statement would have been of the true motives and feelings of the persons then dominant at Washington. It is curiously reinforced by the observations of a foreign officer of the highest character, of whose notes on the campaign of the Peninsula I have made free use. Colonel Lecomte declares that the Report of the Joint Committee "entirely perverts the facts relative to Jackson's campaign, and the intense terror which it inspired in Washington, which was the true cause of the failure on the Peninsula. On quitting Washington, before having been deprived of a part of his command, General McClellan had given the most exact and judicious instructions for the defence of the capital. He had pointed out Manassas and Front Royal as points forming a good advanced line, and had ordered Banks to intrench himself

While the administration and its friends at Washington were taking these jocose views of war, its responsibilities and its conditions, General McClellan at Fortress Monroe was earnestly endeavoring to ascertain the truth in regard to the rebel forces before him, resolved to do his best.

His task was not a light one.

The Merrimac, which the President had promised him should be neutralized by the navy, he found still so far mistress of the James River that the naval forces at Hampton Roads were entirely unable to assist the army in the reduction of the water batteries of Yorktown and Gloucester. His engineers under General Barnard reported the strength of the enemy's lines to be so great that it would be impracticable to break them, and too hazardous to attempt to carry them by assault.

In short, the commander of the Army of Potomac found himself in the position of Lord Raglan and Marshal St. Arnaud before Sebastopol, but with a relatively stronger enemy in his front,* and with no such "confidence" and "cordial sup-

there, distinctly forbidding him to advance further into Virginia. But as soon as General McClellan's back was turned they wished to make Banks a rival of him, and, supposing that the Army of the Potomac would attract all the force of the enemy, it was thought that Banks might gather some cheap laurels if he were sent *into the upper valley of the Shenandoah. The Aulic Council at Washington thought they might in this way strike a master-stroke and cause Richmond to fall before McClellan had time to appear before it.* * * *

"Jackson might have moved between Warrenton Junction and Winchester; he might have pushed cavalry detachments into Western Maryland; but he could have attempted no serious enterprise. Instead of this it was thought that a good trick might be played upon Jackson, and that he might be "bagged," to use an American expression. To form a notion of this plan of the campaign manufactured at Washington, and of the confusion which attended its execution, one should read the series of telegrams by which the President informs General McClellan of the progress of this wise manœuvre."—*Translation in Hillard's Life of McClellan*, p. 219.

* The fact that General Magruder reports himself to have held Yorktown, on the first appearance of General McClellan's army, with a force of but eight or ten thousand men, is often most absurdly and unjustly cited as proof that the Army of the Potomac was detained before that

port" in his rear as the Duke of Newcastle and Napoleon III. gave to the allied armies.

All the conditions of the position in Virginia, indeed, were now become, through the course of the President and his counsellors, so completely different from those upon which General McClellan had been officially led to count, that his whole plan of campaign was now to be recast in the face of the enemy.

The new situation cannot be more fairly stated than it is in the following letter, written at the time by General Keyes, one of the officers appointed by the President himself to the command of an army corps:

HEADQUARTERS 4TH CORPS,
WARWICK COURT HOUSE, VA., April 7, 1862.

MY DEAR SENATOR,—

The plan of campaign on this line was made with the distinct understanding that *four* army corps should be employed, and that the navy should co-operate in the taking of Yorktown, and also (as I understood it) support us on our left by moving gunboats up James River.

To-day I have learned that the 1st Corps, which, by the President's order, was to embrace four divisions, and one division (Blenker's) of the 2d Corps, have been withdrawn altogether from this line of operations, and from the Army of the Potomac. At the same time, as I am informed, the navy has not means to attack Yorktown, and is afraid to send gunboats up James River for fear of the Merrimac.

The above plan of campaign was adopted unanimously by General McDowell and Brigadier-Generals Sumner, Heintzel-

place by a handful of men. Connected with Richmond directly by rail, Yorktown was practically held by the whole army of Johnston, so long as Johnston chose to hold it. He chose to hold it so long as it should be tenable without a battle. When the batteries of General McClellan compelled him to abandon it, he abandoned all the intervening country between Yorktown and Richmond, and gave the latter city up to be besieged.

man and Keyes,* and was concurred in by Major-General McClellan, who first proposed Urbanna as our base.

This army being reduced by forty-five thousand troops, some of them among the best in the service, and without the support of the navy, the plan to which we are reduced bears scarcely any resemblance to the one I voted for.

I command the James River column, and I left my camp, near Newport News, the morning of the 4th instant. I only succeeded in getting my artillery ashore the afternoon of the day before, and one of my divisions had not all arrived in camp the day I left, and, for the want of transportation, has not yet joined me. So you will observe that not a day was lost in the advance; and in fact we marched so quickly and so rapidly that many of our animals were twenty-four and forty-eight hours without a ration of forage. But, notwithstanding the rapidity of our advance, we are stopped by a line of defence nine or ten miles long, strongly fortified by breastworks, erected nearly the whole distance, behind a stream or succession of ponds nowhere fordable, one terminus being Yorktown and the other ending in the James River, which is commanded by the enemy's gunboats. Yorktown is fortified all around with bastioned works, and on the water side, it and Gloucester are so strong that the navy are afraid to attack either.

The approaches on our side are generally through low, swampy, or thickly wooded ground, over roads which we are obliged to repair or to make, before we can get forward our carriages. The enemy is in great force, and is constantly receiving reinforcements from the two rivers. The line in front of us is therefore one of the strongest ever opposed to an invading force in any country.

You will then ask, why I advocated such a line for our operations? My reasons are few, but, I think, good.

* General Keyes, it will be understood, is referring here to the action of the council held after the evacuation of Manassas by Johnston.

With proper assistance from the navy, we could take Yorktown, and then, with gunboats on both rivers, we could beat any force opposed to us on Warwick River, because the shot and shells from the gunboats would nearly overlap across the Peninsula, so that, if the enemy should retreat, and retreat he must, he would have a long way to go without rail or steam transportation, and every soul of his army must fall into our hands or be destroyed.

Another reason for my supporting the new base and plan was, that this line, it was expected, would furnish water transportation nearly to Richmond.

Now, supposing we succeed in breaking through the line in front of us, what can we do next? The roads are very bad, and if the enemy retains command of James River, and we do not first reduce Yorktown, it would be impossible for us to subsist this army three marches beyond where it is now. As the roads are at present, it is with the utmost difficulty that we can subsist it in the position it now occupies.

You will see, therefore, by what I have said, that the force originally intended for the capture of Richmond should be all sent forward. If I thought the four army corps necessary when I supposed the navy would co-operate, and when I judged of the obstacles to be encountered by what I learned from maps and the opinions of officers long stationed at Fort Monroe, and from all other sources, how much more should I think the full complement of troops requisite, now that the navy cannot co-operate, and now that the strength of the enemy's lines and the number of his guns and men prove to be almost immeasurably greater than I had been led to expect!

The line in front of us, in the opinion of all the military men here who are at all competent to judge, is one of the strongest in the world, and the force of the enemy capable of being increased beyond the numbers we now have to oppose to him. Independently of the strength of the lines in front of us, and of the force of the enemy behind them, we cannot advance until we get command of either York River or James River. The efficient co-operation of the navy is, therefore, absolutely essential, and so I considered it when I voted to change our base from the Potomac to Fort Monroe.

An iron-clad boat must attack Yorktown, and if several strong gunboats could be sent up James River also, our success will be certain and complete, and the rebellion will soon be put down.

On the other hand, we must butt against the enemy's works with heavy artillery and a great waste of time, life, and material.

If we break through and advance, both our flanks will be assailed from two great water-courses in the hands of the enemy; our supplies would give out, and the enemy, equal, if not superior in numbers, would, with the other advantages, beat and destroy this army.

The greatest master of the art of war has said that "if you would invade a country successfully, you must have *one* line of operations and one army, under one general." But what is our condition? The State of Virginia is made to constitute the command, in part or wholly, of some six generals, viz.: Fremont, Banks, McDowell, Wool, Burnside, and McClellan, besides the scrap, over the Chesapeake, in the care of Dix.

The great battle of the war is to come off here. If we win it, the rebellion will be crushed. If we lose it, the consequences will be more horrible than I care to foretell. The plan of campaign I voted for, if carried out with the means proposed, will certainly succeed. If any part of the means proposed are withheld or diverted, I deem it due to myself to say that our success will be uncertain.

It is no doubt agreeable to the commander of the First Corps to have a separate department, and, as this letter advocates his return to General McClellan's command, it is proper to state that I am not at all influenced by personal regard or dislike to any of my seniors in rank. If I were to credit all the opinions which have been poured into my ears, I must believe that, in regard to my present fine command, I owe much to General McDowell and nothing to General McClellan. But I have disregarded all such officiousness, and I have, from last July to the present day, supported General McClellan and obeyed all his orders with as hearty a good will as though he had been my brother or the friend to whom I owed most. I shall continue to do so to the last, and so long as he is my commander, and I am not desirous to displace him, and would not if I could. He left Washington with the understanding that he was to execute a definite plan of campaign with certain prescribed means. The plan was good and the means sufficient, and, without modification, the enterprise was certain of success. But, with the reduction of force and means, the plan is entirely changed, and is now a bad plan, with means insufficient for certain success.

Do not look upon this communication as the offspring of despondency. I never despond; and when you see me working the hardest, you may be sure that fortune is frowning upon me. I am working *now*, to my utmost.

Please show this letter to the President, and I should like also that Mr. Stanton should know its contents. Do me the honor to write to me as soon as you can, and believe me, with perfect respect,

Your most obedient servant,

E. D. Keyes,

Brig.-Gen. Comd'g Fourth Army Corps.

Hon. Ira Harris,

U. S. Senate.

CHAPTER IX.

THE SIEGE OF YORKTOWN. RETREAT OF THE CONFEDERATES UPON RICHMOND. EVACUATION OF NORFOLK AND DESTRUCTION OF THE MERRIMAC. THE BATTLE OF WILLIAMSBURGH, AND ADVANCE TO THE CHICKAHOMINY.

THE reports of General Barnard and of General Keyes having made it necessary now to open regular approaches against the defences of Yorktown, the work was at once begun and vigorously pushed forward.

His excellency, the commander-in-chief, however, contemplating the situation by telegraph from Washington, suggested a shorter method of dealing with the enemy. On the 6th of April he telegraphed to General McClellan:

"You now have over one hundred thousand troops with you, independent of General Wool's command. *I think you had better break the enemy's line from Yorktown to Warwick River at once. This will probably use time as advantageously as you can.*

"A. LINCOLN, President."

"The enemy's field-works," says General Barnard, Chief of Engineers, in his report, "are far more extensive than may be supposed from the mention of them I make; and every kind of obstruction which the country affords, such as abattis, marsh, inundation, was skillfully used. *The line is certainly one of the most extensive known to modern times.*

"The country on both sides the Warwick, from near York-

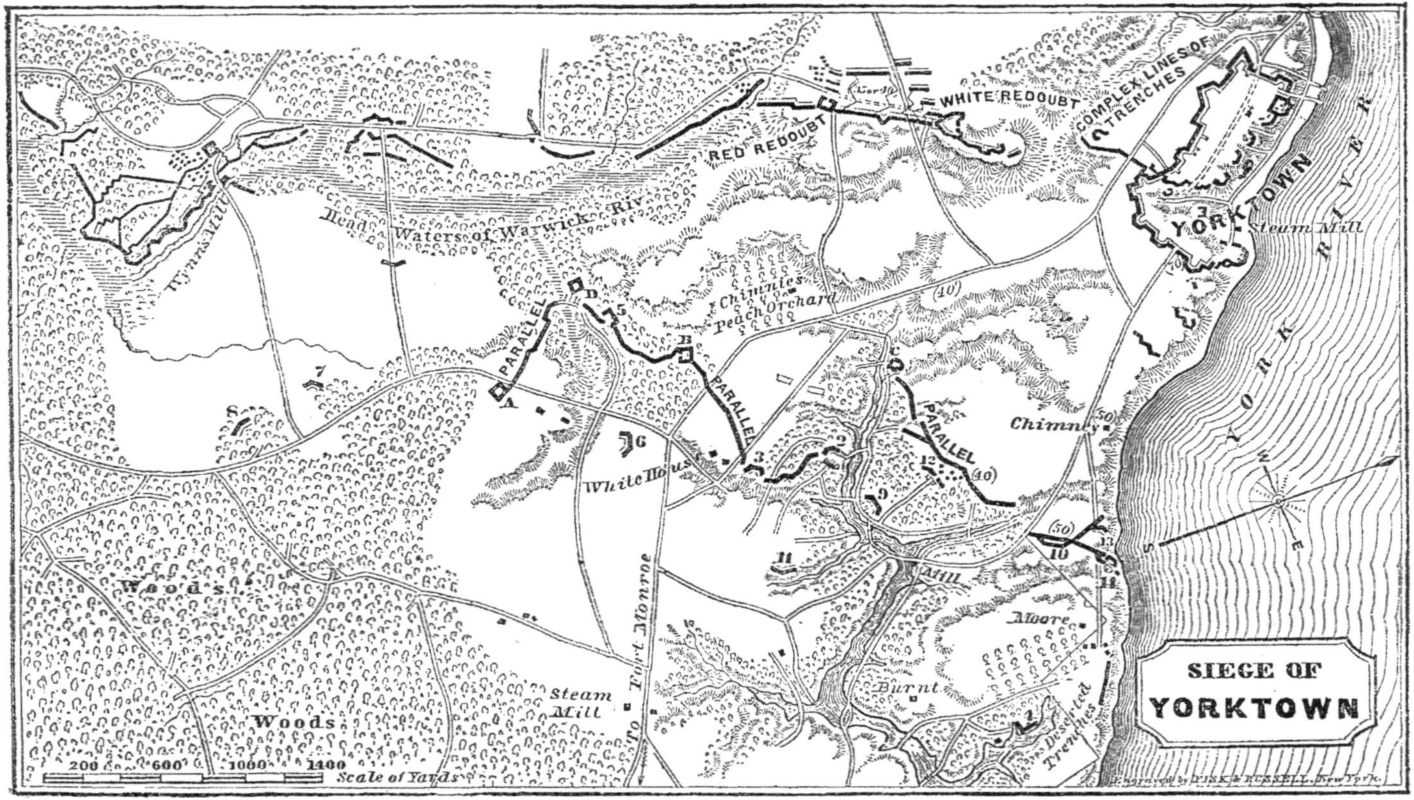
SIEGE OF
YORKTOWN
YORKTOWN
YORK RIVER
Steam Mill
COMPLEX LINES OF TRENCHES
WHITE REDOUBT
RED REDOUBT
Head Waters of Warwick Riv
Wynns Mill
PARALLEL
PARALLEL
PARALLEL
Chimnies
Peach Orchard
White House
Chimney
Mill
Moore
Burnt
Deserted Trenches
To Fort Monroe
Steam Mill
Woods
Woods
200 600 1000 1400
Scale of Yards
Engraved by FISK & RUSSELL, New York.

town down, is a dense forest, with few clearings. It was swampy, and the roads impassable during the heavy rains we have constantly had, except where our own labors had corduroyed them. If we could have broken the enemy's line across the isthmus, we could have invested Yorktown, and it must, with its garrison, have soon fallen into our hands. It was not deemed practicable, considering the strength of that line, and the difficulty of handling our forces, (owing to the impracticable character of the country,) to do so. If we could take Yorktown, or drive the enemy out of that place, the enemy's line was no longer tenable. This we could do by siege operations. It was deemed too hazardous to attempt the reduction of the place by assault."

This was the deliberate opinion of the chief of engineers of the Army of the Potomac, given at the time. In a subsequent report* the same officer, General Barnard, retracts this opinion, and remarks, "My opinion now is that the lines of Yorktown should have been assaulted." This palinode has been quoted with approbation by the committee on the conduct of the war. It is quoted also, but not by any means with approbation, by Colonel Lecomte, of the Swiss army, who served through the Peninsular campaign on the staff of the Army of the Potomac, and who has since published in Paris a condensed translation of the Report of the Committee on the Conduct of the War, illustrated with notes by himself. This professional soldier observes: "We are the more astonished at this retrospective confidence of General Barnard because we believe that the engineers who were with him, and he himself, repeatedly expressed very different opinions on the spot."

It is unnecessary to add that the opinions of General Barnard, "given on the spot," were the only opinions then of value, or even accessible to General McClellan, whose duty it was, as commander-in-chief, to be guided by those opinions,

* Army of the Potomac. Engineers and Artillery. Barnard and Barry. New York: Van Nostrand, 1863.

formed, as it was to be presumed, by General Barnard, after a proper examination of the enemy's works, and expressed with a conscientious sense of his grave responsibility.

Remembering that the lives of thousands of his soldiers as well as "time" must certainly be "used" in trying to "break" this impracticable line, and reposing more confidence in the opinions of his own generals, given from observations taken on the spot, than in the inspirations of the President at Washington, General McClellan resolved to take Yorktown by a siege.

To take this resolution required not a little moral courage, in the face of the following letter from a commander-in-chief who "could order whatever he pleased," and who had already at so many critical moments flung the weight of his imperial will, borne down by an "outside pressure," into the scale of the enemy's force.

WASHINGTON, April 9, 1862.

MAJOR-GENERAL McCLELLAN:

MY DEAR SIR,—Your dispatches, complaining that you are not properly sustained, while they do not offend me, do pain me very much.

Blenker's division was withdrawn from you before you left here, and you know the pressure under which I did it, and, as I thought, acquiesced in it, certainly not without reluctance.

After you left I ascertained that less than twenty thousand unorganized men, without a single field-battery, were all you designed to be left for the defence of Washington and Manassas Junction; and part of this even was to go to General Hooker's old position. General Banks' corps, once designed for Manassas Junction, was diverted and tied up on the line of Winchester and Strasburg, and could not leave it without again exposing the upper Potomac, and the Baltimore and Ohio Railroad. This presented (or would present, when McDowell and Sumner should be gone) a great temptation to the enemy to turn back from the Rappahannock and sack Washington. My explicit order that Washington should, by the judgment of *all* the commanders of army corps, be left entirely secure, had been neglected. It was precisely this that drove me to detain McDowell.

I do not forget that I was satisfied with your arrangement to leave Banks at Manassas Junction; but when that arrangement was broken up and *nothing* was substituted for it, of course I was constrained to substitute something for it myself. And allow me to ask, Do you really think I should permit the line from Richmond via Manassas Junction to this city to be entirely open, except what resistance could be presented by twenty thousand unorganized troops? This is a question which the country will not allow me to evade.

There is a curious mystery about the *numbers* of the troops now with you. When I telegraphed you on the 6th, saying you had over a hundred thousand with you, I had just obtained from the secretary of war a statement, taken, as he said, from your own returns, making one hundred and eight thousand then with you and *en route* to you. You now say you will have but eighty-five thousand when all *en route* to you shall have reached you. How can the discrepancy of twenty-three thousand be accounted for?

As to General Wool's command, I understand it is doing for you precisely what a like number of your own would have to do if that command was away.

I suppose the whole force which has gone forward for you is with you by this time, and if so, I think it is the precise time to strike a blow. By delay the enemy will relatively gain upon you—that is, he will gain faster, by *fortifications* and *reinforcements*, than you can by reinforcements alone.

And once more let me tell you it is indispensable to *you* that you strike a blow. *I* am powerless to help this. You will do me the justice to remember I always insisted that going down the bay in search of a field, instead of fighting at or near

Manassas, was only shifting, and not surmounting, a difficulty; that we would find the same enemy, and the same or equal intrenchments, at either place. The country will not fail to note—is now noting—that the present hesitation to move upon an intrenched enemy is but the story of Manassas repeated.

I beg to assure you that I have never written you, or spoken to you, in greater kindness of feeling than now, nor with a fuller purpose to sustain you, so far as in my most anxious judgment I consistently can. But you must act.

Yours, very truly,

A. LINCOLN.

In publishing this extraordinary letter in his report General McClellan contents himself with calling attention to the statements made by General Keyes and General Barnard as to the strength of the lines on which he was thus invited to "move" by way of avoiding a movement against himself of "senators and representatives;" and he adds, with characteristic calmness: "I could not forego the conclusions of my most instructed judgment for the mere sake of avoiding the personal consequences intimated in the President's dispatch."

The unofficial reader, however, may take the liberty of observing the curious inconsistency between the "precise reason" which the President here gives for "detaining McDowell" and the less precise reasons which the President himself and the President's friends elsewhere suggest for the same proceeding. Nor can the unofficial reader forbear to note that if the President really supposed the enemy behind Yorktown was destined to gain "by reinforcements" during the delay of a siege he cannot have had any reasonable fear of the same enemy's moving at the same time northward to take advantage of the "open line from Richmond via Manassas to Washington;" the railroad bridges on the said "open line" furthermore having been destroyed by the said enemy on his retreat from Manassas.

On reading such a letter indeed one is tempted to turn from the story of the Peninsular campaign with a feeling of sickness and shame. The spectacle of a great army and its commander launched upon a distant and perilous expedition, at the mercy of an executive power so incapably or so criminally administered, may be full of instruction for a future age. But those who, living in the present, must bear, in one or another way, the burdens which such an administration of authority imposes upon the people can scarcely contemplate it without a blinding and choking sense of indignation.

Nor will that indignation be diminished by the reflection that, since the removal of General McClellan from command, the lives and services of a larger number of faithful soldiers of the Union than he then commanded before Yorktown, have been uselessly sacrificed to the President's dread lest the "country should note" a "hesitation to move upon an intrenched enemy."

Fredericksburg, Chancellorville, Chicamauga, Spottsylvania, Cold Harbor, Petersburg, through such dread lessons as these names have taught, it has been necessary for the "commander-in-chief" at Washington to drive heroic armies before he could be made to comprehend the prescience and the sound judgment which he thus insulted in the trenches of Yorktown.

Finally, on the 4th of May, 1862, the overwhelming batteries of the Union army having been completed, and being ready to open from all quarters their irresistible fire upon the rebel positions, General Johnston commanded the evacuation of Yorktown.

The news of this event was hailed with delight at the North, and with indignation by the southern press. The Confederates left behind them all their heavy artillery, and a large supply of ammunition. This, however, was not the most serious part of the loss inflicted upon them by the capture of Yorktown. As this capture opened to General McClellan the road by the

York river to Richmond, it compelled the Confederates to evacuate Norfolk, from which port, after destroying an immense amount of public stores, General Huger, with 18,000 men, a part of whom had been engaged in the defence of Yorktown, was withdrawn upon Richmond, to strengthen the defence of the capital on the Chickahominy: and the evacuation of Norfolk in its turn made it necessary for them to blow up the *Merrimac*, and thus to open the lower James to the Federal navy.

Within a month after his arrival on the Peninsula, and in spite of the unparalleled folly—to use no harsher word—with which the interests of the campaign had been trifled with at Washington, General McClellan had thus won advantages which offered to himself and to the Government speedy, triumphant, and decisive results, upon the single condition that the force of the nation should be so concentrated as to enable him to turn these advantages to account.

The evacuation of Yorktown was followed immediately by an advance of the victorious army as rapid as the horrible condition of the roads and the necessity of establishing a new base of supplies on the York River would permit. Having the advantage of the railway in his rear, and being much too strong in point of numbers to be easily pushed, in retreating through a friendly country, General Johnston fell back, fighting.

General Sumner, in the front of General McClellan's pursuit, came, with a small part of his corps, upon the enemy, strongly intrenched, in front of Williamsburgh. Such was the state of the roads, "narrow, and full of frightful morasses, from which it was difficult to extricate the cannon," says the Prince de Joinville, "although the weather had been fine and dry for several days, that no such thing as a general action was to be thought of in these virgin forests." The Confederate intrenchments were gallantly but fruitlessly assailed by General Sumner's cavalry, under General Stoneman. The infantry of Sumner came up too late in the evening to effect anything, and during the night one of those tropical rains began which in the early spring so often convert whole square miles of country in Eastern Virginia into one immense lake. The next day was fought the battle of Williamsburgh, begun practically by accident, while the commander of the army was where his duty called him to be, in the rear,* arranging and pushing forward the tremendous work of the general advance. The Union troops of General Hooker were first engaged, and although they behaved, fighting in the close thickets and almost pathless woods of that marshy wilderness, with extraordinary gallantry, they suffered terribly, and had began to fall back, when the battle was re-established by General Hancock, and by General McClellan, who, having been notified of what was going on, had made his way through incredible difficulties, to the front, and appeared in person on the field at the decisive moment to secure the victory to the army of the Union. The Prince de Joinville thus paints in simple but burning words, this critical and glorious scene:

* It may seem, perhaps, hardly worth while to notice those imputations upon the personal courage of General McClellan, which ignorance or malignity alone could have founded upon the fact that the commander-in-chief of the army in the field was not always in the van of every action fought by his troops. But a passage in which Mr. Kinglake *apologizes* for Lord Raglan's casual exposure of himself at the battle of the Alma, so aptly meets these silly charges that it may well be given here: "It was not right—nay, if it were not that success brings justification, it would have been scarcely pardonable—that a general charged with the care of an army, should be under the guidance of feelings akin to the impulses of the chase. By the stir and joyous animation of the moment, Lord Raglan was led on into a part of the field which he would not have sought to reach in cold blood. He would have regarded as nothing the mere difference between being struck by shot in one part of the field, and the risk of being struck by shot in another: but he knew that, in general, it is from a point more or less in rear of battalions actually engaged that a chief can exercise the most constant and extended control over his army: and an ideal commander would not suffer himself to ride to so forward a spot as to run the risk of losing the government of his troops for many minutes together in the critical period of an action."—*Invasion of the Crimea, Vol.* 1, p. 544. Am. Edition.

"The Federal General Hancock, seizing the moment, cried to his soldiers, as he waved his cap, 'Now, gentlemen, the bayonet!' and charged with his brigade. The enemy could not withstand the shock, broke and fled, strewing the field with his dead. At this very moment General McClellan, who had been detained at Yorktown, appeared on the field. It was dusk; the night was coming on; the rain still falling in torrents. On three sides of the plateau, on which the general was, the cannon and the musketry were rattling uninterruptedly. The success of Hancock had been decisive, and the reserves, brought up by the General-in-chief, charging upon the field, settled the affair. Then it was that I saw General McClellan, passing in front of the 6th cavalry, give his hand to Major Williams, with a few words on his brilliant charge of the day before. The regiment did not hear what he said, but it knew what he meant; and from every heart went up one of those masculine, terrible shouts, which are only to be heard on the field of battle. Those shouts, taken up along the whole line, struck terror to the enemy. We saw them come upon the parapets and look out in silence and motionless upon the scene. Then the firing died away, and night fell on the combat, which in America is called 'The Battle of Williamsburg!"

The Battle of Williamsburg was but an episode in the march upon Richmond; and in the circumstances of the case could not possibly have been any more than an episode in that march. But it threw the electric light of battle over that love of the Army of the Potomac for its commander which had already developed itself, and which has since inwrought itself so deeply into the moral substance of that army, that in spite of two years of incessant obloquy, misrepresentation, and calumny poured out upon his head, the name of General McClellan rings still like a trumpet through its heart.

"It seems," observes one of the most brilliant historical writers, "that although by human contrivance a whole people may be shut out from the knowledge of momentous events, in which its armies are taking a part, there is yet a subtle essence of truth which will permeate into the heart of a nation thus kept in ignorance."

Through all the clouds which partisan passion has raised about the name of General McClellan, through all the rolling and swelling slanders of a partisan press, and the wordy mists of partizan Reports on the Conduct of the War, this truth has made its way into the nation's heart, that the real history of that arduous march through the swampy forests of the Peninsula, and of that great siege which has made the rude name of the insignificant Chickahominy immortal, is written in the love which the soldiers of McClellan bear to their commander.

Criticism may assail this love, malignity may denounce it; but impartial history has only one verdict upon such affections. Their root is in reality—reality proved and tested by all that is sharpest and sternest in human experience. Their meaning is incontrovertible. He who wins such affections is worthy to have won them.

The feeling of the country in regard to the operations before Yorktown and the battle of Williamsburg, found expression at the time in the following resolutions, which were unanimously adopted by the House of Representatives, on a motion made by Mr. Lovejoy of Illinois, a well known and extreme leader of the Republican party, though not a member of the committee on the conduct of the war:

"*Resolved*, That it is with feelings of profound satisfaction to Almighty God, that the House of Representatives from time time hear of the triumphs of the Union armies in the great struggle for the supremacy of the Constitution and the integrity of the Union.

"*Resolved*, That we receive with profound satisfaction intelligence of the recent victories achieved by the Armies of the Potomac, associated from their localities with those of the Revolution; and that the sincere thanks of the House are hereby tendered to Major-General McClellan for the display of those high military qualities which secure important results with but little sacrifice of human life."

Two days after the evacuation of Yorktown, General Franklin, sent by water to the right bank of the Pamunkey River, disembarked his division, and, after repulsing an attack in force of the enemy, secured the occupation of West Point, the terminus of the York River Railroad.

Nine days afterwards, the 16th of May, the headquarters of the army were established at White House, the head of navigation on the Pamunkey; and here, under the protection of the gunboats, a great depot for the army was established.

Immediately after the battle of Williamsburg, General McClellan had pressed the government anew for reinforcements, which would enable him to make a decisive attack upon Richmond. A few days later, on the 14th of May, on learning of the destruction of the Merrimac, he again addressed a similar appeal to the authorities at Washington:

"Casualties, sickness, garrisons and guards, have much weakened my force, and will continue to do so. I cannot bring into actual battle against the enemy more than eighty thousand men at the utmost, and with them I must attack in position, probably intrenched, a much larger force—perhaps double my numbers. It is possible that Richmond may be abandoned without a serious struggle, but the enemy are actually in great strength between here and there, and it would be unwise, and even insane for me to calculate upon anything but a stubborn and desperate resistance. If they should abandon Richmond, it may well be that it is done with the purpose of making the stand at some place in Virginia south or west of there, and we should be in condition to press them without delay. The confederate leaders must employ their utmost efforts against this army in Virginia, and they will be supported by the whole body of their military officers, among whom there may be said to be no Union feeling, as there is also very little among the higher class of citizens in the seceding States.

"I have found no fighting men in this Peninsula—all are in the ranks of the opposing foe.

"Even if more troops than I now have should prove unnecessary for purposes of military occupation, our greatest display of imposing force in the capital of the rebel government will have the best moral effect. I most respectfully and earnestly urge upon your excellency that the opportunity has come for striking a fatal blow at the enemies of the Constitution, and I beg that you will cause this army to be reinforced without delay by all the disposable troops of the government. I ask for every man that the government can send me. Any commander of the reinforcements, whom your excellency may designate, will be acceptable to me, whatever expression I may have heretofore addressed to you on that subject.

"I will fight the enemy, whatever their force may be, and whatever force I may have, and I firmly believe that we shall beat them, but our triumph should be made decisive and complete. The soldiers of this army love their government, and will fight well in its support; you may rely upon them. They have confidence in me as their general, and in you as their President. Strong reinforcements will at least save the lives of many of them. The greater our force the more perfect will be our combinations, and the less our loss.

"For obvious reasons, I beg you to give immediate consideration to this communication, and to inform me fully at the earliest moment of your final determination."

GEO. B. McCLELLAN,
Maj.-Gen. Comm.

An immediate response to this appeal, in the form of an order sending forward the corps of General McDowell by water, would have enabled General McClellan, at once, to transfer his base of operations to the James River, by enabling him to oblique upon that river, and attack the newly constructed forts at Ward's or Drury's Bluff, to which the guns and the crew of the *Merrimac* had been transferred, and by which the federal gunboats were beaten off on the 15th of May.

No response whatever came until the 18th of May, when the secretary of war telegraphed, refusing to send General McDowell by water, because it would "uncover the capital entirely," and also, because it would "require more time," but announcing that, "in order to increase the strength of the attack upon Richmond, at the earliest moment General McDowell had been ordered to march upon that city by the shortest route, and keeping himself always in position to save the capital from all possible attack, so to operate as to put his left wing in communication with the right wing of General McClellan's, who was further "instructed to co-operate by extending his right wing to the north of Richmond."

This order demands our attention. It determined the whole course of the siege of Richmond, and to it may be directly traced all the misfortunes which attended that siege.

In the first place, it peremptorily extinguished all hope of reaching the James River as a base of operations.

In the second place, it made it certain that the Confederates, seeing so powerful a force as that of General McDowell's manœuvred with an evident eye to the safety of Washington rather than to the capture of Richmond, would understand that a very slight demonstration towards the former capital would secure for them an undisturbed liberty of concentration against the unsupported Army of the Potomac.

In the third place, it compelled General McClellan to expose his army to great danger from such a hostile concentration, by requiring him to extend his right wing in a very hazardous manner beyond the Chickahominy, thus greatly weakening his line, and in the event of any failure on the part of General McDowell to join him, positively inviting the blow which, upon that failure, was, indeed, eventually struck.

The instructions issued to General McDowell at the same

time with this order to General McClellan, indicate a firm belief at Washington that the enemy were likely to advance in force by Fredericksburg upon Washington, thus uncovering their flank to General McClellan. General McClellan, who knew his antagonists better, by no means shared this belief, but annoyed as he was at the refusal of the government to reinforce him properly by water, he determined to hope everything from the advance of McDowell by land, knowing, as he well knew, the capacity of that officer, and his anxiety to play a prominent and decisive part in the war.

He learned nothing positive, however, in regard to the details, or the probable time of this advance, on which so much depended, until Saturday, the 24th of May, when the President telegraphed to him, that although "Banks was yet in some peril at Front Royal," (where Jackson was then operating for the precise object at which General McClellan had foreseen that the enemy would aim,) still "McDowell could, and positively would, move on Monday morning to join the Army of the Potomac."

The telegram which brought this good news, bore with it, unfortunately, abundant evidences of the President's undiminished confidence in his own capacity as a commander-in-chief, such as certain hints to General McClellan about things which he might "do almost as well as not" while building the Chickahominy bridges. Still in such matters happily "the hearer was one and the speaker another," and if McDowell was really coming, the President's brilliant military suggestions could do no great harm.

But McDowell was not really coming. Late in the evening of the same day, May 24th, came the following telegram in his stead:—

May 24, 1862.
FROM WASHINGTON, 4 P. M., '62.

MAJ.-GEN. G. B. McCLELLAN:

In consequence of Gen. Banks' critical position, I have been compelled to suspend Gen. McDowell's movements to join you. The enemy are making a desperate push upon Harper's Ferry, and we are trying to throw Gen. Fremont's force and part of Gen. McDowell's in their rear.

A. LINCOLN,
President.

"Stonewall" Jackson was doing his work effectually. Such was the panic spread by his dashing and eccentric demonstrations, and such the profound obfuscation which he contrived to breed in the official mind at Washington, that he actually wrung from Mr. Lincoln, on the 25th of May, the following telegram:—

WASHINGTON, May 25, 1862, 2 P. M.

MAJ.-GEN. McCLELLAN:

The enemy is moving north in sufficient force to drive Gen. Banks before him; precisely in what force we cannot tell. He is also threatening Leesburg and Geary on the Manassas Gap Railroad from both north and south—in precisely what force we cannot tell. I think the movement is a general and a concerted one, *such as could not be if he was acting upon the purpose of a very desperate defence of Richmond. I think the time is near when you must either attack Richmond or give up the job, and come back to the defence of Washington. Let me hear from you instantly.*

A. LINCOLN, President.

Possessed with an extraordinary infatuation as to the probability of the enemy's swooping down upon Washington by the way of Fredericksburg, the President for some days could not be made to comprehend that there was anything important in the world to be done excepting to cut the Fredericksburg and Richmond Railroad. In vain did General McClellan urge some attention to the true principles of the defence of Washington as laid down by him before leaving the Potomac.

The whole alarm of the administration centred upon the city of the Rappahannock.

On the 26th General McDowell advanced beyond the Rappahannock, and the enemy in that quarter began to fall back towards Hanover Court House and Richmond.

This rebel force, commanded by Generals Anderson and Branch, was considerable enough in numbers to threaten the right and rear of General McClellan's extended line, and he at once ordered General Fitz John Porter, then justly described by the *New York Times* as one of the "noblest, most painstaking and trustworthy of our officers," to attack and dislodge it.

General Porter performed this duty with signal success. The battle of Hanover Court House was fought by him on the 27th of May. The whole division of General Branch, about 10,000 strong, was utterly routed, and General Anderson, who was supporting him at Ashland, hastily retreated upon Richmond. The fugitives from these points carried the news of the disaster into the rebel capital, where it was universally supposed that Jackson's diversion had failed of its great object, and that the action indicated the junction of the army of McDowell with the army of McClellan. This belief threw the city into the greatest alarm and confusion. The road leadings to the south were crowded with escaping citizens, household goods, official archives, women and children; and had the junction of the two Union armies been really now effected, and General McClellan been thus enabled to force a decisive battle for the possession of Richmond, it can scarcely be doubted that the place must have fallen into his hands. So well aware of this was General McClellan, that immediately after the victory he telegraphs to the government:—

"There is no doubt that the enemy are concentrating everything on Richmond. I will do my best to cut off Jackson, but am doubtful whether I can.

"It is the policy and duty of the government to send me by water all the well drilled troops available. I am confident that Washington is in no danger. Engines and cars in large numbers have been sent up to bring down Jackson's command.

"I may not be able to cut them off, but will try; we have cut all but the F. and R. R. R. The real issue is in the battle about to be fought in front of Richmond. All our available troops should be collected here, not raw regiments, but the well drilled troops. It cannot be ignored that a desperate battle is before us; if any regiment of good troops remain unemployed it will be an irreparable fault committed."

On the next day, the 29th, having gained information that there was positively no rebel force between Hanover Junction and Fredericksburg, he telegraphed this also to Washington. The President and secretary of war, however, on the authority of "certain contrabands," preferred to believe that the rebels were not concentrating on Richmond, but on the contrary re-enforcing the terrible Stonewall Jackson, who might at any moment destroy Gen. Banks, devour Gen. Fremont, and annihilate Washington.

They accordingly threw away all the results of the battle of Hanover Court House by not only refusing to permit McDowell to join the Army of the Potomac, but by absolutely ordering him to "burn the bridges" by which that junction should have been effected.

Two years of wasting and fruitless efforts have since atoned for the colossal blunder then committed.

The golden opportunity offered to the country at the end of May, 1862, by Porter and McClellan, has never since returned.

The Confederates were not slow to avail themselves of the advantages held out to them by the bewilderment and vacillation of the Washington government. Gen. McClellan, as we have already seen, had been obliged to extend his line dangerously in order to meet the overland advance of McDowell, and to attempt to hold both banks of the Chickahominy, in order to secure his own communications.

As soon as it was ascertained that Stonewall Jackson had

arrested the advance of General McDowell, General Johnston, at Richmond, at once determined to throw himself upon the weakest point of General McClellan's position.

A rain-storm of unparalleled violence, on the night of May 30th, favored his designs. In a few hours the Chickahominy became a roaring torrent. All the bridges of the Army of the Potomac,* with a single exception, were rendered impracticable; the roads were destroyed. On the morning of the 31st of May the Confederates furiously assailed the left wing of General McClellan's army. At Fair Oaks, General Casey's redoubts, in the advance of the wing, were stormed and carried, and after a desperate battle, in which the advantage rested with the Confederates, their victorious progress threatening the absolute destruction of the whole left wing, was arrested with difficulty just at nightfall, by the artillery of General Sumner.

Night put an end to the conflict. During the night an attempt was made, under the instructions of General McClellan, —who, rising from a sick bed, passed nearly the whole night on horseback—to throw new bridges across the stream, and pass over the whole right wing of the Army of the Potomac. It was too late, the floods increasing prevented the execution of the work.†

* Testimony of General Barnard. Report on the Conduct of the War. Vol. i., p. 401.

† The Confederates miscalculated the moment when these floods would be at their highest. They began to rise most furiously about twenty-four hours after the commencement of the storm, and rose with great force during the night of the 31st of May and first of June. "About eleven o'clock P.M. on the 31st of May," says an engineer officer, "I received orders to construct a bridge, and proceeding to the spot found the stream somewhat swollen, and rising rapidly. * * * I commenced laying the bridge three feet above the level of the water. The water continued rising very fast, and the current became so swift as to render the work extremely difficult. At about four o'clock I had succeeded in placing three lengths of trestles, when I was relieved by Captain Ketchum. At that time the water had risen so as nearly to submerge the bridge."—Report of Captain Brainerd in Barnard's Report, *ut. sup.*

The battle began again in the morning on the side of the Federal troops, with all the valor of desperation; on the side of the Confederates in a fierce, confused, disorderly fashion attributable to the fact, not then generally known to either army, that General Johnston, exposing himself with his usual gallantry, had fallen dangerously wounded. This circumstance left the rebel army for a time without a recognized leader.

Failing to overcome the determined resistance of the Federal troops, the Confederates, about noon on the 1st of June, fell back in extreme confusion on Richmond.

Thus ended the battle of Fair Oaks. Had it been possible for General McClellan at this time to throw his right wing, with his artillery, across the Chickahominy, and to advance upon Richmond during the two or three days of confusion, which followed the failure of the Confederate attack, and the fall of General Johnston, Richmond might have doubtless been seized and occupied.

Thanks to the confused and contradictory orders from Washington, by which his army had been forced to assume the position which it held before the battle, and to the tremendous rains of the 30th of May, this was, however, impossible.

General Lee succeeded immediately to the command vacated by the fall of General Johnston; the Army of the Potomac strengthened itself in its positions, and on the 3d of June we find Mr. Lincoln considerately telegraphing to General McClellan to keep a close eye on the Chickahominy River!

The first days of June passed on, continual rains surrounded the operations of the army with difficulties which, as Mr. Stanton, on the 11th, telegraphed to General McClellan, "no art or skill could possibly avoid but only endure." The rein-

p. 96. "Changed direction of bridge. Everything went on smoothly until I reached the sixth trestle, when, in endeavoring to raise the abutment, owing to rapid rise of the water, the whole structure surged in shore, and fell with a crash."—Report of Captain Ketchum. Ibid., p. 98.

forcements so urgently needed still failed to arrive, although the battle of Fair Oaks had plainly revealed the determined concentration of the enemy on Richmond.

So weak had now become the extended lines that on the 13th of June the rebel General Stuart, with fifteen hundred cavalry and four guns, was able to make a clever circuit of the whole army.

Mortifying as this occurrence was to the army, and creditable as it was to the hostile cavalry, it was naturally invited by the great extension of the lines, and was after all a much less daring feat than the dash of the Confederate General Hampton in September, 1864, through the powerful front of Lieutenant-General Grant's position on the James River, with its resultant capture of the whole supply herd of the Federal army.

On the 10th of June, having been notified by the secretary of war that General McCall's division was on its way to join him, General McClellan sent the following dispatch to Washington, in which it will be seen that he recommends, as a means of counteracting the enemy's concentration on Richmond, precisely that movement on Atlanta, which has since, under the orders of General Grant, been adopted:

JUNE 10, 1862—3:30 P.M.

I have again information that Beauregard has arrived, and that some of his troops are to follow him. No great reliance, perhaps none whatever, can be attached to this; but it is possible, and ought to be their policy.

I am completely checked by the weather. The roads and fields are literally impassable for artillery, almost so for infantry. The Chickahominy is in a dreadful state; we have another rain storm on our hands.

I shall attack as soon as the weather and ground will permit; but there will be a delay, the extent of which no one can foresee, for the season is altogether abnormal.

In view of these circumstances, I present for your consideration the propriety of detaching largely from Halleck's army to strengthen this; for it would seem that Halleck has now no large organized force in front of him, while we have.

If this cannot be done, or even in connection with it, allow me to suggest the movement of a heavy column from Dalton upon Atlanta. If but the one can be done, it would better conform to military principles to strengthen this army; and even although the reinforcements might not arrive in season to take part in the attack upon Richmond, the moral effect would be great, and they would furnish valuable assistance in ulterior movements.

I wish to be distinctly understood that whenever the weather permits, I will attack with whatever force I may have, although a larger force would enable me to gain much more decisive results.

I would be glad to have McCall's infantry sent forward by water at once, without waiting for his artillery and cavalry.

If General Prim returns *via* Washington, please converse with him as to the condition of affairs here.

In his response to this dispatch, the secretary at war seems to have been visited by a momentary gleam of practical wisdom as to the situation. He promises to communicate General McClellan's suggestions at once to General Halleck, with "a request that he shall conform to them;" promises to send forward McDowell's force speedily; and adds, "it is clear that a strong force is operating with Jackson, for the purpose of detaining the forces here from you."

On the 20th, in reply to General McClellan's request to be informed of the "numbers and positions of the troops not under his command in Virginia and elsewhere," information of direct practical importance as aiding him to estimate the probable force of the enemy in his front, the President replied that he could not give the information accurately, and if he could, would rather not transmit it, for fear of its "reaching the enemy."

Thus left in the dark again; McDowell not coming forward as promised by Mr. Stanton; his army thinned by disease and by duty, General McClellan had to contemplate the impending certainty of a collision with the whole force of the enemy. On the 24th of June a deserter brought the news that Jackson, having thrown the Departments of the Mountain and the Rappahannock into a hopeless state of confusion, had been reinforced from Richmond, had retraced his steps, and was rapidly moving upon the weakest point of the Army of the Potomac.

Telegraphing to Washington on this subject, General McClellan was answered that "neither McDowell nor Banks nor Fremont appeared to have any accurate knowledge" as to where Jackson was or what he was doing.

On the next day, June 25th, General McClellan, his bridges and intrenchments being at last completed, took the initiative, with the determination of bringing on a general action, in which he would now be able to command the services of his whole army. He ordered a general advance of his pickets, which brought on a stubbornly contested engagement between the enemy and General Heintzelman's forces. The advantage rested with the Federal troops, and at night the general telegraphed to Washington "all goes well."

During that night, however, information came in confirming the story of the return of Jackson, thirty thousand strong, upon the right and rear of the army. The next morning, the right was attacked in force.

The problem now presented to General McClellan imperatively demanded an immediate solution. That the enemy was superior in numbers to himself was proved by his offering battle on both sides of the Chickahominy at once. Should the Army of the Potomac concentrate to meet this offer on the left bank, thus abandoning the attack on Richmond, and risking in case of defeat a retreat on Yorktown; or should it concentrate on the right bank, abandon its depots, its communications with the York River, and undertake to swing itself boldly around to the James, where with the gunboats at its back, it might resume the offensive more rapidly than in the other event, and more formidably indeed than ever?

General McClellan promptly decided to adopt the latter alternative. In view of his long-cherished desire to make the James his true base, he had more than a week before ordered supplies to be sent to City Point; and he now at once set about the task of blinding the enemy as to his intentions.

How successfully this was done cannot be more clearly or impressively told than it has been told by the Prince de Joinville, an eye-witness of all the trying and terrible scenes through which for seven days and nights the army marched and fought its way from peril to safety:

"The distance from Fair Oaks to the James River was not great; it was but seventeen miles. But the stores and baggage had to be moved upon a single road, exposed in front to the enemy, who by several different roads radiating from Richmond could throw a considerable force upon several different points at once. The speed with which the operation was conducted upset his calculations: he probably supposed that we should feel the ground before we acted, and perhaps he thought that McClellan would find it hard to make up his mind to abandon his lines at White House. He acted at least as if this were his view. The troops of General Hill, mentioned above, having crossed the Chickahominy at Meadow Bridge on the 26th, the day after the affair with Hooker, in the afternoon attacked the troops of McCall, the advance of Porter, on the left bank. The first conflict was very severe; but McCall occupied a strong position at Beaver Dam, a sort of ravine bordered with beautiful catalpa trees, then in flower. There he had made abattis and thrown up some earth so that he could not be overcome, notwithstanding the length of the fight, which lasted until nightfall. This vigorous resistance compelled the enemy to throw numerous reinforcements across the river. This was exactly what General McClellan desired. His intention was to fix the attention of the enemy here while on the right bank he prepared his movement to the James River.

"The night was spent in passing over to this bank the whole of Porter's baggage and uniting it with the long train which was to set out in the evening of the 27th. The orders were given to re-embark or destroy all the stores and magazines along the railway to White House, and to evacuate that depot. General Stoneman with a flying column was charged with the execution of this order. He was to delay the advance of the enemy, and fall back, when he had done his duty, upon Yorktown. All this was carried out exactly. At daybreak on the 27th, McCall was ordered to fall back on the bridges thrown across the Chickahominy at Gaines's Mill. Followed up rapidly, as he had expected to be, he joined the other troops of Porter's corps, the division of Morell and the regulars commanded by General Sykes. Porter's duty, demanding as much self-possession as vigor, was to make a stand in front of the bridges, in order to give the army time to accomplish its general movement. He was not to cross the bridges till the evening of the 27th, and was then to destroy them. His three divisions were attacked early in the day. The corps of Jackson coming in from Hanover Court House, took part in the action. The battle was fought in a rolling country, extensively wooded, but upon certain points open and cleared. The struggle was arduous; the Federals resisted with success; there was even one moment at which Porter might have thought himself victorious.

"This would have been a great advantage, and might have profoundly modified the position. Accordingly, during this moment of hope, McClellan hastened to throw upon the left bank all the troops not absolutely necessary to guard the lines in front of Richmond. One division, that of Slocum, crossed the bridges before four o'clock and joined in the action. Another, Richardson's, reached the scene only at nightfall. At the moment when these reinforcements began to take part in the fight, the scene had an imposing character of grandeur. We had thirty-five thousand men engaged, a part in the woods, a part in the plain, forming a line a mile and a half long. A numerous artillery thundered upon every side. In the valley of the Chickahominy the lancers, with floating pennons, were stationed as a reserve; and this whole animated picture of the battle was set in a picturesque landscape illuminated by the last rays of the sun going down below a horizon as crimson as blood. Suddenly the volleys became extraordinarily intense. The reserves, which had till now been lying in the hollows, were called up, excited by shouts, and sent into the woods. The musketry becomes more and more violent, and rolls away towards the left. There can no longer be any doubt that the enemy is making a final effort on that side. The reserves are all engaged, there is not a disposable man left. It is six o'clock, the daylight is fast disappearing; if the Federal army can hold out an hour longer the battle is won, for at every other point the enemy has been repulsed, and Jackson, Hill, Lee, and Longstreet will have urged up their troops in vain. For lack of infantry, Porter has put three batteries *en potence* on his extreme left to support the troops who are there sustaining an unequal fight; but these troops have been in action since early morning, they are worn out, and have fired almost their last cartridge. Now in their turn come up the Confederate reserves; they deploy regularly into line against the Federal left, which gives way breaks, and disbands. The disorder grows from point to point till it reaches the centre of the Federal lines. There is no panic; the men do not fly in the wild excitement of fear; but deaf to every appeal, they march off deliberately, their muskets at the shoulder, like people who have had enough of it, and do not believe success possible. In vain do the generals, the officers of the staff, among them the Count of Paris and the Duke of Chartres, ride sword in hand into the *melée* to stop their disorderly movement; the battle of Gaines' Mill is lost. There is nothing left but to prevent a rout. The enemy, indeed, was advancing on the plain still in the same order, his infantry deployed by regiments *en echelon*, and every minute he was closing in upon the confused masses of the Federals. Such is the fury of the cannonade and the musketry fire that the cloud of dust struck up from the ground floats steadily over the battle. Then came the order for the cavalry to charge. I happened at this moment to be near its position. I saw the troopers draw their swords with the sudden and electrical impulse of determination and devotion. As they got into motion I asked a young officer the name of his regiment. 'The Fifth cavalry,' he replied, brandishing his sabre with a soldier's pride in his regiment. Unfortunate young man! I saw the same regiment next day. From the charge of that evening but two officers had returned. He was not one of them.

"The charge failed against the dense battalions of the enemy, and the broken regiments galloping through the artillery and the flying infantry in the clouds of dust only increased the general disorder. The artillery horses were killed, and I saw, with painful emotion, the men working with the courage of desperation at guns which could no longer be removed. They dropped one after another. Two alone were left at last, and they continued to load and fire almost at point-blank range upon the enemy. Then the deepening twilight hid the scene All these guns were lost.

"General Butterfield had made in vain the most superhuman efforts to save them. On foot, his horse having been shot, struck in the hat by the fragment of a shell, and his sabre hit by a ball, surrounded by his aids-de-camp, of whom several fell at his side, he had tried to rally the infantry around a flag planted in the ground. He succeeded, but only for a few moments; the precipitate rush of the retreat carried everything away. Happily night came on, and after losing a mile of ground, the army reached the fresh brigades of Meagher and French, which were formed in good order. These brigades sent up a vigorous hurrah, and a few guns put anew in battery opened their fire upon the enemy, who paused at last, checked by this final and determined resistance.

"As the last guns of this action were firing, we heard a lively rattle of musketry from the direction of Fair Oaks, on the other side of the river. It came from the Confederates, who were attacking the Federal works; but the attack, which was probably only a demonstration, was vigorously repelled.

"The day had been severe. In the main battle, that of Gaines' Mill, thirty-five thousand Federals had failed to defeat sixty thousand Confederates, but they had held them in check. More could not have been expected.

"During the night the Federals repassed the bridges of the Chickahominy in perfect order, destroying them after they had passed. They left behind them the field of battle, covered with the dead (for in this fierce conflict the losses on both sides had been considerable) a great number of wounded, too much hurt to be moved, a dozen guns, and a few prisoners, among whom was General Reynolds. The corps of Keyes, which was in the advance, fell back towards the James River, and took possession of the passage of a large morass, White Oak Swamp, which is traversed by the road the army was to take as well as by the principal lines of communication which could be used by the enemy to harass us.

"The 28th and 29th of June were passed in sending forward the train of five thousand wagons, the siege train, a herd of twenty-five hundred oxen, and other *impedimenta.* The reader may judge what a piece of work this was, when he reflects that it was all to be done upon a single narrow road. The first day we were undisturbed; the enemy was exhausted by the previous day's battle; he seemed, moreover astonished and disconcerted, and did not yet fully understand the object of the Federal army. The whole of this army was united on the right bank of the Chickahominy, whilst the bulk of the Confederate forces was upon the left bank, and the bridges were down. To recross the river they would be forced either to build new bridges or to fall back some distance to the Mechanicsville bridge; either of which operations involved time. Now, time was everything, and the retreating army put it to good use. It was not until the 29th that the Southern columns came in sight of the Federal rear-guard. A battle at once began, at Savage's Station, but the enemy were vigorously received, and after repulsing them the Federals waited till nightfall before recommencing their march. The last duty done by the telegraph the day before was to inform us that the Confederates were at White House. This post they had found abandoned. The morning of the 29th had been spent by us in destroying all that could not be carried away from the camps. A complete railway train, locomotive, tender, and cars, which had been left on the rails was sent headlong over the broken bridge into the river. Nothing was left for the foe but three siege guns, which could not be moved, and which we neglected to bury.* These were the only siege guns he captured, although the story has been everywhere repeated that he took the whole Federal siege train with the exception of these three pieces. The whole of that train reached the James River in safety. Our great misfortune was, that we were obliged to abandon so many of our wounded, not only at Gaines' Mill and at Savage's Station, but along the whole line of retreat. This misfortune was inevitable. It was only by ceaseless fighting that we could protect our retreat, and the transportation of so many wounded men would have required conveniences which we did not possess.

* The Prince is here in error. The army, by the official statement of General Barry, lost but one siege gun, the carriage of which broke down so that it could not be moved.

"General McClellan, during the 29th, and the morning of the 30th, remained near White Oak Swamp, urging on the passage of his enormous train. The heat was overwhelming. His aides-de-camp, continually galloping from the rear guard to the advance, were utterly exhausted. So long as this huge train divided the different parts of the army we were in great danger. But nothing disturbed the serene self-possession of the General-in-chief. On the 29th he had stopped, I remember, to rest in the verandah of a house by the wayside, when the mistress of the establishment came to complain to him that the soldiers were eating her cherries. The general rose with a smile, went himself and put a stop to the pillage. But he could not prevent the shells, next day, from setting fire to the house of his pretty hostess.

"At daybreak on the 30th McClellan had the satisfaction of seeing all his troops and all his trains in safety beyond White Oak Swamp, which was to oppose a new barrier to the pursuit of the enemy. By the evening of the next day, Generals Keyes and Porter were in communication with the gunboats on the James. The trains had moved upon roads pointed out by the negro guides. The heads of the columns had met nothing but small detachments of cavalry, which they had easily dispersed. The hardest part of the work was done, but it was to be supposed that the enemy would renew his attempt to disturb the retreat. So the general took his measures in time. He left Sumner and Franklin to act as the rear guard, and hold the passage of White Oak Swamp; and put Heintzelman with the divisions of Hooker, Kearney, Sedgwick, and McCall, across the point of intersection of the roads leading from Richmond. They protected the trains and reached the James River at the exact moment when the transports with provision and ammunition, and the hospital ships, which, with wise foresight, General McClellan had ordered up ten days before, arrived from Fortress Monroe.

"Meanwhile, as had been expected, Franklin and Sumner

were sharply attacked in White Oak Swamp, to which point the Confederate generals had brought a large force of artillery. They fell back step by step. Later in the day Heintzelman also was attacked at the Cross-roads. Here the battle raged with varying fortune, in the woods. The divisions of McCall suffered severely, and its commander was made prisoner; but Hooker and Kearney, coming to his help, repulsed the assailants with great loss. They did not, however, succeed in rescuing the general, who was sent into Richmond to join Reynolds.

"Finally, a third attack upon the corps of Fitz-John Porter failed utterly under the combined fire of the field artillery, and the gunboats. Porter occupied a superb position at a place called Turkey Bend, by some persons, and Malvern Hill by others. This position was a lofty open plateau, sloping gradually down to the roads by which the enemy must debouch. The left rested upon the river, where lay the Galena, the Monitor, and the flotilla of gunboats. The Federal army then had nothing to fear from this side, and had consequently only one flank to protect, which was easily done with abattis and field works. On the evening of the 30th, all the divisions of the army were united in this strong position, and here the whole train, including the siege guns, was sheltered. The army was in communication with its transports and supplies. The grand and daring movement by which it had escaped a serious danger, and changed an untenable base of operations for one more safe and sure, had been accomplished; but after so prolonged an effort the troops were worn out; for five days they had been incessantly marching and fighting. The heat had added to their excessive fatigue; many men had been sun-struck; others quitted the ranks and fell into the lamentable procession of sick and wounded, which followed the army as well as it could, and as fast as it could. Doubtless, during this difficult retreat, there had been moments of confusion and disorder, but of what army in like circumstances would not this have been true? *This one fact remained unassailable: that, attacked in the midst of a difficult and hostile country by twice its own force, the Army of the Potomac had succeeded in gaining a position in which it was out of danger, and from which, had it been properly reinforced, had the concentration of the enemy's forces been met by a like concentration, it might have rapidly resumed the offensive.*

"As we have said, each of its necessarily scattered sections had for five days been called upon to resist the most furious assaults, and had done so with vigor. Now that it was assembled as a whole upon Malvern Hill, the Confederate army, also reunited, might possibly make a last effort against it. So in the night of the 30th of June and 1st of July, McClellan prepared himself for this eventuality. He put his whole artillery, at least three hundred guns, into battery along the heights, arranging them in such wise that their fire should not interfere with the defence by the infantry of the sort of glacis up which the enemy would be obliged to advance to the attack. The artillery fire was to be reinforced by the 100-pounders of the gunboats, which were ordered to flank the position. It was mere madness to rush upon such obstacles; but the Confederates attempted it. Again and again, during the day of the 1st of July, they undertook to carry Malvern Hill, but without the slightest chance of success. The whole day for them was an idle butchery. Their loss was very heavy; that of the Federals insignificant. This success was due to two causes: First, to the fortunate foresight of the general, who, in spite of numerous natural obstacles to the passage of artillery, had spared nothing to bring his on, and next to the firmness of his troops. Men do not make such a campaign, and go through such experience as they had endured, without coming out more or less formed to war. If their primitive organization had been better, the survivors of this rude campaign, I do not fear to assert, might be regarded as the equals of the best soldiers in the world.

" On the evening after this battle, the exhausted enemy retired to appear no more, and the Army of the Potomac took up a position and sought rest at Harrison's Bar, a spot chosen by the engineers and the navy as the most favorable for defence and for receiving supplies. The campaign against Richmond had ended without success, but not without honor. The honor of the army was safe; but those who had looked to success for the early restoration of the Union under an impulse of generous and patriotic conciliation, saw their hopes unhappily fade away."

CHAPTER X.

CLOSE OF THE PENINSULA CAMPAIGN. THE ARMY ORDERED TO ACQUIA CREEK.

OF the military qualities revealed by General McClellan in the conception and the execution of the brilliant and daring movement by which the Army of the Potomac was swung away from the overwhelming attack of the confederates on the line of the Chickahominy, and re-established upon the new base of the James River, but one opinion has ever been expressed by competent critics. Dazzled by the vastness of the area over which the present war is fighting out, by the numbers of men arrayed in it "for mutual slaughter," and by the transcendent importance to ourselves, at least, of the issues involved, we are apt to forget what is nevertheless the fact, that the bloody record of the past few years in America is, for the most part, a record rather of desperate and indomitable fighting than of striking strategic skill. It has been marked by many fierce encounters of hostile armies, but by few great battles. It is not necessary here to enter into an elaborate analysis of the causes of this fact, causes which are to be looked for as well in the topographical conditions of the war as in the constitution of the armies engaged.

The fact itself is unquestionable, and if, rejecting that sound Roman maxim that victories won in civil strife should be looked back upon with a solemn sadness rather than with the glow of pride naturally kindled by the recollection of triumphs snatched from a foreign foe, the Americans of the next generation shall seek to measure the skill in arms and the military virtue of their fathers by the highest standards of civilized war, there will be found few passages of the great conflict for the Union on which such stress may be safely laid as can be borne by the story of the retreat to the James.

To the general who led that great retreat, his brave army, at least, anticipating history, has already done such justice as only an army can do to its general.

On the 28th of June, being then at Savage's Station, surrounded by the columns of his heroic army, shattered by the terrible battle of Gaines' Mill, but undaunted and firmly fronting still the foe; and shocked into a rare outburst of profound and passionate indignation by the fatal confirmation of all that he had feared and vainly fought against, as the almost inevitable consequence of the conduct of the administration, General McClellan had telegraphed to the secretary of war at Washington.

"If we have lost the day we have yet preserved our honor, and no one need blush for the Army of the Potomac. I have lost this battle because my force was too small. I again repeat that I am not responsible for this, and I say it with the earnestness of a general who feels in his heart the loss of every brave man who has been needlessly sacrificed to-day. I still hope to retrieve our fortunes, but to do this the government must view the matter in the same earnest light that I do. You must send me very large reinforcements, and send them at once. * * * * * * I feel too earnestly to-night. I have seen too many dead and wounded comrades to feel otherwise than that the government has not sustained this army. If you do not do so the game is lost. If I save this army now, I tell you plainly that I owe no thanks to you or to any other person in Washington. You have done your best to sacrifice this army."

Stern and terrible words! such words as no man speaks or can speak save under the strain of a reality as stern and terri ble, words in which the heart of the whole army throbbed within the heart of their general, and made him "strong in speaking truth."

Upon these words, which, condensed into a single fierce, emphatic charge the accumulated evidences of folly, recklessness, jealousy and incapacity which have steadily gathered in upon the course of this story, the biographer of Mr. Lincoln remarks that he does not believe "any subordinate was ever before permitted to say such a thing to his superior officer without instant dismissal."

A more complete admission than this, of the irresistible justice of the charge, it would not be easy to imagine. Mr. Lincoln's biographer is in the right; no subordinate probably was ever before known, in the history of the world, to make such a charge as this against his superior without instant dismissal, and had the charge been anything else than the thing it was, the downright uncontrollable assertion, namely, of an absolute fact, felt to be a fact in the just and indignant heart of him who asserted it, and felt to be a fact in the conscience-stricken and paralyzed spirit of those of whom it was asserted, the failure of the secretary of war and of the President to dismiss General McClellan from the service of the United States immediately upon the receipt of this telegram, would brand these officials as ineffaceably with the stamp of utter unfitness to administer a great war, as their trembling acquiescence in the charge now does. For so far were they from dismissing the general who thus brought home to them, as by a flash of electric passion from the lurid bosom of that thunder-cloud of battle then rolled and heaped around him, the anticipative judgment of a nation upon their guilty trifling with a people's honor and a people's life, that the secretary was stricken into silence, and the President replied with this lamentable plea in mitigation of the charge :—

WASHINGTON, June 28, 1862.

Save your army at all events. Will send reinforcements as

fast as we can. Of course they cannot reach you to-day, to-morrow, or next day. I have not said that you were ungenerous for saying you needed reinforcements. I thought you were ungenerous in assuming that I did not send them as fast as I could. I feel any misfortune to you and your army as keenly as you feel it yourself. If you have had a drawn battle or a repulse, it is the price we pay for the enemy not being in Washington. We protected Washington, and the enemy concentrated on you. Had we stripped Washington, he would have been upon us before the troops sent could have got to you. Less than a week ago you notified us that reinforcements were leaving Richmond to come in front of us. It is the nature of the case, and neither you nor the Government is to blame.

A. LINCOLN.

Never, it may be safely said, were the relative positions of a superior officer and of a subordinate so completely reversed as in this presidential response to General McClellan's indictment of the administration; and never, it must be said, has a less successful attempt been made to evade an indictment so overwhelming.

More than a fortnight before this telegram was sent, the secretary of war, as we have seen, had been visited with a brief interval of military common sense. On the 10th of June he had telegraphed to General McClellan, "It is clear that a strong force is operating *with Jackson, for the purpose of detaining the forces here from you.*"

Yet this purpose of Jackson, thus recognized by the secretary of war, the secretary of war had permitted Jackson fully to accomplish. Again, on the 25th of June, the secretary of war had admitted to General McClellan his "suspicion" that "Jackson's real movement" was directed against Richmond. The notice which the President asserts that General McClellan had given the Government—of troops leaving Richmond, to "come in front" of Washington, was a notice of no such thing; it was a notice given, as the President and the secretary of war well knew, to reinforce the evidence already become morally irresistible when it was given, of the reinforcement of Jackson from Richmond, in order to enable him to strike, with more tremendous effect, that blow upon the weakened and extended right wing of the Army of the Potomac, that right wing weakened and extended by their fault, and theirs alone, under the force of which the Army of the Potomac had finally been driven from its positions on the Chickahominy.

The "misfortune" which had happened to the Army of the Potomac, was not the "price paid" by the President and the secretary of war for "being in Washington."

It was the "price paid" by the country, indeed, for the presence of those officials in Washington. To those officials it was the "price paid" by them for their own license to laugh to scorn, and trample upon, the first principles of the art of war. To the "progressive Republicans" it was the "price paid" by them for their success in "pressing" the President to create worse than superfluous "departments" of command for one and another officer in whom they delighted. To the "joint committee on the conduct of the war," it was the "price paid" by them for their elevation to the dignity of Aulic Councillors, dispensing wisdom from books of military science, and "organizing victory" by the light of political inspiration.

But so dear and precious to these many purchasers of the pomps and vanities of power were these objects, bought with so much blood of brave men, spilled in vain, that, as we shall see, they esteemed the price thus paid not yet sufficiently ample.

The magnificent victory of Malvern Hill enabled the army of the Potomac to fall back safely upon the new base which had been selected for it on the James River, at Harrison's Bar, by General McClellan, and Captain Rodgers, the commander of the naval force, on the co-operation of which it was now able to rely. This movement was committed to, and successfully carried out, under the direct supervision of General Keyes; and on the Fourth of July, 1862, the following address was issued by General McClellan to his troops from his headquarters on the James:

SOLDIERS OF THE ARMY OF THE POTOMAC!

Your achievements of the last ten days have illustrated the valor and endurance of the American soldier. Attacked by superior forces, and without the hope of reinforcements, you have succeeded in changing your base of operations by a flank movement, always regarded as the most hazardous of military expedients. You have saved all your material, all your trains, and all your guns, except a few lost in battle, taking in return guns and colors from the enemy. Upon your march you have been assailed day after day, with desperate fury, by men of the same race and nation, skillfully massed and led. Under every disadvantage of number, and necessarily of position also, you have in every conflict beaten back your foes with enormous slaughter.

Your conduct ranks you among the celebrated armies of history. No one will now question that each of you may always say, with pride: "I belong to the Army of the Potomac."

You have reached the new base, complete in organization and unimpaired in spirit. The enemy may at any moment attack you. We are prepared to meet them. I have personally established your lines. Let them come, and we will convert their repulse into a final defeat. Your Government is strengthening you with the resources of a great people. On this our nation's birthday we declare to our foes, who are rebels against the best interests of mankind, that this army shall enter the capital of the so-called Confederacy—that our national constitution shall prevail, and that the Union, which can alone insure internal peace and external security to each State, "must and shall be preserved," cost what it may in time, treasure, and blood.

GEORGE B. McCLELLAN.

Those alone who believe that by no expenditure whatever of "time and treasure and blood" can the Union be preserved and the national Constitution be made to prevail, will question the fitness of this proclamation to the new position in which the Army of the Potomac now found itself.

Upon the single condition that the Government of the United States should redeem the promise given to the army by its commander, and truly "strengthen it with the resources of a great nation;" and with better reason than ever before since those fatal days of May in which the victory of Hanover Court House had been neutralized by the withdrawal of General McDowell to protect the unimperilled capital of the Union, the Army of the Potomac might still hope to enter in triumph the "capital of the so-called Confederacy."

The new base which the army had reached upon the James was the base originally designed for it by General McClellan in planning his campaign of the Peninsula. This new base had been reached, at last, through much tribulation and at the cost of many lives of gallant men. But it had been reached; and the army rested upon it unbroken in spirit, with its organization unimpaired, and glowing with the consciousness of a great sustained and triumphant effort.

Its true condition on the day when this proclamation was issued, was summed up by its commander in the following dispatch to the President:

HEADQUARTERS ARMY OF THE POTOMAC,
HARRISON'S BAR, JAMES RIVER, July 4, 1862.

TO THE PRESIDENT:—

I have the honor to acknowledge the receipt of your dispatch of the 2d instant.

I shall make a stand at this place, and endeavor to give my men the repose they so much require.

After sending my communication on Tuesday, the enemy attacked the left of our lines, and a fierce battle ensued, lasting until night; they were repulsed with great slaughter. Had their attack succeeded, the consequences would have been disastrous in the extreme. This closed the hard fighting which had continued from the afternoon of the 26th ult., in a daily series of engagements, wholly unparalleled on this continent for determination and slaughter on both sides.

The mutual loss, in killed and wounded, is enormous. That of the enemy certainly greatest. On Tuesday evening, the 1st, our army commenced its movement from Haxall's to this point. Our line of defence there being too extended to be maintained by our weakened forces. Our train was immense, and about 4 A. M. on the 2d, a heavy storm of rain began, which continued during the entire day, and until the forenoon of yesterday.

The road became horrible. Troops, artillery and wagons, moved on steadily, and our whole army, men and material, was finally brought safe into this camp. The last of the wagons reached here at noon yesterday. The exhaustion was very great, but the army preserved its morale, and would have repelled any attack which the enemy was in condition to make.

We now occupy a line of heights about two miles from the James, a plain extending from there to the river. Our front is about three miles long. These heights command our whole position, and must be maintained. The gunboats can render valuable support upon both flanks. If the enemy attack us in front, we must hold our ground as best we may, and at whatever cost.

Our positions can be carried only by overwhelming numbers. The spirit of the army is excellent. Stragglers are finding their regiments, and the soldiery exhibit the best results of discipline. Our position is by no means impregnable, especially as a morass extends on this side of the high ground, from our centre to the James on our right. The enemy may attack in vast numbers, and if so, our front will be the scene of a desperate battle, which, if lost, will be decisive. Our army is fearfully weakened by killed, wounded, and prisoners. I cannot now approximate to any statement of our losses, but we were not beaten in any conflict. The enemy were unable by their utmost efforts to drive us from any field. Never did such a change of base, involving a retrograde movement, and under incessant attacks from a most determined and vastly more numerous foe, partake so little of disorder. We have lost no guns, except 25 on the field of battle, 21 of which were lost by the giving way of McCall's division under the onset of superior numbers.

Our communications by the James River are not secure. There are points where the enemy can establish themselves with cannon or musketry and command the river, and where it is not certain that our gunboats can drive them out. In case of this, or in case our front is broken, I will still make every effort to preserve at least the personnel of the army, and the events of the last few days leave no question that the troops will do all that their country can ask. Send such reinforcements as you can. I will do what I can. We are shipping our wounded and sick, and landing supplies. The navy department should co-operate with us to the extent of its resources. Captain Rodgers is doing all in his power, in the kindest and most efficient manner.

When all the circumstances of the case are known, it will be acknowledged by all competent judges, that the movement just completed by this army is unparalleled in the annals of war. Under the most difficult circumstances, we have preserved our trains, our guns, our material, and, above all, our honor.

Geo. B. McClellan,
Major-General.

To this dispatch the President sent the following reply:

WASHINGTON, July 5, 1862. 9 A. M.

Maj.-Gen. G. B. McCLELLAN,
Commanding Army of the Potomac:

A thousand thanks for the relief your two dispatches of 12 and 1 P. M. yesterday, gave me. Be assured, the heroism and skill of yourself, officers, and men, is and for ever will be appreciated.

If you can hold your present position, we shall hive the enemy yet.

A. LINCOLN.

If by "hiving" the enemy yet, the President meant to imply capturing the city of Richmond, the substance of his excellency's hope was certainly sound, and it was echoed in the fears of the enemy themselves.

With the news of the Confederate victory at Gaines's Mill, and of the retreat of the Federal army from its positions immediately around Richmond, the heart of the beleaguered capital had greatly dilated. So complete had been the concentration of the Confederate forces upon the supreme work of destroying the Army of the Potomac, and so well were the Confederates advised of Stonewall Jackson's astonishing success in deceiving the Federal commanders-in-chief at Washington, and thereby in reducing General McClellan to an absolute dependence upon his own diminished and over-tasked strength, that during the six days of incessant battle which attended the Federal change of base, few men in Richmond suffered themselves to doubt their speedy and utter deliverance from the foe who had so long insulted and invested their city.

By degrees, however, it began to be whispered that the Federal army had not been annihilated; that McClellan, far from being cut to pieces in detail on a disastrous retreat by the White House to Yorktown, had succeeded in effecting the concentration of his whole army at the expense of his depots and supplies; and that, after accomplishing an unexpected manœuvre of extreme brilliancy, and after a series of fiercely contested actions, resulting in terrible slaughter on both sides, but in persistent and continuous victory to the arms of the Union, the young general of the North had established himself in a new position on the river James, more advantageous to himself and more dangerous to Richmond than the positions from which his government had permitted him to be driven.

That his government would repeat with the army at Harrison's Bar the dangerous and so nearly fatal experiments upon which it had ventured with the army on the Chickahominy, was hardly to be anticipated.

Reinforcements from all available quarters were accordingly ordered up to Richmond by the Confederate authorities. Attempts were made to drive the Federal transports down the river. Fort Darling was strengthened, as well as the long line of defences stretching from Drewry's Bluff to Manchester. In short, while the people of Richmond and the Confederates generally rendered all honor to General Lee and to General Jackson for their success in forcing the Federal army to abandon its first attack upon their capital, not a little disappointment was felt and expressed at their failure to effect the complete discomfiture of their antagonists; and the rebel city prepared herself for a new and still more formidable siege.

On his part General McClellan was encouraged by the President to believe that the Peninsular movement against Richmond would now be properly appreciated, and the necessary steps taken to secure its success.

On the 4th of July the President had promised to send him at once ten thousand men from the troops around Washington, ten thousand from the corps of General Burnside, and five thousand from the expeditionary force in South Carolina.

Though this was but a paltering and insufficient way of meeting the emergency, there being no sound reason whatever that could be given why the whole of General Burnside's corps and twice ten thousand men from Northern Virginia should not at once have been concentrated upon the James, still as it was a movement in the right direction, and as it was accompanied by the President with an urgent entreaty that General McClellan should save the army by staying where he was if practicable, and think of "removal" only if he "must," General McClellan could only infer from it that the President honestly meant to aid him in making the supreme effort which all things now at last conspired to favor.

The thought of leaving Harrison's Bar and giving up the campaign never for a moment entered his mind. His consultations with Flag Officer Goldsborough convinced him that the gunboats would be able to keep the river open; and, working assiduously at the fortification of his new position, he found himself strong enough by the 7th of July to telegraph to Washington that if not that day attacked he could "laugh at the enemy."

As it was, however, altogether probable that if the enemy could muster the necessary force, they would that day attack him, General McClellan prepared himself against all contingencies. He knew that if a battle was fought at Harrison's Bar, it would be fought on both sides with desperation, for a defeat in that position must be ruin to the vanquished.

On that day, accordingly, General McClellan wrote to the President a most remarkable letter, embodying the ripe results of his experience as a commander of the armies of the Union; reasserting those sound principles of military politics which he had proclaimed in his first addresses at the head of an army to the invaded people of the South, and by which he had strictly governed himself and his troops throughout all his campaigns; and urging upon the President with a manly earnestness and solemnity of feeling befitting the crisis, the absolute necessity of obedience to that first law of order and success in war which makes unity of authority and concentration of force the indispensable conditions of victory.

This letter General McClellan had been asked by the President in a telegram of June 21st to write. All that had happened in the brief fortnight which had since elapsed gave treble weight and meaning to its words. Upon what ears they fell and how they were answered we shall presently see.

The following is the letter alluded to:

HEADQUARTERS ARMY OF THE POTOMAC,
CAMP NEAR HARRISON'S LANDING, VA., July 7, 1862.

MR. PRESIDENT,—

You have been fully informed that the rebel army is in our front, with the purpose of overwhelming us by attacking our positions or reducing us by blocking our river communications. I cannot but regard our condition as critical, and I earnestly desire, in view of possible contingencies, to lay before your excellency, for your private consideration, my general views concerning the existing state of the rebellion, although they do not strictly relate to the situation of this army, or strictly come within the scope of my official duties. These views amount to convictions, and are deeply impressed upon my mind and heart. Our cause must never be abandoned; it is the cause of free institutions and self-government. The Constitution and the Union must be preserved, whatever may be the cost in time, treasure or blood. If secession is successful, other dissolutions are clearly to be seen in the future. Let neither military disaster, political faction, or foreign war, shake your settled purpose to enforce the equal operation of the laws of the United States upon the people of every State.

The time has come when the Government must determine upon a civil and military policy covering the whole ground of our national trouble. The responsibility of determining, declaring, and supporting such civil and military policy, and of directing the whole course of national affairs in regard to the rebellion must now be assumed and exercised by you, or our cause will be lost. The Constitution gives you power sufficient even for the present terrible exigency.

This rebellion has assumed the character of war; as such it should be regarded; and it should be conducted upon the highest principles known to Christian civilization. It should not be a war looking to the subjugation of the people of any State in any event. It should not be at all a war upon population, but against armed forces and political organizations. Neither confiscation of property, political executions of persons, territorial organization of States, or forcible abolition of slavery should be contemplated for a moment. In prosecuting the war, all private property and unarmed persons should be strictly protected, subject only to the necessity of military operations. All private property taken for military use should be paid or receipted for; pillage and waste should be treated as high crimes; all unnecessary trespass sternly prohibited, and offensive demeanor by the military towards citizens promptly rebuked. Military arrests should not be tolerated, except in places where active hostilities exist, and oaths not required by enactments constitutionally made, should be neither demanded nor received. Military government should be confined to the preservation of public order and the protection of political rights. Military power should not be allowed to interfere with the relations of servitude, either by supporting or impairing the authority of the master, except for suppressing disorder, as in other cases. Slaves contraband under the act of Congress, seeking military protection, should receive it. The right of the Government to appropriate permanently to its own service, claims to slave labor, should be asserted, and the right of the owner to compensation therefor should be recognized.

This principle might be extended, upon grounds of military necessity and security, to all the slaves within a particular State, thus working manumission in such State; and in Missouri, perhaps in Western Virginia also, and possibly even in

Maryland, the expediency of such a measure is only a question of time.

A system of policy thus constitutional and conservative, and pervaded by the influences of Christianity and Freedom, would receive the support of almost all truly loyal men, would deeply impress the rebel masses and all foreign nations, and it might be humbly hoped that it would commend itself to the favor of the Almighty.

Unless the principles governing the future conduct of our struggle shall be made known and approved, the effort to obtain requisite forces will be almost hopeless. A declaration of radical views, especially upon slavery, will rapidly disintegrate our present armies.

The policy of the Government must be supported by concentrations of military power. The national forces should not be dispersed in expeditions, posts of occupation, and numerous armies, but should be mainly collected into masses, and brought to bear upon the armies of the confederate States. Those armies thoroughly defeated, the political structure which they support would soon cease to exist.

In carrying out any system of policy which you may form, you will require a commander-in-chief of the army; one who possesses your confidence, understands your views, and who is competent to execute your orders by directing the military forces of the nation to the accomplishment of the objects by you proposed. I do not ask that place for myself. I am willing to serve you in such position as you may assign me, and I will do so as faithfully as ever subordinate served superior.

I may be on the brink of eternity, and as I hope for forgiveness from my Maker, I have written this letter with sincerity towards you, and from love of my country.

Very respectfully, your obedient servant,

George B. McClellan,

Maj.-Gen. Com'dg.

On the 8th of July, the day after this letter was written, the President visited Harrison's Bar in person, and discussed with General McClellan the whole military situation, coming again to the conclusion expressed in his telegrams of July 4th, that Richmond was the real point of rebel concentration, and that this concentration ought to be met by a similar concentration of the Federal forces on the James. The question of the actual available force of the Army of the Potomac was also, of course, discussed at this time; and the President went back to Washington with the information that the whole force on the Peninsula amounted to about 86,000 men. He had scarcely reached the capital, on his return, when he responded to General McClellan's letter of July 7th, by appointing General Halleck, on the 11th of July, to the command-in-chief of the national armies; and two days afterwards, on the 13th of July, a consultation on the subject of course having been had in the interval with the new nominal chief, he sent the following telegram to General McClellan:

EXECUTIVE MANSION, WASHINGTON,
July 13, 1862.

MY DEAR SIR:—I am told that over 160,000 men have gone with your army on the Peninsula. When I was with you the other day, we made out 86,000 remaining, leaving 73,500 to be accounted for. I believe 23,500 will cover all the killed, wounded, and missing, in all your battles and skirmishes, leaving 50,000 who have left otherwise, and more than 5,000 of these have died, leaving 45,000 of your army still alive, and not with it. I believe half or two-thirds of them are fit for duty to-day. Have you any more perfect knowledge of this than I have? If I am right, and you had these men with you, you could go into Richmond, in the next three days. How can they be got to you, and how can they be prevented from getting away in such numbers for the future?

A. LINCOLN.

It is difficult to understand what creditable motive can have dictated such a telegram as this from a President, who had just gone over the whole condition of an army, to the commander with whom he had gone over it. The implication of its most significant clauses clearly was that General McClellan was personally responsible for the absence of a large part of his effective troops, an implication which the commander-in-chief, perfectly well acquainted as he was with the way in which the authority to issue furloughs was administered among the subordinate officers of the army, a way substantially endorsed and approved by the government itself, must certainly have known to be unjust. Nor can it well be imagined that Mr. Lincoln can have really been at a loss to know how the troops, whose absence he deplored " could be got to" General McClellan, when he was well aware that among these absentees of the Army of the Potomac were whole brigades, acting by his own order, under the command of other generals, in Northern Virginia!

It may be as well to state here, therefore, the officially recorded strength of the Army of the Potomac, including troops present with General McClellan, and troops absent from duty on the Peninsula under authority conflicting with his own, at three different periods:

	PRESENT.							ABSENT.		Grand Aggregate present and absent.	
	For Duty.		Sick.		In Arrest or Confinement.		Aggregate.	By Authority.	Without Authority.		
1862	Officers.	Men.	Officers.	Men.	Officers.	Men.					
April 30	4,725	104,610	233	5,385	41	356	115,350	11,037		126,387	Including Franklin.
June 20	4,665	101,160	496	10,541	44	320	117,226	27,700	887	145,813	Including McCall, not [Dix.
July 10	3,834	85,715	685	15,959	60	213	106,466	34,638	3,782	144,886	Including 2 brigades of Shield's division, about 5,354 men.

How to get men to the Army of the Potomac, however, and how to keep men once got to the Army of the Potomac from " getting away" again, were by no means now the leading questions which occupied the mind of the President.

Unless we are to assume that the government at Washington has habitually organized, disorganized, and re-organized the great armies of the Republic with less thought and care than men commonly bestow upon the least important of their ordinary business transactions, it must be held to be perfectly certain that the President, at the time when he dispatched this telegram to General McClellan, had made up his mind to recall from the Peninsula the whole army, which in this telegram he is made to appear so anxious to see reinforced to such a strength as should enable it to "go into Richmond in three days."

For here again dates become of grave significance. This telegram bears date the 18th of July.

About a fortnight afterwards, on the 3d of August, no positive intimation at variance with the President's implied eagerness to see the Army of the Potomac resume the offensive on the Peninsula, having been in the interval communicated to General McClellan, even by General Halleck, who had visited him in person on the 27th of July, the removal of the army to Northern Virginia was commanded in the following brief but emphatic dispatch:

"It is determined to withdraw your army from the Peninsula to Acquia Creek. You will take immediate means to effect this, covering the movement the best you can. Its real object and withdrawal should be concealed even from your own officers."

All the evidence, indeed, as yet accessible to the public, in respect to the military plans and purposes of the commander-in-chief of the army at Washington, during the eventful summer of 1862, combines to compel the conviction that at no moment of the campaign against Richmond did Mr. Lincoln or his most confidential advisers ever really abandon their determination to avail themselves of every possible occasion for demonstrating the soundness of the original presidential plan of that campaign as opposed to the plan of General McClellan. It will be remembered that on the 9th of April the President telegraphed to General McClellan at Fortress Monroe:

"I always insisted that going down the bay in search of a field instead of fighting at or near Manassas, was only shifting and not surmounting a difficulty."

What the President had thus "always insisted on" before the campaign of the Peninsula began, he never ceased to insist upon during the whole progress of that campaign.

In obedience to this fixed idea of the President, it was that the armies of Banks, McDowell, and Fremont had been consolidated on the 27th of June as the "Army of Virginia." Mr. Stanton's telegram to General McClellan, of the 26th of June, that this new army would "operate promptly" in his aid *by land* ought to put this question finally at rest. It was one consequence of this consolidation that the Army of the Potomac was fighting a desperate battle for its very life at Gaines's Mill, on the 27th of June, the very day of the promulgation of the President's order appointing Major-General Pope to the command of the "Army of Virginia;" and it was another consequence of this consolidation that from the time of the re-establishment of the Army of the Potomac at its new base on the James River, the government had resolved completely to subordinate the campaign of General McClellan to the campaign of General Pope, and at a proper moment to absorb the Army of the Potomac into the new Army of Virginia.

This moment, it was now believed at Washington, had arrived.

During the latter part of the month of July, the Confederate commanders had begun to prepare themselves for the decision which the Federal government announced to General McClellan on the 3rd of August. Slow as they naturally were to believe that the Federal government could commit two such gross blunders as to sacrifice the solid advantages which it possessed at Harrison's Bar, and to confide its interests and its hopes in Virginia to an officer so notoriously rash and incompetent as General Pope, the Confederates had yet been gradually compelled, by the manœuvres of the Union forces, to believe that this consummation, by themselves so devoutly wished, was really reserved for the campaign of 1862. They had begun, accordingly, to trifle with the army of General Pope, and to make their arrangements for flinging themselves in force upon that commander as soon as the evacuation of Harrison's Bar should be fairly commenced.

General Pope himself played into their hands, and accelerated his own ruin by insisting upon it at Washington as a fact, of which he was positively assured, that the Confederates, smitten with terror by the decisiveness of his advance, and fully expecting to be soon driven by him into the James, were evacuating Richmond and falling back on Danville and Lynchburg. General McClellan's representations to the contrary were disregarded, and General Halleck's order of August 3rd was issued.

Against this order General McClellan protested with all the earnestness of a soldier who fully understood the true situation of affairs.

"Your telegram of last evening," he replied to General Halleck, "is received. I must confess that it has caused me the greatest pain I ever experienced, for I am convinced that the order to withdraw this army to Acquia Creek will prove disastrous to our cause.

I fear it will be a fatal blow.

Several days are necessary to complete the preparations for so important a movement as this; and while they are in progress I beg that careful consideration may be given to my statements.

This army is now in excellent discipline and condition. We hold a debouche on both banks of the James River, so that we are free to act in any direction, and, with the assistance of the gun-boats, I consider our communications as now secure.

We are (25) twenty-five miles from Richmond, and are not likely to meet the enemy in force sufficient to fight a battle, until we have marched (15) fifteen to (18) eighteen miles, which brings us practically within (10) ten miles of Richmond. Our longest line of land transportation would be from this point (25) twenty-five miles; but with the aid of the gun-boats we can supply the army by water during its advance, certainly to within (12) twelve miles of Richmond.

At Acquia Creek we would be (75) seventy-five miles from Richmond, with land transportation all the way.

From here to Fort Monroe is a march of about (70) seventy miles; for I regard it as impracticable to withdraw this army and its material except by land.

The result of the movement would thus be a march of (145) one hundred and forty-five miles to reach a point now only (25) twenty-five miles distant, and to deprive ourselves entirely of the powerful aid of the gun-boats and water transportation. Add to this the certain demoralization of this army, which would ensue, the terribly depressing effect upon the people of the North, and the strong probability that it would influence foreign powers to recognize our adversaries, and there appear to me sufficient reasons to make it my imperative duty to urge, in the strongest terms afforded by our language, that this order may be rescinded, and that, far from recalling this army, it be promptly reinforced to enable it to resume the offensive.

It may be said that there are no reinforcements available. I point to Burnside's force, to that of Pope, not necessary to maintain a strict defensive in front of Washington and Harper's Ferry, to those portions of the army of the west not required for a strict defensive there. Here, directly in front of this army, is the heart of the rebellion; it is here that all our resources should be collected to strike the blow which will determine the fate of the nation. All points of secondary importance elsewhere should be abandoned, and every available man brought here—a decided victory here, and the military strength of the rebellion is crushed--it matters not what partial reverses we may meet with elsewhere. Here is the true defence of Washington; it is here, on the banks of the James, that the fate of the Union should be decided.

Clear in my convictions of right, strong in the consciousness that I have ever been, and still am actuated solely by love of my country, knowing that no ambitious or selfish motives have influenced me from the commencement of this war, I do now, what I never did in my life before, I entreat that this order may be rescinded.

If my counsel does not prevail, I will with a sad heart obey your orders to the utmost of my power, directing to the movement, which I clearly foresee will be one of the utmost delicacy and difficulty, whatever skill I may possess.

Whatever the result may be, and may God grant that I am mistaken in my forebodings, I shall at least have the internal satisfaction that I have written and spoken frankly, and have sought to do the best in my power to avert disaster from my country.

G. B. McCLELLAN,
Maj.-Gen. Comd'g.

This appeal was made in vain. In an elaborate reply to it General Halleck assumed the responsibility of ordering the withdrawal of the army from Harrison's Bar while he admitted that he had "tried every means in his power to avoid withdrawing it."

How wise this reluctance was on the part of General Halleck, and how fatal his final decision, events were not long in convincing all the world.

The one substantial reason on which General Halleck, in his letter to General McClellan, rested his decision, was the fact that "the old Army of the Potomac was now split into two parts, with the entire force of the enemy between them." "They cannot be united by land," General Halleck went on to say, "without exposing both to destruction, and yet they must be united. To send Pope's forces by water to the Peninsula is, under present circumstances, a military impossibility. The only alternative is to send the forces on the Peninsula to some point by water, say Fredericksburg, where the two armies can be united."

In the face of the subsequent history of the war it is probable that General Halleck would hardly care to admit that he felt himself shut down to this solitary alternative by the force of purely military considerations. To do so would be to convict himself of an absolute incapacity for the conduct of a great campaign. The real impossibility of sending General Pope's forces by water to the Peninsula, as General Halleck well knew, was not a military, but a political impossibility, it was the political impossibility of permitting General McClellan completely to prove, by the capture of Richmond in August, how Richmond might have been captured in May, had the "overland" theory on which his excellency, the commander-in-chief, had from the first "insisted," been frankly abandoned.

General Halleck repeating peremptorily his orders for the removal of the army, there was nothing left for General McClellan but to obey them.

The wharf facilities at Harrison's Landing were very limited, nor could the heaviest transport steamers come up so high on the James River; and the chief quartermaster, Colonel Ingalls, reported to General McClellan on the 7th, that after the transports already engaged by order of General Halleck, in moving the sick and wounded, should have returned, it would be possible to move at one time 25,000 men of the Army of the Potomac, but that in the actual condition of the transportation that day available, it would be impossible to move more than 5,000 infantry. He accordingly advised the sending forward of the troops to Fortress Monroe, and their shipment from that point. All that could be done was done to accelerate the movement, but from the moment when it began General Mc-

Clellan was plied with telegrams from General Halleck reproaching him for his alleged delay in executing the order of removal, telegrams which are interesting to the student of this campaign only as they reveal the positively hostile feeling of the authorities at Washington towards the recalled commander.

On the 9th of August, for example, three days after his final orders had been given for the removal of the army, General Halleck telegraphed :—

MAJ.-GEN. McCLELLAN,

I am of opinion that the enemy is massing his forces in front of Generals Pope and Burnside, and that he expects to crush them and move forward to the Potomac. You must send reinforcements instantly to Acquia Creek.

Considering the amount of transportation at your disposal, your delay is not satisfactory, you must move with all possible celerity.

H. W. HALLECK,
Major-General.

On the next day, August 10th, the general-in-chief telegraphed again, "the enemy is crossing the Rapidan in large force. They are fighting General Pope to-day; there must be no further delay in your movements. That which has already occurred was entirely unexpected and must be satisfactorily explained."

The enemy was indeed crossing the Rapidan in large force and "fighting General Pope." Having learned early in August, as in some mysterious manner they always learned them, the military decisions come to by the Aulic Council at Washington, the Confederates had forthwith seized their opportunity, and were precipitating the main body of their army upon the headlong commander of the "Army of Virginia." As General McClellan had never been notified of the intention of the government to transfer his army northward until the 3rd of August, and had never been finally commanded to execute that intention until the 6th of August, this refusal to him of proper confidence had resulted in giving the Confederates, operating upon interior lines and by railway, such an advantage over the two armies of the Union in point of time, as could not possibly have been neutralized had the transportation service at Harrison's Bar been as perfect as General Halleck, in these imperious and insulting telegrams assumed it to be. But that service, as we have seen, was far from being at all adequate to the sudden demand now made upon it. On the 10th of August the officer in charge of the quartermaster's department at Harrison's Bar compelled General Halleck to retract the substance of his charges of "delay" by a despatch confirming General McClellan's statement that the capacity of the transportation service of the Army of the Potomac had been entirely exhausted by the demands made on it for the movement of the sick and wounded, and of General Burnside's heavy artillery. It was, furthermore, to have been supposed that as General Halleck had expressly requested General McClellan to keep his movement "a secret from his own officers and men," the necessary transportation service would have been prepared at Washington. But the miserably petty nature of these charges cannot be better shown than it is by the fact that while General McClellan was now taken sharply to task for failing to send forward ninety thousand men to the Rappahannock from an expeditionary base of operations on the James within four days from the date of the final order requiring him to do so, the war department itself had occupied more than a week in sending forward five thousand men from the great national base of supplies to the James River. On the 5th of June Mr. Stanton had telegraphed to General McClellan, "I will send you five regiments as fast as transportation can take them." These regiments joined the army on the 12th and 13th of June.

To move the Army of the Potomac safely from Harrison's Bar to Acquia Creek and Alexandria, with such facilities as were supplied to General McClellan, was the proper work of a month at least. Anxious that no unnecessary delays should occur, either in embarking or disembarking his men, General McClellan, on the 12th of August, went in person seventy miles to the telegraph office at Jamestown Island, and sent a telegram to General Halleck, announcing his wish to confer with him on such subjects as the following:

"I learn that wharf accommodations at Acquia are altogether inadequate for landing troops and supplies to any large extent. Not an hour should be lost in remedying this. Great delays will ensue there from shallow water. You will find a vast deficiency in horse transports; we had nearly (200) two hundred when we came here. I learn of only (20) twenty provided now; they carry about (50) fifty horses each. More hospital accommodations should be provided. We are much impeded here because our wharves are used night and day to land current supplies. At Monroe a similar difficulty will occur. With all the facilities at Alexandria and Washington, (6) six weeks about were occupied in embarking this army and its material."

General Halleck telegraphed from Washington:

WASHINGTON, Aug. 14, 1862. 1.40 A. M.

I have read your dispatch. There is no change of plans. You will send up your troops as rapidly as possible. There is no difficulty in landing them. According to your own accounts there is now no difficulty in withdrawing your forces. Do so with all possible rapidity.

H. W. HALLECK,
Maj.-Gen.

Immediately after sending this reply, General Halleck left the Washington Office without informing General McClellan of the fact, or waiting for any further communication from him, thus insolently signifying his profound indifference to the wishes, the counsels and the feelings of the officer to whom, within a brief fortnight, he was destined to be indebted for his deliverance from the chaos of danger and despair into which the Aulic council and himself were now rapidly hurrying the affairs of the state.

Late in the afternoon of the 16th of August, when the last soldier had left the deserted camp, General McClellan and his personal staff bade farewell to the spot upon which he had planted the banner of the Union in such a formidable proximity to the rebel capital as since that day no army of the United States has occupied.

Part of his troops moving by land on Yorktown and Fortress Monroe, and part descending the James River, the commander of the Army of the Potomac had thus pushed forward his ninety thousand men to the relief of General Pope within a fortnight's time from his receipt of the first positive intimation that such a movement would be required of him.

On the 24th of August, three weeks after this intimation had reached him, General McClellan reported for orders at Acquia Creek. The corps of General Porter; pushed forward through the tangled wilderness of the Peninsula with unsurpassed rapidity by that officer, on his learning, by a letter inter cepted at Williamsburgh, that the enemy were massing themselves tremendously against Pope; had reached Northern Virginia two days before, and was already in the front of battle endeavoring to ascertain where the commander of the "Army of Virginia" really was, and what his plans of action were.

CHAPTER XI.

THE REMOVAL TO ACQUIA CREEK. THE FAILURE OF POPE'S CAMPAIGN. GENERAL McCLELLAN TAKES CHARGE OF THE ARMY. THE CAMPAIGN OF MARYLAND.

THE history of the eventful week which followed the arrival of General McClellan at Acquia Creek in August, 1862, cannot be adequately set forth within the limits of this volume. That week was such a carnival of incapacity as the world has seldom seen. The Aulic council at Washington and their favorite commander in the field, General Pope, had now invited upon themselves precisely such a blow as that which they had enabled the enemy a month before to deliver upon the Army of the Potomac.

Recalling General McClellan from Harrison's Bar, they had liberated Lee for a campaign in the North. So swift had been the movements of the Confederate general, and so stolidly stubborn were the Aulic council and General Pope in the belief that Lee was not moving at all, that the Federal "Army of Virginia" was struck by his decisive advance after the 18th of August as by a thunderbolt. Beaten wherever he was found, utterly bewildered by the manœuvres of his enemy, and clinging firmly to the one notion which happened to be of all notions possible to him the most dangerously erroneous, that he was dealing not with the main body of the rebel forces but with a flying column, General Pope had so completely entangled himself with his own line of operations, that when

General McClellan arrived at Acquia Creek and telegraphed to General Halleck for information as to the whereabouts of General Pope and as to his own future position and responsibilities, the general-in-chief could only reply ignominiously enough: "You ask me for information which I cannot give. I do not know either where General Pope is or where the enemy in force is. These are matters which I have been all day most anxious to ascertain."

Matters worth knowing to a general-in-chief these certainly were; but the legitimate curiosity of General Halleck was destined to be gratified only by the newly-arrived general upon whom he had been unable to find time, ten days before, to bestow the commonest courtesies of official life.

On the 27th of August General Halleck again telegraphed to General McClellan: "I can get no satisfactory information from the front, either from the enemy or our troops. There seems to have been great neglect and carelessness about Manassas. Franklin's corps should march in that direction as soon as possible. A competent officer should be sent out to take the direction of affairs in that vicinity." Of the commander of the "Army of Virginia" he telegraphed on the same day this astounding piece of information: "Pope's headquarters are at Warrenton Junction, but I cannot ascertain the present position of his troops!"

A "competent officer" was evidently needed still nearer the headquarters of the army. Two days afterward General McClellan was again applied to for information concerning the army which he had been displaced from command to reinforce, and this time by the President himself, who had given that army its being, and had himself selected its commanding officer. The President's telegram is quite pathetic in its utter helplessness:

Maj.-Gen. McClellan,—

What news from Manassas Junction? What, generally?

Abraham Lincoln.

Now in these four days of utter bewilderment and despair at the headquarters of the army in Washington, General McClellan had received from those headquarters an abundance of contradictory and for the most part flagrantly inexecutable orders, emanating sometimes from the gallopping headquarters of the Army of Virginia, and sometimes from the befogged administration of the war office. Precisely what forces he commanded, or whether he still held any command at all, he was utterly unable to ascertain.

To move any troops to the assistance of General Pope, unless in such force and under such conditions as should enable them to make an independent fight of their own, was clearly to expose the army to annihilation, for General Pope had completely lost all conception of anything like a general plan of operations. On the 23d of August he had burned Rappahannock Station without giving any notice to Generals Morell and Sykes, of General Porter's corps, who were then watching the fords of the Lower Rappahannock; and on the 27th of August he had destroyed Gen. Taylor's New Jersey Brigade by flinging it into the face of a whole Confederate army corps at Bull Run, under the firm belief that he was marching it against a scouting party of cavalry.

Such was the utter incoherence of the operations of General Pope indeed, and so feverish the alternation of senseless confidence and equally senseless alarm at Washington, that both the capital and the army must have been sacrificed, had a less clear-headed officer or one of less moral courage in the face of an ill-defined responsibility and an imminent peril, occupied the anomalous position held by General McClellan at Alexandria, whither he had been summoned nominally to superintend the forwarding of troops to General Pope, but really, as the President in another lamentable telegram of August 29th had notified him, to "assist General Halleck by his counsels in controlling affairs."

This telegram was sent in reply to one from General Mc-

Clellan, calling upon the President to decide upon one of two courses, and either to concentrate all the available forces not yet involved by General Pope in his bewildered retreat, for the purpose of opening communications with that general; or to abandon the attempt to ascertain what General Pope was trying to do with his army, and to concentrate upon Washington, making the capital safe as a place of refuge for Pope's beaten forces, and as the base of new operations to recover the ground lost by him.

The President, who had been so eager to act as commander-in-chief, when the skies seemed to be clear and auspicious of victory, shrank from his duty now, and threw the responsibility of action upon General Halleck, his nominal general-in-chief, and upon General McClellan, whom he had just deprived of his army.

In the exercise of this somewhat vaguely defined authority, General McClellan ventured to save the forces under General Franklin and General Sumner from marching out, as General Halleck had ordered them to do, quite in the dark, and in an inadequate state of preparation against an enemy of unknown strength. For doing this he was reprimanded at the time by General Halleck, and has since been frequently taken to task by the partisans of the administration. But nothing is more certain than that an immediate and unquestioning execution of General Halleck's first, and by no means peremptory, directions in regard to these forces would simply have involved them in the disastrous finale of General Pope's campaign, which culminated in the second battle of Bull Run, fought on the 30th of August; and that Washington itself would, in that event, have been exposed, in a state of absolute helplessness, to the triumphant Confederates.

How this battle of Bull Run was fought and lost can only be understood from a careful study of two reports not now fairly accessible to the public, the reports of General Fitz-John Porter and of General Sykes.

Suffice it to say, that at two o'clock in the afternoon of that fatal day General McClellan was telegraphed to from Washington to send forward "ammunition for artillery" to General Pope, he having neither ammunition wagons nor even any information as to the calibre of Pope's artillery. When it is remembered that General Pope's army had been organized at Washington in the month of June; that its commander had been in high favor with the authorities at Washington, and in direct communication with them until, by his own signal incapacity, he had involved himself helplessly in the toils of Longstreet and of Lee; and that General McClellan had reached Alexandria a deposed commander, under the cloud of official displeasure, only three days before this second battle of Bull Run was delivered, it must be admitted that no such tribute has ever been paid to the military genius of a commander as is paid to that of General McClellan by those friends of the administration, who insist that he ought to have been able to intervene at the eleventh hour without a soldier at his back, or a ray of official light on his path, between the distracted forces of General Pope and the ruin upon which their leader was hurrying them!

This of course he could not do, nor was he permitted to do what alone he could have done and what he earnestly desired to do, pass to the front with his old soldiers of the Potomac and share their fate with them.

Late on the night of August 30th, as the tidings of Pope's complete overthrow began to come in, General McClellan telegraphed to General Halleck:

"I cannot express to you the pain and mortification I have experienced to-day in listening to the distant sound of the firing of my men. As I can be of no further use here, I respectfully ask that if there is a probability of the conflict being renewed to-morrow, I may be permitted to go to the scene of battle with my staff, merely to be with my own men, if nothing more; they will fight none the worse for my being with them. If it is not deemed best to intrust me with the command even of my own army, I simply ask to be permitted to share their fate on the field of battle. Please reply to this to-night.

"I have been engaged for the last few hours in doing what I can to make arrangements for the wounded. I have started out all the ambulances now landed."

General Halleck replied the next morning that he could give no orders, as "General Pope was in command of the department." On the previous day, indeed, at the very moment when the Army of Virginia was falling to pieces in General Pope's incompetent hands, the secretary of war had issued an order giving General Burnside command of his own corps, giving General Pope "command of the Army of Virginia and of all forces temporarily attached to it," and giving General McClellan command of "that portion of the Army of the Potomac not sent forward to General Pope's command," the whole Army of the Potomac being then under orders to join General Pope!

This was on the 30th of August. At ten o'clock of the next night, August 31st, the general-in-chief, Halleck, was telegraphing to the commander thus derided and insulted twenty-four hours before:

"I beg of you to assist me with your ability and experience. I am entirely tired out."

No thought but his country in his mind, General McClellan responded at once to this Macedonian cry. At midnight of the 31st, learning that the rebel cavalry were on the Fairfax road, that the right wing of Pope's beaten army was entirely exposed, and that his whole left wing had been that day driven in, he telegraphed to Washington:

"I recommend that no more of Couch's division be sent to the front, that Burnside be brought here as soon as practicable, and that everything available this side of Fairfax be drawn in at once, including the mass of the troops on the railroad. I apprehend that the enemy will, or have by this time, occupied Fairfax Court House, and cut off Pope entirely, unless he falls back to-night, *via* Sangster's and Fairfax Station. I think these orders should be sent at once. I have no confidence in the dispositions made, as I gather them. To speak frankly, and the occasion requires it, there appears to be a total absence of brains, and I fear the total destrnction of the army. I have some cavalry here that can carry out any orders you may have to send. The occasion is grave, and demands grave measures. The question is the salvation of the country. I learn that our loss yesterday amounted to fifteen thousand (15,000).* We cannot afford such losses without an object. It is my deliberate opinion that the interests of the nation demand that Pope should fall back to-night, if possible, and not one moment is to be lost. I will use all the cavalry I have, to watch our right. Please answer at once. I feel confident you can rely upon the information I give you. I shall be up all night, and ready to obey any orders you give me."

Within an hour General Halleck had responded, acquiescing in General McClellan's suggestions, authorizing him to "establish an outer line of defence," and begging him for more "reliable news." Such news was indeed desirable—for at 4 P. M. of this very day General Pope had contrived to get word to Washington that he "was all right!"

On the next day, September 1st, General McClellan was sent for, to come to Washington and take command of the defences, his command to be strictly limited to the garrison of the works. He accepted the duty thus ungraciously thrust upon him; but suggested that General Halleck should send out some "reliable" person to ascertain whether General Pope was indeed "all right."

The general-in-chief sent one of his own staff; and shortly after requested General McClellan to come to his headquarters to meet the President. Utterly prostrated by the disasters which he had brought upon the country, the President had

* This was equal to the whole loss of the army in the "Seven Days' battles" before Richmond.

suffered himself to be persuaded into insulting the whole army of the Potomac by supposing that its soldiers, angry at the injustice done their commander, were not cheerfully co-operating with General Pope. Unnerved, and tremulous with emotion, he assured General McClellan that he had "always been his friend," and begged him to telegraph to "Fitz-John Porter, or some other of his friends," and try to do away with the alleged reluctance of the Potomac Army to act with Pope. General McClellan, as positively as was consistent with a proper respect for the President's official station, assured him of the gross absurdity and indecency of these allegations: but finding that nothing less would calm the perturbed spirit of the commander-in-chief, he finally sent a telegram to General Fitz-John Porter, urging him, for his own sake and that of the country and of the old Army of the Potomac, to "lend the fullest and most cordial co-operation to General Pope." Of course General Porter replied that he and all the Army of the Potomac had done, were doing, and would always do, their duty as soldiers of the Republic.

It is a lamentable illustration of the rancorous and petty nature of partisan passion, that this telegram, wrung from General McClellan by the entreaties and almost by the tears of the President, and acknowledged at the time by the latter as a "service he should never forget," has been since adduced as a proof that General McClellan had bewitched the officers and soldiers of the Army of the Potomac out of their allegiance to the nation.

On the next morning, September 2d, General Halleck's messenger returned with authentic news of General Pope's humiliating defeat, and of the utter confusion in which his army was retreating. Upon this the President came in person, with General Halleck, to General McClellan's house, and begged him to go out, meet, and take command of the retreating army, to organize the defence of the capital, and in short to act as generalissimo once again—for the salvation of the State.

Upon this moment of the conduct of the war hung its whole future fortunes. Never before nor since has it been so vitally important to the nationai honor, to the safety of the capital, to the very existence of the national government, that the command of the armies of the Union should be lodged in the hands of a man perfectly loyal, perfectly sound of heart and clear of brain, as it was on this second day of September, 1862.

The defeat of McDowell at the first battle of Bull Run had for a time imperilled all these things. But the victors of July 21st, 1862, were raw troops, and the Confederate Government of that day was a raw government, with an undeveloped policy before it and an unconsolidated people behind it. The conquerors of General Pope, on the contrary, were the veterans of a year of battles, flushed with the successful defence of the rebel capital, and with the triumphs not of one or two insignificant skirmish fields, but of a whole campaign in Northern Virginia; while the policy of the Confederate Government was now beginning to acquire a certain positiveness and cohesion, and the people of the Confederate States to feel themselves in some sort committed as a nation to war.

The selection by the Government at Washington of General McClellan for the command of the army in July, 1861, is excused by those who pronounce that officer's career to have been "a failure," on the grounds that he was recommended by his recent success in Western Virginia, that the Government knew as much of him as of any one of its generals, and that the time was necessarily a season of experiments.

No such excuse can be given for his re-selection in September, 1862. Then the government knew more of him than of any of its other generals; then he was recommended by the untoward conclusion of the siege of Richmond; then to risk experiments was a crime.

When, on the 2d of September, 1862, the President and General Halleck—the commander-in-chief who "could order what he pleased," and the general-in-chief whom he had himself selected—put the whole power of the state into the hands of Major-General McClellan they by that act distinctly absolved him of all responsibility for the national disappointment before Richmond, and as distinctly acknowledged their full sense of his superiority as a commander, not merely to themselves but to all the generals whose services were within their disposal.

The accredited biographer of Mr. Lincoln declares it to be his belief that General McClellan was unfitted for command either because he "intentionally avoided decisive engagements in order to accomplish certain political results which he and his secret political advisers deemed desirable," or because he was, "by the native constitution of his mind, unable to meet the gigantic responsibilities of his position when the critical moment of trial arrived."

If either of these hypotheses be well-founded, it is needless to say, that whatever judgment posterity may pass upon General McClellan, there can be no doubt as to its verdict upon the President of the United States, and the general-in-chief who thus flung all the military responsibilities of these positions upon the shoulders of General McClellan at the moment when these responsibilities were most "gigantic," and when most a man decisive of temper and resolute in action was needed to meet them!

Of one rare and great quality, at least, General McClellan on this memorable 2d of September, proved himself to be possessed. "One single thing," says a brilliant writer,* "has been lacking to Italy, a thing in appearance humble, but in reality of all things the greatest—honesty! * * * * * Patriotism itself has been unscrupulous in Italy; her most virtuous citizens have professed their disdain for the human species, and have acted upon the principle, that as the world is peopled by fools one must ape madness in order to rule it.

* Renan. "Les Revolutions d'Italie." Essais de Morale et de Critique. Paris, 1859, pp. 267–8.

* * * There have been reactions against this strange eclipse of the moral sense, but no where in Italian history do I find a St. Louis, a Washington or a Lafayette. These, the Italian will tell us, were not masters of policy, they were simply honest men. Perhaps so, but would to heaven, for Italy's sake, that she had possessed more of these timorous consciences and these narrow minds!"

Without a comment on his treatment in the past, or a condition to secure justice in the future, this young general, before whom power thus prostrated itself with all the temptations which official imbecility has ever offered to vaulting ambition, accepted the command of the armies, not even exacting its formal transmission into his hands.

Getting at once into the saddle, he rode out to meet the retreating forces. He came upon General Pope in person at no great distance from the capital, but could learn nothing from him as to the position either of the enemy or of his own men. It was not till long after nightfall that he succeeded in gaining such a definite idea of the condition of things as enabled him to begin to issue his orders. But his re-appearance at the head of affairs was the signal of such a sudden and astounding change in the *morale* of the retreating troops as proved that these stout soldiers of the Peninsula, at least, fully understood the difference between the deliberate retreat of a skilful and successful general, constrained by circumstances, not of his own creating, to change his positions, and the rout of an army sacrificed by the incompetency of its commander. The troops everywhere hailed him with cheers; the disorganized battalions, as if by magic, became a formidable host again; and before midnight, on the 2d of September, Washington was once more safe against any attack of the enemy.

The ulterior plans of Lee now began to develop themselves. His movements on the 3d of September indicated to General McClellan his intention of crossing the upper Potomac, and carrying the war into Maryland and Pennsylvania.

General Halleck and the administration could not believe this possible, and urged a strictly defensive policy upon the soldier in whose hands the hope of the nation once more rested. But General McClellan, governed by sounder principles, determined at once upon an aggressive movement. In four days he had re-organized the army sufficiently to enable him to take the field, had put General Banks in command at Washington, and was marching in watchful pursuit of the enemy.

The same authorities who had harassed his operations during the spring and summer with incessant charges of "slowness" and "delay" now began to torment him with suggestions that he was moving too fast and too far.

On the 9th of September General Halleck earnestly warned him against an attempt of the enemy to attack Washington from "the Virginia side." On the 12th the President was sure that the enemy was "recrossing the Potomac," and urged General McClellan not to "let him get off without being hurt." On the 13th General Halleck scolded him for "uncovering the capital," as he was sure that the "enemy would suddenly move on Washington with the forces south of the Potomac," and on the 14th the same officer feared that he was "exposing his left and rear."

We know now that on the 9th of September General Lee issued orders to his army to "resume its march, taking the Hagerstown road. * * * General Jackson to take the route towards Sharpsburg, cross the Potomac, take possession of the Baltimore and Ohio Railroad, capture such of the enemy as may be at Martinsburg, and intercept such as may attempt to escape from Harper's Ferry." This at the time General McClellan did not know, but with only his own military judgment to guide him, and under a constant fire of discouraging and delusive telegrams from Washington, he divined the truth and pressed on. How much the country owes him for his self-possession, self-reliance and energy at this juncture of events can only be fairly estimated by those who will give themselves the pains to reflect on the consequences which must have followed had he bowed to the President's assurance of September 12th, that the enemy was going back to Virginia, an assurance given, as it chanced, at the very moment when Stonewall Jackson was appearing in force before Harper's Ferry.

The disgraceful surrender of Harper's Ferry by Colonel Miles and Colonel Ford almost immediately followed, the post being given up to the Confederates at eight, A. M., on the 15th of September. The garrison there had not been put under the orders of General McClellan until the 12th, by which time all communication between himself and the Ferry had been cut off. But he had at once ordered General Franklin to its relief, and this officer, at the moment of the surrender, was actually within three miles of the position of Maryland Heights, and within seven miles of Harper's Ferry, at a point in Pleasant Valley where his advance had rested the night before from the combat and victory of Crampton's Gap.

On the same day with the combat at Crampton's Gap, the battle of South Mountain was fought and won for the possession of Turner's Gap. In this battle, one of the best contested of the war, about 30,000 men were engaged on each side. Here fell General Reno, in whom, says the commander, "the nation lost one of its best general officers."

The President acknowledged the tidings of this victory in the following characteristic manner:—

War Department,
Washington, Sept. 15, 1862—2.45 P. M.

Your despatch of to-day received. God bless you, and all with you. *Destroy the rebel army if possible.*

A. Lincoln.

To Maj.-Gen. McClellan.

The "rebel army" which the victors of South Mountain

were thus requested to "destroy," was the same army, it will be remembered, which had destroyed Pope's "Army of Virginia," and thrown the capital at Washington into a paroxysm of terror. The army invited to "destroy" it was an army which had become almost a mob but a fortnight before, and which had only been brought and held together, in the advance upon a victorious enemy, by the moral power which the name and the character of its commanding general exerted upon the men.

Two days afterward was fought the signal battle of Antietam Creek, near Sharpsburg, by which the whole Confederate plan of campaign was broken up; Maryland and Pennsylvania were delivered from the presence and the terror of the foe; and the triumphant and aggressive enemy, driven across the Potomac, was put once more upon the defensive. Never before had two such armies contended for victory on a single field in the new world. For fourteen hours nearly two hundred thousand men and five hundred pieces of artillery had shaken the solid earth, with their thunder of battle, among the Maryland hills.

The position of the Confederates was one of unusual strength. General Lee, thrown upon the defensive by the determined advance of General McClellan, had fixed himself here with the hope that the army of the Union, still suffering, as he well knew, from the demoralizing influences of Pope's recent campaign, worn down by a week of incessant marching and by two days of almost incessant fighting, and separated from its supply trains, would be dashed to pieces in its onslaught upon his lines; in which case, holding his communications open with Virginia, he might be rapidly reinforced and supplied, and resume his advance upon the North unobstructed by any formidable force.

To overcome and destroy the powerful army thus posted with the army then actually in his hand, General McClellan could not expect. It would require his utmost efforts, he knew, so to cripple Lee as to drive him back into Virginia.

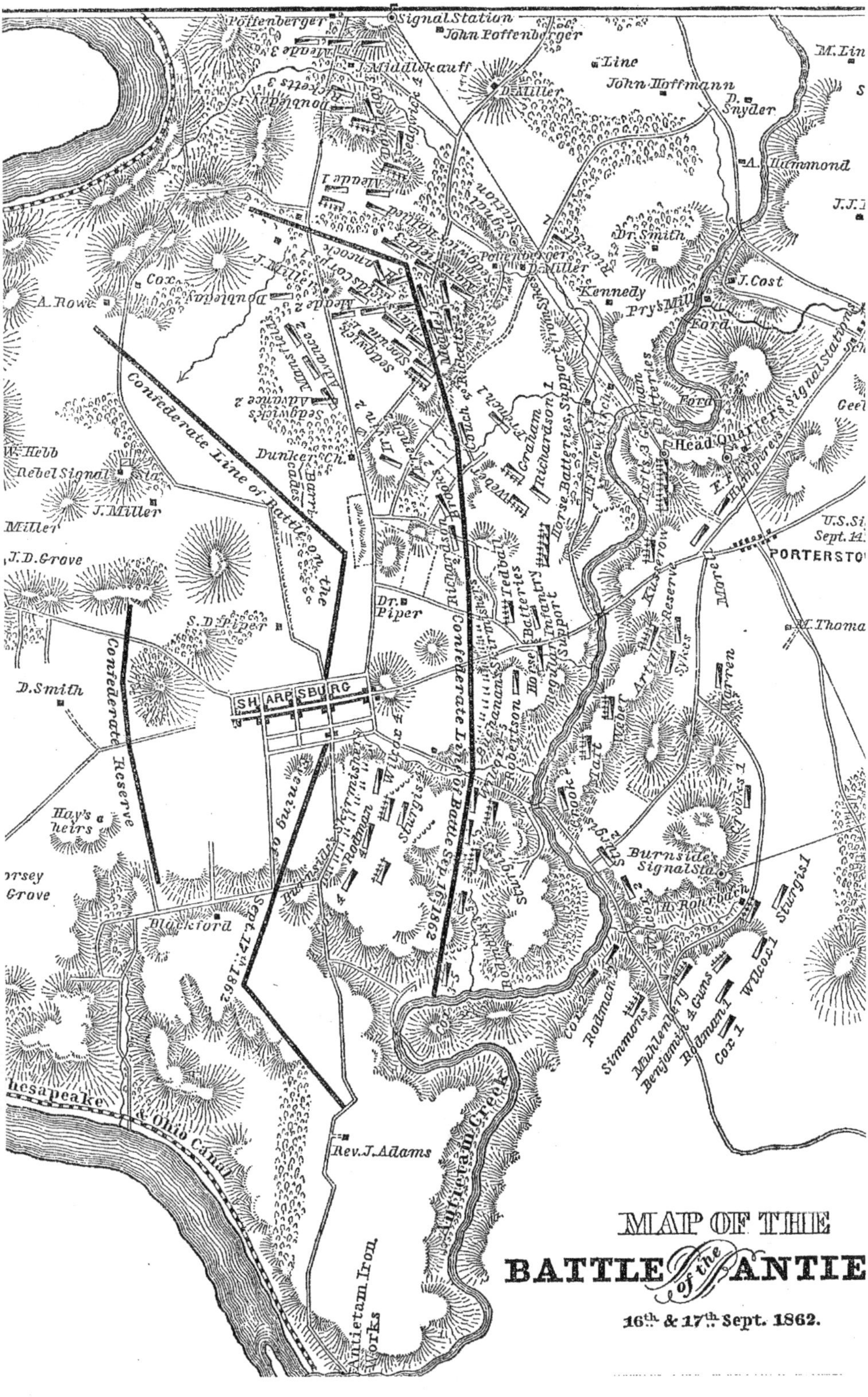

MAP OF THE
BATTLE of the ANTIE
16th & 17th Sept. 1862.
Signal Station
Poffenberger
John Poffenberger
J. Middlekauff
D. Miller
Line
John Hoffmann
D. Snyder
M. Lin
A. Hammond
Dr. Smith
J. Cost
Pry's Mill
Ford
Kennedy
Head Quarters
Signal Station
Cox
A. Rowe
J. Miller
Confederate Line of Battle on the
Dunker Ch.
W. Hebb
Rebel Signal Sta.
Miller
J. D. Grove
S. D. Piper
Dr. Piper
SHARPSBURG
D. Smith
Confederate Reserve
Confederate Line of Battle Sep. 16 1862
Evening of Sept. 17th 1862
Hay's heirs
Grove
Blackford
Burnside's Signal Sta.
H. Rohrbach
U.S. Si
Sept. 14
PORTERSTO
M. Thoma
Chesapeake & Ohio Canal
Rev. J. Adams
Antietam Iron Works
Antietam Creek
Kennedy
Sedgwick
Meade 1
Doubleday 1
Ricketts 3
Meade 3
Hancock
Richardson 1
Horse Batteries
Graham
French 1
Weber
Tedball
Regular Infantry Support
Robertson
Sykes
Artillery Reserve
Warren
Morell
Kingsbury
Crook
Tait
Sturgis
Rodman
Wilcox
Cox
Simmons
Muhlenberg
Benjamin 4 Guns
Crooks 1
Sturgis 1
Wilcox 1
Rodman 1
Cox 1
Humphreys

This accomplished, it was certain that the Confederates, recrossing the Potomac, would make a fresh stand at the first available point, and safely defy pursuit until the exhausted army of the Union should have had time to reorganize itself for a new campaign of invasion.

The battle of Antietam, then, was on the part of the Union forces an offensive-defensive battle, and on the part of the Confederates a defensive-offensive battle. It was the culminating effort of General McClellan to drive from the Northern soil an enemy against whom the government had avowed itself but three weeks before quite powerless to make head. With General Lee, on the contrary, who had had time to choose his position, it was an effort to dispose of the only remaining obstacle in his hitherto victorious progress from Richmond towards Washington, Baltimore and Philadelphia.

Under these conditions the action began at daylight on the 17th of September, 1862, with a vigorous assault upon the enemy's left by the right wing of General McClellan's army, which was to have been followed up by a similar assault of the Union left wing upon the right of the Confederates. The centre of the Union lines was held by two divisions of General Porter's corps, the divisions of Generals Sykes and Morell, which had suffered so severely under General Pope in the second battle of Bull Run. These divisions constituted the only real reserves of the army, filled the interval between the right and left wings, and protected the supply trains of the army in the rear. It was of course greatly important that the front of this force should be maintained firmly in any event, and more particularly that it should be so maintained in the event of any failure on the part of either of the Federal wings to make a due impression upon the enemy.

The attack of the Federal right began at the hour appointed, and was pushed with promising success. At 8 o'clock General Burnside, commanding on the left, was ordered forward in his turn to carry an important part of the heights on the enemy's right. This order was not obeyed until nearly noon, and its object having been partially achieved, General Burnside halted his advance until 3 o'clock in the afternoon. During this inaction of the left wing the conflict had raged with great fury on the right; several general officers had fallen, and so severe had been the losses of that wing that two brigades of General Porter's corps, already weakened by detachments to the right and rear of Burnside, were ordered up from the centre to reinforce it, at the risk of exposing that vital position to attack.

Under repeated orders from General McClellan, General Burnside at length resumed his attack, carried the heights upon the enemy's right and drove his men from their guns. But this advantage, which, had it been won three hours before, might have gone far towards rendering the victory more decisive than there had been any antecedent reason for believing that it could be made, was won too late. The enemy, reinforced just before dusk by Jackson's troops from Harper's Ferry, assailed Burnside in his turn, and forced him back from the crest upon the lower range of hills near the bridge which he had carried at noon.

Night, however, closed upon a victory which had saved the North from invasion and the nation from humiliation. Thirteen guns, thirty-nine stand of colors, upwards of fifteen thousand stand of small arms, and more than six thousand prisoners, attested the brilliancy of the triumph—a brilliancy undimmed by the loss of a Federal color or a Federal gun.

To renew the attack on the next day, in the then condition of the troops, was pronounced impossible by the corps and divisional commanders, and the Confederates sending in a flag of truce for permission to bury their dead, the permission was granted, and the day spent in preparations for resuming the offensive on the following morning.

But during the night of the 18th, Lee, whose position, almost on the river bank, gave him great facility for the manœuvre, evacuated his intrenchments on the Maryland shore and retreated into Virginia.

The glorious sun-burst of this victory at Antietam lighted up the whole North. For the moment partisan spite and passion themselves were dumb, and the gratitude of a nation rewarded the gallant soldiers to whom under Providence it owed its escape from a great peril and shame.

It is painful to know that this feeling of gratitude was by no means shared by the government at Washington.

On the 20th of September General McClellan was obliged, in reply to several captious telegrams from General Halleck, complaining that the administration was "left entirely in the dark as to the movements of the enemy," to say,—

"I regret that you find it necessary to couch every despatch I have the honor to receive from you, in a spirit of fault-finding, and that you have not yet found leisure to say one word in commendation of the recent achievements of this army, or even to allude to them."

This contemptuous indifference to the feelings which make up and maintain the military spirit and the morale of an army was not now for the first time exhibited by the authorities at Washington.

One of the greatest of military writers has said, "it is the duty of a prince to reward his men for a fine retreat as highly as for the most brilliant victory; for firmness under reverses is more honorable than enthusiasm under success, since it requires courage only to carry a position, while it demands true heroism to make a difficult retreat in the face of a victorious and enterprising enemy without being disconcerted, and steadily meeting him with a front of iron."

Yet to the following telegram, which General McClellan sent to General Halleck just before his return for the Peninsula, no reply was ever made, nor was any notice ever taken of its suggestions:

HEADQUARTERS ARMY OF THE POTOMAC.
August 18, 1862—11 P. M.

Please say a kind word to my army, that I can repeat to them in general orders, in regard to their conduct at Yorktown, Williamsburgh, West Point, Hanover Court-House, and on the Chickahominy, as well as in regard to the (7) seven days, and the recent retreat.

No one has ever said anything to cheer them but myself. Say nothing about me, merely give my men and officers credit for what they have done. It will do you much good, and will strengthen you much with them if you issue a handsome order to them in regard to what they have accomplished. They deserve it.

G. B. McCLELLAN,
Major-General.

Maj.-Gen. HALLECK,
Comd'g U. S. Army, Washington, D. C.

CHAPTER XII.

AFTER ANTIETAM. GENERAL McCLELLAN CROSSES THE POTOMAC. THE EMANCIPATION PROCLAMATION ISSUED BY THE PRESIDENT. GENERAL McCLELLAN RELIEVED FROM THE COMMAND OF THE ARMY.

SOMETHING of course must be pardoned to men who, being no more than mortal, found themselves in the humiliating position into which the official superiors of General McClellan had now, by their real inferiority to that officer, been brought. The campaigns of Pope in Virginia, and McClellan in Maryland, had demonstrated this inferiority, not merely to all other competent observers, but to these official superiors themselves. The President and General Halleck knew that but for General McClellan and the army which he alone had been able to hold together, the beginning of September would have seen them fugitives from Washington or prisoners in Richmond: and it would be asking too much, perhaps, of human frailty to find fault with them for a certain degree of restlessness and discomfort in his presence.

But that they should have set themselves at work as soon as the safety of the North was assured, to find or make an occasion for depriving its saviour of his command was a crime against the State, the magnitude of which is only to be measured by all that the nation has since been thereby called to bear of loss, of suffering, and of shame.

Yet the events which now took place are difficult of explanation upon any other theory than this.

Five days after the battle of Antietam the President issued

his proclamation of emancipation, declaring a general war against the social system of the seceded States, to begin on the 1st of January, 1863.

This proclamation of course was utterly inconsistent with all those principles in obedience to which alone General McClellan, in his letter from Harrison's Landing, had expressed his belief that the war could be honorably and successfully conducted. And as it is now known* that the publication of this proclamation had been delayed, by the advice of Mr. Secretary Seward, until a glow of triumph should have dawned upon the Union arms, it is a new and curious illustration of the President's notions of "confidence" and "cordial support" that he should have availed himself of General McClellan's victory of Antietam to fulminate a "bull" on the politics of the war, diametrically hostile to all that officer's often and earnestly expressed convictions in respect to our military policy.

General McClellan, however deeply he may have felt the inopportuneness of this proclamation, dealt with it in the spirit of a soldier and a citizen, who recognized the just limits of civil and of military authority, respectively.

"The principles upon which, and the object for which, armies shall be employed in suppressing rebellion," he said, in a General Order to his troops, October 7th, 1862, "must be determined and declared by the civil authorities; and the chief executive, who is charged with the administration of the national affairs, is the proper and only source through which the needs and orders of the Government can be made known to the armies of the nation. Discussions by officers and soldiers concerning public measures determined upon and declared by the Government, when once carried beyond temperate and respectful expressions of opinion, tend greatly to impair and destroy the discipline and efficiency of troops, by substituting

* See the facts in this case stated in the explanatory prospects of Mr. Carpenter's picture of the President and his Cabinet preparing this proclamation.

the spirit of political faction for that firm, steady and earnest support of the authority of the Government, which is the highest duty of the American soldier. The remedy for political errors, if any are committed, is to be found only in the action of the people at the polls.

"In carrying out all measures of public policy," added the general, in conclusion, "this army will, of course, be guided by the same rules of mercy and Christianity that have ever controlled their conduct towards the defenceless."

General McClellan's abstinence from interference in the civil policy of the administration was not reciprocated by a similar abstinence on the part of the administration from interference in his own military plans.

His efforts to strengthen his army for offensive operations were constantly thwarted. Troops promised to him to-day, were suddenly diverted to-morrow to distant and independent commands.* The transportation of necessary supplies and material to his army was impeded by carelessness, or worse than carelessness, in the bureaux of the war department, and the office of the general-in-chief at Washington. The ancient spectre of an invasion by the way of Manassas rose again to trouble the rest of the President and his councillors.

On the 1st of October the President visited General McClellan at his headquarters, went through the camps, and went over the battle-fields of South Mountain and Antietam.†

The condition of the army was fully explained to the President, who recognized, or seemed to recognize, the absolute impossibility of moving immediately upon a new campaign of invasion in the face of an organized and powerful enemy, and

* For example, Sigel's troops were first put at his disposal, and then without his knowledge sent into West Virginia.

† It was upon this occasion that the President shocked the army and the nation by calling upon one of his suite to entertain him with certain comic songs while riding among the fresh graves of the soldiers who had fallen in the terrible battles of September.

who expressed his renewed and grateful confidence in its commander.

The army under General McClellan was indeed utterly worn down by the efforts which it had made. The main body was composed of the troops which General Pope had exhausted in his fatal campaign at the end of August. Hastily reorganized by General McClellan in the first week in September, the army had been marched through the mountains of Maryland to fight the fierce battles of South Mountain and Antietam. It needed everything that an army can need, horses for the cavalry, shoes and equipments for the men,* supplies, in short, of all kinds, without which it would have been sheer madness to move into an enemy's country at the approach of winter.

The President, however, on the 6th of October, directly after his return to Washington, caused his general-in-chief to issue an order commanding General McClellan to "cross the Potomac, and give battle to the enemy or drive him south."

The President, the secretary of war, and General Halleck must have known, when this order was issued, that it would not be obeyed, for they knew that it could not be obeyed.—Whether they expected, by issuing it, to drive General McClellan into a resignation, or were merely preparing a "record" to which they might afterwards appeal in proof of his "tardiness" and their own "energy" is, perhaps, a question. There can be no question, however, that the order itself was an outrage alike upon common sense and all military propriety. It

* Corps commanders upon receiving notice from the quartermasters that they might expect to receive their supplies at certain dates, sent their trains for them, which, after waiting, were compelled to return empty. Several instances occurred where these trains went back and forth from the camp to the depots as often as four or five different times without receiving their supplies; and I was informed by one corps commander, that his wagon train had travelled over one hundred and fifty miles to and from the depots, before he succeeded in obtaining his clothing.

The corps of General Franklin did not get its clothing until after it had crossed the Potomac, and was moving into Virginia.—*Report*, p. 411.

was followed up, a week later, by another of those astonishing military letters of advice and instruction which President Lincoln seems never to have ceased writing until the success of General Grant in taking Vicksburg, a year afterwards, on a plan which his excellency had not suggested, induced him to admit that a general in the field might sometimes understand what he was doing better than a politician in the White House.

Some of the propositions of this letter, dated October 13th, deserve immortality.

"As we must beat him somewhere or fail finally," said his excellency, speaking of General Lee, "we can do it, if at all, easier near to us than far away." The results of General Pope's experience at "beating the enemy near to" Washington, recent as they were, would seem to have quite passed away from the presidential memory when this brilliant maxim was evolved from the depths of the presidential mind!

Again said the presidential commander-in-chief, "if we cannot beat the enemy where he now is *we never* can." This dogma was the more discouraging that neither the President nor General McClellan himself exactly knew where the enemy at this moment was.

Fortunately, however, for the country, after expatiating in a highly wonderful manner over the map, and displaying an amazing facility at making geometrical war, the President wound up with the saving clause, "this letter is in no sense an order."

A weary interchange of telegrams now went on between the headquarters of General McClellan and the Aulic council at Washington, the latter urging an immediate movement, the former insisting, as it was his duty to insist, that the army should not be hurried into the field unprepared for the serious work before it.

The merits of this tedious controversy are well summed up in the following passage from General McClellan's report:

WASHINGTON, Oct. 21, 1862—3 P.M.

Your telegram of 12 M. has been submitted to the President. He directs me to say, that he has no change to make in his order of the 6th inst. If you have not been, and are not now in condition to obey it, you will be able to show such want of ability. The President does not expect impossibilities; but he is very anxious that all this good weather should not be wasted in inactivity.

Telegraph when you will move, and on what lines you propose to march.

H. W. HALLECK,
General-in-Chief.

MAJ.-GEN. G. B. MCCLELLAN.

"From the tenor of this dispatch I conceived that it was left for my judgment to decide whether or not it was possible to move with safety to the army at that time, and this responsibility I exercised with the more confidence, in view of the strong assurance of his trust in me as commander of that army, with which the President had seen fit to honor me during his last visit.

"The cavalry requirements, without which an advance would have been in the highest degree injudicious and unsafe, were still wanting. The country before us was an enemy's country, where the inhabitants furnished to the enemy every possible assistance, providing food for men and forage for animals, giving all information concerning our movements, and rendering every aid in their power to the enemy's cause. It was manifest that we should find it, as we subsequently did, a hostile district, where we could derive no aid from the inhabitants, that would justify dispensing with the active co-operation of an efficient cavalry force. Accordingly, I fixed upon the 1st of November as the earliest date at which the forward movement could well be commenced.

"The general-in-chief, in a letter to the secretary of war on the 28th of October, says: 'In my opinion there has been no such want of supplies in the army under General McClellan as to prevent his compliance with the orders to advance against the enemy.'

"Notwithstanding this opinion expressed by such high authority, I am compelled to say again that the delay in the reception of necessary supplies up to that date, had left the army in a condition totally unfit to advance against the enemy; that an advance under the existing circumstances would, in my judgment, have been attended with the highest degree of peril, with great suffering and sickness among the men, and with imminent danger of being cut off from our supplies by the superior cavalry force of the enemy, and with no reasonable prospect of gaining any advantage over him.

"I dismiss this subject with the remark, that I have found it impossible to resist the force of my own convictions, that the commander of an army who, from the time of its organization, has, for eighteen months, been in constant communication with its officers and men, the greater part of the time engaged in active service in the field, and who has exercised this command in many battles, must certainly be considered competent to determine whether his army is in proper condition to advance on the enemy or not; and he must necessarily possess greater facilities for forming a correct judgment in regard to the wants of his men, and the condition of his supplies, than the general-in-chief in his office at Washington city."

Before moving upon the enemy, General McClellan was extremely anxious so to guard the line of the Potomac as to put a stop to the possibility of those raids by the Shenandoah, which have since inflicted, through three consecutive years, so much shame upon our army, and so much loss upon the people of the Pennsylvania and Maryland border. The importance of taking these precautions was increased in the mind of General

McClellan by the fact that Bragg's rebel army was then at liberty to reinforce Lee, and so to enable him to do precisely what he has since done, not once nor twice, but regularly with the recurrence of the harvest season of the Shenandoah.

General McClellan urged this matter upon General Halleck at Washington. The only reply which the general-in-chief vouchsafed was the information that "no appropriation existed for permanent intrenchments," and a silly sneer to the effect that Bragg was four hundred miles away while Lee was but twenty.

On the 26th of October the army finally began to cross the Potomac, and marching on a line east of the Blue Ridge, by the 7th of November its several corps were massed at and near Warrenton. "The army," says General McClellan, "was in admirable condition and spirits. I doubt whether during the whole period that I had the honor to command the Army of the Potomac it was ever in such excellent condition to fight a great battle." The Confederates, under Longstreet, were directly in front at Culpepper, and the rest of Lee's army lay west of the Blue Ridge. The army and its general alike expected, with confidence and hope, the issue of a new and near impending passage-of-arms with their antagonists.

In this expectation the army and its general alike were destined to be disappointed.

Delivered from the terror of Lee's presence in the North; reassured for the safety of Washington by the position of the army, and persuaded that victory must crown its next efforts, the administration seem to have judged the moment come for striking down the general whom they hated, as men hate those whom they have injured.

Late on the night of November 7th, 1862, in a storm of wind and rain, General Buckingham, arriving post haste from Washington, reached the tent of General McClellan at Rectortown. He found the commander surrounded by his staff and by some of the generals of the army, and handed him a despatch of which he was the bearer.

Opening the despatch and reading it without a change of countenance or of voice, General McClellan passed over to General Burnside a paper which it contained, saying, as he did so, "Well, Burnside, you are to command the army."

CHAPTER XIII.

NOMINATION OF GENERAL McCLELLAN TO THE PRESIDENCY. THE CONDUCT OF THE WAR. MR. LINCOLN AND HIS AULIC COUNCIL. GENERAL McCLELLAN'S POLICY OF THE WAR. HIS TRUE RECORD AS A COMMANDER.

On the 28th of August, 1864, two years after his final removal from the command of the Army of the Potomac, General McClellan received at Chicago a unanimous nomination from one of the largest political conventions ever assembled in America, as the candidate of the Democratic party for the Presidency of the United States.

During those years the conduct of the war for the Union had been surrendered up entirely into the control of those Aulic councillors of President Lincoln whose efforts to undermine the military and the political influence of General McClellan at Washington we have seen beginning almost at the moment of his nomination to the command-in-chief of the national armies in November, 1861, remorselessly prosecuted during the whole campaign of the Peninsula, and finally triumphant after the campaign of Maryland in November, 1862.

Under the control of these councillors the Republic had gradually become one vast camp. Armies such as the civilized world had never seen arrayed for battle since the downfall of the first Napoleon, had been summoned into the field. The debt of the nation and of the States had been swelled to proportions rivalling the burdens imposed by the ambition and the folly of many successive generations upon the most cruelly misgoverned empires of the Old World. Restrictions foreign to the habits of the people and to the spirit of the Constitution had been imposed upon liberty of speech and of the press. In many sections of the country, quite beyond the sphere of hostilities, life had been made almost intolerable, not only to those who differed from the dominant party in respect to the wisdom of its war policy, but to those also who impugned its capacity for administering that policy. It had been openly proclaimed by those who had a right to be heard as speaking for the administration, that rebels had no rights which loyal men were bound to respect; that the war begun for the enforcement of their constitutional obligations upon the seceded States ought to be waged in contempt of the constitutional rights of those States; that the rebellion of the South justified and demanded a revolution by the North.

In the course of these two years of Aulic power men had gradually come to see that, in the language of Mr. Lincoln himself, "the civil war had radically changed the occupations and habits of the American people;" but it was by no means so clear that, in the language of Mr. Lincoln, this change was effecting "for the moment" only. The war had been so ill-managed, in a military sense, by the presidential commander-in-chief and his councillors, that notwithstanding repeated victories of the national armies in the stricken field, no substantial progress appeared to be making towards the dispersion of the great Confederate armies and the pacification of the Confederate populations. Richmond, after defying repeated attempts at its reduction according to the plan of campaign which the Aulic council at Washington and the President had vainly endeavored to coerce General McClellan into adopting, still held out against the concentrated force of the national armies moving at last as that commander had two years before urged that they should move. Vast regions of territory west and east of the Mississippi, which had once been occupied by the troops of the Union, had been abandoned again to the Confederate arms. The solemn petitions put up to the Divine Majesty in executive proclamations that He would "subdue the anger which had produced and so long sustained a needless and cruel rebellion, and change the hearts of the insurgents,"* had been turned almost into a mockery by measures directly calculated to inflame the anger of the populations in rebellion and to harden the hearts of the insurgents against the government and the people of the Union.

In contemplating this condition of affairs men who, as Mr. Jefferson said of himself in the dark hours of the alien and sedition laws, "retained unadulterated the principles of 1775," had begun seriously to tremble for the future of the Republic. Of the war so conducted, in such a spirit and for such objects, they saw but two possible issues: the subjugation of the South and the degradation of its States to the condition of conquered provinces; or the collapse of the national resources and the consequent recognition of the Confederate States as a rival and victorious power.

Both of these issues were abhorrent to the minds of such men.

To the former issue no specious representations of the moral glory and the national health to be acquired by the abolition of the institution of slavery could reconcile even those among them who held slavery in the deepest detestation. They saw that a sincere hatred of slavery could no more excuse a social war in its name upon communities originally independent than a sincere hatred of heresy could justify the enforcement of the Catholic religion by the sword upon such communities. Nor could they look forward to the prolonged struggle which such a war would necessitate, without the gravest concern as to the effects of such a struggle upon the character of the American people and upon their political institutions. Mr. Lincoln had already announced that "the dogmas of the quiet past were

* *Proclamation of a Day of National Thanksgiving, 15th July, 1863.*

inadequate to the stormy present." If the storm was to be protracted indefinitely, not the dogmas only, but the whole social order also of the quiet past must vanish before its violence. Mr. Lincoln, it is true, had also announced that he was not "able to appreciate the danger that the American people" might come, by familiarity with military rule, "to lose the right of public discussion, the liberty of speech and the press, the law of evidence, trial by jury, and the *habeas corpus*." But those who remembered that Mr. Lincoln and his Aulic councillors had been conspicuous for years among those who could not "appreciate the danger" that sectional controversy, conducted in a temper of unfraternal passion, might lead to civil war, were more likely to take warning from the dismal experience than to find comfort in the cheerful confidence of the President. Mr. Lincoln's easy faith that "our strife pertains to ourselves, to the passing generations of men, and can, without convulsion, be hushed forever with the passing of one generation,"* seemed to such men somewhat at variance with the facts of history and the characteristics of mankind. It has been well said by one who had himself passed through the fiery furnace of civil war: "The most frightful feature of a civil war is not the blood which flows on every side, nor the dead who strew the streets and roads, nor the shattered walls of once happy homes; it is the passions which ferment in men's souls. * * * The sombre legend which begins the story of the world, the legend of Cain and Abel, seems to hover over these fratricidal conflicts, and to stamp them with a seal of infernal rage." To transmit these fermenting passions through indefinite years to come, is a crime against the human race which has an associated and progressive destiny. For men are not isolated to the point they occupy in space or time. "They hold on one to the other; they act one on the other by ties and means which do not require their personal presence and which survive them, so that successive generations of men

* Message of President Lincoln, December, 1862.

are inter-connected with each other and linked together by the act of succession."

Mr. Lincoln's quaint notion of a geographical nationality, his dogma that the "land we inhabit would ere long force re-union, however much of blood and treasure the separation might have cost," may perhaps be a formidable indictment of himself and his administration for spending blood and treasure to do the work of the equator and the poles; but it could hardly be expected to reconcile those who believe a nation to consist of men and not of acres, to seeing the life of a generation given up to a war of moral or material domination.

To the issue of the recognition of the Confederate States, those who shuddered at the idea of a prolonged social war against the South, were equally averse. They looked upon such a recognition as a calamity both to the North and to the South. They saw in it the copious seed of future strife, as well as a present source of national humiliation. They believed that it could be avoided by a prosecution of the war at once soldierlike and statesmanlike, by the prostration of the military strength of the seceded States, and by the protection of their political rights.

In argument with those who thus believed and felt, the Aulic council was powerless. The force of its appeals to the vehemence of the Southern resistance, and to the reiterated demands of the South for absolute independence, was broken by the simple fact that throughout nearly the whole of its course the war had not been fought for the Union, nor under the control of men who held the maintenance of the Union paramount to all other considerations. It was idle to say what the South would or would not do in a contingency which had never been presented to the South, the contingency of a complete overthrow of the military power of the South accompanied by a strictly constitutional assertion of the authority of the Union.

To raise to power a Federal administration capable of presenting this contingency to the South became the great animating purpose, not of the Democratic party alone, but of thousands upon thousands of conservative citizens of all parties, as the time drew near in the summer of the present year, for the nomination of a presidential candidate in opposition to Mr. Lincoln.

In obedience to this purpose it is that Major-General McClellan has been summoned from his enforced retirement into the foreground of the political field.

The record of General McClellan's connexion with the conduct of the war most assuredly justifies the confidence thus reposed in him.

We have seen that at the outset of his career as a Federal commander in Western Virginia, he clearly set before himself, his soldiers and the people of Virginia, the specific objects of the war, and the limitations imposed by those objects upon the duty of the government in arms.

We have seen that in his counsels addressed to the President, at the request of that functionary, in his general orders to his troops, in his instructions to the generals acting under him, he steadily and consistently adhered to those objects and reasserted these limitations.

Since his removal from duty with the army, he has again and again taken various suitable occasions to reiterate his conviction that "while the war is fighting, all citizens should see that the war is prosecuted for the preservation of the Union and the Constitution, for their nationality and their rights as citizens."*

Holding these convictions as to the politics of the war, General McClellan, as we have seen, was actively engaged in the military conduct of the war from the summer of 1861 to the fall of 1862. During that time he conducted only two campaigns in a comparative freedom from the practical interference of the administration with his plans.

* Speech at Trenton, N. J., Nov. 13, 1862.

CPSIA information can be obtained
at www.ICGtesting.com
Printed in the USA
LVHW101345160422
716387LV00003B/176

9 783752 592078